Swell: A Different Path

Account of the Change, Volume 3

J.G. Johnson

Published by J.G. Johnson, 2019.

SWELL: A DIFFERENT PATH

First edition. August 16, 2019.

ISBN: 978-1393381099

Written by J.G. Johnson.

Also by J.G. Johnson

Account of the Change
Swell
Swell: A New Beginning
Swell: A Different Path

Watch for more at nascentbooks.com.

Table of Contents

Crazy Friends | Saturday, June 26 1

Whiners | Sunday, June 27 4

Lucky Jerk | Monday, June 28 27

A Real Buddy | Tuesday, June 29 34

Different Path | Wednesday, June 30 45

Life's Wrench and Battle Axes | Thursday, July 1 70

Who I Am | Sunday, July 4 98

The End is Nigh | Friday, July 9 129

Ravens! Worse than Chihuahuas | Sunday, July 11 149

Stand Together or Hang Separate | Monday, July 12 166

Surprise Guests | Thursday, July 15 172

What Lays in the Dark | Thursday, July 15 192

Price of Love | Thursday, July 15 203

Rebound | Wednesday, July 21 209

Awoooo | Thursday, July 22 222

What Lays in the Dark Again | Thursday, July 22 234

Dancing in the Moonlight | Friday, July 23 252

Heart's Conviction | Friday, July 23 260

Killing Field | Sunday, July 25 278

Dedication:

I want to say thank you to all of the people that have supported and encouraged me to chase my dreams and my heart. Without you, I never would have been able to go the places I have, seen the things I have seen, and learned just how big the world really is. This book is for you and it is for everyone that still believes that dreams aren't dead. Don't let anyone tell you what is impossible, only you know what is impossible for you. So, live your dream and follow your gut. Lastly, never fear chasing the squirrels and bunnies of your life. They may just lead you to your destiny and even if they get away, you will have learned something. You have a brain, a heart, and a soul never stop feeding them.

P.S. I also would like to say thank you to, Michael, over at silverfoxphotography.net for his help with the cover and helping bring this book to life.

Crazy Friends
Saturday, June 26

A stiff elbow to the ribs pulled Mick out of his daydreaming as the jet taxied towards the runway. He shot a reproachful glare at his neighbor and 'friend' who not only wasn't fazed by it but didn't even seem to notice. It would have miffed him if anyone else did that, but with Jake, it was just who he was. "What!?"

"You ever wake up one day and think 'Today is the day that everything is going to change?' I mean like really change, the kind of change that did in the dinos, wiped out the mammoths, ate the dodos?"

"Dude, no more anime for you! Just because we're all on the way to Japan doesn't mean that something daunting is going to happen that requires the rise of a champion to lead the starved, beaten, and weary to victory against all odds, Jake!" Mick Renalds retorted with a snort from his window side seat. Blond hair, blue eyes, 23, and pushing 6"5' and with a physique that would make a mountain troll princess swoon. Like the dreamer next to him, he was on his way to Japan to work as an English Assistant Teacher or EAT for short. He was also a realist. Had he watched his fair share of Anime? You bet. And he'd enjoyed tearing holes in the plots. *Yah, sometimes things happen which stand convention on its head but all that really is, is the undeniable truth making its presence known. Try to tell that to a dreamer like Jake and you were in for a long argument with someone that could almost make the unbelievable sound believable. Imagine if he ever learned the truth.*

On second thought, better that he stays unawares. He's already too perceptive for his own good.

Mick wasn't quite sure how Jake could do it, but on the drop of a dime, he could lead you down a most plausible sounding rabbit hole and then drag you not only through Wonderland but make you accept that you weren't tripping and that the Caterpillar was actually a larval telepathic alien that was learning about how messed up the human psyche really was. In a lot of ways, it was a wasted talent. Had Jake ever applied himself to something like politics or business, he would have been a force to reckon with. *Alas, every time I even mention such an idea to him, he gets a very serious look on his face and says something like 'You do not want a person like me in a position like that. I might just succeed.' Which is probably for the best. Honest dreamers meet bad ends and things could become ticklish for his continued existence should he show up on other's radar.* He sighed while giving his friend a sideways look. *Some secrets are best left sleeping.*

One of these days something is going to happen that shatters that protective dome of reality that Mick relies so heavily upon. I only hope that it isn't to his detriment when it does. Because I'd hate for Mick to be dodo-ized. "Where's your sense of adventure, man?" Jake Jameson said with a frown, shaking his head.

Jake Jameson was the epitome of normal looking. Look in the dictionary for a picture of average white American and there he was. 5"10', short brown hair, with an average, if slightly athletic, build. Check, yep normal. The only thing a little different was his eyes. They were a marbled hazel green that gave those that stared the feeling that a swirling galaxy was gazing into their soul. He also looked a good five years younger than he actually was at 26. He could never decide if that was a good or bad thing.

"What do you call what we are about to do?" Mick demanded. Considering what they were currently doing, Jake's question made little sense. "It's not like you, me, and the fifty or so others with our group alone, aren't moving to another country where the culture, language, and environment are starkly different from anything most of us have experienced before! Some of us may even stay and start whole new lives here!" he said, watching as his chastisements bounced harmlessly off of Jake's chipper mood.

"Well, yah. But that's a little adventure. I'm waiting for the big one to come along!" Jake replied, practically bouncing up and down in his seat with anticipation. He couldn't really explain it but somewhere deep down, maybe in his atoms themselves, there was something that screamed that there was more, much more, out there than mankind had ever imagined. *"or forgotten,"* the voice whispered, half heard, in his head. He did his best not to think about that. The voice had been there for as long as he could remember but he had been smart enough not to let anyone know after that one time he had freaked out his family. He didn't want people thinking he was crazy.

"Well let's hope that your grand adventure is kind enough to wait until we land in Japan. I don't have any desire to wind up like those people in the TV show having a shared final delusion. Oh, and wake me when we land!" Mick asked, promptly passing out before the Jet had even taken off.

Whiners
Sunday, June 27

Mick had not gotten much sleep for the last two hours of the approach into Tokyo. None but the dead had, and even theirs probably wasn't that sound. To say that the turbulence was bad would have been an understatement on par with saying that they only hadn't crashed yet because the wind was so strong that they couldn't fall from the sky. The seatbelt light had been on full time and the two fools that had tried to get up had found themselves bouncing off the ceiling of the fuselage as the jet had hit a particularly bad spot and suddenly dropped several thousand feet in altitude. In fact, that was the only reason they were being allowed to land instead of being diverted. The restless dead man didn't help either.

Go to Japan, gain a little experience, and have some fun. Escape family obligations and heritage. Mick chuckled as he clutched at his armrest. The jet lurched sickeningly, eliciting a moan from the injured man and a new volley of puking from the passengers. To say that the jet would need a thorough cleaning, if it managed to survive, was an understatement. *If this keeps up, crashing may be preferable, if only to bring an end to this stench. Fell-hound stool stinks less than this!*

"Well Mick, it looks like we won't end up like those folks in the show. According to the map we are over Japan now. Granted we still need to land. Preferably on land and on a runway. Bad things happen when jets do crunchies on buildings and with these waves a water landing would be pure suicide. In one piece would be nice but alive will do," Jake said as the jet began to shudder, emphasizing just how dubious that proposition was quickly becoming. There was no doubt that they would be on the ground here soon, but in one piece? Well, that was another question altogether.

4

The jet jerked again, eliciting a moan of pain from mister 'seatbelt signs don't mean nothing' and a bit of flopping limbs from the dead one.

"Jerk!" Mick retorted, white knuckled. *The maniac is smiling!!! Man was not meant to fly!*

"Attention!!! We are now banking in for our landing. Remain seated! And a little prayer might be a good idea," the Pilot gritted out. You could hear the strain in his voice from hours of fighting like a one-armed strongman trying to bench a squirming elephant in freefall to control the jet. In fact, if you listened at all, you could hear the strain going through the fuselage in shudders, creaks, groans, and what sounded distinctly like cracking and rivets popping.

"Did the Pilot really just suggest that we seek divine intervention for a safe landing?" Mick asked, going even whiter than Michael Jackson.

If he gets much whiter, he'll either be a ghost or a pop star. Though at this rate we might all be right there along with him. What fun. Jake smiled gleefully as he looked over at Mick. "You see, if you had a little faith, that would have given you a little reassurance. For today is either your time or it's not!" he explained in a most matter-of-fact tone. *In the end that is what it always comes down to!*

"Dude, you are so not helping," Mick growled, through clinched teeth, worried about biting his tongue as he glared at his 'friend.' *Why did I ever think being his friend was a good idea? Oh, because usually he is only an amusing amount crazy.*

A sudden gust swatted the jet almost 45° off of the course it had been on. Which was bad. It was only made worse by the fact that the jet had been about to go wheels down. This meant that where the jet, by some miracle, had been coming in almost straight on with the runway, it was now coming in just shy of sideways. Before the Pilot had a chance to correct, the jet touched down and things were going good. For about .003 seconds. Then the right-side landing gear collapsed in a screech of torn metal and exploding pneumatics and hydraulics. Granted, it was barely audible over the screaming of the passengers. The wing quickly followed suit, folding under in gouts of flames that would have done a cranky dragon proud as the jet tumbled over it. It was soon joined by the other wing as the jet completed the roll and it too snapped off. Surprisingly the fuselage had been taking it pretty well so far but being treated like a seesaw over two wings was more than it could take. Just behind the rear wing joint, a third of the way back in coach, and right in front of where Jake and Mick were sitting, the two halves of the fuselage separated. It was a bad day for the pilots and first classers as they rolled away and right into a fuel truck. Jake only got a glimpse of the ensuing fireball as they continued to roll over. The two halves had been separating in a more or less V-pattern. After several more rotations, Jake's half began to slow and finally came to a stop with them sitting at only a slight angle with the storm baring its fangs directly into their faces. Seeing as how the rows in-front of them had torn free they were now effectively moved to the first-class and had plenty of extra legroom. Mick stared out into the fangs of the storm as the warm rain washed over him. *At least it doesn't smell like vomit any more.* Mick looked to his side as he caught motion, and found Jake getting out of his seat.

"I've always wanted to fly first-class. Now that I'm here, I don't see what all of the hype is about." Jake turned in his seat and smiled to Mick. "Well, we're on the ground, we crashed in a storm, and on an island in the Pacific. Yep, sounds just like that show. Pinch me quick and see if this is a hallucination," Jake joked as he stopped the recording he'd been making on his phone since just before things went sideways, horizontally so. Getting out of his seat, he pulled his Indiana Jones style leather messenger bag out of the overhead and grinned out into the fury of the storm. As the lightning flashed, Mick could see him clearly and even the devil himself, after reaping a world, would have been scared to tread near him. And then he was gone. Just gone.

Mick sat there blinking against the torrent of water cascading down on him and quickly inundating the fuselage as he came to grips with everything that had just happened and the truly sane insanity of his friend. The strobes of the emergency vehicle's lights jarred him out of his reprieve from reality. *What am I doing!? Yah, Jake ditched me, but that was just Jake being Jake. I'm uninjured and over the shock. It's time I got a move on and it's not like that is even the closet that I have ever been to death.* He stomped down hard on that train of thought before it could get any more traction. He had left that life behind. And for very good reasons.

Mick climbed out of his seat and made his way to the gaping maw of the fuselage. Given the choice of wading back through the remaining passengers to get to the remaining emergency slide at the rear hatch or following Jake's example and climbing down, he chose to climb. *And I don't even have to worry about carrying anything because my bags were in the overhead a few rows up and that section is gone now. I really hope that my check bags were in the rear half of the jet.* It wasn't like he had brought anything really irreplaceable with him, but finding clothing for a man of his stature was nigh impossible in Japan. Even Amazon.jp didn't carry his sizes.

Mick turned around as his feet met the asphalt only to find himself face to face with a perturbed looking man that positively exuded authority.

"Are all of you passengers crazy!?" he demanded. "What part of sit, stay, and await aid from emergency personnel don't you all understand? I'll make it as simple as whitewash on a picket fence. Jet. Crash. Sit. Wait. Get rescued. Real simple. No?" he explained using exaggerated hand motions before shaking his head in frustration. "But, oh no, no, you all just come sauntering out without a care in the world!" He glared over his shoulder at the sound of a rumble that was just barely perceptible over the rage of the storm. It became a frown as he spotted a departing bus through the squall washing out the tarmac. "You have got to be kidding me!" He let loose a slew of expletives in at least five languages that would have made Mother Tereasa blush and Mark Twain and Shakespeare swoon with envy at the sheer poetry and inventiveness of it.

By that point, some other personnel had gathered round and were staring at who was apparently the response team's chief. "You, take this lost little," Chief gave Mick another glance, "make that big lamb to the bus," he ordered, nudging Mick over to the waiting man. "The rest of you start getting the remaining passengers out and onto the busses. Be on the lookout for anyone suffering from shock. I have to go track down the one that got away before he causes any more problems," he finished, standing there expectantly as no one moved. "Now would be a good time to start!" he barked and the responders jumped back into action while he rubbed his temples and trudged off, muttering invectives, to a waiting car that seemed primed to take flight in the gale-force winds that were tearing across the tarmac. All Mick could catch was a portion about 'raving mad foreigners,' the rest was drowned out by the roar of the storm.

Mick jerked as he felt a hand clamp onto his elbow. It wasn't painfully tight, but it was solid and informed him that 'resistance was futile. He would be assimilated into the rescue effort.' *Great, now I have Star Trek going through my head. Could be worse. It could have been Galaxy Quest.* He gave up with a shrug and followed the man without putting up a fight. *Not that they really could do anything to stop me if I wanted to resist. All things considered, I would rather get out of this deluge and something says resisting would only prolong my stay. And it isn't like I really want to draw any undue attention to myself either. I'm pretty sure that I lost them at this point, and it would be a real shame to find myself back on their radar because of some pesky reporter and a camera or a police report.* His stomach let out a rumble as they neared the buses. What with the turbulence, they hadn't been able to serve any of the inflight meals - which was not really food and everyone knew that it was better to not eat on flights anyways - or refreshments after the first go around shortly after they took off and he was getting beyond hungry. "Any chance that there is some food and dry clothes waiting for me at the end of this ride?"

His keeper turned and gave him an appraising look. "Food, yes, probably. You are pretty big, so clothes may pose a bit more of a problem. We should be able to find you something, but no guarantees."

I hope they have plenty of food because I could eat a whole cow at this point. Mick stepped up into the bus and took the seat nearest the exit by right of conquest. "Any idea how long I will need to wait?" he asked, trying not to cringe at the feel of his sodden clothes while still wrapped in the oppressive heat and humidity of the storm. He liked to be clean and hated wearing wet clothes. You'd think that after growing up in Seattle, that he would be used to being wet, but he'd always hated it and was one of the rare and devout umbrella users in the Pacific Northwest.

"Shouldn't be long. We don't have that many people to recover," the man replied, before realizing what he had just said. He looked back with a fear for his career in his eyes.

"I understand," Mick said, giving him a tired shrug. "Those of us that made it are lucky to be alive. Some of the others may not feel the same, but when all of the rows in-front of you shear off, and you're left staring out at the flaming front half of the jet and the jaws of the storm responsible for it, you develop a very clear appreciation for just how lucky you are to be alive."

"Right."

Mick turned away and looked out the window as the first shaky survivors were being shepherded towards the bus. Despite no real signs of injuries, many of the survivors were being carried on stretchers or practically being dragged between two responders. *I may not have taken it with a smile like Jake did, but at least I don't think I looked as shocked as those people. Granted, there are more than a few wires loose in Jake's head. Although, now that I think of it, it may be more of a case of a different wiring template altogether and not just loose wires.* He shook his head reproachfully as the first of them reached the bus and fell into a seat in a sobbing daze. *Something says that I am going to regret not having joined Jake in his exodus!*

By the time his bus pulled out, he was more than ready to leave and be rid of the pity-party he now shared the cab with. It had only taken thirty minutes to load, but it had been a maddeningly long thirty minutes filled with the incessant sobbing and whining of the other survivors. It usually wouldn't have bugged him so much, but between his soggy clothes, low blood sugar, sleep deprivation, and all-around cranky mood, he was definitely a less than happy camper.

"Would you all just shut up already!?" Mick commanded in a holler, cutting through the sniveling hoard as he stood and rounded on the rest of the passengers. Heads snapped up and fear filled many of their eyes as they recoiled away from him and his words. With the dark backdrop of the storm outside and the dim bus lights he must have looked like some kind of towering barbarian or monster to them. "You are alive. Unless you had family in the other section of the jet, you have nothing to whine about, and everything to be thankful for! Next one of you snivelers that I hear, I'm throwing you back out in the rain and I'm not going to ask the driver to stop before I do it. Then you will really have something to whine about!"

Mick sat back down with a huff as the entire bus went quiet and stared at the back of his head since the head rest, unfortunately and painfully, only managed to reach the top of his shoulders. The bus driver started whistling happily.

***

Mick was the first off of the bus when it reached the terminal. In his haste to be free of the 'sniveling hoard,' *better to be back out in the rain than stuck another minute with that lot,* he almost ran over the small Japanese man that greeted him at the door with a wool blanket. He forced himself to take a breath and put on a smile as he took note of the worried look on the man's face as the probably 5'2" little man craned his neck to look up at him. "Thank you!" he said, accepting the blanket with as much grace and courtesy as he could muster. He must not have looked very convincing because the man wilted before him as he moved the rest of the way inside. He was just in time to see a TV clip of Jake giving a quick and vague statement. Despite his current irksomeness, he found himself smiling and shaking his head. *Lucky jerk. He may get burned for that, but at least his visibility just got a big boost and it looks like he will make it clear of the airport before the safety Nazis can detain him. Who knows, he may even be able to get a girlfriend now.*

Mick's brief reprieve was interrupted by the arrival of the other survivors, who were still maintaining a wide berth around him. The remaining support staff had moved in and were, with little success, trying to shepherd the confused herd in the proper direction. He let out a sad sigh and hung his head as he shook it, before rounding on them once more. *Why me?*

"Persons in flashy orange and blue outfit will lead you where you want to go. Follow persons!" Mick barked at the lemmings. They jumped a little, but after his threat on the bus they obeyed and fell upon the surprised staff in a gibbering mob. Apparently feeling protected now, they wasted no time starting in on their demands, complaints, and other plebeian jabberings. Of which, unsurprisingly, more than a few seemed directed at him; as shown through their jabbing fingers and vile sneers in his direction. Mick let the shadows build and extend around him ominously. They quickly found their other complaints more pressing.

One of the staffers quirked an eyebrow at him and sauntered over. "What was all of that about?"

Mick turned on the man with a sigh. "Lemmings," he answered flatly, walking away in the direction of the smell of hot food while the man stood there confused.

He quickly snapped out of it and turned to stop Mick. "Hey, wait! You're going the wrong way."

"No, I'm not! There is food this way and I mean to get at it!" Mick said, continuing on without missing a step.

"But you have to get examined..." The man drew up short as Mick rounded on him. He had long since learned to read people and for just a moment he found himself faced with the unfathomable. It made that inner part of the brain that ran purely on instinct freeze as if it had suddenly found itself confronted with a predator that it couldn't hope to fight or escape. So, as any prey found in such a situation, he froze in hope that the predator might pass him by.

"When would I get to eat!?" Mick asked, taking note of the cold sweat that the man had broken out in. *Not good if that much is peeking through. I need rest and food soonest. I can't afford any accidents now.*

The man paused as the waves of fear passed and whatever monster had suddenly loomed before him sunk back down into the depths from which it had reared, leaving in its place just a mountain of a man before him. He knew that the memory of that brief glimpse into the dark would stay with him for the rest of his life, though. At last his brain re-engaged and he registered the terse question. "Probably after a check-up and once we get everyone sorted out and through customs. About an hour. Maybe two," he answered, dubiously.

Mick smiled and walked away leaving the man to tail him at what his brain considered a slightly less dangerous distance. Most of the restaurants and stores were already closed thanks to the late hour, storm, and therein non-existence of customers, but he somehow managed to find an Udon shop that was still open. "Rice and a large Kitsune Udon with extra green onions, please," he ordered, dropping into Japanese and stepping up to the window. The proprietor just stood there surprised for a moment while giving the wet giant before her an appraising look.

"Coming right up," she said, breaking into a smile and a nod as she set to work. It wasn't people's usual reaction on first meeting or seeing him, but the smile gave him a bit of a warm feeling. She moved like a leaf caught in the wind as she flitted about the tiny kitchen, barely seeming to touch the floor. Although, it was her skill with the blade which held Mick's eyes captive. The ingredients seemed to fall to pieces without even a hint of force being used. It spoke to a level of training and experience far beyond what a person working in a place like this should have had. It was par with, if not superior to, the skill of any knife user, inside or outside of the kitchen, he had ever seen. She surprised him further when, instead of just handing him his tray, she came out and brought his order to one of the nearby tables.

Mick made to pull out his wallet to pay but she cut him off before he had the chance.

"You were on 'The Jet', right?" she asked, as he took a seat and pulled the tray a little closer and tucked a napkin into his collar. Past experience had shown that noodles were rather dangerous food to eat with chopsticks. Not that his soppy clothes would be much worse for the wear should he happen to fumble a noodle and cause a splash, but he didn't know how long he would be stuck in them and didn't much like smelling or looking like a sloppy person.

"What gave it away?" Mick asked. There was sarcasm in his voice but also amusement and curiosity. *Never met anything like her before.*

She laughed. "You look like a ghost, you're sopping wet, you don't have any bags, and there is a perturbed looking staff guy glaring at you from around the corner. I think he is trying to decide if he should stick his own neck out and drag you back or if he should pass it up to his boss. Given that he's getting out his radio, I figure he decided on the latter and you have between fifteen and thirty minutes before they come for you."

"Plenty of time." Mick smiled and snapped apart his chopsticks.

"Heh. You are an odd one," she said, taking a seat. It wasn't like there was anything else that she needed to be doing at the moment and she highly doubted that there would be any more customers tonight.

Mick finished his slurp of noodles and looked up with a smile. "You should see my friend. Then again, you may have seen him already if you were watching the TV. No sooner than we stop rolling, he gets up, cracks a joke, and heads out into the storm like it's a sunny day in the park. Then he somehow manages to get past all of the red tape, which should have hogtied him with a pretty bow, and winds up on TV."

"Oh, I saw him. He seemed like a real odd fellow. I got the feeling that there was a lot more to him than most people ever see," she said, with a curious smile.

Mick gave a shrug but watched her a little closer all the same. *She's rather perceptive. I'll have to be careful not to let anything unwonted slip.* "I don't think he really even understands himself." *Not that I understand him much better than he does. It's a good thing that I found him first and that whatever it is that lurks inside him has never reared its head or there may have been issues.*

"Enough about him for now. What brought you here?" she asked, giving him a curious eyebrow.

To be sarcastic or not to be sarcastic? I'm too tired for sarcasm and she gave me the food for free. Well, that and she is rather pretty. Admit it! Fine, she's beautiful. "I came over as a CE-J or Culture Exchange Japan employee."

"Oh, I've met a few of them before and I had one at a school I attended when I was growing up. If you don't mind me asking, where were you placed?" she inquired.

"On the shores of Lake Towada in Aomori Prefecture," Mick answered. He was a little surprised when another question didn't immediately follow and looked up to find her smiling. It was now his turn to give her a curious eyebrow to which she laughed. *She has an exquisite laugh.* There was a rakish beauty to her laugh that reminded him of a wolf's serenade in the deep woods. *But I'd best not let it distract me too much. But maybe a little bit is okay.*

"Sorry, it's just that I guess we will sort of be neighbors. My family lives in that general area. Granted, general areas are a mite bit bigger up in the north than they are down here in the more civilized areas," she chuckled, like it was an inside joke. "Some areas are somewhat cutoff up there and a touch insular but for you, I might consider hopping the border and stopping in for a chat or a coffee," she added, smiling coyly at him and trying not to blush and give up all of her cards. *He's not what I expected but maintaining proper decorum is still only proper in this situation.* "I was just working here as a part-timer for my uncle during the summer while I did some research here in Tokyo. My research is over now, and I'll be heading home tomorrow if the weather cooperates," she explained.

"Imagine that! I mean, what are the odds!?" Mick mused before giving himself a shake. *Rather low I would think. And you remember how coincidences tend to turn out. Especially under these kinds of circumstances. Be caut... Oh forget it. I left that life behind and I'm not going to let it chain me down any longer!* "In that case, it is a pleasure to meet you. I'm Mick Renalds, and I'd love to share a cup of coffee and a good talk with you or whatever you would like. I have a feeling that talking with you could become addictive," he said, giving her a sheepish smile. He could feel the blush reaching to his ears. And rightfully so. The more he looked, the more he recognized just how amazingly beautiful she was. She was beautiful but also carried an 'I work for a living' bearing about herself. She had well developed, but not oversized muscles, was around one-hundred-sixty centimeters tall. Her face was just slightly rounded in a heart shape with strong cheeks and tiny but proud chin. Her hair was a little long, just reaching past her shoulders, but you could tell that she was confident, because she wore it tied back, revealing her face. And there was something about her smile, with her just slightly pouty lips, and big eyes that made him stare despite himself.

She smiled at the offer of his name, his slight blush, and his obvious 'covert' re-appraisal of her. "Uesugi Ai, a pleasure to meet you and I look forward to being neighbors. It's a big area, but I look forward to sharing a cup of joe and a good talk with you once you get settled in. In any case, I'm sure you will fall in love... with the town and way of life I mean," she assured him, smiling coyly.

"I think you may be right," Mick agreed, feeling his blush deepen even further. *Stupid! You don't stand a chance.*

He's rather cute when he is blushing and there is something different about him. A darkness but also a light. Ai started to say something, but a depressing shadow suddenly descended over their table.

"Was the flight full of crazies or was it just your row?" The newcomer demanded.

Mick didn't need to look to recognize the Chief's voice. He sounded even more peeved than the last time. "Not crazy, just famished. What with the turbulence, they missed all but the first drink and snack run," he commented absently, setting his chopsticks down on his empty bowl, not that he really remembered having finished it or his rice off, and turned to face the Chief.

Chief glared down at him but soon gave it up when it became apparent that Mick wasn't about to be intimidated and threw his hands up in frustration. He was a big guy, but next to Mick he looked average. "Crazy Americans," he grumbled. "Well, now that you seem to be fed!!! I am going to have to 'Insist' that you rejoin the others so that we can give you a proper check-up! That one crazy that slipped free was bad enough."

Mick had to cover his laugh with a cough at the mention of Jake. "Yes, Jake is a little bit of an oddball," he agreed, smiling at the chief's surprise.

"I should have known that you two knew each other. Birds of a feather indeed," Chief shook his head sighing. It had been a long, wet, and trying day and the paperwork, interviews, and meetings on today's events were going to take days to get through and many long nights of work. And the sooner he got this lost 'lamb' returned to the flock, the sooner he could get to it and get home. "Now, am I going to have to get some help to drag back the obviously 'confused' and 'distraught' passenger or will you come quietly?" Chief asked, nodding to the two; large-ish Japanese men flanking him.

Mick smiled and stood up. He was a full head taller than the tallest of them and probably out massed them by at least a third if not double. And, in his case, it was all muscle. "Tempting, and I'm sure the lawsuit would pay out splendidly, but you are in luck. I hate lawyers and now that I have had some food, I will come back quietly. It was for the good of everyone that I got fed. You really don't want to be around me when my blood sugar gets too low or I get a bit anemic. So where to?" he asked, looking between and down at them with a smile.

Had it come to a tussle, he doubted that they would have prevailed unless they were willing to do things like shoot him, and even that wouldn't have guaranteed them victory. He had long since faced far, far worse than them and had the faded scars to show for it. He wasn't just strong and massive. He was trained and had perfect muscle memory as well as a photographic memory. He could easily have gone pro MMA, Karate, Judo, Boxing, or several other armed and un-armed martial arts. To the annoyance of most all of his masters and trainers, he had refused on the grounds that if he ever had a reason to fight, it was to destroy his opponent and there wouldn't be any rules dictating what was allowed in the fight. The only Master that hadn't been annoyed, and had wholeheartedly agreed with him, had been his Iai-master. A broken sword, chest plate, and three broken ribs had more than convinced that master that competition was a no-no. *And let's not be forgetting the family reasons either.*

"Um..." Chief looked up and up at the tower of muscle, and it wasn't show muscle but the thick build of real working strength, looming before him now. *Was he always this big?* He gave his head an internal shake to clear the cobwebs. Years of training and experience were the only thing that kept the doubt from showing on his face. "From here it would be faster if we cut across the terminal instead of heading back the way you came," he explained. *I'm in charge here, why in the world am I explaining this to him!?I need a break.*

Mick smiled, knowing full well what the Chief had thought. *Realized you bit off more than you could chew didn't you!* "After you then." Chief twitched a little but turned to leave without showing any other signs of apprehension.

"Wait!" Ai ordered before they made good on their departure. They all stopped in their tracks like the President himself had given the command. She grabbed a sticky pad and a pen from under the counter, scribbled something on it really fast, tore it free, and handed the note over to Mick. "I hope you fall in love with the area and if you ever need help or are in trouble, go here," she whispered into his ear where the others couldn't hear her. There was a twinkle in her eyes as she stepped back that spoke of enjoyable mischief. She gave an equally demure smile before turning back to the task of closing up shop. *Fate is a weird thing.*

Mick glanced down at the note and smiled. There was a basic map with some scribbled landmarks on it. It looked more like a trail map than a town, but he recognized enough of them at a glance that he was confident that he could find his way. *Just what kind of town does she live in?* "Same." He smiled, wishing that he could stay and chat with her more but knowing that it was time to go. He turned and followed the Chief and his improv-goons as he led the way. There was a little extra spring in his step. *Just what game is Fate playing now? Maybe my luck is finally changing. Right, and wouldn't the others just flip if that happened. Then they would really have something to be torqued about.*

Good to his word, the Chief buzzed them through all of the security doors and cut clean through the heart of the terminal instead of taking the long way around through the civilian areas. Why there wasn't a bypass for civilian traffic that did the same was one of those mysteries that he figured there was no satisfactory answer to beyond stupid design practices and sales quotas at the kiosks. They exited out of one of the baggage handling areas and back into a common area, which looked like a small gymnasium or conference hall, where the other survivors were already gathered and milling around like a herd of squawking sheep. There weren't as many as Mick had expected. The chief apparently could read stoic expressions or thoughts better than most con-artists, because he answered the question before he even asked it.

"Of the one-hundred-eighty-seven passengers on Allen Air's 626, only seventy-three survived the 'landing.' Or a little over a third. The front half of coach is always the most crowded," the Chief explained.

"Given that I was in the front row when we came to a stop, I probably have a better idea of just how lucky to be alive we all really are than most of these people," Mick stated, sighing tiredly. "So, what line do I go stand in first?"

"Crazy Americans. If I didn't have a passel of perfectly normal ones, whining away, making demands, and calling for their lawyers, I would have had to think that our media had been grossly misrepresenting you. But I have those aplenty. So, I can just write you and your friend off as strange rule breaking anomalies. Or, in your case, maybe 'mutant aberrant' would be more apt," he mused with a grin. Mick chuckled appreciatively at the jest, even if it was rather closer to the mark than he would have liked to admit. "That line by the doors is the one that you need to start in. They will direct you from there."

"Thanks. So now for my one American question. Any ideas on our luggage? I'd really like a change of clothes and something says that they probably don't have my size," Mick asked, squaring his already square shoulders and making his bulk evident.

"In your case, I'll take that as a reasonable question. Sadly, I don't have a good answer at this point. At a best guess, if your bags survived, we will probably get to them late tomorrow. The storm has us pretty much completely shut down. No point risking anyone else out in the storm now that we have recovered the passengers," Chief answered.

"Thanks for trying and sorry for inconveniencing you," Mick apologized, he was even a little sincere, before heading for the line.

"Ticket, passport, other identification, or name please?" the person at the intake table, which was covered in folders, asked without looking up as Mick came to a stop at the table.

Mick fished his ticket and passport out and handed them over. He was lucky that he had at least kept his wallet, passport, and cash on him instead of leaving them in his lost carry-on.

The man checked them really fast then seemed to do a double take before finally looking up and handing them and a folder back to Mick. "You're lucky. You are the furthest forward survivor. Well, there was that other guy that somehow got out, but he's not here to claim the position," he added conversationally. "Anyways, take this and wait in that line, the doctor will give you a quick checkup. Once you are done there, just keep following the directions and you should be done fairly quickly."

"Thanks," Mick said, taking the folder and stepping into the line. While he waited, he went ahead and flipped through the folder that they had given him. It was more than a little disturbing just how much information it contained on him. There was everything from his 'minimal and false' medical history to his academic history in there. *Jake is right to be paranoid about doctors and electronic records. Once it's in the system, it is nigh impossible to get it completely out again. Good thing that there are places which the system still can't reach and those who work for the system that are willing to make adjustments if you know how to ask right.*

"Are you okay?" a nurse asked, noticing his shiver and was obviously concerned that he was hypothermic or going into shock.

"All good. I just had a little bit of a disturbing thought and found myself in agreement with the sentiments of one of my friends," Mick answered, shrugging.

The nurse gave him a quizzical look that said she wasn't quite sure if she believed him, but she moved on after a moment.

Mick shook his head as she walked away to see to another passenger that was on the verge of hyperventilating. *Dude's alive! What does he have to be so worked up over?*

"Folder?"

Mick's head snapped back around as he realized that he had reached his destination. "Do I get it back?" he countered. "No offence, but there is a lot of personal data in here that I would just as soon not have get lost or misplaced in filing somewhere or worse logged into public records when this court case blows up." *Or cross-checked against my actual condition.*

The doctor blinked a few times in surprise. "It will be filed away with the rest of the records once this is all over with!"

"That doesn't work for me. You can make your notes and record the results but the file stays with me!" Mick retorted, just loud enough to draw a few curious looks, adding to the pressure on the doctor not to make a scene out of it.

"You won't be able to make a claim for injuries if the chain of control is broken!" the doctor warned.

"I'm more worried about reimbursement for my belongings than about injuries. So, thank you for the warning and I'll take my chances," Mick informed him as he handed over the folio with his medical records alone. He held it tight enough that the doctor had to give a little tug to get it free. It was a little petty, but he didn't much like the doctor's attitude either and despite eating he was still hungry and feeling a touch cranky. His soggy clothes were doing little to improve his disposition either.

With a slightly disturbing creak from the gurney, he took a seat while the doctor fussed over him and made some notes in the folder while mumbling under his breath. *I must be channeling my inner Jake or something. Probably a good thing Jake isn't here. He would be bored out of his mind and would have flipped when he saw the file on him. Then again, his file would probably have been almost blank, and he would have seen to keeping it that way.*

The doctor made a few quick checks, looking for any injuries and taking his vitals before consulting the folio and scrunching his forehead and frowning. He was still frowning as he looked back at Mick. "Are you on any kind of depressants?" he asked, flatly.

Mick was caught off guard by the question but recovered quickly. "No, I don't take any medicine except for coffee and tea - and drugs are just stupid."

The doctor's frown deepened. "The truth now!?" he repeated, a dark flicker lighting in his eyes as he figured that he could get back at Mick for his previous actions.

Mick wasn't in the mood to play petty games. "Cut to the chase already. I'm tired, soggier than a Lejeune bullfrog, and I was just in a plane crash. I don't really care for the verbal jousting at the moment!" He let a little heat slip into his voice and leaned a little forward, towering over the doctor to make his point. Usually he was a distinctly level-headed person but that had less to do with his natural tendencies and more to do with a highly developed amount of self-control to keep his inner 'Mr. Hyde' at bay. Jake was one of the few people that had any idea of the sheer volume of emotion that he constantly kept under lock and key, but even he didn't really know the half of it. For that matter, even his own family didn't. On the flip side, Jake was the only person that he knew of that possibly had even more going on inside of him and in his head than he did. *Even if Jake doesn't know it. It's probably for the best that that particular chasm never sees the light of day, lest it open its maw and swallow the light completely.*

The doctor felt the heat and saw the embers in Mick's eyes but wasn't convinced and apparently, he had somehow already lobotomized the areas of his brain that should have been telling him that this was not someone you wanted to get on the bad side of. Some people were just that way. Super type 'A' personalities with inflated egos. "That is exactly the problem. Even if this was a completely normal situation, your vitals are far too low and calm. They are almost at the same point as someone in deep sleep. The only way that that is possible is if you are on depressants of some kind! Those are highly regulated in Japan and illegal to possess without a doctor's permission. In light of current events, I am willing to overlook all of this as long as you tell me the truth right now and hand over any remaining drugs. If you refuse, I will be forced to seek assistance from security, reports will be filed, and you will most likely face deportation at the bare minimum!"

"Draw a blood sample if you must, but I'm telling you I'm not taking or on anything, and I don't much like being called a liar and a junky!" Mick said, getting up off of the exam table and towering over the tiny doctor. Apparently, some part of his brain had escaped the lobotomy.

The doctor blinked, finally backing down and stepping back a little. He quickly set about getting out some blood drawing equipment. "When this comes back, you can expect that you will be arrested and that charges will be filed!" he said, with more than a little dark glee and anticipation in his voice and eyes.

Mick smiled, sat back down, and held out his arm. "You're lucky I hate lawyers and media, or this would be a fine lawsuit. As it is, I just really don't care except that you are holding me up and I'm sick and tired of pushy people with inflated egos an ideas about their own authority. So, hurry it up!" The doctor gave the tourniquet an extra tight tug and wasn't all that friendly about inserting the needle. But his aim was decent enough and he found the vein on the first try and the vial filled quickly. "Happy now?" he asked as the needle was removed and he held a cotton swab over the spot. *Blood draws are always tricky. Wouldn't do to have him notice anything out of place.*

"You can leave," the doctor ordered scribbling a note on the tube with gleeful malice and waving him out the exit.

Mick didn't need to be told twice and left, rubbing out the spot so that it wouldn't bruise too badly. The next area had some people handing out blankets, towels, toiletries, and clothes to those who were missing their carry-ons or clothing. He processed past each pretty quickly, getting two blankets instead of the customary one since he was so tall. It was smooth sailing until he reached the person with the clothes. There was a jumble of different designs and styles apparently donated/appropriated, from the terminal shopping areas. The person took one look at him and walked away to a side area and came back with a little old lady. She wordlessly walked up and quickly took a few measurements and notes before disappearing for a few minutes. When she came back, she was carrying several layers of cloth and hung it up on a rack by a changing stall.

"Sorry, but it's going to have to be a summer kimono for you. No one really stocks clothes in 'giant size.' On a plus side, you will soon be the proud owner of what is a several thousand-dollar kimono. Just please don't tell the others, because it really isn't preferential treatment," the man explained. The little old lady had finished laying out the parts and dragging over a step stool by that time. She shot them a look that said she was ready and despised waiting.

With a nod, Mick made his way over to the changing room and began to strip out of his sodden clothes. He was a bit startled when the little old lady came in behind him, as quiet as a mouse, with a layer of cloth and her step stool while he had on nothing but his boxers. She didn't even pause as she started fitting him out. He could have sworn that she rolled her eyes at his reaction. After the underlayer was on, she directed him out of the changing room and started adding the other layers. She was almost painfully thorough and made sure that he could see what she was doing. Despite not uttering so much as a sound at him, she apparently wanted him to at least know how to put it on right the next time that he needed to.

In the end she'd decked him out in a night green outer layer with a subtle checkered print that looked a mite bit like stars while a shadowed forest pattern dominated the hem. It was truly marvelous, and he was pretty sure that he had caught a slight smile cross her otherwise expressionless face as she gave a content nod and handed him two extra sets of washable liners so that he could at least cycle the inner layer. With that all done, it was off to staking out a cot, bench, or comfortable looking stretch of floor to call his for the night.

It only took him one look at the cots to tell him that they would be a non-starter. Almost all of them were a solid eight inches shorter than him which left him with trying to find a bench without armrests that he could use. In the end he had to cheat by dragging two of the benches together. Given that it was the middle of summer, he didn't need a lot in the way of blankets. After pulling off the outer layers of his kimono and carefully folding and setting them aside, he rolled up his blankets as a pillow and got as comfortable as he could. He was out cold as soon as his head touched down. It was one of his gifts. He could immediately fall asleep anywhere and anytime he needed to. Within a few minutes he was in a deep sleep and snoring gently.

Lucky Jerk
Monday, June 28

Mick awoke to the warmth of the sun on his face. He'd slept like the restful dead but was a touch creaky and cranky thanks to his improv bed and not looking forward to the next few minutes. With much effort he managed to pry his eyes open and squinted at the blazing ball of warmth beaming through the terminal windows. It was nice to see that the storm had broken, but between it only being 5 o'clock and the scene straight out of a disaster movie that was revealed outside the window, there was little joy to be found at the breaking of a new dawn. Their jet may have been the only one to crash but it was not the only wreckage. At least two other jets that had been parked had been torn free of their tethers and flipped. Two others in sight had broken wings, three had snapped landing gear, and another had a broken fuselage. The fury of the storm had been even more daunting than he had originally thought. It really was a miracle that they had managed to land and a terrible shame that the pilots who had managed to pull it off had perished.

His stomach let loose a grumble that shook the bench informing him that it was starving and if he didn't feed it soon, it would start eating him. A quick survey of the area showed that most of the survivors were still asleep and that there were only a few shepherds about to watch over the dreary flock. Figuring that they may have a lead on some food, he got up, dressed, and made his way over after gathering his few belongings in a cinch knapsack that he had been given the previous night. It had the Allen Air logo on it.

"Any chance that there is somewhere to get some food around here?" Mick asked the slightly surprised shepherd who was still trying to categorize the kimono clad giant now towering over him. "Oh, and maybe a shower?"

"Ah...?" *Oni! He must be some kind of foreign Oni. I knew I never should have left the village.*

"Food? Is? Where?" Mick prompted again, using single word Japanese to get past the locked state that the man had obviously entered. *By his expression, you'd think he was facing a monster or something. Heh.*

The shepherd gave himself a shake and craned his neck way up to look at Mick. "It's only five-thirty," he stated like that answered everything.

Mick bit down on a hunger induced angry retort and took a deep breath instead. *I forgot about that. Blasted Japan and their late opening hours.* He knew the dilemma well from his first assignment in Japan. He was naturally a morning person. Japan was an early start country, so they got along great except for one little thing. Nothing but convenience stores opened before 10 o'clock. Unless you cooked your own breakfast, you were stuck starving until brunch or lunch. "Then coffee and vending machines?" he inquired, leaning a bit further into the man's bubble. It was a more aggressive approach than he usually used, but he was starving, and this man had information that he needed.

The shepherd tried to back up a little, but the wall had him trapped. He quickly pointed to a hallway. "There are a few vending machines over there. There is also a little Lawson's. They said that they would bring breakfast between 8 and 9 o'clock. And there are some rental showers a little further down the same hall. I think they cost 500?," he answered, adding the shower comment in hopes that it would distract the giant Oni before him from eating him.

"Thank you," Mick replied, smiling and taking a step back to the obvious relief of the man. He started to turn to leave but thought better of it. "You might want to call your boss and tell him that they should probably think about getting that breakfast here a bit earlier unless they want a bunch of even more upset survivors on their hands," he warned, leaving to claim his hold-me-overs before the rest of the sniveling hoard awakened and descended upon the unsuspecting vending machines and convenience store.

The selection was so-so. In the end, he settled on a machine cappuccino, salmon and mayo onigiri, and a meat bun. It wasn't enough to fill him up by a longshot, but it was enough to hold him over until the promised breakfast arrived. By the time he returned to the 'holding area' there was a little bit of a ruckus starting up. Apparently, more people had awoken and now that they'd had some sleep and their brains were 'working,' they had demands. Not caring for the drama, Mick made his way by and found a seat looking out at the tarmac and the torn remains of their jet that still laid out on it. There was now a little bit of activity out there as work crews started the cleanup, survey, and salvage operations.

It really is a miracle that any of us survived. Mick smiled, looking up to the ceiling while he chewed on a SoyJoy. He wasn't nearly the atheist that Jake assumed he was. Point in fact, he was rather devout. Jake just never really saw that part of him past his realist character.

While he ate, he went ahead and turned on the TV near his area. It was set to the news and, what wonders never cease, they were the news. He tried a few other channels also and stopped on one with an interview just starting. The headline read 'What's happening.' He went ahead a clicked the volume up a little and sat back to listen.

Wonder if Jake is watching this, because she is so his type. He smirked as the petite expert took her seat.

"Thank you, Ms. Aida, for taking some time out of your busy schedule today to help shed some light on the events of yesterday for our viewers. Let's get started. The main question that I'm sure is on many of our minds is 'what does geology have to do with meteorology?'"

Now there is a stupid question! Mick chuckled as he saw the 'guest' do her best to not sigh in exasperation.

"Thank you for having me here. The answer is, quite a bit, actually. For instance, did you know that compared to the yearly gas outputs of geological events, vehicle emissions barely even show up as a blip? There are even rather good models that indicate that it is only the emissions of vehicles that are keeping us from slipping into a new Ice Age. Between the sun and the planet, pretty much all of the weather is created. In this case, the direct cause looks to be ocean warming due to volcanic venting," Kyoko explained.

"So, Ms. Aida, you're saying that the cause of the unprecedented Typhoon last night that caused the crash of Allen Air's 626 out of Portland and the death of one-hundred-and-fifty people was a volcano?" the reporter asked.

"Well, not quite, and the last I heard it was one-hundred-fourteen that tragically perished in the crash, but the nationwide death-toll was tragically close to a thousand last I saw before this meeting. The crash was tragically spectacular, but I would hate to marginalize all the other deaths and tragedies that this storm has wrought," Kyoko corrected. "As to your question, please take a look at this," she said, bringing up a slide showing the string of vents along the ocean floor while blatantly ignoring the reporter's apparent angst at being corrected.

It had been a while since his last geology class in college, but he remembered enough to recognize what he was seeing faster than the reporter. *Jake may have been closer to the truth then he knew. He just may get his adventure.* He turned his attention back to the reporter who looked more than a little miffed about being corrected. *'Honest newsy' and 'fact checked news' should be listed under oxymoron.*

"Could you please explain, for our viewers, what we are looking at?" the reporter asked, knowing better than getting in a spitting match on live-TV, and turning her attention to the slides. You could tell from the doe in the headlights look that the reporter was really the one in need of the explanation.

"Why yes, it would be my pleasure." Aida said, almost rolling her eyes. Her distaste for reporters was fairly evident. "What you are looking at, based on the heat plumes, which have opened up along this previously unknown fault, is a new range of active volcanic vents. The heat venting has caused unusually high water-temperatures across a large area of the Pacific Ocean. When this cold front ran into the abnormally warm waters," she overplayed the weather forecast, "it caused a Typhoon to develop with frightening speed and power," she answered, using many simple, a little too simple really, pictures and diagrams.

"Why was a fault line this important unknown?" the reporter demanded, jabbing her finger at Aida like it was somehow her personal fault for not knowing about it and that she was therefore responsible for the storm and crash.

"Because it was un-know-n!" Aida replied, letting some sarcasm leak in. "Before yesterday, there had been no indications that there was any reason to look into the area. For all intents and purposes, it was just a stretch of deep ocean floor. Flat and barren except for some fish and crabs. Then yesterday, this!" She pointed at the display with the plumes again.

"Okay, I guess that is understandable. At least the storm has blown itself out," the reporter said, trying to change the subject. She may not have been the sharpest tool in the shed, but she could tell when she was being mocked.

"Okay?! Okay?! Do you have any ideas of what the long-term effects of having a major active thermal vent right off our coast could be?" Aida asked. The reporter started to respond but she cut her off before she had the chance. "But wait! There's more," she mimed, using her best telemarketer impersonation. "Why?

"Excuse me?" the reporter asked. "Why what?"

And Aida face palmed on national television. Mick chuckled. *Have to like her spirit.* "For starters the storm may have passed but the vent is still pumping out heat. Heat causes evaporation, thereby increasing the moisture in the air. If even a moderate cold front moves in, you get clouds. Get enough clouds and you have a storm. Maybe the next one won't be as bad as the last. Or maybe it will be worse. But as bad as that is, it's still just the surface problem!" A touch of her inner terror was clear in her voice for any with ears to hear. She reigned it in quickly and was smiling as she asked, looking directly at the camera instead of at the reporter, "Why has a vent, an active fault, opened up where there shouldn't be one? What does it mean?" She asked.

"Um?" the reporter responded. It was clear that she wasn't sure how she was supposed to deal with this. Her job was to ask questions not answer them. And the interviewee hadn't even directed the question at her. Her relief as she evidently got a 'cut it' signal was almost painfully evident. "Well it looks like we have run out of time. So, to the audience. What does it all mean? Thank you, Ms. Aida, for your help!" The feed quickly cut back to the main newsroom, cutting off any reply which Aida may have made.

"Very interesting?" Mick commented, fishing for another bite of food and getting nothing but finger and wrapper for his effort. *All gone already!* A whiff of cheap bacon, powdered eggs, and terrible coffee drifted by his nose. "That smells wretched. I think I'll go get a plate." He quickly deposited his trash in one of the cans and gathered up his meager belongings before heading off in search of more food. *I really wish my metabolism would demand just a little less intake. I wonder what exceedingly dull things they have planned for us today.*

"Following lunch, there will be consultation sessions with a psychiatrist, your consulate, and Airline officials that will handle any questions of reimbursement for losses and will add your name to a joint suit should you desire to be part of it. They will also issue you a return ticket on an airline of your choice or a voucher for a later flight and two first class roundtrip flight vouchers. If you have any other questions, please consult with one of the representatives in an orange vest," a man instructed from the front of the chow line with a loud hailer.

I guess that answers that. I wonder if they will let me just take the vouchers and leave?

A Real Buddy
Tuesday, June 29

"There are enough busses and taxis for all of you. Please wait your turn and we will help you leave as quickly as possible," a guide shouted, as Mick and the remaining survivors funneled out.

It was now Tuesday. Two full days had passed since Mick had 'landed' in Japan. He had 'requested' some additional toiletries the previous day when they had shown up with the remains of his belongings in a plastic bag. A sneaker and his swim trunks were all that was left. When he had asked about reimbursement for the lost clothing and other belongings they had simply asked for a general value, doubled the amount and rounded up. He had come to Japan with 300,000 Yen. He now had 1,000,000 Yen lining his wallet and tucked safely away in his knapsack with his lucky trunks and shoe. It would more than cover the cost of his lost belongings, but finding clothing in his size here in Japan was going to be a royal nightmare. There were some excellent reasons why he had packed heavy. He'd had more money, but given his newfound fondness for kimonos, he had sought out the little old lady again, to her surprise, and requested two more sets of liners and one more kimono, a yukata, and a jimbe. He'd left the color and style choice to her again and she had selected a burgundy colored kimono and sea blue yukata. She had gladly accepted his 400,000 Yen and promised that they would be waiting for him when he reached his town. Since she had more time and was getting paid this time, she did a full fitting and was going to get the sizing perfect. It was really only luck that the first kimono had happened to be in the right size.

More than anything, he was going to miss the few books that had also been lost. They had been hardbacks and finding replacements for them was going to be expensive and take time. When it came to fiction, he mainly read Science Fiction and Fantasy because they were the genres that were willing to really talk about serious social issues and say what needed to be said and it was fun to check their accuracy against reality.

He was forced out of his lamentations as he reached the head of the line. They stuck him on a micro bus with the few remaining CE-J's who had decided to stick around. There had been at least twenty of them left when they had first arrived. There were now only seven including him. The other cupcakes had cut and ran home to mommy or whatever namby-pamby land they called home.

The ride was long, hot, and sticky with the soupy thick humidity that had followed the storm and now hung like a soggy blanket over Tokyo. It was so thick that you could almost drink the air. Even Mick, whose dad had been a career Marine - on the side - and who had grown up mostly at camp Lejeune, found it almost unbearable. It didn't help that, for whatever reason, the driver seemed to only think that the low setting existed on the AC. Add to that that apparently the other people in the bus hadn't taken advantage of the airport showers and you had the makings of the bus ride to hell. *Shoot me now and let it be over with.*

At long last, the bus rolled to a stop at the hotel. Mick didn't waste a second throwing open the door, to the annoyance of the driver. It was an auto door and had started to open but had been taking far too long. There was a CE-J staffer waiting to greet them as they swam out of the sauna bus.

"Is this all of you?" she asked, giving the now empty bus a quick check to verify that it really was empty. "There were supposed to be four more..."

"They're not here and won't magically appear just because they are on your list. So, if it's all the same, can we move this inside where it is air conditioned!?" Mick said, already moving for the entrance before she could argue or find some way to delay the inevitable.

It was like the breath of life smacked Mick in the face as he crossed the threshold and was greeted by dry, cool air. It was only then, after the brief shock from the drastic change abated, that he could hear the whine of the ventilation system that hinted that the reprieve could be short lived as the system burned itself out trying to maintain the cool. If the heat and humidity didn't break soon, then the compressors would.

"If you would 'please' follow me, we can get you your room key. It will only be for tonight, since you will be leaving for your placements tomorrow," the CE-J lady said, coming in behind them when it became apparent that waiting for nonexistent people to show up was not high on their lists.

Mick collected his key and headed straight for the room. There was a 'dinner/meet your neighbors' event later that night, but right now he wanted a long shower and maybe even a soak in the tub if it was big enough. He slid the key into the lock and stepped in. The TV was on, so apparently, he had a roommate. A head poked around the corner and he let out a groan. "For real?" He glared balefully at a grinning Jake who was now hopping to his feet. "Dozens of empty rooms and they stick me with you!" he groaned, dropping the bundle with his meager possessions in it.

"Mick!" Jake exclaimed, giving Mick a bear hug and patting him on the back. "Glad to see that they finally released you from purgatory," he said, stepping back and grinning broadly.

"You have no idea!!!" Mick growled, trying really hard to be angry and failing miserably as a smile betrayed him. It wasn't like he could blame Jake for doing what he had done. That was just who Jake was. And, he only had himself to blame for not following along. He finally gave it up with an annoyed shake of his head at his jovial 'friend.' "I never will understand why I ever thought it was a good idea to become friends with you."

"If I remember right, it was because I was the only person that was willing to argue with you and poke holes in your precious logic 'Spock,'" Jake ribbed. "Well, me and your sister," he added, looking around for the Amazon, only halfway for effect.

Mick's older sister was a lithe beauty that stood even taller than Mick and was just as strong. You didn't really understand lethal beauty until you got in a fight with her. Calling it a fight wasn't really fair either since what it really was, was a slaughter. She moved with a grace and flexibility that made ballerinas and gymnasts look like drunk newborn horses with roller-skates for hoofs and struck with a sharpness that made a Katana look about as sharp as wet clay. Even Mick, who was highly trained and had a similar dexterity, could barely hold his own against her. For about fifteen seconds that was. Then it would all be over and there would be stars or tweety birds doing circles about his head. What was even worse was that she was smart and, like Mick, had both a photographic and motographic memory. So, you may be able to pull a new move over on her once and then she would not only learn it but improve it.

Then again, unlike hers, Mick's heart was never really set on winning when they had fought and he was just as smart if not more so. She may have beaten him at sparring every time, but never once had she bested him at strategy.

Jake shook his head to keep from going down an old rabbit hole that he had long since learned was lined with razor wire. There was something distinctly odd about the Renalds family. They played normal far too well for being so abnormal. But he wasn't about to go poke that sleeping lion in the nose to see if it was a Nemean Lion.

"Yet another good reason as to why I decided to stay rather than return. Aliya never would have let me live it down if I had chickened out." Mick shivered at the very thought of how she would have reacted. *And the others wouldn't have been overjoyed at my return either. Especially since they finally managed to facilitate my exile.*

"Putting those nightmares aside for the moment, what's up with the new threads?" Jake asked, cocking an eyebrow at Mick's new threads. "Is that as comfortable as it looks?"

"If Aliya ever heard that you referred to her as a nightmare, she'd walk across the Pacific just to throttle you," Mick warned, shooting Jake a dangerous grin.

"I thought we were friends?"

"Oh, we are. Which is why I won't tell her on the condition that you buy dinner!" Mick threatened, knowing that Jake was already good and trapped.

"Real buddy you are!" Jake grumbled, grabbing his wallet. "Back to the previous question...?" he asked, grabbing the door.

***

"You know, you're a real buddy Jake," Mick said, as they slurped ramen noodles and had a few drinks at a nearby ramen shop. It was a hole in the wall, but those also had the best food, were the easiest to get a seat in, and had the lowest prices. Granted, it was a little like Russian Roulette and you had best keep aware of the toilet locations from the restaurant to wherever you were heading. Just in case the porcelain throne, or more like trench seeing as how this was Japan, put forth an urgent summons for you to immediately present yourself under threat of utter humiliation.

"How ya figure?" Jake asked, as he downed his drink. *Oh, how I have missed real ramen, and while beer may not be my first, second or fifth choice, there is no denying that it goes good with ramen. Only problem is that it really makes me have to pee.*

"Well, we survived a major accident. Which is all good and dandy but then you get up and look down at your shaken buddy, me, and make a blasted reference to a TV show and walk out into the storm like you're having a stroll in the park without a care in the world. Do you have any idea how long I sat there trying to rationalize the insanity of the whole situation?" Mick asked as he refilled Jakes cup. After all, it was only proper to refill your drinking partner's glass when it got low.

Jake pondered that for a moment while he slurped up some more noodles. "More or less than two minutes? And it wasn't that insane, it was just reality. Though the two are close cousins and often times interchangeable," he answered in all honesty. "Still don't see how that makes me a real buddy?"

Mick shook his head. *Yep, there is something seriously wrong with my friend. His brain's wiring just doesn't follow the proper diagram.* "Fine! You're a real pal, but I was being sarcastic in this case. You just up and left. One little comment and you were gone. What was up with that?"

Hmm? "Since you asked, to tell you the truth, I was on a bit of an adrenalin high and my clothes were soaked. I could tell that you were okay, and truth be told, the rest of the passengers didn't mean much to me and it wasn't like there was much my staying could have done to help the situation except by being in the way. I needed to keep moving and really wanted to get some dry clothes. So, I left. And being your pal, I won't lambaste you with just how much of a pain being the only person from the flight trying to leave was. You'd think they all thought I was crazy or something," Jake confessed.

"Dude! News flash. You are one-hundred-percent certifiable," Mick said with a laugh, "Not that I am complaining. That is what makes you interesting. And it isn't all that bad," he chided with a look that completely said, 'I know something you don't know.'

Jake didn't like not knowing. *What's it got's in its pockets!* "Spill!" he demanded.

"Let's just say that that non-existent shadow you have been casting has become a lot opaquer. Have you really not noticed the way that ten times as many random people have been coming up to talk to you as before, and almost everyone else stares at least a little?" Mick asked with a smug grin, casting a quick glance around them.

Jake thought back on the last few days and took a quick glance around and noticed several people abruptly finding some spot on the wall or their food to be incredibly fascinating. The ramen was good but not that good and the paint on the walls was painted in a fashion that would have made a modern art painting look tackier than sap in a dog's fur on a cold morning. Worse was the smattering that didn't look away. A few of whom were rather cute, and he felt a blush which had nothing to do with the beer creeping into his cheeks. "No!" he moaned. *May the media return to the seventh level of the seventy-seventh ring of hell from which it was spawned. I hate that kind of attention!*

"Oh yes. Like it or not, you are the official face of the crash. Just about everyone with a TV has seen your little speech at least once. Sure, they'll forget what you said, even that that was where they first saw you. But just about everyone now kind of recognizes you even if they can't place where from," Mick said, clapping Jake on the back. "Oh, stop moping! It's not all bad."

"Huh, you're going to have to run that by me," Jake replied. His drink was empty again. *Just when I need you, you aren't there for me.*

"You're smarter than that," Mick chided. "Then again for all your smarts, you do seem a little slow in one area."

"As I said, enlighten me oh grand master of all that is human nature," Jake prompted as Mick poured. *And my cup has returned to a proper state.*

"Simple! Your non-existent dating life just took a major turn for the better. You lucky devil," Mick answered, giving a silent nod to the gaggle of giggling cuties that kept glancing at the two of them. *The wingman affect is not without its benefits.*

Jake almost did a nosedive into his drink before rounding on Mick to make a snide remark. The smattering of giggles at his antics were not lost on him and it took every ounce of his control not to look. He stopped there with his mouth agape as the remarks died and the cogs in his brain finally engaged. The couple of cuties who had been looking at him took on a whole new reality and he felt like a man who had ordered a hotdog and the waiter brought out a New York steak with all the fixings and wondering if he would have to pay the difference if he ate it. *Dating?* The rusty cogs of the untouched area of his brain began to grind free as he mulled the basic mechanics of it. *Starts with recognition. Agreed, before my existence was almost non-existent unless you for some reason stuck around long enough to get to know who I really am. Now, there is a hook.* "Oh."

"'Oh' indeed," Mick said with a smile. "I'd be jealous if I didn't know that you could use all the help you can get. You know you wouldn't have to resort to such extremes, becoming the face of a crash caused by a major event thereby becoming the face of both, if you'd just speak up a little more." He pointedly didn't mention the lady from the interviews. Jake had mentioned her twice in their conversations and it was clear that he had a touch of a crush. He didn't want to derail him now by reminding him of someone that he was likely never going to meet. "And stop thinking so much about everything! Just act. Be like you are after a couple drinks all the time, and you wouldn't have any problems. Oh, and stop being so damned picky about your type. Though I guess that isn't quite the issue here as it was back in the states," he said, pointedly glancing to the few lookers. "Still, you're too picky!" Mick replied, downing the rest of his drink. *It really is a shame that so few people really get to know my crazy friend. He's an odd one for sure, but once you get to know him, he isn't easily forgotten.* "And remember to smile."

Am I really that stiff? Yep. "Fine! So maybe you're right," Jake replied. Mick simply gave him a raised eyebrow. "Okay, so you're right. No ifs, ands, buts, or maybes about it. I still don't think this is going to have as big of an effect on my popularity as you think it is.

I mean, have you seen the town I'm going to? It doesn't even have a train. I'd be surprised if there were ten eligible women, close to my age, in the whole town! And with the marriage rates in Japan that means more like five," Jake replied, as he polished off his drink, and this time found his bowl empty.

"True enough. But at least you will have a little bit of a leg up with those five. And don't even try to pull the small town and no train card. It isn't like my town is any better and the nearest train station is over an hour away!" Mick retorted, downing his drink and getting up. "Gochisousama deshita," they both said before Jake paid and they left.

"True," Jake conceded. His town was marginally bigger and about ten minutes closer to a train station. "You don't have to answer if you don't want to, but I have to ask... Why'd you stick around?" He split his attention between eyeing Mick and not getting trampled or ran over as they made their way down the packed street. Thankfully, the cars and scooters were few and far between, and what with the crowded streets, were creeping along at an ADHD snail's pace.

"Figured you'd be asking that soon. See what I mean about liquid fortification?" Mick said stalling.

"Pot calling the kettle black," Jake shot back.

True enough. "You know that conversation, the one just before takeoff, where you were talking about grand adventures?" Mick asked.

Ooo, now that's interesting. "Yah, I remember. You counseled me to be more of a realist and to hope that the adventure didn't kick off until we landed," Jake supplied. *In this case I wonder if that pre-landing marks the kickoff or if the crash does? Mick may have been right about the start point if it was the crash. Hmm?*

"Well, I still don't think much of living with your head in the clouds, but things look like they may get interesting around these parts and I'd hate to miss it," Mick responded with a shrug. *And is isn't like going back is really a choice at this point. I'm rather fond of keeping my blood.*

Jake stared at Mick sideways for a few seconds. *Nope, not even going to comment on that. Maybe there is hope for him yet.*

"You know, I can practically hear what you're thinking right now," Mick said giving Jake a friendly shove.

"Yah, but I haven't said it, so you can keep on going like it was never said," Jake supplied with a smirk. "And you still hit like a girl."

"Heh, tell that to my sister the next time you see her," Mick shot back.

"Oww." Jake said like he'd been slugged to the gut. "Never tell your sister I said this, but I think even Tyson would be afraid of her."

"Now..." Mick started to reply. *On second thought? Yep he's right. The man would leave with no ears, knees or balls.* "You're right. In the indomitable words of Sergeant Schultz, 'I hear no-thing, no'ting.'"

"You know, I think you are the only person I have ever met that not only got the reference, but used it," Jake said with a smirk. "Now let's see if poodles really can fly."

"Think we'll need some badges or badgers?" Mick shot back.

"Oh, most definitely." Jake agreed.

"And if there's rocks ahead? We'll all be dead," they both chorused, their laughter redoubling at the befuddled looks of those around them. Loud foreigners had that effect. Especially when one of them was a kimono clad giant and the other one seemed like someone that they should recognize. More than a few took some stealthy photos, convinced that the two of them must be famous or something.

"You know it really is too bad that we are going to be posted so far away from each other. It's going to be a real pain finding another person that gets the quotes or who I can indoctrinate in the ways of awesome. I think I'll call them Grasshopper." Jake said as he reined in his laughing fit and wiped some tears from his eyes.

"Yah, but if it's your girlfriend I suggest you not call her Grasshopper," Mick warned.

"Good point. So, was it more or less than two minutes?"

"Less."

Different Path
Wednesday, June 30

Morning came early. Beer, jetlag, glaring sunlight, and a not so comfy bed did not make for good mornings. "Down with that flaming ball of happiness in the sky. Oh, how I loathe thee thy incessant life-giving illuminator. May you fall beneath the horizon, preferably stubbing your little toe on the bed frame as you lay down in about thirteen hours and make way for the return of darkness," Jake muttered from his bed.

"Dude, it is too early in the morning for you to be this weird already," Mick growled, rolling over and covering his ears with his pillow.

Did I say that out loud? Whoops. "My bad," Jake said. "Dibs on the shower," he said, stalking past Mick's bed. Mick made a noise and gave him a shooing motion.

Dude needs to learn how to sleep in. Mick grumbled as he heard the shower start. He may have been an early riser but that didn't mean he liked waking early when he didn't have to. *And hotels in Japan need thicker walls!* He complained as Jake began singing in the shower. Against his will, he rolled over to glare at the clock. 5:34am! *Too stinking early in the wee dawn hours to be awake. Sleep? ... Nope, not happening now, and that turkey already beat me to the shower.*

With a huff, he rolled out of bed and set about getting what few belongings he now had put away while he waited for Jake to get done with the shower. What with everything that had happened and the funky weather, they had been told to dress practical. Aka, do whatever you like. It wasn't a hard choice in his case given that all he had for clothes was the clothes that he had flown in, a Kimono, swim-trunks and the shoe.

***

Seven o'clock found them both down in the main dining area along with the other early risers and early departure people. Breakfast was almost the same as the first day - serviceable, but with little else going for it. Mick was in the 8 o'clock group bound for Tohoku, while Jake was in the 9:30a.m group headed for Kyoto prefecture.

"Well, I guess this is where we go our separate ways," Mick said, sticking out his hand.

Jake took it. "Yep. So, when the grand adventure really kicks off should I call you or you going to call me? Then again, ya think the phones will still be working?" he asked with a Cheshire grin.

Mick just shook his head. "Dreamers. One little comment and it goes right to their heads and that blimp sized imagination that lurks there. Then again, who knows and if it does kick off, I figure we both make it and then maybe after many years and grand journeys we unexpectedly meet up in a little bar somewhere and share our stories over a couple of drinks," he answered with a shake of his head. "I can't believe I just said that."

Oh, I'm not that far gone. You'll notice the inclusion of an 'if' in my statement. It never hurts to plan for the unexpected. Even if it is highly improbable," Mick answered.

"Oh, good. You had me worried there for a moment. In that case. See you in a roadside bar in about... one and a half years sound about right? Should be on a Saturday," Jake supplied, making a note in his planner just for kicks.

"Sure. Just peachy," Mick answered with a grin. *Let's hope his uncanny intuition isn't up to its old tricks.* "Well then, I guess I'll see ya then," he said gathering his bags, after likewise making an entry in his planner, and heading for his departure group.

"Yep, and we can regale each other of our adventures over a few drinks. You're buying this time," Jake said with a smile and waved bye.

Mick shook his head and gave a dismissive wave bye as he wandered towards his group. Given the distance from Tokyo, they usually would have flown, but what with the funky weather and the recent 'traumas' of one member, they had opted to take the train this time. Once they had finished gathering the last few strays, they headed out for the station.

"Be careful not to get separated from the group or you are liable to get left behind," their leader warned as they wormed their way through the other waiting groups.

"Hey man. What's up with the kimono? I mean, I know they said dress comfortable, but don't you think you are living the Japan dream a little too much," the guy next to him asked as they set off for the station.

"It was all that they had in my size," Mick answered noncommittally. He'd met enough stoners and mental cases over the years to be able to know one when he saw one. This one definitely fit the stoner bill to a T.

"Where are your bags anyways? You send them all ahead? You know that they might get lost or delayed and you could find yourself in a pinch?" Stoner commented, like he was an authority on all things.

Or, in your case, searched by the mail service when they set off an alarm? "Japan post is even more reliable than the trains. But, for your information, I don't have any bags to send," Mick commented, letting a touch of annoyance into his voice. He could deal pretty well with most people, but stupid people and junkies, who were automatically grouped into the stupid camp, just rubbed him wrong.

"You came to Japan without any luggage? That wasn't too bright. I mean it's hard enough to find clothes here if you are normal size and you's definitely not normal size," Stoner prattled on with a smug smirk. Given his pupils' dilation, Mick figured that he had done a joint sometime that morning. The smell of weed coming off of him definitely gave that impression but that could have just been 'baked' in.

Mick was good at keeping his emotions in check, but stupid just brought out the worst in him. "Maybe if you had spent a few more brain cells on thinking instead of figuring out where to huff your next fix, you could have been smart enough to put two and two together you dunce. Seeing as how that is beyond your remaining limited capacity for worthwhile thought, I will explain it, in the simplest terms that even an amoeba could understand, so that you can hopefully find two brain cells to rub together and understand what I say so that you can return to minding your own business. When you fly on a jet and the jet crashes, and your bags are in the part of the jet that is on fire, you wind up without bags. Were you able to understand that, or do I need to repeat it with single word sentences and pictures?"

"You can't talk to me that way!" Stoner shouted loud enough to catch the attention of the rest of the group. His face was turning cherry red with anger and embarrassment as he turned and squared off with Mick.

"Can, am, and should are very different things. If you really planned to help teach English, then you should be well aware of that. And, you really want to think long and hard with those few brain cells that you have left about what your next move here is going to be," Mick warned, sensing dummy getting ready to prove his point.

"What's the issue here?" the prefectural rep for CE-J asked, coming up next to them.

"He..." Stoner started.

Mick turned to look at the rep. "You really want a junkie in this program? I mean he's got a pouch of weed in his pocket and I'm sure a stash in his bag. Wouldn't surprise me if he'd brought some seeds with him also. Last I checked, weed was still a big no-no here in Japan," he explained, quirking an eyebrow. There was an officer that had been moving in on the disturbance that had just caught that last part also.

Before the CE-J could comment, the officer stepped in. "Your passport, residence card and the contents of your pockets!" he ordered.

Finally realizing just how toast he was, stoner panicked and made to run for it. Unfortunately, for him at least, Mick was still in his way.

Mick's hand shot out and latched onto Stoner's collarbone as he drove his thumb down into the gap between it and his neck. Stoner dropped to his knees as the officer quickly stepped in and secured his hands. He then proceeded to empty Stoner's pockets. Sure enough, there was a hefty pouch and wraps.

The CE-J rep was still recovering from the shock at the whole turn of events as the officer called it in and hefted a now deflated stoner back up to his feet. He shakily turned to face Mick. "How'd you know?"

"You didn't?" Mick asked, shaking his head. "His eyes were dilated, he was stupid, and he reeked of weed. I'm amazed that he even made it through the interview process. You should really think about adding a drug test," he suggested, shaking his head. "Will you be needing anything more from us officer? We have a train to catch up to Tohoku," he informed him in Japanese.

The officer craned his neck up to look at Mick, seeing as how he only came up to Mick's mid-chest. "Some contact information for your group in-case we need any further information."

Mick looked back to the rep. "I think he'd like your business card," he suggested, startling the rep back into action. The officer looked confused between the two of them. "He's the boss, I'm just a new guy," Mick explained, shrugging.

The officer took the card and handed one of his own over after scribbling the case number on it. "We will contact you if we have further questions. Should you wish to provide us with information or provide a representative, call this number and provide the case number," he instructed, hauling a now crying and pleading Stoner to his feet and dragging him towards an awaiting patrol car that had just pulled up. The door closed, cutting off his pleading sobs.

"So..., wouldn't want to miss the train," Mick reminded the still shocked group as he began chipperly strolling towards the station.

***

Thanks to the delay, they barely made the train. The conductor had had to hold the door to let the last of them board and Mick had caught the scathing look he had shot them when he thought no one was looking. From there, it had been a five-hour train ride up to his area and an hour-long local train ride to his nearest station. He would have preferred to fly, but even though Mick was the only one that had been on "The Jet," he seemed the least concerned about the prospect of taking a plane. It had been a long ride.

Mick let out a sigh of relief and stretched as he exited the last station. His whole body ached from inactivity and far too many hours of sitting. There was a small truck, the only vehicle in sight, waiting to pick him up. Leaning against it and waving him over was a guy in rather plain clothes. He looked more like a farmer than any City Hall person that he had ever seen.

"Welcome," the man said, sticking out his hand and looking up at Mick as he drew near. "I'm Sayako Yosuke, the mayor and proprietor of 'Sayako's Inn' in the town that is hosting you." There was something different and yet familiar about Yosuke that Mick just couldn't quite place.

Mick accepted the hand firmly and with a smile. "So, you're my boss?" He gave Yosuke another onceover, trying to place where he may have met him before, searching through his memories. *Nope, I definitely haven't met him before, but there is also more to him than meets the eye. And what did you expect!? That you would just waltz into this new land and immediately understand all of its workings!? Well no. But I can see that I have a lot of catching up to do.*

"I guess you could call me that if you want. Most people just call me Yosuke. We have a bit of a drive into town and I can explain along the way as I show you around. That is, if you fit in the truck?" He gave Mick an appraising look. *Worse case, he rides in the back.*

It was close. Through a combination of hunkering and slouching, he had just managed to fit. They were now tearing down the road at a higher speed than he really would have preferred. Especially considering that every bounce caused him to hit his head on the roof. "About that explanation...?" he prodded as they rolled towards what he assumed was the town.

"So, as you can see, our town is pretty small. We mostly make our income off of a mix of farming, freshwater fish-farming, selling mountain delicacies and game, and tourism. Also, a little skiing in the winter months. It's not like we really need a lot of income though. We are almost completely self-sufficient. In winter that serves us splendidly because when bad weather comes through, it is not uncommon for us to be completely cut off for days or even a week. Sometimes you can't even get out of your house if a bad storm comes through. Not that that is such a bad thing if you aren't alone. The boredom can inspire you to find inventive ways to stay entertained." Yosuke's grin left little doubt as to what he was implying.

"Sounds remote. I mean, I read the little bit that I could find on the area and looked at the maps. I wasn't able to find much useful information beyond some tourist brochures and a one-page website. I couldn't even find a population," Mick explained, looking around a bit more now that they had entered town and weren't driving at Mach 42. The town was bigger and more populated than he would have expected from the brochures and for being so remote, there were more young families and younger residents than he had expected.

Yosuke shot him a sidelong look. "It is, and we like it that way. Not everyone stays here year-round, but the population is right at about fifteen hundred in the greater area. I hope that won't be a problem for you? There is plenty to do, but you'll have to do without most of the modern amenities like malls and most stores. We do have a grocery store that stocks mostly local produce and there is a general store that has clothing and other household goods. They can also order in things that they don't have on hand. Given your current attire, I take it that they failed to retrieve your luggage from the jet?"

"This was all that was recoverable," Mick replied, brandishing his swim trunks and sneaker. All I have are the clothes on my back and what I mailed ahead.

"That's too bad. Although, given that you mailed a second one to your home, you must have taken a liking to kimono?" Yosuke asked, with a smile as he pulled into a driveway.

"Ya, they are..." Mick's train of thought cut off as he noticed the distinctly un-Japanese house that they were pulling up to.

"I can see that you like it," Yosuke commented proudly, grinning from ear to ear. "It may not be the biggest Inn in Japan, and I know I am more than a little biased in this, but it is the best Inn."

Sure enough, Mick had seen bigger and fancier Inns before, there was definitely something different about this one though. And, something about the way that Yosuke had said 'best Inn' made Mick feel that he wasn't just talking about the local competition. It was a sprawling three story building of solid wood construction with a wraparound porch on each level which overlooked the well-manicured grounds. There wasn't a trace of the plaster and concrete that inundated so much of Japan's 'modern' construction. The second and third stories stair stepped back, giving it a slightly castle like appearance. How he hadn't found a review or picture of it in his searches of the area and how it wasn't listed as a major vacation location, he wasn't sure, because on looks alone it rated four stars. "I'm amazed that I didn't see any photos or mentions of this place in my searches." His curiosity was perking by the second and it was clear that this town was much more than met the eye.

Yosuke let out a laugh. "I should hope not. We go to no small lengths to keep out of those things. Our clientele value their privacy and having everyone and their blathering hoard trying to book a stay here would mess that up bigtime. We are pretty picky in who we will let stay and doing the checks on that many people would be a bit much, especially when most wouldn't meet the requirements. Enough about that though. Let me show you to your place," Yosuke said, hopping out and waving for Mick to follow.

"I'm staying here?" Mick asked, a little confused as he did what looked like interpretive dance to extricate himself from the little truck.

"Here? No, well yes. Just wait a second and I think it will make more sense."

Mick agreed with a shrug and followed, rolling his shoulders and rubbing the kinks out of his neck. His eyes continued to play over the Inn and its construction as they made their way around it. He barely had time to stop from running into Yosuke's back as he suddenly came to a stop.

Detached and looking rather small compared to the main building was a smaller home. It wasn't until they had walked rather farther than he had thought it was at first, given the scale and his misperception, that he realized that the house wasn't nearly as small as it had first appeared. It was a two-story home built in the same style as the main Inn.

"I know it isn't much, but the rent is free, and no one has been using it since the last grounds keeper and his family moved. If you really don't like it, feel free to use it until you are able to find another place to stay," Yosuke said, as he kicked off his shoes at the entry.

"Right..." Mick replied, a little awed by his new home. *The only way that I would pass this up is if the inside is a whole lot more trashed than the outside would lead me to believe or if it is it already 'occupied' and in that case, there are ways to fix that.* "Is there a catch?" he asked, curious what Yosuke would answer. Japan seemed to be a lot more open than he had first assumed or seen the last time that he had been through.

"Catch? No catch. We don't have plans to get a new keeper, so it is just sitting here unoccupied. It is a little dusty from being unoccupied and the facilities are a little old, but we have maintained the upkeep and the pipes are solid. If there is any catch, it is that you are bumped up against the woods, but as long as you don't go wandering around in them at night and check before opening the door at night, you should be fine," Yosuke assured him. "So, you want to see the inside?" he asked, by way of going inside.

Let's see just what I have gotten myself into. The inside was far more open than he had suspected, missing most of the interior walls that were the common stock of Japanese design. Instead it was tracked with a plethora of sliding dividers to adjust the spaces into different size and shaped rooms to fit your needs and taste. The only truly separate room was the attached bathroom and king size bathtub that bulged out of the side of the otherwise rectangular home. *Oh ya, that tub is going to get some serious use. It might even be big enough for me to really stretch out or even float in.*

Except for the bath area, which was flagstone tiled, the rest of the floors were solid wood timbers worn smooth from decades of feet that didn't betray a single squeak as they walked through the first floor. There was a nice kitchen in one corner; that, if not new, more than made up for it with ample counter space and robust kitchen grade appliances. There was also an open fire pit dominating the center of the floor with a kettle rack hanging over one side of it and a hooded chimney. Running parallel to the back wall was an open stairway that led up to the second story. Like the first, the floors were still solid wood timbers. Unlike the first floor, there were three spacious rooms with sturdy walls dividing them and a small wash closet. The master dominated the far end of the floor opposite the stairs. There was a porch wrapping three sides of the second floor and connecting all three rooms. While only half the size of the master, the other rooms which flanked it were still adequately sized. There was a bed with a decent feeling mattress in the master room and futons, with bedding, for the rest as well as potbelly stoves for use during the cold winter months. The only bad thing was that there weren't any air-conditioners, but with the altitude and the mountain and lake breezes, he wasn't too worried about that.

"So?" Yosuke asked after they had finished the tour. "The only thing that is a bummer is that you will need to fall some timber before winter sets in and keep a fire going to keep the place heated," he explained, looking to the foothills and mountains rising up behind the house with a complex mixture of emotions that Mick couldn't quite parse. "You can cut the timber behind the house but be sure to scatter your falls and plant replacements, so the mountain doesn't get any bald spots. Oh, and don't go wandering too far off into the woods either. They aren't particularly safe, and it is frightfully easy to get turned around and lost in them."

"No biggy. We cut our own timber back in the States and I am pretty handy with an ax. I rather like the workout anyways," Mick assured. *Now I wonder why he's so leery of the woods. I think I'll have to take a little walk.*

Crap! He looks like a fox that just spied a hen house with a broken latch. He is definitely going to try and take a stroll into the dark timber now. "Well, as long as you are in the woods, be sure to take an axe with you. You never know how it might be handy," Yosuke warned, making sure to hold Mick's gaze. *For what little good it might do you. Then again. You are a big feller. You might just make a stand of it. For a few seconds.*

He totally figures I'm puppy kibble if I run into whatever it is up in those mountains that has him concerned. Now I really want to find out what has him so worried. "I'll keep that in mind." Mick leered up into the woods, letting his senses roam but couldn't pick much of anything out except the standard weight of old trees and the secrets they shared. Shelving it for the moment, he clomped back downstairs maintaining the noisy giant character that he affected to keep people from wondering why someone his size could move quieter than a ghost.

His meager belongings had already been dropped off so there wasn't much organizing to worry about at the moment, which left the question of dinner and some cooking supplies. His stomach let loose a rumble that punctuated that point and elicited a chuckle from Yosuke.

"I'll see to taking you to the grocer to get some food tomorrow," he said, holding up his hand to forestall Mick's question. "You don't need to worry about cooking tonight. Even if you are dead on your feet, we have a bit of a welcome dinner planned for you up at the inn. We went ahead and invited a few people from the area so that you can start getting to know your new neighbors," he explained with a grin that made Mick a touch leery.

"As long as there is food and maybe some drinks, I am good," Mick agreed, watching carefully.

"Drinks? Oh, I think we can accommodate you there," he assured, grinning from ear to ear.

Ah, so they plan to test my mettle, do they?! Well, I hope they brought pillows to cushion their falls as they hit the deck.

***

If anything, the main Inn felt like what the fantasy of an Inn was supposed to be like. The interior was decorated with a mix of Japanese and European art in a turn of the century style. The halls were wide and designed for ease of movement. There was also a good mix of tabletop, card, and board games in the lounge area. The one that caught his eye right off the bat was a Go board where two older gentlemen were in a heated battle for control of the center and what looked like an original tabletop Pac-Man. Mick wanted to stay and watch how the battle played out between the old men but Yosuke seemed intent on showing him around and he reluctantly pulled himself away. What really set the Inn apart was the accommodations and the atmosphere. The rooms were spacious, and they came in a variety of styles. Everything from what seemed like a long stay apartment, to elegantly simple futon rooms that made five-star hotel rooms seem shoddy in their stark calm and tranquility. The atmosphere also seemed more like an overlarge home than an Inn. Or, at least like visiting a relative's home.

Mick rounded the corner and followed Yosuke into another section of the Inn. He was a touch surprised to find that it was the kitchen. Several people were bent over prep-stations, pans, and dishes getting what looked to be a feast ready. In that storm of activity, it wasn't hard to spot who was the boss.

"ATSUKO!" Yosuke hollered over the din.

"If you burn the butter while I am gone, you had best be prepared to spend the next decade as a busboy," Atsuko warned, before turning to see just what was important enough to prompt Yosuke to trespass upon her domain. "You know the rules! If you are going to be in my kitchen, then you are going to be working. There is a pile of dishes over there that need doing and I just found the doers," she ordered, shuffling them over to the sinks. "Now that your hands aren't idle, what brings you here?"

"I'd figure that the big feller next to me would have made that apparent!?" Yosuke replied, applying elbow grease to a particular sticky stain on one of the pans.

Mick turned to wave from his position at the counter, handling the knives.

Atsuko furrowed her brow when she saw what he was working on, then her eyes went wide and her hand lanced out in a blur, snatching the blade out of his hands. Without even a word of explanation, she set to examining the blade. Apparently unable to find any visual faults, she grabbed a pumpkin and set to taking it apart in a blur of fluid motion. Just where one cut ended and the next began, was something of a mystery. With the pumpkin skinned, sliced, and chunked, she moved on to a Daikon and cut it into one continuous transparent ribbon. Still apparently finding no fault, she grabbed a fish and set to slicing it into hair thin slices which she skillfully folded into miniature roses.

The kitchen had become deathly still and quiet as she had worked. "What are you all lollygagging about for? Get back to work. Ren, for your sake, I hope that that butter isn't burning!" Atsuko barked, sending the kitchen staff back into a scamper of activity before she rounded on a sweating Yosuke and an inquisitive Mick. Atsuko set the knife aside gently and with the same speed that she had been using just moments before, she clasped onto both of Mick's hands and rotated them palm up. After a moment's examination, she released them and finally looked Mick in the eyes. "Who are you?!" she asked, skepticism and intrigue writ large on her mobile face.

"Like I was trying to say. This is the new CE-J," Yosuke explained, both relieved and surprised at Atsuko's reserve and curiosity. He hadn't expected Mick to recognize the wet stone and start honing the knives either. If he had, he would have told him not to even look in their direction. Of all of the tools in the kitchen, Atsuko's knives were the one thing that no one else was allowed to touch.

Atsuko held up her hand to forestall any further interruptions from Yosuke. "So?"

"Mick Renalds."

"Yes, that is your name. I already knew that much. What I asked is 'who you are' and you still haven't given me an answer yet. So!" Atsuko demanded.

Mick cocked his head to the side as he considered how to answer. He had been able to tell just as much as she had when she had examined his hands and even more from watching her work. "I have worked in more than a few kitchens and studied weapon combat extensively. I know my way around a blade and blade maintenance."

Atsuko held his eyes for a moment longer before relenting and breaking eye contact. "Right... Well in any case, I should probably be introducing myself. I'm Saiyako Atsuko and this is my kitchen. In this kitchen, everyone works. I don't have time or effort to spare on slackers. Besides that, there is only one rule in this kitchen. No one touches my knives!!! Except me. Or, at least that used to be the rule. I'm not sure what you did or how you did it, but this is the best shape that this knife has ever been in. Even better than the day I got it. From now on, you have my permission to sharpen and care for any cutlery that needs tending to. The rate is 5,000 yen for a full-size blade and 2,500 yen for a mid or small size blade," she explained.

The kitchen had become a quiet hustle of activity as everyone strained their ears to listen in on how she would react. Apparently, they had been expecting something different because they let out an audible gasp at her proclamation. The quiet didn't last long as the kitchen descended into hushed chatter as they continued working on plating dish after dish.

"Do I get to cook also?" Mick asked, intrigued at the prospect of learning a thing or twenty. *And maybe teaching a few things also.*

"Have bit of confidence now don't ya. A little cheeky too. I like that. But if you want to cook in this kitchen, you are going to have to earn your knives and pans like everyone else," Atsuko challenged. Her words and posture left no room for complaint or argument.

Earn my knives and pans? Now that is intriguing. I'm not sure how this will all fit in with my cultural exchange work, but I am sure that that can be worked out. Helps that the one doing the work is my Boss's wife. "I'm up for it. That is, when my other work for your husband and the town allows for the time needed," Mick replied, tossing the ball squarely at Yosuke's head.

Yosuke frowned. "And here I thought we might be friends," he said, frowning and looking hurt. He started answering before looking back at Atsuko. "You don't have to give me the look so don't even start. I know that arguing and reasoning are already lost causes so, I'll go finagle the paperwork tomorrow morning so that you can have your new kitchen slave... I mean helper," he corrected, shooting a Mick a warning look. "It's on your head now. If you're wise, you'll run."

"And miss all the fun?" Mick shot back with a raised eyebrow. Yosuke simply shook his head in pity.

"Right... but you don't start until breakfast shift tomorrow. That means you need to be here and ready by 5:30 am. But, for today, you are a guest and have no more work to do beyond enjoying the evening and answering a small mountain of questions. So, the two of you layabouts had best be getting out of my kitchen so that us working folk can get back to getting dinner ready!" Atsuko ordered, shooing them out at knife point.

Yosuke, let out a tired and relieved sigh as the door closed behind them. It didn't stay closed for long as they were bumped out of the way as someone carried out a tray of food. He shot Mick a look that seemed to be equal parts curiosity, pity, jealousy, and amusement. "You really stepped in it now," he chuckled. "And, you had best be expecting a lot more of that from now until you earn your knives and pans. If you can show that you really have the talent, they will respect you, but until then, you will be treated as an interesting anomaly. And, don't feel bad if you fail. Most do. So, no one will hold it against you."

"I look forward to finding out just what is involved in doing just that," Mick replied chipperly.

"Hold onto that attitude for as long as you can. You'll need it," Yosuke warned. "But, for now, we have a meet and greet to get through tonight. So, just relax and enjoy yourself," Yosuke said, grinning as he led the way. *And won't your first day on the job be great with the hangover that you are going to have after we get through with you.*

He is so going to try and get me wasted. This should be fun. Mick chuckled earning himself a sideways glance from Yosuke. "Nothing. Just a funny thought. So..." He cut off as they entered the next room and he realized that their little meet and greet with some of the locals really meant with most of the town. The room wasn't packed but that was only because the room was so big and the town was so small, although the rambunctious locals seemed determined to make up for their sparse numbers with sheer volume and merry making.

What's more, Mick was surprised to see that it was a rather equal mix of age groups and genders. He was scanning the crowd when his eyes landed on one guest in particular who was relaxed against a wall and his heart skipped a beat. It was Ai. She shot him a quick smile before the parting of the crowd closed back in, cutting off his line of sight. When it parted again, she had disappeared. He was still looking around for her when Yosuke gave his shoulder a little shake.

"I know they are a little bit on the rambunctious side, but they are all great people. So, no worries. You'll be fine," Yosuke assured, misreading the cause of Mick's surprise.

"Right." Mick gave himself a shake, casting one last glance in search of Ai, before he followed Yosuke over to his seat. He continued to scan the crowd, only partially out of habit but mainly in hopes of catching sight of her again. *Get it together man. I mean, what are the odds that she'd actually be here? Tonight?*

Low. But since when has that ever stopped you? It's a small, big area. You can worry about this later. For now, you are a guest and it is high time that you started acting the part.

Mick gave his head a quick shake to clear his thoughts and turned to Yosuke for a little chit-chat to distract himself. Only problem was that Yosuke wasn't there. In his place, there was a grandma who was giving him a rather thorough appraisal. "Hi," he said, temporarily at a loss for words as his vocabulary took a vacation.

Grandma frowned. "Hmm," she intoned before giving him one last squint and wandering back off into the crowd with a rather distinct waddling gait that reminded him of some small fluffy animal trying to walk on two legs instead of four.

Yosuke passed her, with a quick but troubled glance, as he returned with drinks. "What did Ba have to say?" he asked, not at all sure that he wanted to hear the answer. *Just who is this guy?*

"Huh?" Mick asked, a little surprised by the question and Yosuke's grave tone. "I mean, Hmm. She was sitting there before I knew it and I said 'Hi' and all she said was 'Hmm' before she got up and left," he answered, trying to get a feel for the room and keeping an eye out for Ai. "Is she one of the town elders or something?"

"Or something," Yosuke agreed before waving it off and setting down the glasses and bottles that he had been carrying. "It's..." he started to explain only to be cut short by Atsuko's arrival.

"Food's going to get cold. Sit," she ordered. Within a blink, every aisle was cleared, and seat filled. Mick had hoped that that would allow him to reacquire Ai, but he still couldn't seem to pick her out of the crowd. "That's better." She gave the crowd one last reproachful look before nodding to Yosuke and taking her own seat.

Yosuke wasn't one to keep her waiting. He climbed to his feet. "Since my lovely wife has already browbeat you all into silence, I think I'll keep this short." There was a brief round of chuckles and Snidely Whiplash sounds at that.

"That will be the day," someone muttered from a corner of the room.

Yosuke scowled in their general direction. "You melanocytes will rue the day but, for the moment, as a civilized man, I am willing to let bygones be bygones and enjoy this welcoming dinner for the newest member of our community. I hope that you all have a chance to get to know him well. So, without further ado, Kampai." He raised his glass in toast.

Mick raised his own to meet Yosuke's and his neighbors in cheers as the sound of clinking glasses reverberated throughout the room. He had been a little surprised to find that someone had already managed to fill his cup without his noticing. With the clinking coming to an end, and taking his cue from Yosuke, he rocked back his own glass. White fire rolled down his throat and stars burst in his eyes, as the whole room swam. He'd quaffed half of his glass in that initial swallow and he was glad that he hadn't tried for more. Whatever was in his glass, it wasn't Sake or any other alcohol that he was familiar with. It made 151 looks like beer by comparison. At the same time, as the fire receded, it carried an amazingly complex taste that could best be described as the sweetness of nature in a bottle. He caught sight of an anticipatory eyebrow from Yosuke as the night sky full of stars that had erupted in his eyes subsided.

"Well I'll be. He's still sitting," Yosuke said into the surprised silence that had descended upon the room.

It was only then that Mick realized that they all had been waiting for this moment.

"Looks like we won't be needing the buckets of ice water after all." Yosuke smirked as he patted Mick on the back. The party broke into cheers and laughter as their surprise broke and the room descended into the chatter of eating, drinking, and jovial conversations.

Mick saw more than a few bills change hands at lost bets as he continued to survey the room for Ai. He decided to ignore it as he took another, much more reserved, drink before turning back to Yosuke. It still lit up his world, but after that initial shock, his body was primed and ready for it this time and he was able to gain a much clearer appreciation of the drink. He still didn't have the foggiest idea about just what it was though. "Yosuke, what am I drinking?" he inquired, continuing to sip away at it.

"Tengu whisky. It's a local brew that you are unlikely to find anywhere else except for a few select shops and establishments in Japan that only serve select clientele. It has never been exported or been made widely known and we prefer it that way," Yosuke answered, taking a rather more reserved sip from his own glass. "Legend goes that a Bacchus Tengu spent a thousand years circling the globe and learning the secrets of all liquor before returning here and forming all of his knowledge into the creation of the perfect liquor, Tengu whisky," he explained, smiling at the tale. "Or at least that is what they say. I'd suggest that you take it slowly, though. Most people pass out on their first try with only a sip. It can sneak up on even a regular drinker if he isn't careful," he warned, with a challenging eyebrow. "Granted, some people can drink it like water, he said draining his glass with a smile."

So that's how he wants to play. Couldn't put me under with the first blow so now you're figuring on driving me under with a war of attrition. You really should know your opponent before you throw down the gauntlet. Or at least send in a sacrificial lamb to check him out before you go storming in all on your lonesome. And, if I'm not mistaken, that face-palm that Atsuko just gave means that you have been beaten at this game more than a time or two already. Soo... Mick finished off his glass before grabbing a bottle to refill Yosuke's with a wicked grin. "I happen to be an accomplished pacer and there is plenty of tasty looking food and I plan to sample all of it tonight," he stated, picking up the gauntlet.

"I'm sure that this will prove to be an evening that exceeds your expectations," Yosuke agreed, raising the bottle to reciprocate.

***

Mick was on his fifth glass and working his way through a delicious stir-fry of green peppers, beef, ginger, and bamboo shoots when one of the grandpas of the party made his way over. He politely extracted Yosuke's wallet as he snoozed away and pulled out ¥2,000 yen.

"Itadakimasu," he said, grinning as he set down his own Growler, replacing the emptied bottle of Tengu whisky, and deposited his obvious spoils of a bet in his wallet. "Thanks for your hard work," he said, giving Mick a grin. "Now that we have that out of the way, why don't you try a glass of some really good stuff and not that low brow swill that Yosuke was pawning off on you?" he offered, un-stoppering the jug.

The smell alone was seductive and intoxicating as it quickly pervaded the whole room and the chatter died off as heads rounded on them. Atsuko was on her feet in a flash but stopped at a raised hand from the Grandpa. Mick was surprised to see the look of concern in her eyes trying to convey the warning that had been left unsaid. Whether it was respect, fear, or something else that stilled her tongue, Mick didn't know. What he did know was that this little old man was far more than he appeared and that this was a pass/fail test. Mick had a distinct aversion to failing.

"I'm willing to give it a try," Mick replied. The silence was quickly replaced with the rustle of clothing and paper as wallets were pulled out and bills were openly placed on the tables. *Apparently, some bets are too good to pass up.* Not one to be left out, Mick fished into his kimono's sleeve pocket and pulled out a small, thumb sized, silver, platinum, and gold pendent on a black gold chain that rippled and swirled between the different metals that was fashioned after a crow in flight. "A crow for a Tengu," Mick said quietly, earning a surprised gasp from the rest of the dining room and a smile from the grandpa with the jug.

"Oh, I like this one a lot," he said, with a toothy grin as the air behind him shimmered, revealing black as night wings of steel with hard and razor-sharp feathers that peaked over his shoulders and slightly to the sides. "You seem to have me at a bit of a disadvantage. You obviously know what I am, but as of yet I haven't been able to determine that you are anything but exactly what you appear to be. A rather stout human," Gramps observed, continuing his appraisal. "Not that I'm about to hold that against you. I've known a few decent humans over the years. Even had the odd Onmyouji drinking partners. But I've learned it is best to learn just what is roosting next to you, lest what you thought was a sparrow turns out to be a Shrike."

Mick smiled. *If only I was the Shrike. Unfortunately, I'm the bramble.* "I'm human enough. My family just has a longer and somewhat more storied history than most," he answered.

Gramps regarded him levelly for a few seconds while the tension in the room continued to ratchet up. At last he shrugged and the relief in the room was palpable. "As it happens, I have even met a Druid or two in my time," he smirked and arched an eyebrow as he went fishing. Druids were the European equivalent of the Onmyouji though they tended to be far more fatalistic, and black and white in their practices than the Onmyouji's gray. Also, far more proactive and offensively bent when they felt threatened. There were good reasons why the Fair Folk of Europe, werewolves, dragons, and vampires in particular, no longer existed in large numbers and where they did, lived in what amounted to reservations that they only exited at their own peril. The Druids, for some compelling reasons, tended to take the shotgun and group responsibility outlook on things. Modern times had so far done little to temper the fervor of the traditional Druids either. The newer philosophical order of Gray Druids was a little bit of a different matter. Although, the decline in the prominence of shadow and the spread of man had reduced all of the various Order's numbers and their effective reach a great deal. Granted, there was also far less to watch over and fearing their overbearing ways and loose interpretations, others had seen to putting the majority of Druids under the heel and were moving them into more of a support role and monastic record keeping community.

"Then you were lucky to either catch them when they were drunk or asleep. After the black plague, the Druids have been the bane of crows, though some of the darker ones still associate with ravens," Mick said, shivering. "No offence, but I've never much cared for ravens. They are far too mercenary and rogue for my peace of mind."

"A wise policy," Gramps agreed. "But I take it from your tone that your connection to our world is of a different sort!?"

"No, more of a different path. The Druids are a branch, but my path is more of a root. A tap root in-fact," Mick said, watching as Gramps's eyes narrowed with a hint of trepidation.

"They are a myth!!!" he whispered, though it still reverberated loudly in the stilled room.

Mick quirked an eyebrow at Gramps. *And what exactly are you to be nitpicking myths. Although there are myths and 'Myths.'* "Almost, but not quite. The numbers have dwindled even further than the druids, and only a few families remain, but I can assure you that the Order of the Knight's Keepers still lives and while their numbers may be decreased, their reach and power has only expanded," he answered. A pin drop would have clapped like thunder in the silence that filled the dining room. More than a few of the older patron's hands were looking a mite bit fidgety.

"And they have finally decided to spread their influence to the East?!" Gramps lamented, looking at Mick in a newer and darker light. *In the worst case, not many of us will make it clear of this room, but we should at least be able to deal with this one.*

"Not quite," Mick chuckled. "Really, quite the opposite in many ways. For starters, I came west, not east. My family is from Washington. Also, the Order is not currently robust enough to consider expansion at this point, though it is growing for the first time in a millennia and there are those that have hopes of restoring it to its prominence of yore, and beyond. But mainly, there is the fact that I am no longer avowed by the Order. I am an exile and in an even more precarious position with the Order than the Fair Folk. You see," he raised his hand for all of them to see as what looked like black sand began to accumulate on his palm, "I'm something of an embarrassment. While the Order may be a tap root, there is a heart to its history that was utterly exhumed and burned to cinders in fire. One known as Night. It is one of the powers that gave birth to the Order, but it is not of the Order. It is of the Fair or something else and is looked down upon as a taint that was supposed to have long ago been destroyed or locked away where it could never again see the light of Day. The story of its return is long and twisted, but the simple answer is that I understudied with the Gray Druids on the east coast and it turns out that the Templers, read 'Order,' with the aid of the Vikings, happened to have reached the New World far in advance of Columbus and they left buried and guarded that which was meant to never be found or wielded again. Alas, I was bound to that history before birth and one thing led to another, people died, rules were broken, seals were breached, people sought power beyond their understanding and control, a choice and fate predestined was accepted, and Night stepped once more into day and it couldn't be put back again. But a blight like that couldn't be allowed to remain. Especially when I was suspect already thanks to my family, choice in friends, non-standard education in beyond the commonly accepted, and most feared of all, because of my knowledge of the true history. That taint above all else could not be allowed to remain, lest the taint spread. Unfortunately - or fortunately - because of the political landscape, neither could it be quietly disposed of either. Which left but one option: discredit, dishonor, and exile to locations where eventually a knife may be able to find its way into my back without undue amounts of suspicion or evidence of foul play," Mick explained and shrugged while he drew the inky black sand back in. "Unfortunately for them, I snuck off to Japan and locations unknown before they could arrange a proper exile to someplace like the dark woods of Ireland. I'm sure there is still a good bit of tooth gnashing going on over that," he grinned, wolfishly. "But that is then and there and this is here and now and I believe that there was a bet with a Tengu over a drink that remains to be settled," he said, smiling. He could feel a good bit of the tension in the room drain out as Gramps barked out an amused laugh.

"I knew there was a good reason for me to come down off of my mountain tonight," Gramps said, grinning as he poured. "Something says that things are about to get exciting for the first time in a long time."

"You sound just like a friend of mine." Mick shook his head and smiled as he drank deeply of the Tengu Private Reserve.

"What did I miss?" Yosuke asked, sitting up and holding his pounding head as his vision swam.

Life's Wrench and Battle Axes
Thursday, July 1

4:30 am came early and with a slight fog from having drank too much. In the end, he'd drank even Gramps, whose real name was 'Yamada Tobio' although he happened to go by Gramps, into a draw. It turned out that the old bird had just as much tolerance for alcohol as he did. Given the outcome, Mick had been happy to settle for a jug of Tengu private reserve in exchange for the pendant. The only problem now was to find someone to share it with who could handle and appreciate it.

For the moment though, he needed to get a move on. Atsuko may have stayed up just as late and drank her fair share also, but before departing she had made it clear that he was still expected in the kitchen bright, early, and ready to get worked to the bone. With a groan of discontent, he rolled out of bed and set about getting ready.

The fog hadn't just been in his head. There was a heavy fog blanketing the whole area and cutting down the visibility to a few meters as Mick made his way outside and towards the main building. He wasn't much of a fan of fog and this fog set his skin to crawling as soon as he stepped out into it. Remembering Yosuke's warning from the day before, he went ahead and collected the ax that was propped up next to the porch and made his way towards the Inn.

He was maybe halfway across the field when the fog suddenly grew thicker, the visibility plummeting down to little more than the reach of his hand and was still fuzzy even at that distance. Unsure what to expect, he shifted his grip on the ax a little closer to the ax head. It reduced the amount of power that he could put behind each swing, but it also increased the speed at which he could react. In this soup, speed was the far more important aspect. Despite the low visibility and the unease in the air, his pace never wavered as he continued forwards; calm and alert.

He caught a shadow of movement out of the corner of his eye. It hadn't been much, but the fog swirled ever so slightly as if touched by a breeze that didn't exist anywhere else. His grip and muscles relaxed as he readied to react. It came from dead ahead. He whipped the ax up in an arc to take it at the neck. The fog shifted again revealing his quarry. Muscles and tendons threatened to snap as they dragged his momentum to a standstill a hair's breadth shy of its neck.

Sweat beaded Atsuko's brow as she looked down at the bite of the ax that all but kissed her skin. She needed to swallow, but that seemed ill advised at the moment.

Mick looked up in shock as the fog cleared revealing the inn behind Atsuko. *I must have been more keyed up than I thought if I was that far off in judging my distance traveled. Doesn't mean that I was wrong to be keyed up though.* With a calm breath, he pulled the blade back down to his side. "Sorry, there was something in the fog."

Atsuko swallowed and let her breath back out as she cast furtive glances out into the fog and back at Mick. "Then we should best be heading back inside. There are still things in these mountains that even we don't know about or can explain, and they are best left undisturbed by our passing." She turned and headed back up onto the porch. Keeping an eye out the whole time until they were back inside.

Almost gets decapitated and doesn't even bat an eyelash. Sure seems like this whole town is a little beyond explanation. Between drinking bouts the night before, he had learned a little more about the town. About half the people of the town were honest to goodness humans. They might have had a little mixed blood, but they were still humans. As for the rest, they ran a gamut, but Cats, Tanuki, and Itachi, particularly of a wind weasel clan, seemed to be the dominant groups. There was also a handful of village Tengu and a few foxes, none with more than two tails, to round out the party. More remarkable than that, the town was stable. The intra-species-communities still existed, which made sense considering the different needs and issues that each group faced, but all of them also mingled in a most non-standard fashion. Even more striking was the number of mixed marriages between species and even with humans that he had seen. It was unlike any place he had ever been, seen, or heard of before and definitely beyond the quaint mountain lakeside town that he had expected. Sure, he had figured that he might run into a Fair Folk or two in his town but nothing like this. It was unprecedented.

Mick set his ax down, leaning it against the wall as he closed the door behind them. "Again, sorry about that."

"Sorry, would have been if you had done any damage. You didn't and you were wise to be leery. I should have said something as soon as I realized that it was you approaching," Atsuko reassured, subtly reminding him that she was not a helpless lady. "But that is in the past now. You are a good half hour early and I happen to have some coffee and fresh orange and cinnamon glazed scones. That is if Yosuke hasn't eaten them all yet."

"Thank you," Mick nodded, following her into a small side dining room that he hadn't seen on his previous visit. Yosuke was already there and reading the newspaper while munching on a scone. By the number of crumbs on his plate and shirt, it definitely wasn't his first, second, or probably even third.

"You're up awfully early," Yosuke jibed, smiling until he met Mick's eyes. "What?"

"There were Whispers in the fog today. It looks like they are back," Atsuko answered, flatly.

The color and joviality drained from Yosuke's face as it faded into a mask of concern as he set down the newspaper and scone. "I need to make some calls," he said, climbing back to his feet and leaving the room without further explanation.

Mick watched the door swing closed behind him before taking a seat and turning his attention back to Atsuko. He cast her a questioning eyebrow.

Atsuko sighed as she took her own seat. "You're in luck. It's going to be an easy day today. I'll be able to really take some time to test you and see how your skills are before I toss you into the fire. Usually, I prefer the temper that a straight fire bath gives to the new help. But, after last night and this morning's 'adventures,' I can see that you have all the temper and seasoning needed already. Don't get your hopes up after that little bit of praise though. I am still going to work you to the bone!"

"Appreciated. But I think there is something just a little more pressing at the moment," Mick said, leaning forwards while he absently picked up a cup of coffee that she had poured for him. "What are the Whispers? And, why did they scare the bejeebers out of Yosuke?" He took a sip of the coffee and was hard pressed not to cough as he discovered that it was reinforced. It was only as the burn clawed its way down into his gut that he noticed the bottle of cream liquor that had manifested itself on the table. 'Tengu Fire Brand Cream Liquor' was shouted across the label by a torqued looking crow.

"We don't know," she answered flatly, holding her coffee closely, as if to absorb its warmth. "There is almost nothing that we know about the Whispers. They have been here since before this area was settled. For the most part, they leave us alone. That is, so long as we don't trespass too far into the forest. For those that do, there are only two results. They never return or if they do, then it is only achieved by great personal sacrifice or through sheer luck. But no one has made it more than three kilometers deep into the woods and returned to tell of what they've found. How they managed to cut the road/trail into the lake and establish this village in the first place is still something of a mystery."

Mick leaned back, absorbing the new information and trying to recall anything from his own learnings and experiences that might help explain it. He was drawing up a blank. Werewolves and some of the ape races were known as being rather territorial of their woods or hunting grounds but hard boundaries weren't in their MO. Maybe a flock of harpies, they liked the woods and could be pretty touchy, but they also were fairly easy to identify thanks to their shed feathers. "So... Any idea what spurred them to come out now? The fog seems a little unnatural. Is it something that draws the Whispers out or something that comes with them?"

"The fog isn't natural. That much we are sure of. And as to why they have come out..." Atsuko arched an eyebrow at Mick. *He's the only thing that changed around here as of late. And he does seem to have a rather peculiar history. If anything was liable to pique the Whispers curiosity, it would be someone like him.* She cocked her head to the side in puzzlement. *For that matter, regardless of the cause, if the Whispers are about, how did he ever manage to make it here through the fog?*

She figures it is because of me. Mick opened his mouth to reply but was cut off as Yosuke re-entered the room. His face was contorted in a mask that Mick had already seen far too many times in his life. "What happened!?" he and Atsuko asked at the same time.

"Mai is missing," Yosuke replied flatly.

"Mai? But they never take or harm children. Maybe scare them, but never take them!" Atsuko exclaimed.

"Apparently they want to make sure that they really have our attention this time," Yosuke agreed. "And they aren't done breaking all the assumptions that we thought we knew about them either. They left a note," he explained passing it over to Atsuko. She read it thrice before handing it over to Mick.

Knight Outcast of the Order, Mick Mär Renalds,

I hope that this letter finds you well. As you read this letter, know that we mean you no harm and we will return the child to the town as soon as the fog lifts. Our intention was never to take her, and we only did it for her own protection. More than we were concealed in the fog today. We beseech you with a simple request. Come to us. You will need to bring one week's supplies and proceed into the forest behind your house. Follow the signs from there. You should come armed. The dangers of the woods are great and not to be underestimated. We are not the threat within the woods. The ones who plague the town are another and it is wise to fear them. They are an ancient evil who we detest. We are those who live in the dark to protect the light. Come to us, child of Night.

Ever vigilant,

Mick read the letter a second time to make sure that he hadn't missed anything and that he fully understood it. "I guess I won't be making it to work today. I'm going to need some things though. A pack, food, bedding, and the like. A sturdy knife or three would also be appreciated...," he started before he noticed the shocked looks on the other's faces. "What?"

"What?!!!" Yosuke asked incredulously. "It's a trap and you are talking about blithely walking into it without the least bit of concern for yourself."

Mick arched a questioning eyebrow at him. "Then it's a trap. If they wanted me, they could have just extorted me with the safety of the little girl. They know I am a member, or at least was, of The Knight's Order. I may not be held to my old oaths of that order anymore, but that doesn't mean that I don't still live by them. It was the order that betrayed me, not the other way around. And the oaths I took are pretty cut and dry on my duty when the life of an innocent is weighed against my own. But instead they indicate that they will return the girl as soon as the fog has lifted and it is safe," he held up a forestalling hand against the counter argument killing it on Yosuke's lips. "Yes. They could just be using this to lull me into a false sense of security. But then you need to ask, 'what is there to be gained for them in doing that?' I mean, they will have already turned over the best tool that they could have used against me if that was their intention. But that isn't what they have done. That points me towards believing that they aren't playing games and are making this request in good faith. So, I am going. If you won't help me, well then, I'll figure something else out on my own," he finished explaining. He looked up with a wolfish smile after shaking his head. "And I've never much liked leaving mysteries unsolved and this is far from my first time confronting the unknown. I've lived and learned in the darkest and most remote areas of the nine continents Africa, Antarctica, Asia, Atlanti, Australia, Europe, Mu, North America, and South America." Atlanti and Mu had been interesting and more than difficult to reach given that one was at the bottom of the ocean and the other was right where it was said to be but somehow separated from everything else and unperceivable unless you were invited.

Yosuke threw up his hands and turned on Atsuko. "Are you just going to let this happen?" he demanded. "This isn't just about his life. This is about the safety of the whole village. He may be an outcast, but he is a high-profile outcast. There is every chance that if something bad happens to him and his 'Order' finds out about it that they will descend upon our town seeking answers and I fear that they won't be too kind in how they go about asking them."

Atsuko continued to sit there motionless for a moment longer. "Yes, they may. And if they venture into the woods to recover him or seek revenge when we tell them what has happened, they will meet their own ends," she agreed. Yosuke looked smug, until he noticed that she wasn't done yet. "But this is a chance that we cannot let pass us by. For the first time in over five-hundred years, some part of those in the woods are reaching out. I would truly like to know what has prompted this move by them. Something has changed and I don't much like this talk of ancient evils. I'm perfectly content with ancient remaining in the past and leaving us to our nice present and future. We in Japan did a better job of living with humans than most, but it is only because we were able to convince them that it was all just myths and fantasy. If they remembered, and given how we have been reduced over the years, it is doubtful that we could survive the confrontation. If there is something unrestrained out there that is stirring again, then it could mean the end of the peace that we have worked so hard to create. You know as well as I do what humans do when they run into something that they can't understand, and which makes them feel weak."

Yosuke hung his head, not wanting to admit that she was right, but knowing that she was.

"You all seem to be forgetting that this isn't your choice. It is mine and I have already decided to go," Mick said into the silence. He had spent enough years already having others decide what he should and shouldn't do and he was done with it. *My life is my own now.* He breathed a sigh of relief as that fact finally clicked into place. *Now I can live. And the fog is lifting.* "The day is still young, and I need to make preparations. So, help me or get out of my way, but I am going!"

"He's going! Yosuke, go get the old pack. I'll take care of getting the food together. Rouse Oga and have him get together an outfit for a week's trek. Tell him to think old-school travel from the 'good old days' with all of the old precautions in mind. He is free to add on more modern equipment where it makes the most sense, though,"

Atsuko ordered, laying out the groundwork. "I'd suggest packing more, but a week's supplies are about ideal anyways. Anything over that will only be cumbersome and if you haven't gotten where you are going by then, then you probably won't be going because you'll already be dead," she stated flatly. Mick shrugged. "Good. Now for the hard part... Follow me," she snapped, marching out of the room. A moment later her head popped back in. "Coming??"

Mick glanced to Yosuke, who just shrugged, beaten. He got up and turned for the door but stopped to reach back for his coffee cup. *Might be the last good cup that I get.*

He found that he was smiling as Atsuko led him down a set of stairs, into a side room, and down into a sub level of the Inn that he hadn't seen the night before. All things considered; he couldn't help but feel excited. This was the kind of thing that he had been doing until his exile. It was what he was born for. It was literally in his blood and his destiny, and if there was one thing that he had learned, it was that destiny wasn't keen on letting any of those that it had entwined escape without paying a dear or deathly price.

The few rooms that were open and had a light on, revealed organized rooms of various supplies. Everything from silverware to pianos were stored down there. When they reached the end of the hall, Atsuko pulled a keyring from her pocket and opened the second to last door. It was pitch black to his eyes and he lost sight of her as soon as she stepped in. He wasn't about to turn back now and followed her in with only a moment's pause. He'd expected a room but instead found that it led to another staircase leading down to a deeper level. Atsuko was only a little ahead of him and flipped on the lights. The stairs ran deep.

"You see nothing!" Atsuko said, her suddenly cold eyes filled with the promise of violence.

Mick nodded an okay. *I see no'ting.* It was hard to stifle the statement and the laugh that followed close on its heels. *Jake would be loving this. Who am I joking! I love this. I was literally born for this. And unlike Jake, bless his complete lack of skill at keeping a secret, I know how to keep a secret and keep it I shall.* There were some things that you just didn't talk about and this was apparently one of them. *Time to channel my inner Schultz.*

Heat started raising up to meet them as they traveled deeper. After the first twenty steps, the stairs had shifted from wood, to cut stone. The floor leveled out onto a landing at the two-hundred and forty-fourth step. The path forward was barred by a heavy iron and wood door with an intricate iron inlay depicting a forest and a great battle shrouded beneath the trees. The key ring jingled again, and the door swung outwards without a single squeak. Mick took a small step back as waves of heat released by the door rolled out at them and struck him like a hammer blow. After the initial shock had abated, even if the heat had not, he realized that he could indeed hear hammer blows coming from within.

Without explaining, Atsuko led the way into a large and dusky warren below. It rather reminded Mick of the Labyrinth or the Portland Underground, which was an extremely freaky place, but far older.

There was a clamor of hammer blows sounding from deeper within. It died with a deafening suddenness as Mick crossed the threshold. The perfect silence was shattered with the crash of falling tools and metal. "Visitors!!!" a hoarse voice boomed out at them. It carried power and age, yet also spoke of great loneliness. "That door has laid shut for eighty-eight years. I have to wonder just what portents or going-ons must have transpired to compel you to come down here in person after all of these years, Atsuko?"

Atsuko twitched at the use of her name and seemed to be fidgeting like a middle-schooler with their first love letter.

"Hmm???" the voice prompted again. A shadow shifted and started around the corner towards them.

Mick instinctively tensed as he saw the movement. The fact that the shadow was rippling like water or fire did little to assuage his fears. Although, the little old man that soon followed it did plenty to. He had the look of being in his late sixties or early seventies and he was sporting a full head of silver hair, a cane, and, despite the heat, had on a tweed sweater. Mick's eyes immediately started splitting their attention between the old man's eyes and the cane. He knew better than to assume that things were as they appeared. The inquisitive eyebrow that the old man gave him as he neared, did little to relieve his doubts. *I am standing before a predator and it just realized that something, not a sheep, has entered its domain. This could get ugly.*

Atsuko noticed the exchange and carefully moved herself onto an intercept course. *Now if I only knew which of these two was actually the greater threat. Best defuse this fast.* "Daddy, this is, Mick. Mick, Daddy, also known as Kentaro" she said, making the introductions. "He's new to the area and already neck deep into waters where even we don't tread and about to go even deeper..." Kentaro cut her off with a hand on her shoulder and a twinkle in his eyes.

He had covered the five meters separating them within a blink and without a whisper of movement. "And you are still thinking of him as a human because he looks like a human. Because of that you fail to see that he is the biggest Fear in the room. You see the 'what' and not the 'who'. You come seeking help and protection from that which you do not know for that which you do not comprehend. You came seeking a weapon for one who is a weapon. Its blade may as yet be sheathed and unseen, but it is a blade unrivaled," Kentaro finished, looking not at Atsuko but directly into Mick's eyes. "A blade which cuts both ways."

Pops is either far too perceptive or he knows a lot more than I had thought possible for anyone outside of The Order or maybe those mystics in Africa. Who am I kidding, The Order isn't even that worried. They don't understand Fear anymore. They have been the top dog for too long and have grown too arrogant to see the world in any light except for one which pleases them. Mick let out a calming breath, letting his tension bleed away. "A pleasure to meet you, Kentaro," he said, giving a brief bow. "He's right, Atsuko," he said, turning to face her. "I don't let it out except when I have to. Last night was little more than a parlor trick and purely non-threatening. Offensive abilities are far more volatile and less predictable. Defensive abilities are almost as bad, because they can trigger offensive actions. See previous statement. So, yes. My blade is unrivaled. But it is also unchained and best only drawn when there is no other choice. So, a chained blade is not that bad of an idea. Swords are handy and look cool. Axes are deadly and infinitely more useful. Also, people look at a sword and see a weapon. When they look at an axe, they see a tool. Any chance that you have anything like a short axe? About forty centimeters long, with something like a hammer head or spike on the reversed side? One would be good, but two would be better," he inquired.

"Oh, I like this one," Kentaro chuckled. "He didn't even have to see my wares and he could already smell that this was a place of steel. Also, he apparently has a good eye for maximizing."

"You and Ten-chan both," Atsuko grumbled from a table. Apparently, she hadn't much cared for being treated like the kid in the room. Mick could sympathize.

"That old crow still flapping around and causing mischief!?" Kentaro asked.

"He's still just as much bluster as he's ever been, and he still has his claim on the mountain. A few city Tengu tried to muscle him out a few years back when they started dispersing back out from the cities. I think their tail feathers are still frozen to some mountain in Siberia that he blew them off to. Beyond that, he is still his old mischievous and cantankerous self," Atsuko answered. Her father was a dangerous and unpredictable fellow and he had powerful enemies and friends. That was why he had taken his self-inflicted exile into the basement. The town couldn't afford to get dragged into his fights and he knew it. So he had disappeared as best as he could and let people think that he was gone.

"Good to hear. I'll have to make sure to go visit him sometime," he replied absently from around the corner. It sounded like he was looking for something. "Battle axes. Weapons of brutes and deadly in the hands of even a peasant. Looking at it that way, I guess it makes sense why nothing like them really ever caught on over here."

"Plate armor had a bit to do with that also. Axes make the best can openers. The nobles and knights weren't huge fans of them either. Having peasants that had bows was bad enough. They were rather happy that low level steel production kept their numbers down, except for with the Norse. Now there was a race that knew that a battle field is carnage and the side that can rain down the most of it in the shortest amount of time is usually the winner. If it hadn't been for their bad luck with the climate and them ticking off Jörmungandr, I still say that North America would have been theirs. I shudder to think of what they would have invented had they lasted until black powder and firearms were introduced," Mick said, shouting to be heard over the cacophony coming from the other room.

"Probably true. That Erick fella certainly made a big enough impact over here and in China when he came sailing over out of the northeast," Kentaro chuckled. The clattering came to a sudden stop. "Ah, there you are!"

Mick rocked as that little cavalier statement of a bomb struck; trying to fit what he had just heard into everything that he had thought that he had known. *Jerk, Leif never mentioned that. Certainly explains a few things. If I ever get back to Main, I am going to have to have a nice long talk with him.* That train of thought came crashing down as Kentaro came back out with an oiled leather wrapped bundle. The leather spoke of Europe, but the metal shrouded within sang of Japanese iron and of a longing that he knew all too well. Without meaning to, he stepped closer. Atsuko, spurred on by a more natural curiosity, followed suit.

Kentaro had his arm draped over the bundle in a restraining manner. He lifted up his hand to stop them as they got near. "That is close enough. You see, I find it rather odd that you are here, Mick. I have a hard time believing that it is only through chance. You see, I recognize you. You aren't the same, some of the features are different, as well as the language, but I know you! It is why I could recognize who and what you really were from the start," he explained. Mick couldn't help but knit his brow and give him an odd look. He chuckled. "You know a lot and a little at the same time. It's not surprising in one as young as you. You see," he began to slowly peel back the shroud, "Night has visited these lands before and she left these behind in thanks for our help when she left," he said, looking up at Mick as the last fold fell away, uncovering two short heft axes. One had a rounded hammer on the reverse while the other sported a spike. Beyond that, they were completely the same. The metal had the swirls of Japanese folded steel, but the designs were Northern European. Built into swirling patterns of the dark steel were the delicate lines and shapes of Ivy. "When she left these, she also left a message. It warned that the blades were dangerous to any that handled them without the proper training and foretold that in the far-off future, a distant descendent of hers would appear in a time of 'upheaval' and that only they would be able to handle them. All others that ever tried to touch them or handle them have suffered severe burns and spikes of living black metal driven through their hands. So, think before you reach out. If you are false, only pain awaits you. If you are true, I don't know what will happen. She forgot to include that little fact in the user's manual," he finished with a shrug, extending the bundle to Mick.

Mick gently gathered the bundle and moved over to the table that Atsuko had been sulking at and deposited it there, just running his eyes over the weapons for a moment; taking in their shape, size, and potential. They scared him. They spoke to that part of him that he kept buried and locked away. They spoke to Night. They spoke to the Berserker within. And there was absolutely no way that he could walk away now that he knew they were here.

"What's that written on the handle?" Atsuko asked, pointing more closely than he really felt was safe.

Kentaro edged in and frowned. "Where did that come from? It's never been there before!"

Mick sucked in air. "'Gun Státh' and 'Cuideam,'" he whispered. Atsuko and Kentaro both gave him a questioning look. For the first time, it was clear to see that they were indeed father and daughter. *You're stalling! They expect an answer.* He took a steadying breath before reaching out and wrapping his hands around the heft of each ax. Nothing happened. He had just started to sigh with relief, when it felt like lightning flashed through his whole body. But it wasn't a flash. It was a New, Old Knight of Night. The searing flash continued coursing through him. Up one blood vessel and down another until every vessel and capillary in his body sung. He had experienced this once before. The day that Night had awoken. It continued for an eternity, contained within a second. When he could finally re-focus his thoughts and eyes, he was surprised to find both Atsuko and Kentaro still staring at him, awaiting his answer to their question. *It happened so fast that they didn't even notice! I guess that that is better than the first time where I was unconscious for a week.* He gave his head a little shake to clear the last of the cobwebs and set the axes back down. His hands were a little shaky as he drew them back. Atsuko and Kentaro were now giving him a concerned look as his body finally caught up with what had happened, and he broke out in a heavy sweat.

"Are you okay?" Atsuko asked into the stretching silence.

"Yah. Yah, I am okay." *No! No, I am really not.* Memories and information from an eon past were flooding into his brain. His body shivered so fast that they couldn't even see it as muscle memories, not his own, ingrained into the fiber of his being. The reason that no one else could handle the weapons was that they had been imbued with Night. Night remembered all that its host did. Even time and distance couldn't separate them. Mick already had the memories of the founder from his first encounter and this second contact had just given him those of yet another. *And I just got over the headache of sorting out all of the last set. I am curious as to how a descendent happened to wind up traveling with Leif? Oh, wait. I remember now. Oh, I really hate that.*

"*You and us both.*"

"*Shh. I'll deal with you and the new guy...*" Mick blinked as a flood of perturbed and rather direct memories welled up, flipping his world sideways. "*Beg pardon! New lady. Later! I don't have time to sort out the new boundaries and a whole new lifetime of memories right now.*" *Why do all of us users of Night have to go and have photographic memories? Is it too much to ask for only a normal person's worth of memories!?*

"*Well... just don't take too long. She is trying to redecorate.*"

"*No redecorating the inside of my head. I had best not find doilies lying about when we talk later!*"

"*Hmm!!*" a soprano voice sniffed but didn't reply.

I really don't have time for this. Mick turned his attention back to his external concerns. "As I was saying, these aren't your run of the mill weapons. They were forged by a user and descendent of Night and retained a portion of their power," *along with other things.* "Night is Iron of a sort. If you really know what you are doing and have taken the time to properly train, you can use Night in the forging of weapons. Through it, you can control the matrix of the elements down to the atomic level. For that matter, if you have the energy and strength, you can perform Alchemy by stripping or adding electrons and neutrons. In general, it is easier just to use it to gather the trace amounts of those elements together, but if that isn't an option because of time or really weird geology of an area, you can do it. But back to the point, if you know what you are doing and have the mental fortitude, you can imbue weapons with Night and give them abilities that go far beyond what metallurgy alone can do. Unfortunately, what makes them special, also makes them unusable by any but their maker or another descendant of Night. As I told you last night, The Order doesn't much like Night. So, they have gone to great lengths to find all of the Ancient Arms of Night and see them disposed of. Usually that requires the likes of a volcano. The threat that they pose of awakening the descendants of Night is viewed as too great a threat to overlook. As far as I knew, the Sword of the First Keeper, which is what awakened my own connection to Night, was the only weapon still intact. The only reason that it hasn't been purged, like all the rest, is that it can't awaken any more people. Each artifact is like a capacitor for Night. Once it has been used to awaken someone, it loses the ability to do so to anyone else. It does maintain its imbuements and lack of usability for any but those of the 'Fallen Branch.' So, even most normal members of The Order could use it now. That is, if they knew where it was. It sadly disappeared only a short time after I had re-discovered it. I sincerely hope that it never needs to be found. Some weapons have seen too much."

He gave his head a shake. There was power and danger down the path that that Sword pointed. Some day he would probably have to walk that path, but that day wasn't today. "Which makes these two interesting. Since I touched them, they can't awaken anyone else, but they are still highly useful and beyond rare. The craftswomanship alone speaks to the skill of the craftswoman and the quality of the weapon."

"Right. Well thank you for the socio/political history lesson about archaic Orders and their internal drama. It was rather enlightening and makes me glad that we only have to deal with the Onmyouji. They can be sticks in the mud, but at least they take a coexistence stance for the most part and keep their drama in-house and rather low key," Kentaro said, scratching at his head.

"I fully agree. As you can probably guess, the Onmyouji's stance has rather disturbed The Order over the years. Granted, the Tigers running the show in China are far more troubling to them. After the Brits got kicked out of Asia, The Order pretty much lost its foothold in Asia and they are still peeved at the Royals over that. But I am digressing. These will be perfect for my needs and I thank you for their safekeeping over the years and for entrusting them to me," Mick said, giving a polite bow.

"No worries. As far as I can tell, they already belonged to you as inheritance. And frankly, I am happy to be rid of them. They had a way of clattering sometimes that could be downright annoying," Kentaro said, waving him off.

Mick nodded his thanks and set about securing the harness for his new tools on his back. He was a touch surprised to find that the harness had another empty mount for a sword. Since it hadn't been offered, he didn't ask and figured that it was no longer about. But it did pique his curiosity as to just what had become of the missing member. *A question for another time.*

"Well then... I think that is everything. The day was young when we came down here, but by now the sun is sure to have climbed high and I should really be going," Mick said with a final nod.

"Best you had, but a moment," Kentaro said, grabbing Mick's arm by the elbow. His voice dropped into a hush as he spoke. "Trust nothing but your heart in those woods. An ally, a friend, an enemy, and an assassin. In those woods, they can all be the same. They have a use for you, and they want something out of you. I know not of what awaits you there but know that sometimes the guards can be just as bad if not worse than that which they are guarding. If you are as talented as you seem and more than a little lucky, we may someday see you again. Until then burn bright and don't stop," he warned. "Now get out of my shop. I have much work to do and little time to do it!"

Mick grinned and nodded his thanks again. "Till we meet again," he said and headed for the door and stairs, leaving Atsuko alone with her father for the first time in decades.

In that brief moment of silence, the looks of concern and curiosity on their faces were exact mirrors.

Kentaro broke it. "That one," he pointed to Mick's ascending back, "is going to make some really big waves."

"I hope we all still remember how to swim! Ready your forge. I fear we will have much need of it," Atsuko said.

"Aye."

***

Yosuke had a pack stuffed to the gills with supplies waiting for him when Mick reached the top of the stairs. His eyes went a little wide when he noticed the hardware riding on Mick's back. "I thought those things hated everyone?"

Mick grinned as he adjusted the straps. "They kinda do," he answered, but didn't elaborate. The ongoing conversation in his head was getting a bit on the noisy side and juggling all of the different languages that were in play was giving him a splitting headache. He was going to need some alone time to get this all worked out and the easiest place and way to get there was for him to be on his way. "No time like the present!" He said, giving the straps one last tug and a bounce before heading towards the back door and onto the path towards his house and the woods beyond. Yosuke came boiling out of the inn after him followed closely by Atsuko.

"You have no idea what you are walking into!" he said, catching up with Mick. *I doubt that he will listen, but this is likely the last chance that I will have to try and save him from this folly.*

Heh. Apparently, my feet were already on this path even before I arrived here. There is no turning back. Not after the choices that I have made and the fate I have accepted. Forward is the only direction left to me! "Neither do you and that scares you. I understand that and respect it. But this is a path that no other can walk or has walked before. I have been on the 'Path Apart' a 'Different Path' for a long while now and the direction it has been leading me is finally starting to take shape after wandering through the wilderness. I can't go back, and I can't step off of it. Forward is the only direction left to me!" Mick explained.

"It is to death that you go!" Atsuko pitched in. Voicing her doubts for the first time. "We can't stop you, but that doesn't mean that we will rest easy knowing that you walked into your death!"

"To Death is where we all go eventually. What is important is that when you meet him, you can stand tall. Sleep well. 'I'll be back!'" Mick said, only adding a slight Austrian accent. Some chances were just too good to pass up. He ducked into his house of one whole night, took one last look around, and left with the bundle of his belongings that was all that remained lashed to his pack. He wasn't the least bit surprised to see them worrying over a confused and disoriented little girl when he came back out. *Good to their word so far. Let's see if it lasts.* "That should be it. I'd appreciate it if you can cover for me with CE-J so they don't throw a hissy fit when I drop off the radar!?"

"You mean when you disappear, never to be found or heard from again?" Yosuke rebuked with a tired sigh.

"Or that," Mick shrugged with a smile. "See you when I see you," he said, and plunged into the shadows of the trees without looking back. The trees enshrouded the path behind him, cutting him off

from going back after a bare twenty meters. The forest held its breath
as it quietly watched. He just shrugged, adjusted his axes, and walked
on, eyes scanning and ready to face destiny once again.

***

Hours passed by in a dream under the towering canopy. The birds
chirped, the bugs buzzed and bit... hard, although the ones that tried
it on him dropped dead as soon as they started, and the animals
scurried about their daily lives. It was all perfectly normal and 100%
a lie. Well, except for the bugs. He was pretty sure that they weren't in
on it and were just being their buggy selves. If they were in on it, then
he was really in trouble. So far, the path had been rather clear. It was
more of a game trail than a path, but that was to be expected. Fair
folk didn't make paths. Paths were made by and for humans. That,
and predators hunted on paths and roads. Trails were usually safer.
Unless you were in Africa. Then nowhere was safe. Mick shivered,
despite the high temp, at the memory of his one mission in Africa
and getting stuck between the locals and the Chinese. Even the deep
Amazon and South of the USA wasn't as harrowing as that had been.
Although Louisiana hadn't been a cakewalk either, and did those
bugs ever bite in the most inconvenient places.

Bloody spying birds. Mick grumbled looking up at a passing
raven. He debated taking a swing at them, just to make them a
touch leerier, but decided better of it. They were not to be trusted.
Mercenaries with loyalty as solid as the highest bidder. They could
always be bought, and he had even known them to sell out their own
mother if there was a shiny in it for them. Or, if they figured it would
tick-off a crow, they would do it for free.

The question wasn't if they were reporting to anyone, but how
many different people they were reporting to. The guarantee was that
those that they were reporting to were either desperate or severely
lacking in scruples. Or both. The kind of Fair that were definitely

going to try and stab you in the back. With the crows, at least you knew that their word was good, and they tended to only work with the kind of Fair that, if they meant you harm, would come at you head on and in a more or less honorable fashion. Even if it wasn't a fair fight based on size or abilities, but they were at least 'sportsman like.'

A crisp breeze set the trees to rustling and pulled Mick's eyes up to the horizon, at least the little that he could make out of it through the canopy, and the low-lying sun that would soon be kissing the horizon.

"Best be making camp and get ready for what comes," Mick sighed, looking about for a good place to pitch his tarps. It took a little searching, but he managed to find a small, broken hill with a Titan of a pine growing alongside it that faced away from the trail that he had been using. Defensibly, it was so-so, but short of a bunker, that was going to be true for everything that he found and at least it would block the majority of the wind.

As soon as he had his camp properly arranged with the small rock face of the hill to his back, the pine to his right, and a small raised bed of boughs for his sleeping bag, he set about gathering a stock of firewood for the night and making his fire. He decided to make a trench fire with a round base at the far end. It would work to cut off the bigger of the two easy approaches and would keep him warm throughout the night. Stealth wasn't what night called for. The things that hunted in the night, did so because the dark was their element. Trying to be stealthy wasn't only pointless, but left you even more vulnerable. It was far better to advertise your presence, drive back the dark as much as you could, minimize your easy approaches, and be ready when the time came. If they would come wasn't the question either. It was 'when' they would come. Tonight, or another, but it was as inevitable as the rising and setting of the sun. When they came Night would face darkness and the greater shadows would reveal by light which lived on. "But that comes after it is full dark. For now, it is time to see about a bit of dinner," Mick said into the listening breeze and started rummaging through his pack for some fixings.

There was a decent mix of freeze-dried meals that had what looked to be an Oni in an Onsen as a mascot and 'Oni Brand' stamped on them: cured vegetables, meats and fish, eggs, rice, and some oats, as well as the necessary cooking tools. There was also a rather heavy but necessary whetstone for maintaining the knives, which he was pleased to find had been included. There was one extra as well. Although saying that it was a mark of his indentureship may have been more accurate. Wrapped in an oil cloth bundle at the base of his pack was a small multi-use kitchen knife of virgin steel that had never seen use before. The make was unmistakably the same as those in Atsuko's kitchen. There was even a letter wrapped around its hilt.

Mick,
A down payment on years of work owed. I expect a return on my investment.

Atsuko

"How nice. You know, I was indentured once!?"
"Seeing as how I have all of your memories, I do know. I still have rather vivid nightmares, based on more than a few of those memories," Mick grumbled. They'd been playing nice, but apparently there was no putting this off much longer.

"If you think that is bad, try being a slave," a soprano growled back in his head.

"I'd rather not, but I now know what you are talking about and it sucks. Moving past that and seeing as you have decided to open a dialogue, I guess now is as good of a time to be about this as any. Starting with a name would be nice. You know who I am and I'm sure

that by now you are acquainted with MacAllen. Yes, I could just dive into all of those memories that came along with you, but I would rather not. So?"

There was a pause in his thinking while the new roomie made up her mind. *"Ai'yana. Daughter of Orlan. First Watch of the Order of Night. Cleaver of the lost," she finished.*

Mick scrunched his forehead. *Order of Night? I have a feeling that I just ran into one of those things that is bound to complicate my life in un-wanted ways.*

Mac whistled.

"Something that you have been holding out on me?" Mick asked, slipping through the fabric of reality and into the Realm of Night where all that once was still lived and took his seat at the long table in his head. The room, which had been a castle chamber, now had some distinct Viking flare to it. The tapestries and wall hangings had been replaced with round shields and the suit of armor that had stood in the corner now had a target on it and an axe embedded in the bullseye.

This sealed realm was only accessible to holders of Night. It contained all of the memories of those who carried Night and allowed him to learn from them. Those like Mac and Ai'yana, were the only ones that had to answer his questions and he could only call them up because their memories were now mixed with his own, but everything existed here if you knew where to look and what questions to ask. He was also only able to talk with them without coming here because they had connections to him.

But as with all things, when you wanted to hammer out a good usage contract, face to face was always best.

"Oh, nothing much. Just a few reminiscences that I may have once jotted down. Ideas really, listing my contacts amongst the Fair, safe houses, families that could be trusted, and the such. All in a Journal you see. Towards the end was an idea for a new order to counterbalance the Knight's Keepers. I intended to pass it on to my sons when I passed. Apparently, they got it and followed through with some of the ideas. I hid it well but those two could always scrounge out my hiding places. They were real terrors on the sweets when they were growing up," Mac explained, smiling fondly at some past memory.

Mick scowled. *Odd that I've never run across any mention of them. Had they been wiped out by the Keepers, I would know about it. They would have used it as pretext to get rid of me permanently. Which means that the Keepers don't know about it. So, what happened to it and is it still around today? But how? The Circles that this world run in aren't so big that they could have stayed hidden. Everyone knows somebody and the big players may work in the dark, but they are all known. There would have been whispers at least.*

"Dead!"

The single word split through Mick's head like a lightning bolt.

"They are all dead. Betrayed by one of their own. My axes saw him fall, but there were only two of us left. Leif rescued me after that. Gave us a home and a new mission. We never managed to bounce back from it," Ai'yana answered.

The night's air had turned cold and still. "I see," Mick answered. There really wasn't anything else to be said. A twig snapped back near his camp. It was time to return. With an effort, the fabric tore again, and the world expanded. He loosened his axes in their sheaths and took a slow, deep breath. The time had come.

Red eyes caught the firelight. The shadows pressed in, driving back the fire's light and suffocating it down into an ember's glow. Except for the eyes, the body remained shrouded in inky darkness. A stench of rotten meat and wet dog clung to the air. With it came a flood of memories from three lifetimes. This was an opponent that they all knew and loathed. They were powerful, fast healing, fast, devious, vile, lying, betraying, and all-around no good. And they stank!!!

"Don't you mutts ever bathe?" Mick protested, doing his best to keep his mouth shut and to breathe shallow. It wasn't just the smell that he had to worry about. The miasma that they exuded carried paralytic particles. It wasn't as effective against him as it would have been on a normal person, but in high enough concentrations, it would slow his reactions a touch.

"Brave words from a mountain of kibble," it barked back. "You'll make a nice addition to the carrion heap in our den."

"Sure, you know what you are trying to bite off? Could be that you're biting into a bowl of stone laced kibble that might just choke you?" Mick warned. "You sure that you want to take the risk? For that matter, can you still smell past your own stench? Because the only fear you're smelling is your own."

Its eyes burned brimstone as it rushed forwards, but not quite into reach, before swinging back around in a snarl. "Brave kibble has a spice all its own!"

Mick nodded his head. "Figured you wouldn't take the easy route and I'd prefer to not have my stuff get all thrashed in the scuffle and covered in your stench." He stepped out from under the tarp, away from the fire's embracing light, and let the darkness enfold him. "Call your mate around and let's be about this! A real shame that I am going to have to move camp tonight once we are all done. I really liked this spot," he lamented, smiling madly in the glow of the moon as the embers lit the night behind him. He slid his axes free, holding them low and slightly away from his sides as he peered out into the darkness. He could use any weapon to lethal effect, but the axe and one and a half-hand sword were the master brushes of his art.

Predictably, the first attack came from behind him as the Black Dog's mate lunged through the air at him from the crest of the hill. He was ready when it came. *They never learn. The cowards always try to attack from the back.* He tucked his right shoulder and dropped to the ground in a role just centimeters beneath its septic snapping fangs and raking claws. At the same time, he brought his left axe around in a cartwheeling, backhanded swing that caught the Black Dog in the ribs behind its left foreleg and, biting deep, flung it over and away from him. The dog landed hard, jamming its snout into the loam, as its legs collapsed, and it tumbled and made a rasping yelp as the pain finally registered.

"I tried to handle this peacefully," Mick remarked into the shadows as the remaining black shadow converged on its injured mate.

"I can..." The response cut short in a yelp as fangs sunk deep into its neck and the lights burned out in its red eyes.

"You will pay for this human," it swore after dispatching its weakened mate. Weakness was not to be allowed. It would have to seek another mate. It was always a pain killing a leader to capture a new mate. The fleshling would pay for this. It would see that it putrefied alive, both for the taste and the entertainment of its suffering.

"Real loyalty there. I'm sleepy! How's about we wrap this up!" Mick replied and closed in. The Dog circled. Its honor too damaged to retreat but now aware of the scale of beast that it was facing. In a desperate move, it released the complete store of the toxic air that it had, trying to slow him. He wobbled to invite the attack and was just about to bring up his strike when he rolled to the side and came up looking behind himself. The Dog lay dead with an arrow sticking out of its mouth and the back of its head. He stood up, fully exposing himself, but no further arrows manifested out of the darkness. "I had it under control but thanks anyways," he shouted off into the night. The hoot of a passing owl was all that replied. "Right."

He turned back from the darkness and began repacking camp. It wasn't like he was going to get anymore sleep tonight, and with the stench staying wasn't much of an option either. *Nothing like a stroll through the dark woods by the light of the moon.*

***

The dawn broke crisp and cool. The night had seen him out of the valley and up into the surrounding hills. The trail had faded into nothingness during the night, but the signs remained. It was less of a physical sign, although those still existed also, and more of a feeling in his blood that cried out to him, dragging him along whether he wanted to or not. On the other side, the lizard part of his brain longed to curl up in a little ball and suck its thumb. He settled for a big yawn and making camp to eat breakfast and catch a few hours of rest under a small maple tree. It wasn't long before his eyes grew heavy and fell closed as he watched the waves of clouds washing over the valley below.

Who I Am
Sunday, July 4

There was a dark wood paneled and smoke-stained ceiling above him, the gurgle of a decent sized creek and the patter of rain on a tiled roof when Mick next woke. His hands, elbows, knees, and feet were bound snugly, but not uncomfortably so, by silk ropes. He could have escaped them easily enough, but he was curious to meet his host on their terms. He found that people tended to be more talkative when they thought that they were in control and he was curious as to just how they had subdued him without him noticing or Night reacting. The room had the smell of wood smoke, mountain vegetables, and tea about it. But most important, there were the hushed sounds of a conversation coming from the room next door.

"You really think that he can stop it?" a somewhat familiar female voice asked.

"No, I don't think anyone could stop it. But he may! May! Be able to minimize the fallout," a gruffer and older male voice answered.

"And a stone accidentally dropped by an overflying crow brained the shogun during the final battle," she retorted. Mick couldn't help but grin at that image. Stranger things had happened before.

"That actually happened. Anyhow, he has far better odds," he said dismissing her. Mick could practically hear the pandering wave of his hand.

"How much better?" she demanded.

"Oh, at least ten percent."

"And that he lives?" she pressed.

There was a harrumph. "No better than two percent in any case. Granted, those aren't much different from the odds that every human in the world is facing right now and it isn't like none of our kind won't be lost in the changes to come either. At least this way, we may be able to limit the worst of it to Japan."

The fear was palpable and now that Mick recognized it, the very air seemed to hum with angst and anticipation of something. It was looking more and more like Jake was right.

"You saw the numbers. You're the one who sought out the one long chance that we had to stop this. You're the one who double checked that he was legitimately a descendent of Night. Who snuck into the embassy and arranged for his placement here! You even arranged to meet him at the airport just to be sure. And, you're the one who argued for all of this. It's too late to turn back now and the choice isn't ours to make anymore. We gave up that right when we summoned him here. The choice is his and his alone!"

There was a long pause. "But the weight of his life is on us," she retorted. Her anguish and fear clear in her shuddering voice.

Mick listened into the silence, wondering what they would say, but no reply came. *That sounded distinctly not good. Just what are they guarding that they figure could cause a 98%* die-off and is related to Night? *Whatever it is, I have a feeling that I may have just stepped into something a lot bigger than I expected too. Returning Darkness? Sure, no problem. Done that before. World ending power? Now that sounds a little out of my league. But they seem to know about Night and it seems to be connected which means that I don't really have that much of a choice. The Order is going to defecate a flail sideways if they find out about this.*

The pitter of footsteps closed in on his door. He didn't even try to play like he was still asleep and readied to meet his visitor's/ captor's eyes as the door creaked open. *They should oil those hinges and square that door.* Creaky doors were nightmares when you needed to sneak through a house. All other thoughts ceased, and his breath caught, as she turned around and their eyes met.

"Ai!" Mick exclaimed, his heart beating fast. He could feel the flush rosy-ing his neck, ears, and cheeks, but there was no use denying the pitter-patter of his heart and no easy way to compose himself while his hands remained bound. He should have felt angry at the way that she had played him but all he felt was happiness at seeing her again. The world could burn for all he cared at that moment. She was here and that meant that everything was as it should be.

Ai cast her eyes to the floor as a flush pinked her own cheeks. "Mick."

"So... You... I mean this... It was all..." Mick cut his sputter short as his reaction surprised a giggle out of Ai. "Well, excuse me for being a little flustered."

Ai covered her mouth to hide her smile and smother her giggles as she replied "That's not it. I was just surprised. I didn't expect you to have a cute side like this," she smiled, her eyes twinkling with mischief.

Mick made to stick out his lower lip and cross his arms in annoyance but with his arms bound, all he managed was his lip and an awkward wiggle. Ai broke into a full bout of laughter that forced her to take a seat on the floor, lest she fall down. "It's not..." Mick started but gave it up as a smile cracked his own lips and soon became a full-blown belly laugh that would leave him feeling sore the next day. *Just what have I gotten myself into? Again! On second thought, whatever it is, seeing her again is totally worth it.*

Ai regained her feet slowly as their laughing fit abated and did her best to regain her composure. She was afraid but somehow, seeing him, she just couldn't believe that this was the end and that she would never get the chance to know him. She opened her mouth to start talking but paused as Mick beat her to the punch.

"You really were at the inn on that first night, weren't you!?" Mick asked, turning his eyes to look at her.

She sighed before she answered. "Yes. What with you being in 'the Town,' we had to be sure before we dared move openly and I stood the best chance of remaining unseen. It surprised me when you noticed me. Your training must have been rather peculiar for you to have been able to manage that."

You could say that.

"Helps when you have a few lifetimes of experience of dealing with odd stuff to draw upon also," Mac piped in.

"I learned to spot Shadows and Mist long before I ever met either of you. Now be quiet!" Mick warned the squatters in his head. "And it was really just luck that we ran into each other at the airport?" he asked, wanting to hear the truth of it directly from her. He had a healthy belief in fate and destiny, but he also knew that not everything was always as it appeared, and he wanted to get to the bottom of this before he made any choices. He'd seen too many good people die because they thought they had destiny behind them.

Ai fidgeted for a moment before taking a deep breath and meeting his eyes. "No and Yes!" she admitted, looking slightly ashamed. There was great happiness in her eyes and yet also a great sadness lurking just below the surface but no dishonesty that he could see. "No, I was there to try to see you and confirm what we thought we knew. Yes, it was luck that we could meet face to face. After the crash..." she cut off letting her fears go unspoken. "That you survived that, it had to be a touch of destiny. I think. Because, what else do you call it when everything in the world conspires to kill the person you are looking for and yet they still manage to reach the place where they are most needed at just the right time?"

"Really horrible, no good, awful luck," Mick answered flatly, while his eyes gleamed of mischief.

"That may as yet hold true. But sometimes the two are the same but just different sides of the same coin. Maybe 'fate' would have been a more apt term. In any case, I take it from your questions that you overheard at least a part of our conversation?" Ai asked, turning serious and smashing down the torrent of emotions that was threatening to breach her resolve. Mick simply nodded that he had. "Then I ask you to reserve your judgment until I have completed explaining everything."

Mick cocked his head to the side. "I can do that under two conditions."

"And those would be...?"

"Can you undo these bindings already? I really would rather not damage such nice ropes as these unless I absolutely have to. Unfortunately, I really have to use the restroom and I'm running out of time for a peaceful resolution to my current situation," Mick answered. He gave her the best pleading smile that he could manage under the situation. It even had the advantage of being 100% true.

"Oh! Sorry about that," Ai said, rushing back to her feet in a rush to release him. She rushed a little too fast. Her legs had had just long enough to fall asleep and as soon as she went to take a step, her balance disappeared and she came crashing down across Mick's chest, putting their faces mere centimeters apart.

Her breath was hot on his cheek, her skin smoother than silk, and her hair and skin had the light scent of mountain berries and a fresh mountain breeze. "Umph. Well, not quite what I had in mind and a little fast, all things considered." He teased, enjoying her flush and fluster.

"Sorry!" Ai exclaimed, turning pinker than Barbie, fresh out of High School, on a date with G.I. Joe and scrambling back to her feet. "I..."

"Restraints... Please..." Mick managed to cough out while restraining his laughter and some discomfort. Her landing and dismount had left more than a little to be desired in some areas and he really did need to use the restroom.

"Sorry!" She rushed over and quickly pulled the ends of the ropes to undo the knots and stepped back.

Mick bent over with as much dignity as he could muster and caught his breath. "Where's the bathroom?" he asked as levelly as possible.

"Uh... Right this way," Ai said, directing him to follow her.

The home, it definitely had that lived in charm of a home and not just a house, was built in a classical Japanese style with wood floors, packed earth walls - where there were walls, sliding divider doors, and timber framing. There was also a mix of more modern features and furniture scattered about. A dining table with chairs. A leather couch. A laptop sitting half open, its power cord running into an outlet in the wall next to the big screen TV. Mick was still letting the cognitive dissonance of it settle down when they reached his destination. It was obvious from the layout that he was only seeing a small portion of the house which meant that this place was in the old school mansion size for Japan.

"Here you are," Ai said, waving to a closed door and meeting his eyes again. She held them for a second before hers slid to the side as her cheeks turned rosy again. "Sorry."

"You don't have any reason to be sorry. I'm okay. Thank you for showing me the way," Mick said, doing his best to reassure her and trying not to over think it as their bodies brushed against each other as he slipped past. It was rather challenging. He took a quiet but deep breath once the door was safely closed behind him. He couldn't be sure, but he thought he may have heard a mumble or matching huff from the other side.

"You got to pee!"

"Right" Mick agreed, giving his head a shake to try and clear the memory of what had just happened from his thoughts. It wasn't working.

"That may make things difficult." Ai'yana piqued in.

"Shh," Mick accidentally said aloud.

"Are you okay?" Ai asked, from outside.

"Just dandy," Mick replied. He gave himself a shake and took another calming breath. It did the trick this time. He had just started to relax when Ai decided to ask another question.

"What was your second condition? I probably should have asked before I let you go, but it's a little too late to tie you back up now," Ai asked.

"I don't know? Getting tied back up may not be that bad," Mac snickered. It was rather fun teasing his great-grand-something.

Mick blushed and did his best to keep his cool. It was kind of hard. *"Get lost!"* he growled. *"There are more important things to be worrying about right now!"*

"Right," Mac chuckled. *"Bubye."*

Mick took another breath. *Stupid. What did I ever do to deserve this?* He quickly finished, washed his hands, and stepped back out into the hall where he was once again almost chest to chest with Ai. She wasn't quite tall enough to be nose to nose with him but the way she looked at him with her wide eyes and that pouting lip almost did him in.

"Are you okay?" Ai asked, when Mick didn't say anything and had been staring at her for several seconds. She liked the attention, but it was a bit embarrassing.

He took a deep breath. "Go out on a date with me!" he blurted, his brain not even processing what he had just said for several seconds. By the time it had, it was already too late. For all that he joshed Jake for his less than stellar performance where dating was concerned, it wasn't like he had much more experience. It wasn't that there hadn't been people interested in dating him, it had just been that he hadn't ever reciprocated the feeling. Jake had high standards. Mick's made them look soft. Ai was everything his heart had ever been looking for and more. He hadn't realized that he was holding his breath as his heart thundered in his ears until she answered after what seemed like an eternity.

"Okay," Ai whispered softly. She felt like if she had said it any louder, then the possibility would be blown away by the wind. "Okay," she said again, louder this time, just to be sure that he had heard her.

Mick let out a heavy sigh and felt like a mountain had lifted off of his chest. "Okay," he replied. It wasn't the romantic way that he had always envisioned these things happening, but Ai had said 'okay' and that was what was really important. Before he could think it through or lose his nerve, he wrapped her up in a hug.

Ai made a little yip in surprise at his sudden embrace, but her arms were soon wrapped around him and her face was buried in his chest. He smelled nice. Reluctantly, she pulled away after the moment stretched on. "We should be getting back to the others," Ai said, before leaving. Her legs felt like rubber and she needed to sit down. *Finally find a guy I like and he's probably going to die. This sucks! Please don't let him die.* She pleaded, clasping her hands and looking up at the ceiling.

Ai flopped down on the couch in the living room and he sat down in the other open chair, not wanting to be too pushy or seem clingy. There was also a rather stocky, in a linebacker kind of way, fellow sitting in the recliner.

"Nice of you to join us. There are some things that we really need to talk about, and it can't really wait. So here goes," the man began, barely giving Mick a chance to sit before he started. "I'm Reigi and I need to know if you are willing to die!"

"Come again, and maybe try to start from the beginning this time," Mick said, reaching up and scratching his temple. Going on suicide or one-way missions wasn't an entirely new thing to him. The Order had been sending him and his family on those types of missions for a long time, hoping that they wouldn't come back. They did. Renalds were like that. After he had acquired Night, they had tried even worse missions than those. Mu and Atlanti were case and point. He was still here. *But I didn't survive this long by going in all half-cocked on those missions. Information is the key to doing the impossible. If you know enough, then the impossible becomes possible.* "This is one of those talks where I'm really going to need you to start from the beginning."

Reigi looked at his watch. "How hungry are you?"

Mick's stomach growled in reply, eliciting a chuckle from both of them.

"In that case, we can start this conversation over dinner," Reigi answered, climbing to his feet. He was just as much of a mountain of muscles as Mick had suspected.

Ai grabbed a book off of the sofa table and smiled when she noticed him looking. "I hope you are rested, because this will take a while," she warned, only somewhat lamenting that they couldn't chat about other things. *What will I wear?*

The dining room was on the opposite side of the house from the room that he had woken up in. It was a nice setup with the kitchen flowing into the dining and living room for easy access. Apparently, the room where they had first talked was the sitting room. Mick made to help with setting up but was shooed away and forced to sit and do his best not to look fidgety as Ai and Reigi put out the dishes and brought out the food. He wasn't really that good at the whole sitting and watching others work thing. Unless he was watching to learn, he was more of a hands-on kind of guy. The only good thing about sitting was that they were eating at a full-size table with chairs that reasonably fit his bulk without too much trouble. He wasn't averse to sitting on the floor, but the tables were always a bit too small when he had found himself in those situations and his butt and back were always sore afterwards. 'What's for dinner' turned out to be curry and tempura with a side of salad and assorted pickles.

He was more than a little surprised when, before eating, he bowed his head to pray and Ai and Reigi made to join hands in with him. They smiled at his surprise as he looked up at them.

"Toyatomi and the other jerk Shoguns that followed after him didn't get all of us," Reigi answered with a smile. "Sad that there are still so few of us in the country, though. Between all of them, they certainly caused a lasting wound in the hearts of the Japanese that refuses to mend."

"I see," Mick said, filing away that information for a later conversation. It may not have done much to change his current situation or fate, but it certainly helped him feel more at peace with it. He joined hands with them and re-bowed his head. "Lord, we come to you in troubled and dark times. Times that may require the greatest of sacrifices. In these troubled times, we ask for your direction and the peace that comes from following it. Grant us wisdom, patience, and understanding. See us down the path that you desire and deliver us from our trepidations. Deliver us and guard us against those that would see evil visited upon us. As you are our shield, let us be your sword and torch in the darkness. And, please bless this meal and evening Lord. In Jesus name we pray. Amen," he finished, lifting his head. Reigi gave him a curt nod as he released his hand, while Ai held onto his hand just a moment longer than necessary and gave it a little squeeze before letting go. Regi didn't comment on that but the slight furrow of his brow made it clear that he had noticed.

"Well, dish up before it gets could. We have a lot to talk about and only so much time to do it in," Reigi ordered, with the slightest of tugging at the corners of his mouth. He let whatever he was thinking pass with a small huff and set to dishing up some salad.

Mick didn't need to be told twice as his mouth watered and his stomach growled as the scent of the curry wafted through the room. They had even included properly sized plates with high edges that were perfect for curry. Reigi let him get a couple of mouthfuls down before he started in.

"To start, we have to go way back. Right up near the beginning. Are you familiar with the legend of how Japan formed?" Reigi asked.

Mick quirked an eyebrow but played along. "Izanagi and Izanami made the base island by churning the sea with the spear Ame-no-nuboko and the drops of salt water that fell from it. Then they came all the way down and had some kids that became the eight main islands. Hokkaido and Okinawa aren't included."

"Correct in the broad strokes. The first part is what is important because it is a little bit inaccurate. The lands of Japan were created by the descent of something from the heavens. It just wasn't a spear. It was an asteroid. A unique asteroid. One that is related to you also," Reigi added, smirking as Mick's head snapped up.

"What?" Ai and Reigi chuckled at the shocked look on Mick's face. Reigi pulled a small blue crystal, about the size of a pinky, out of his pocket and tossed it over to Mick. He caught it and gave it a quick look. He instantly knew what it was, and his blood ran a little colder as he sensed the sheer power that he was holding in his hands. He'd only ever read about them or seen them locked away under heavy guard. Those that had them treasured them above all of their other possessions and all that knew of them feared them and coveted the power that they bestowed upon those that did have them. And Reigi had just tossed him the biggest one that he had ever seen or heard of like it was no biggy. "A Ragnarök stone," he whispered and made to put the stone back down but was distracted as Reigi started talking again.

"We call them 'Ryuu Suishou' or just Crystals. But they are what is really responsible for the formation of Japan. Way back near the beginning, a great big asteroid fell from the sky. It broke up into several large fragments that crashed into the ocean and shattered their way all the way down through the crust until they lodged in the roof of the mantle. They then quickly began absorbing energy and expanding, which eventually deformed the crust and caused fissures to open, causing the formation of Japan," Reigi explained, glancing up at Mick to see if he was following.

Mick looked at the crystal in his hand. It looked a little clearer than it had before. "You're trying to tell me that there are chunks of these under Japan?"

"Chunk is a rather small term and they are quite connected. Mountains would be a much better representation. Mountains that are growing and are connected!" Reigi corrected.

"Growing?" Mick felt another shiver run down his back. It fit so well with what he had seen happening since coming to Japan, but it was still almost too shocking to believe. One crystal could hold the power to wipe out a whole city. He shuddered to think on the amount of power held in a mountain made of the stuff. There was a good reason why they were referred to as Ragnarök stones.

"Yes, growing. They have been almost stagnant since their last expansion that formed Japan. But their energy levels are about to peak and when they do, the crystals will enter into another explosive growth phase. The signs are already showing. When that happens, Japan will be destroyed and the world won't be much better off as the crystals spread, gobbling up any energy that they can access and spreading out to cover the whole mantle ceiling. When that happens the crust of the earth will become vastly displaced causing earthquakes and volcanic eruptions on a scale that has never been seen before. The loss of life is projected to reach cataclysmic proportions. A 95% die-off of human life. Very bad!" Reigi explained. "Even those who survive won't last long. Eventually that much crystal will suck the core cold and then it is bye-bye home."

"And no one else knows that this is going on?" Mick asked, finding it hard to believe that the world as he knew it was at its end and no one had tipped him off until just now. This was the kind of thing that the rumor mills ate up and spat out faster than the speed of light.

"There are others that are aware of the crystals and that they are responsible for the current happenings in Japan, but they are looking at only a piece of the puzzle. Without the whole puzzle to work with, all of the data is off and makes it look like this is just localized and not globalized. They don't understand that the old equations don't fit anymore because a piece of the equation that they don't even know about is about to be shoved right smack dab into the heart of the planet," Reigi answered, locking eyes with Mick.

"I have a feeling that I am not going to like this. Just what does this have to do with Night? That is the only reason that you could need me. Beyond Night, I am just another big, tough, and highly trained person. So how does Night change the equation?" Mick asked, giving the table a light thump for emphasis. A tremor ran through the ground, setting the dishes rattling slightly at the same moment.

Reigi didn't seem to notice or find it odd. "That isn't the only reason at all. But, you are right. We need Night!"

"Why?"

"You are the only living user and holder of Night in the world. How much do you really know about Night?" Ai asked. She set her hands on top of each other to keep from reaching over for his but she was still blushing a little and she didn't seem angry.

Mick paused, debating for just a moment whether he should tell them what he knew. *And if the Order finds out that I shared their darkest secrets with people of the Fair... What? They'll want me deaderer?* He let out a small chuckle at the realization and felt like a weight that he didn't even know that he had been carrying had been lifted off of his shoulders. He was his own and if they wanted him, they could come and get him. He didn't owe them anything. They had cleared that account when they had exiled him.

"MacAllen Renalds founded the Order and was the first carrier of Night. He encountered it in a small glen in the mountains of Ireland, when he went for a swim in a small mountain pool with his brother. It rejected his brother, the older of the two, scarring his hand, but bound freely with him. Their feud can be traced back to that point. The Order was founded by both of them as a counter to the members of the Fair that were preying upon their villagers. For a time, they worked together. To counter the discrepancy in ability between them, the older brother, Rollan, sought more and more abilities and powers which could be gathered and trained and performed whatever tasks that needed to be completed in order to enable not only himself, but his descendants to retain access to those abilities. MacAllen discovered this too late. Some of the things that Rollan had done in the pursuit of power were evil beyond speaking. Rollan was ready for this eventuality though and painted the crimes as MacAllen's doing. The others, believing the apparently untainted by the Fair and older brother, turned on MacAllen. He was forced to flee lest he and his family with him be utterly destroyed. He could have won the battle with his brother, but there was no winning the war without killing or suppressing everyone else and there was no way to guard his family against that threat. Also, for all the corruption of his brother, the Order that they had created was acting as a check against the Fair and protecting the people. Several hundred years after the deaths of him and his brother, the MacAllen side of the family ran back afoul of the Order. Enough time had passed by then that they were granted leniency, seeing as none of the remaining members were touched by Night. How that separation occurred is a little bit of a mystery, but it saved my family from destruction," he said, breaking dozens of vows in one fell swoop. If the Order knew, they would have been more than a bit ticked off.

Now to break the vows with death sentences attached to them. "To answer your questions about Night, I can only speak for what I have discovered about it. "Night is fickle. It is a power like many others, but its limits are hard to define. At times, it acts sentient, more like a symbiont with a will of its own. It can even carry memories. Under the right circumstances, it can live independent of a host, but not if it is separated against the host's will; it can only happen through a controlled and non-distressed action. It is controllable remotely through thought, but some of it is lost due to interference and the greater the distance, the greater the drain on power and the more that is lost. It is iron in base but that is not all that it is made up of. Carbon and graphene are also present as well as pretty much all of the other known elements and a few that I haven't seen identified yet. It is also naturally in a liquid state, but without the presence of heat. Although, it can be formed into all of the other states also. Even a few states that are a little tough to define. It is replicable. Given the right resources, time, energy, and concentration, vast amounts of it can be created. But, without a host to sustain it, in anything over about a kilo quantity, it loses cohesion and dissolves back into its base elements. Even the kilo and lesser amounts suffer degradation unless they are bound up in something or have some source of energy sustaining them," he explained. "Why?"

Reigi's eyes were gleaming with hope. "Because the crystals didn't fall alone. Night and Light fell together."

The world went white as his heart seemed to fall silent and the ringing in his ears drowned out all other sound. He was aware of the concerned reactions of Ai and Reigi, but they were a long way away at the moment, as memories that were one hundred percent his and his alone, carried him back through the years.

***

"We shouldn't be here!" Mick pointed out. "There are excellent reasons why no one comes to this area and even fewer return!"

"Yes, there are. But fear is the greatest threat and the Fear of this place conceals too much. It has blinded not only the Order, but the Druids, and even those of the Fair. Anything capable of that needs to be researched, understood, and properly sealed if it is truly a threat. At a minimum, it needs to be pulled out into the light," Aldwin argued. Everything he said was plausible and correct but the grin he wore said that, once again, breaking the 'rules' was his greatest motivator.

It was all a memory, and no matter how much he wanted to change it, he wasn't in the driver's seat. The past was immutable, and he was only a passenger watching it all happen again. He knew the train wreck was coming, when and how it would happen, how to stop it, and even how to change it, but he was powerless before the immutability of history. Many had tried to change the past, all of them had met bad ends.

Mick shook his head while looking down at his feet. He was smiling when he looked back up. "And this is why the Order has a deep-seated distrust of Druids. Your lot stick your nose into any nook or cranny that you can find!"

"Says the man who is sticking his nose into Druid affairs. I seem to remember that The Order was founded by sticking its nose into a lot of things," Aldwin pushed back. He knew more of The Order's history and other things than was entirely healthy, but that self-same knowledge and his drive to acquire more and more of it was also his greatest asset and armor.

"Yes. I dig and the Order is not exactly happy about that. Although, there is not much that they can do to stop it either; seeing as how I am not breaking any sanctions and I am only seeking knowledge for the betterment of the Order and defense against the eventuality of a Druid uprising led by someone like... well... You. The Order gained their power through digging into the dark cracks and they will not stand to see their dominance questioned or challenged.

Be careful how you push. If they see you as a threat, the Counsel of Rollan will have your head and there will be nothing that I can do to protect you!"

"That blade cuts both ways. The Order's supremacy is not as great as it once was. Asia is open. The Fair have spread, and while hidden and somewhat reduced from their ancient numbers, they have gathered strength that the Order knows not of because they only see from above. We Gray Druids are but one of many orders that are arising from their shadow. They could take my head, put their boot on our throats, as they always have, but a time will come when they will have to grow, or they will be washed over by the flood that is rising. I tell you this now. As your friend. The signs are here. A change will soon be upon us. What it is, what will cause it, and what it will mean, none of us know. But all that are looking agree that it is coming, and we are all afraid," Aldwin warned, turning grave. He may have been young, but he was one of the most learned and powerful of his order. His words and wisdom were to be heeded. It was also the reason that he had volunteered to mentor the young heretical Knight that had come to study with them.

Mick shivered again, as he had shivered then. He had known it was coming also. He could read the signs and projections as well as anyone else. Now he even knew what was probably going to cause it. But at that time, he had shivered for a different reason. He had shivered because he knew that his friend was right and that he was also one of the greatest threats that existed to the Order. Aldwin knew the Fear of the Order. Respected it. Looked at it. And, in looking, could see light and weeds peeking through its once impenetrable walls. He knew that all it would take was a little force on the right crack and the whole wall would come down. Sections may still stand in the rubble, but it would never be able to be restored to its former glory as the flood of everything that it had long held back washed over it. Only the towers would remain to remind those who passed over the rubble of what had once been.

"I know. But you know how my family's position in the Order fares. We have more of a foot in this world than that of the Order anymore and Duke Rollan the XXV has been casting about like a mad dog on a barely tethered leash, just looking for an opening, any chance, to be rid of us. The older families still remember and fear or respect us. They would also happily see us wiped away. The weight that we carry amongst the middle and lower houses barely allows us to maintain our position in the council. We have warned them, but they will not listen. Their foundations built on sand run too deep. They will only move when the sand is scoured away to bedrock and the whole castle comes crashing down." Mick sighed tiredly. *And it doesn't help that Aliya is the best Knight that they have had in a hundred years and has taken the title of the Paladin from their champion and keeps bruising their egos with every successful mission that she wasn't supposed to return from yet does and not only does she return, but comes back stronger.* He gave it up with a huff. "But the future is for tomorrow. As you have dragged us here already, we have an investigation to undertake that is bound to bring the council 'bundles of joy.'" His words dripped sarcasm, but his grin was genuine and born of his adventurous spirit as he stepped into the cleft in the ocean crags of Maine to do something stupid.

The light cut off as soon as the Old Man's Beard that shrouded the entrance was allowed to fall back down. The air had the wetness and carried the sweet smell of peat. The walls glistened with moisture that crawled along its surface in a never-ending ripple. Aldwin cast the dark aside, lighting an eerie blue wisp that did nothing to dispel the trepidation and damp cold that hung in the air. It only seemed to make the shadows that clung to the walls grow deeper and stronger as it reminded them of their eternal battle against the light. It was, surprisingly, a short walk to the back of the cave and their destination. These things tended to be long and harrowing, but today, for all of the hype about the place, nothing out of the ordinary had occurred. The Cave came to a stop in a large chimney room with a single shaft of sunlight shining down in the center of the room. It was rather unremarkable except for the black obelisk that pierced up out of the ground in the center. That and the fact that the chimney couldn't actually have light shining down it right now because it was past noon. But the plants growing in the column of light didn't seem to mind.

"That is not normal!" Aldwin said while he circled the light's perimeter, careful not to disturb it in any way, analyzing it for any information or signs of traps.

"Odd? Yes. But I have seen stranger," Mick agreed, coming closer and getting a look for himself. The stone was glass black and smooth like obsidian, but darker than anything natural. It reflected exactly no light. You could only really make out its shape because the light around it defined its shape. His head hurt just from trying to process the solid void, trapped in a pillar of light. Worse, there were no signs that anything in the room was artificial. Beyond his understanding and perception? Sure. But artificial? Nope. "On second thought... Maybe not. That thing gives me a headache!" Mick said, jabbing his finger at the obelisk. He knew he had made a mistake when Aldwin's eyes went wide. It was soon followed by a lancing pain shooting up his arm from his index finger. It was searing and freezing at the same time. Pulling and smashing in every direction. Flaying and binding. It was like no pain he had ever known, and more than man was designed to process. He jerked his hand free from the ring of light and dropped to his knees clutching it to his chest. His whole body was wracked by a cold sweat and nauseous shivering. Aldwin was at his side almost as soon as his knees hit the stone floor.

"Show me your hand!!!" he ordered, all pretenses of his just being a plucky young man evaporating as he assumed his true role as Master of the Rune.

Obeying was the last thing that Mick wanted to do. He knew his finger was ruined. He could still feel the mangled mess that his finger had become. Aldwin wasn't much for dickering and bedside manner. He was stronger than his size and in Mick's shocked state, he was strong enough to force him to comply.

"It's fine," Aldwin whispered, in astonishment.

"No, it isn't. It won't ever be fine. I saw what was happening and there is no..." Aldwin's slap across his jaw was so jarring and sudden that Mick forgot his pain long enough to feel anger and regain a modicum of his composure. He made to retaliate without thinking and only stopped short of throwing Aldwin across the room when he realized that he was holding him by the scruff of his shirt with his injured hand. It wasn't injured. "How? I saw it. I felt it. That was no illusion," he said as he lowered Aldwin back to the ground and marveled at his hand.

"No, it wasn't," Aldwin agreed, examining Mick's hand once again now that his feet were firmly planted on the floor. The gleam in his eyes did little to calm Mick's frayed nerves. He pricked one of Mick's fingers with a needle without warning him and almost earned himself another flight across the room. Needles were a no-no for Mick. Mick's leer rolled off of him faster than water off of a grunge duck's back. "Well we can rule that out. No signs of spontaneous regeneration, healing, or reversion. Which means it wasn't you. Something in..." He stopped short as he motioned back at the obelisk.

Mick followed his gaze and felt his heart pound as he noticed the Runes now alight on the obelisks face.

Enter the light or leave and be barred from re-entry. Through sacrifice, the way forwards shall be opened. When Night and Light unite....

***

Mick's eyes snapped back open. He couldn't suppress a shiver as the waves of the memory subsided. Reigi was still talking.

"What we are asking..." He stopped as Ai set a hand on his forearm to get his attention.

She leaned forward and took Mick's hand in hers. "You know something... Don't you?"

Mick's heart thumped a little faster. Her hand was soft, yet strong for her size. He could have forced her to let go, but at the moment letting go of her hand was the last thing that he wanted to do. He wanted it to last forever. He took a deep breath and squeezed her hand. Her cheeks flushed a little, but she didn't let go of his hand. *"Why didn't you ever tell me!?"* Mick demanded.

"Tell you what? I know what you are talking about and thinking, but I didn't have anything to do with how we wound up together. Someone who came long after me arranged all of that. Apparently, they knew things that I hadn't learned yet. If you want answers, you'll have to ask them!" Rollan grumbled.

"We didn't know!" Ai'yana whispered.

Mick and Rollan paused. *"Know what?"* They both asked.

"We didn't know what it meant. An elder discovered it. He was the oldest of our order. Ancient even. A founder. A son of your son, Rollan. He spoke of having traveled to a far-off land in the west through the Northwest Passage. There he said that he met a wizard who worked side-by-side with strange creatures of the Fair. He travelled with them for a time. It was then that he encountered a Ragnarök Crystal. Not one of the little ones that we had seen and heard of before, but a tree made completely out of the stuff. His eyes always got a little misty at that point

and he wouldn't speak any further of it. The prospect of finding a tree of Crystal is what drove Leif to make the trip over here. We never did manage to find it though," Ai'yana said, frowning.

Mick opened his eyes again. Their conversation had taken but a blink. *The one who came before, must also be the one who sealed the sword away.* "Maybe. What I know is that there were other descendants that carried Night who came here long ago. One of them apparently found a tree made out of Crystal. I now believe that they are the same person who was responsible for sealing the 'Founders sword' which is also how I came to carry Night. From what I have gathered, they must have discovered something of the connection between Night and Light, which I now gather is the Crystal that you are talking about. What I read when I started down the path that led me to Night would seem to indicate that they knew that Night and the Crystal were connected and that someday they would need to be reconnected."

"He was right. The Crystal is the core. It is like an energy dump. The problem is that while it can hold enormous amounts of power, it does have a limit. If it reaches that limit, it has to expand and grow, or it has to be limited. Night is the only thing capable of that. Crystal is indestructible. It can be reduced into a powder. But it is unbreakable without complete annihilation. If you manage to actually split a crystal atom, the whole structure cascades and it explodes with all of the force contained within the broken crystal. We don't get exactly how that cascade works, but it is proven. Something like that on the scale of the main Crystal would shatter the planet. Its growth is our main problem. Night is the answer to that. Night can eat crystal. It doesn't destroy it. It converts it. The best that we can figure, it stores what it needs and shunts the rest somewhere else through quantum energy. Where and how it does that is unknown. The problem is that Night got dislodged from the Crystal when it arrived, something about oxidization shock, and the Crystal has been feeding unregulated ever since. We need you to reconnect Night and Light and restore the balance. It won't be enough to completely stop this expansion. The expansion is already under way, but if you can reconnect Night, then it should be able to keep the expansion localized to Japan and halt any further expansions," Reigi explained bleakly.

"And the two percent odds are because you realize the amount of Night that will be required to accomplish that?" Mick asked, cutting to the chase.

Ai gave him a sad look. "They are just odds. There is no way for us to really know what will happen. Night and the Crystals are not fully understood. How they do what they do and how they will interact is impossible to predict with any certainty. What we know is that Night can only be created inside of a host. No matter the amount of energy and resources available to it, without a host giving it directions, it remains stationary, continues to shield energy transfer and shunt energy at a set rate, and it won't do any more than that. We also know that in that state, it will lose cohesion with time."

"You're right for the most part, but wrong on one. Night can be created outside of a host. The problem is energy. It has to have energy to be created and as the host, I am that source of energy. I have to be the gateway. Night can even collect energy and feed it back to me if I need. That can actually be a problem when I get into starving territory. Night has automatic protection measures and maintaining our energy needs is one of them. You don't want to be around Night when it is hungry. The problem is that while Night can gather the energy, I have to be the distribution hub. Distance isn't so much of a problem. The energy transfer is perfect. I think it has something to do with quantum entanglement of energy, but I haven't cared to do the science behind that. But, what you are describing would be tough. Just the sheer amount of power that would be required would burn out every cell in my body, and I don't think I could even make a dent before I keeled over," Mick explained, locking eyes with them.

Ai cast a glance over to Reigi "Then that really is our only option," she said, sparing Mick a fleeting and sad glance.

"What?" Mick asked, furrowing his brow.

"We may be able to fix the burnout problem. The issue is that we don't know if it will work with you and it comes with its own risks. It has been tried thousands of times and as far as we can find, has only succeeded twice," Reigi answered.

Mick frowned. *I hate non-answers.* He clinched his hand in frustration. He was a little startled when he felt something go crack. When he opened his hand, the midnight blue crystal he had been holding was gone and only a transparent white powder remained. *That crystal would have gone for billions in the right circles.* A corner of his head that sounded an awful lot like Rollan pondered.

Reigi sucked in air, drawing Mick's attention as he rushed around the table with a small plate. "Dump that here!" he ordered, setting the plate down. Mick complied while Reigi rushed into a side room. A moment later, he came back with a voltage meter and another, even bigger, crystal.

Just how many of these things do they have. He watched as Reigi inserted the probes. At first it read as a zero, but after a moment it ticked up by .00001 and started climbing quickly. At the same time, color also slowly started seeping back into it "What happened?"

"This could really work!" Reigi said looking back up at Ai in surprise and wonder.

"Maybe, but the initial risk will still be huge!" she warned, but couldn't argue his point, this was one of the greatest hurdles that they had been worried about.

"This proves that Night can do what we need it to. It even reduced the mass," Reigi countered.

"Yes, but..."

Mick cut in. "Why did it crumble like that?"

"Night did it. It really can drain, inhibit, and consume the crystal. Creating crystal dust is super hard," he explained, nesting the crystal that he had brought out in the middle of the powder. Almost immediately, the powder started to regain its color, but it remained in a micron-powder state. It was like watching a blood stain spread on a white shirt except it was blue and without the sticky mess. "The dust forms naturally when the crystal is drained completely. Something about the atomic bonds between the molecules collapsing. The atoms retain their structure, but they lose their cohesion. But crystal is a perfect superconductor and capacitor. It can store any form of energy, so managing to completely drain a crystal is almost impossible. It would be like trying to empty a river with a teacup. Theoretically possible, but exceedingly difficult to achieve in reality. It usually requires dozens of dragons working in consort and even then, they can only manage it with miniscule crystals, and it can take days. You just did it over lunch and with a crystal five times bigger than any of those ever done before. And that powder is the key to our whole plan!" Reigi said excitedly.

Mick's frown deepened. "How so?" he asked, cautiously and getting a bad feeling about this.

"We want to inject you with it!" Reigi answered bluntly.

"What?!" Mick demanded, looking between them both and back down at the, now only slightly, less dark blue powder. "That would be..."

"Suicide. Usually," Ai supplied, but tried to convey that the usually was important through a squeeze of his hand. "Your situation is different from any before. At least we hope so. The problem with all those that tired before has been twofold. On one hand those that have tried to perform an implant have been drained by the crystals and died a cold death. On the other, there have been those that are too conductive and have burned out, quite literally. The one successful attempt was a case of someone who was unknowingly pregnant when they attempted it. It failed in them but somehow bound with the child and found a balance with them. How that happened, we still aren't sure, and it only worked once. Others tried after that and paid the ultimate price. But with you, we think that you can achieve that balance. Night is a superconductor and then some, also. With it acting as a regulator and the crystal acting as a gatherer and battery for the energy, we think that you should be able to harness the amount of energy required to propagate Night back to the Crystal without burning out. At least for a little while. We don't know how fast Night will reduce the crystal stored in you or if some kind of balance will be reached. But this gives us a chance!"

Mick contemplated the crystal powder and everything that he had heard so far. *This is crazy!*

"Ya, but it matches pretty well with what your ancestor described," Rollan pitched in. He was dead and nothing but a bundle of memories with the flavoring of the original Rollan and animated by Mick's own consciousness though, so it wasn't like there was much for him to lose.

"It does," Mick reluctantly agree. *"This is a really bad idea!"*

"Ya, but we are right here with you. At least if it goes bad, you won't have to listen to us anymore!" Rollan chiperly countered.

"I'm not quite sure if that was supposed to be motivational or not." Mick frowned and turned his attention back to the others - You know, the living. "So how would you do this?" he asked, cutting to the chase.

"Doesn't really matter how. Direct ingestion would probably be the least dangerous, but it is also the slowest and has a higher chance of non-integration since it would have to be absorbed into your body. Injection is the fastest method but also the most dangerous, because it risks spontaneous reaction and forced integration. It would also probably be the more painful of the two since your body would have almost no adjustment period. It would have to adapt to the new load or fail. But time is running out fast and we may not have the time for a slower and safer approach. Worst case, we shoot you up, throw you at the Crystal, and hope for the best."

"And how much powder would you need to use?" Mick asked, already knowing that his mind was made up and that he was just stalling.

Ai glanced to Reigi, who nodded his approval. "About as much as is on that plate if you included the other crystal in powdered form."

"I see," Mick said, letting out a long sigh and getting ready. Reigi apparently misunderstood it as apprehension.

"There really is no... What are you doing!?" he asked, alarmed as a flow of black powder left Mick's hands, causing him to wince as it enshrouded the plate in a writhing black fog. When it pulled back into his hands a moment later, the plate was empty of the crystals and powder. They both looked up from the scene in shock and surprise.

"What have you done?" Reigi asked, coming to his feet but not moving as he was torn between fear of approaching Mick and the need to be there to administer aid. Not that there was that much that he could do in either case. Either this would work, or they all died.

"I don't need an injection to get the job done. I hate needles anyways and this was all-around faster and more controlled. Night is even now distributing the crystal powder throughout my body," he answered. *Not as bad as I thought it would be. I thought there would be some kind of reaction, but this feels almost normal.* He started to smile reassuringly when the pain hit him like walking on a bed of legos. It was a pain that he knew. A pain that he had experienced only once before. A pain that he had thought locked away and forgotten. It was back.

***

"... balance shall be restored. Enter and be judged in Light and Night."

"Well that sounds ominous," Aldwin said, breaking the silence. "I can guess at some possibilities for Night, your family is one of them, but what do you figure Light is? I don't remember having ever seen a clear reference for Light and Night together that would fit this context."

"I don't know either. But given the context and the warning, something says that this is a Pass or Die test. That is probably why no one has ever reported back on what is here. They decided to challenge it and failed." While they had been talking, the Runes had faded away. On a hunch, he picked up a rock and threw it into the light ring. It came to a stop in mid-air, shortly after it entered the area, and promptly exploded. The fragments didn't exit the area though. They simply continued to break down into smaller and smaller pieces until there was nothing left but a fine dust that fell down to the ground. No Runes had appeared though.

"Interesting," Aldwin commented, getting up and looking over the area. He cut a lock of his hair and tossed it into the area. It reduced in much the same way as the rock, but even faster. Again, no Runes appeared. Without asking, he came back and cut a lock of Micks hair and repeated the observation again. At first it looked the same, but after a moment, it became apparent that the hair wasn't being fully disassembled. It came apart and reformed, time and time again but didn't disappear in dust. Instead, after several cycles of this, it simply fell to the ground. The Runes made a reappearance. "Well that answers that. I'm glad that I didn't touch that area first. I would have been short a finger!"

"Answers what?" Mick demanded, not liking where he had a feeling that this was going.

"That it is somehow connected to you, or your family lineage at least," Aldwin answered, even though he already knew that Mick had reached the same conclusion. "The Night refers to the Night that MacAllen, the forefather of your family, was bound to and that should mean that this test is designed to only allow someone from that family line to pass."

"Possible, but it still doesn't explain what Light is?" Mick retorted, looking for an out. He knew where this was heading. Even back then, he had known some of the trouble that it was bound to bring down on him and his family. And knowing that, and what he knew now, he still wouldn't have changed his mind. The price had been even higher than he had expected, but if there was hope for him and his, then that had been it.

"No, it doesn't. But I'm sure that we can figure it out in time. For now, it is rather obvious that we, or I should say you, need to reach that obelisk and pass this test," Aldwin said, still pondering the black void in the middle of the room.

"And why do we, and by 'we' I mean me, have to or would ever desire to do that?" Mick asked, glaring lasers at Aldwin's back while he absently continued to feel his finger and convince his body that it really was still there. His brain still wasn't quite convinced about that and was having a royal hissy fit. "You saw what it did to my finger and hair. It didn't just take it apart, it put it all back together at the same time. If I go in there, and by some chance I actually survive, there is no guarantee that who comes back out will still be me. Anything could be getting changed or inserted while that kind of deconstruction and reconstruction is occurring. We have no idea what power we are dealing with!"

"And is that going to stop you from walking in there and reaching that obelisk?" Aldwin asked, calling his bluff while he gave him a questioning eyebrow and a crooked grin.

"No. But I thought that I should at least lay out the counter argument in hopes that you wanted to convince me not to," Mick said, getting back up onto his feet and standing at the edge of the light next to Aldwin. "And wipe that grin off of your face!"

Aldwin shook his head. "Is it the mystery, the connection to your family, the fact that we only have this one chance, or is it because you know that whatever happens, it is bound to torque the Order?"

"I am hurt that you think me such a petty man, as to be controlled by whims of spite," Mick said, feigning a scoff. "But yes, I am doing this because it is precisely the kind of thing that they would never sanction. All information on Night and that part of the Order's history is sealed and there is much that my family still doesn't know. This is my/our inheritance and I'm not going to let the Order squirrel off yet another piece of it."

"Dangerous talk. I like it," Aldwin agreed. "I am curious as to just what you may be inheriting though. You know that it could put not just you, but your whole family in the Order's crosshairs?"

"Yes, but they ordered me to supervise and learn under the Druids and to make sure that we have a presence in any breakthrough discoveries or research. There is also a sealed order that I am not to allow you to make any more advancements that intrude upon the Order's power base and to seize any such findings or breakthroughs for the Order. I think this counts." Mick smiled at his feat of logical maneuvering that allowed him to justify under the Order's own orders doing something that the Order would never justify.

"Are you sure you're not a lawyer?" Aldwin asked, chuckling. "In any case, I think this counts under enough of that manipulation to get us by and you seem to be the only option for furthering the investigation. Now for the hard part. Just step through here, have something unexplained and which is apparently extremely painful happen to you, reach that weird obelisk and get us the next clue!"

"Right," Mick agreed, taking a steadying breath. "Remind me why we are friends again?" he asked at the same time as Aldwin gave him a gentle shove that propelled him into the light. You really don't know pain until you feel every cell, every atom, of your being pulling apart and coming back together. It was even worse than hitting your little toe on the corner of a metal bed frame. What was worse, was that he was awake for it all. The amount of pain should have caused him to pass out or at least overloaded his feeling of pain, but it didn't. All he could do was step back out of the light and leave a failure or continue forwards into the unknown.

***

Mick's head cleared, but the pain remained and it was just as bad as the last time he had experienced it. He made to move his arm and was gifted with even more pain. On the other hand, he did manage to lift his arm. Or at least he thought it was his arm. What with the way that his atoms were separating and reforming, it was a little hard to clearly make out what was happening.

Reigi and Ai were kneeling next to him and he was looking up at them so he must have fallen out of his chair at some point. Straining against the pain, he managed to lift his head. Ai and Reigi were saying something but he couldn't hear them through the roar of the pain. He scrunched his forehead as his legs came into view. There was a chair leg sticking out of his leg, but no signs of blood or how he could have wound up with it stuck in his leg. Not really thinking, he rolled to the side, expecting even more pain and for the chair to move with him. It didn't move, but his leg did. Unsure of what he had just seen, he moved his leg back over and watched as it passed straight through the chair leg again. The marvel of it was enough to let him temporarily forget the pain that was wracking him. Ai and Reigi were also watching his little experiment and, despite their concern, also seemed intrigued. On the other hand, he was grinning like a fool as he made to do it again. His shin smacked the chair leg with a crack and a perfectly normal physical pain response that he knew from long experience that brought everything back into sudden focus. "How?" he asked before promptly passing out.

The End is Nigh
Friday, July 9

"Oww," Mick complained as he opened his eyes into a blindingly bright light. It took a couple of dozen blinks before his eyes finally obeyed and focused on something less blinding. It was only then that he noticed that what he had thought was a light was actually the sun and that he was laying back in the bed that he had been in when he had first woken up. The only differences were small, painful, and a little embarrassing. He managed to move his arm behind his back and dragged out whatever it was that had been digging into his back. It was another of the Crystals. A second look and feel showed that there were dozens of the things around him and several of them were poking him in rather inconvenient areas. It was a veritable wizard's dream worth of Crystals. If he had tried to sell them on the gray market, he could have easily pulled in Billions. The embarrassing difference was that he was naked. He made to move and immediately fell back down with a thud as pain wracked his body once again and he landed awkwardly on several of the Crystals. He must have moaned or yelled something because when the pain subsided Ai was by his side and doing her best to reassure him that he was probably going to be okay. *Well, at least she isn't lying to me.* "Thanks," he managed as the pain subsided to a more bearable level.

Ai glared at him for a few moments. There was concern, annoyance, and something else in her eyes that Mick couldn't quite place.

Fool. Yes, it wouldn't really have made much of a difference, but who in their right mind would take such a risk without a second thought? "You're lucky to be alive!" she admonished, finding no better words to convey all of her feelings. The silence between them dragged on for an eternity in a second. Knowing that he would

129

probably be okay, at least for now, would have to be enough. Meeting his concerned eyes was enough to make her cheeks blush a little and her heart pitter-patter like a middle schooler with a crush.

She was really worried about me! She's really cute when she is blushing and a little flustered. Get it under control. Trying to take a cleansing breath without being wracked by coughs, Mick paused, but his heart ignored him as he considered the flow of his thoughts and those that had come before. *I guess I can't die now.* "What happened?" he asked, lifting up his hand and slowly reaching towards hers. He realized that something was wrong when it hit the rays of sunlight shining through the window and the shadow wavered beneath it. Going back and forth between solid and translucent. In search of the cause, his attention shifted to his arm. As he watched, it wavered between being solid and diffused. As he concentrated on it, it snapped back to being solid and the pain that he had been feeling vanished. "What is going on?" he asked, looking back to Ai. The pain was the same as before at both dinner and at the obelisk, but the form was different. Where before the deconstruction had appeared random, this was focused.

Ai shook her head and frowned at both questions. "That is a little hard to explain," she said, pausing for a moment, before taking a deep breath and wiping at her eyes. "You almost died! You should have died," she said quietly, almost afraid that saying it would make it come true. "When you took in the crystal powder, a battle started in your body between Night and Light. Your body was trying to fly apart as your molecules were excited by the sudden explosion of energy as Light, the Crystal, bonded with you. At the same time, Night was fighting to eat and shunt that same energy. Also, to our surprise, it was working to organize it. Devouring it where and when there was too much and integrating - even feeding it - and promoting growth where it could be used. The result, as best as we can figure out, is a kind of controlled atomic instability as your atoms flip between flying apart and being held together. Do you remember the chair?"

The Chair??? How does she know about that? Oh wait, that chair. "Yes. That really happened?"

"Yes. As you can probably believe, we were shocked by what you did. We were also exceedingly wary. At the same time, we were intrigued. You were the first person that we had met with any realistic chance of surviving. What we have been able to gather is that your atomic structure is able to achieve a kind of resonance that allows your atoms to slide past those of other solid things. Or more precisely, things with atoms moving at speeds under a certain threshold. The slower the atomic energy, the easier it is for you to pass through it. Water, air, gases, and the lighter, more energetic atoms stop you, but pretty much anything solid, you can pass through. Given that you have been asleep, we're not sure if it is a conscious or controllable reaction. We don't even know if it will fade. But, given that you have been asleep for almost a week and that it has come and gone and oftentimes coincided with your dreams, we think that it is both controllable and won't disappear." She started to continue but stopped after looking at Mick.

"I was asleep for a whole week?" Mick asked, barely believing it. *A few days, I could understand, but a week?! Just what happened to my body?*

"Not quite. It has been five days. It is now Friday. We are exceptionally lucky that you woke up now. Tonight is the projected deadline to start the procedure for limiting the crystal's growth. If you hadn't woken up, we weren't sure what we were going to do."

"Right," Mick said, putting his weight down on his arms. One sunk a little way through the bed before he pulled it back out. It stayed on top when he tried again. "Useful, but I can see how this could get annoying," he said through gritted teeth as his body screamed out in pain as he sat up. "Can I get some clothes?" he asked, managing a shyly provocative look while on the inside he was screaming from the searing pain of the barely contained energy inside of him fighting to escape. Apparently, his idea of 'within tolerances' and Night's were not quite the same.

Ai blushed and nodded as she left to gather his clothes and Mick did his best to stay modest, while he waited. It quickly became apparent why they had surrounded him with the crystals. They kept him from phasing through the bed and blankets. Ai came back in a moment later. He'd been entertaining himself by experimenting with reaching through the blanket. He felt like a kid caught with his hand in the cookie jar when Ai returned and directed an accusing eyebrow at him. His hand was out of the blankets and innocently folded in his lap only a split second later.

Ai shook her head like a mother finding her kid in the chocolate and set his clothes on the bed beside him. "I know that on some level, this must all be amazing and cool, but please be careful. I'm not being melodramatic when I say that the fate of the world is depending on you," she warned. "On another note, be careful with your clothes. You have a way of falling through them or them off of you that can be rather awkward. On a plus side, it doesn't look like you are going to have to go to the restroom anymore. Apparently now you have zero waste energy pass through your body. After the first day and nothing, we checked. It gets almost all the way to the end and then it gets converted into energy and stored away. We are a little curious if you will be able to reverse the process and use the stored energy to create matter, but that is an issue for another time."

Mick was still sitting on the bed looking up at her with nothing but the covers on. "Um, that is all well and cool and I get that you apparently have seen it all and then some already, and I know that I asked you out before, but..."

"Oh. Ohh. Sorry," Ai said. She promptly walked out the door and closed it behind her. She didn't go any further than that though.

"So just to double check. You can't really explain it all, but it looks like this was a success?" Mick shouted at the door as he finished slipping on his briefs. *I'm glad they didn't give me a Fundoshi. Talk about wedgies.*

"Looks that way. Are the clothes okay? For what you are going to need to do, we figured comfortable was probably best."

Mick surveyed the Jimbe that they had provided for him. "Looks pretty good. I've never worn one of these before, but they always looked really comfortable when I saw them. You mentioned before something about 'integration.' What did you mean by that? I get the bathroom part, but was that the extent of it?"

Ai gnawed on her lower lip a little before she answered. "No. We were going to talk to you afterwards..."

"If I survived?"

"Yes. But I was saying that we really don't fully understand all of this. Night was always just something that we were looking for or only had heard rumors about. The closest we ever got was a lady called Ai'yanna and her husband, but something happened and she was forced to leave before we were able to reach her and we weren't able to learn much. What we are seeing is both good and not what we expected. In your body, Night worked to contain and control Light. It has bonded Night and Light into sets in a lot of cases but also left a lot of separate parts flowing through your blood. It also laced your skeleton with a Night and Light lattice work, making it incredibly strong and providing a ready source of energy for your muscles and tendons. And so on. On an atomic level, you are integrated with Night and Light completely. It is far beyond anything that we ever suspected."

"That is... Well that is a lot to take in. I'm not sure how it changes things, but besides a few peculiarities, like keeping my clothes on, and whatnot, it doesn't change the current situation much," Mick said as he pulled the door open to talk to Ai. Only problem was that she had been leaning against the door and when it opened without notice, she lost her balance. He sidestepped to catch her and wound up with her cradled in his arm and pressed into his chest as he took a knee to break the fall. "Are you okay?" he asked, not letting go of her. His whole body tingled with the warmth of her body pressed up against his and his pain vanished like a cool salve had been put on it.

"Fine," Ai said in a small voice as she looked up at him. She didn't try to move out of his arms. She could feel it in her heart and soul. This was where she belonged. "Um... We should probably get going," she managed to say in a slightly airy voice. *Kiss me already!* Some corner of her mind screamed out.

Mick hesitated for a moment. *This is a path from which there is no going back once I start down it. Would it really be fair to drag her onto that path when I don't even know if I have a tomorrow?* His muscles tensed and then relaxed as he carefully stood, helping her back to her feet. He held her close to his chest for just a moment longer than was really necessary before letting her pull back out to arm's length. She held his hand for a second longer before letting it go and casting her eyes away from his. There was a little bit of embarrassment in her reactions, but he couldn't sense any regret. *If I'm still here once this is done...* "Right." Mick said, not sure what else he could really say under the circumstances.

"Right..." Ai agreed, staring up into his eyes for a moment longer. "Right," she repeated, shaking her head to clear the ideas dancing through it. "I came here to check on you, and the others are probably beginning to wonder where I have gotten off to," she said, turning reluctantly to lead the way.

Mick followed a step behind her. He didn't want to crowd her too much, but at the same time, he was loath to allow any more space between them. *Falling in love when I'm probably going to die tomorrow. Sounds like a country song.*

"Loosen up, lover boy. They said it themselves. They don't fully understand all of this. You survived and are stronger than ever before. No reason for you to already be giving up on the future," MacAllen chirped in.

Mick pondered that for a moment. The light at the end of the tunnel seemed to get a little brighter and now maybe there was something to look forward to once he reached the end. *"Maybe you are right,"* he thought, giving a little nod.

"I should warn you; our people and town have been the guardians of this place for a long time. There are those that still think it sacrilege to interfere with what is about to happen. More dangerous are those that think that we should use the power to our own ends when this is over. To establish a new Empire to rival that of the Yamamoto. Of the two, those will be far more dangerous in the long run. Both groups are in the minority, but their voices still carry weight and they have very loud voices. Be careful," she warned, leading him out of the house for the first time.

The sun hung at about 11 o'clock. It took a moment for his eyes to adjust but when they did, his breath caught in wonder. They were in a broad valley. Around ten kilometers long and perhaps four kilometers wide at its widest. There was also a spur valley in the latter half that looked to extend a little way but was out of sight except for the river that flowed out of it and through the valley. That was all peripheral though. The result of training to take in all of his surroundings. What dominated his attention was the same thing that dominated the whole valley. Surrounded by a small traditional town, fields, and rice paddies, sat a castle. A fully walled citadel castle with both an inner and outer keep, double stepped walls, a moat, and all the other buildings associated with a full-blown Japanese castle. It was all painted Jet Black with silver accents, and it looked to be even bigger than Himeji Castle. What really drew his attention was what sat inside of its walls. A great big tree that reached for the heavens and arched out to cover the whole citadel. A tree made completely out of green and blue crystal. It was impossible and it was staring him right in his face. As he watched, something that he had thought to be a bird angled away from the tree. Given the scale involved, it was something big. And it was heading right for them.

Mick's whole body tensed as the blur neared and gained definition. *I'm glad that she gave me my axes with my clothes.* He tried to look calm as it drew closer and finally circled above them. It was the biggest dragon that he had ever seen. Nearly a hundred meters long and easily fifteen meters across. It lacked the wings of the European dragons that he was more familiar with, but there was no mistaking an Asian dragon. After circling them several times, it began to descend and shrink at the same time. By the time it landed, it had transformed into what looked to be a sixty-year-old, well built, grandpa in an Aloha shirt. Complete with board shorts and flip-flops.

"Ah! The newcomer has decided to rejoin us. And just in time. The big shake up is almost here and the leaders are rattling their sabers something fierce about what to do. He certainly looks to be a big enough wrench to throw at the problem," he exclaimed, appraising Mick who he was just over half the height of in his human form.

Ai looked troubled by the news. "They aren't seriously thinking about trying to interfere? Are they?" There was an edge of pleading in her voice and little quivers in her hands spoke to the distress the idea caused her.

"Depends on whether or not they really believe that they could pull off a coup and if they could get a knife inserted into that one's heart. Preferably while he's still asleep and from behind if they can manage it. Seeing as how you are awake again, they will probably opt for trying to stab you in the back, between the fifth and sixth ribs. Drive it right through the lung and into the heart," he answered chipperly. "You had best hurry though. The winds are shifting, and the foundations of reason are starting to show some awfully big cracks. I have never understood the inclination to throw sound reason out the window when people become afraid. You'd think that they would embrace the one thing that might save them and yet they rarely do. Always figuring that they know better or that they can force reality to match their views simply by ignoring it and shouting loud enough."

"Great!" Ai grumbled. "How long before it is too late to contain this?"

"For the idiots? Sorry, people have tried for a long time and none have succeeded. And eradication only works for short periods of time. They breed like rabbits and somehow manage to get into positions of power and the teaching field so as to be better situated for corrupting others into their ways of stupidity," he said, smiling.

"Not what I meant!" Ai chided, showing a hint of exasperation. After all, it was only the fate of most of the world that they were talking about.

"Oh, you mean contain the world-order-changing Crystal that is about to unleash havoc upon the world like it has only once before experienced? Well for that, we will need to start within the next few hours. Sooner is better though. The longer we wait, the bigger the affected area will be. My models are good but even I can't guess beyond that. A lot of it will depend on him."

Ai chewed on her lower lip a little. She stopped with a resigned sigh. "Then can you take us to the tree? I'll deal with the fallout from the petties, but there has already been enough talk and waiting on more talk. Debate gains us nothing but more destruction and loss of life," she concluded, wishing that they could have avoided this and the bloodshed it would most likely precipitate.

Given how the old man smirked, he had expected that to be her reaction and wholeheartedly agreed and approved.

"Very well then. If that is your choice Princess, I suggest that you allow me to fly you in so as to avoid unnecessary hang-ups with the guards and the council!"

"Much appreciated."

Mick watched as the old man morphed back into a dragon, taking up much of the road. Ai gave a quick bow before, using his leg as a booster, hopping up onto his back. She took a seat behind his forelegs and looked at Mick. "Problem?" she asked leaning over and extending her hand.

"Don't worry. I'm the smoothest ride in the sky and the weather is calm," Mr. Aloha shirt dragon said.

"Sorry. Just sort of surprised me. The European dragons won't let anyone ride on them. They tend to fry those that try," Mick said, looking up at the dragon's head. "And I feel like I should at least know your name?"

"European dragons. Pfft. Egotistical lizards with wings. You ask me, they got what they had coming to them. You have to pay for what you want. Just because you can breathe fire doesn't mean that everything that you want is automatically yours for the taking and that everyone should give it up willingly. You steal enough maidens and sheep and sooner or later, someone is going to figure out how to fight back," he said, shaking his head and rolling his eyes. "For your information, my name is Sen. I'm the electrician for this little town and the overseer for the tree. And don't tell anyone around here, but I also moonlight as a retired man in Hawaii on occasion. But it's a secret, so don't tell the others. Most of them wouldn't know fun if they walked into a wall made of it. It really is too bad that the beaches in Hawaii are about to get really messed up. The whole islands for that matter. A real shame."

Mick blinked a few times while his brain whirled. *Odd, but I get the feeling that he's telling the truth. Although, it is a little worrying about the locals being so wound up that they have forgotten how to have fun.* "Thanks for the tip and will do," he replied, not completely sure which part he was responding to.

"No worries. Now, this next part is a little hard. So, sit still and let us be off," Sen warned. With that, he pushed off gently and they seemed to float up away from the ground.

Once they were about thirty meters up, they started moving forwards in a banking arc that brought them back around to head towards the tree and Mick's mind wandered back to Sen's earlier comment.

"What did Sen mean when he called you Princess?" Mick asked, suddenly wondering if he was in even bigger trouble than he suspected for falling for Ai.

Sen chuckled while Ai sighed. She had hoped that Mick hadn't caught that. "I didn't want to make a big deal out of it."

Mick blinked a few times, until he got it. "So, you really are a princess," he stated, nodding as he fit this new piece of information into his image of her. "I've never met a princess who worked at a Udon shop before," he teased.

Ai glanced over at him. "It's not a problem for you?" she asked, surprised by his reaction.

"Why should it be? I'm sure that us dating will bend plenty of people out of shape but that is because they are too stuck up on the title and forgetting that there is a person behind it," Mick answered, flashing her a smile. "We can talk about it more later. For now, we need to make sure that there is a later."

Ai nodded and knocked aside a tear that had snuck out.

"You tell them!" Sen agreed and chuckled as they flew on.

As they drew closer, a strange sensation settled over Mick. It was almost like nostalgia but with a physical aspect. Like he was being pulled to instead of flying towards the tree. It was only as they flew over the walls that the true scale became apparent. The distance had been an optical illusion created by the scale. The tree and castle were easily twice as big as he had thought, which meant that the valley itself was far larger than he had first assumed, which raised several questions.

"How do you keep all of this a secret? A valley this size would have been noticed and there is no way that you could have kept a castle like that from being talked about. Let alone the gigantic crystal tree that is growing out of it," Mick said, taking in the wonder of it all. "Google Earth has caused problems for a lot of hidden villages that were in even more remote locations than this."

Sen let loose a rumble of laughter that could have been mistaken for thunder or stampeding elephants. It was hard to tell. Ai smiled at him. "You can't find what isn't there," she answered.

Mick scrunched up his brow in thought. "You have some kind of sealing on the area that prevents unwanted guests and pressing eyes?"

"Oh no. That wouldn't have worked," Sen rumbled back. "We didn't just conceal the area, we removed it. By building on the crystals ability to pull in all energy, they managed to amplify the effect and fold the spaces outside the valley together for roughly a four-hundred square kilometers area. From the inside, the outside looks normal, but from the outside, all you can see is the other side and you literally step over it. It took a little creative re-engineering of the terrain to make things match up plausibly on each side and there are a few wrinkles here and there were things manage to slip through every now and then, but that hasn't happened in the last hundred years or so and it has kept this place safe from man and not-man alike. It is also why the woods around the town you were in are so dangerous. Creatures seeking a way in have long gathered in them and take any entry into the woods as someone trying to get ahead of them. They can't get in either, so they take their frustration out on those that they can reach."

"I see." Mick looked around with a new appreciation for just how big of a feat that they had managed. He knew full well the amount of energy that was required to fold space around a single person and just how many had perished because they hadn't properly calculated just how much energy was required and the space had only partially formed - separating them from other parts of themselves, or because the space had collapsed instead of unfolding when they ran out of power before they were ready. Both cases were messy and served as good examples as to why one shouldn't fiddle with space unless they were really desperate and/or fully understood exactly what they were doing.

And that is one of the reasons that people covet crystals. They are one of the few things in existence that can contain the amounts of power required in a small enough space to make things like space folding possible. Mick cast his eyes at the tree with a newfound trepidation as he fully realized just how great of a disaster could soon be upon them. Whatever else he was thinking about cut off abruptly as Sen banked over hard as they approached the crystal and the Citadel's enshrouding walls. He pulled out at the last moment for an abrupt landing a few hundred meters away from the base of the tree. The sheer scale of the tree and citadel took on new proportions as he took in the actual distances involved.

"Sorry, but this is as close as I get. Usually we dragons are pretty fond of Crystals, but the pull of this beast is too great for us. It is too great for anyone. No one has ever managed to get any closer than fifty meters before suffering energy death. In fact, this whole courtyard is strictly off limits because to stay here for too long is also hazardous to one's health and smaller critters and weaker sorts have suffered from hypothermia and entropic death as the energy to provide movement to their atoms has bled off," Sen explained as Mick marveled at the tree. He shifted back to his human shape and gave a shrug.

Mick glanced to Ai for a conformation. "For me too. I passed out at seventy-five meters and didn't wake up for a week. Now that I am a little older, I may be able to get a little closer, but even if I do, there isn't anything that I can do to help. The most we can do is try to keep anyone from interfering."

"Not actually what I was worrying about," Mick said. "But thanks for letting me know. What I was about to ask is if neither of you can reach it, what makes you think that I can?"

Sen and Ai glanced at each other. "You know... that's a good question," Sen said, stroking his goatee. He gave it up with a shrug after a pass or two. "Oh well. Too late to worry about little things like that at this point. Just going to have to assume that if there is anyone that can make it, it's you. It's only the fate of the world resting upon your ability to make it and do what can't be done. No pressure."

Mick blinked his disbelief. Ai at least had the decency to look appropriately concerned and to mouth "Sorry" to him. "Oh, I just love my job!" Mick grumbled and started in.

"The no-man's-land starts ten paces past the edge of the frozen area. Take care not to slip on the ice. The Ice-Blade-Grass is as strong as steel and as sharp as obsidian," Sen yelled after him. "And make it snappy. We don't have much time left!"

Mick waved but didn't look back as he advanced on the tree. After a moment, he paused as he could swear that he heard the distinct fwap of a slap upside the back of a head. He smiled and pressed on.

The air grew more frigid with every step. He reached the edge of the ice after what felt like a minute but according to the sun must have been more than an hour. It was now touching the ridge line ahead of him and it had been a whole hand and change above it when he'd started. It was clear that either his movements and reactions were slowing or that there was some form of dilation at play here. He started to take another step forward only to almost fall over as his leg failed to follow his command. He quickly regained his balance and looked down to see what was wrong. An arrow shaft was staked through the back of his leg, through his shin, and pegging his foot to the ground. A moment later another one whistled past his cheek, close enough that the blade opened a long and deep gash in his right cheek.

Given that they hadn't mentioned arrows spontaneously raining from the sky or sprouting from the ground, and something like that wasn't something that one would usually forget to mention, he assumed that it had come from behind him and looked back to see what was happening. He grunted as pain blossomed from his wounds as he torqued against the shaft.

Sen and Ai had made a good accounting for themselves. There were at least a dozen people laying still and those that were still standing all showed signs of at least minor if not major injuries. Although, there was no signs of Sen or Ai and even stained in blood, there would have been no missing Sen's Aloha shirt. Mick took it as a good sign that he couldn't spot them. From his angle, he was just barely able to glance a few men straining against the courtyard gate, trying to hold back what looked like a concerted effort to batter it back open. Unfortunately for him, there were a few leftovers that appeared to be uninjured or occupied and were currently engaged in attempting to poke holes in him.

"Well this sucks!" Mick grumbled as another arrow tracked in for a chest landing. He pulled one his axes free and fended it off just before it could make impact. The archers seemed to take offence to this unsportsmanlike interference and the lead archer made an animated display to his cohorts before they resumed firing at him. Unfortunately, they had apparently had enough of his defiance and were now attempting to overwhelm him with volley fire. He frowned at this new development.

"Now that's just being mean!" Bringing his axe around, he cut the shaft pinning his leg in half where it protruded between his shin and foot. Wasting no time, he reached behind his right leg, gripped the end of the shaft and gave it a quick yank to get it out. With that out of the way, he took a steadying breath before yanking his leg backwards and up to clear the lower half. He was glad that the one that had stuck him in the leg was a bodkin point instead of a leaf blade or broadhead. Unfortunately, the one that had sliced his cheek open had been a blade type, so he couldn't take that for granted.

The next volley was now upon him. He smacked the first to the side and caught the second with his other axe as it sprang to his hand. He used the momentum of that swing to pull himself around and get almost clear of the third shaft. It sliced an impressive valley along the outside of his right arm, from wrist to elbow. The lack of a finishing blow seemed to frustrate the archers even further as they all stared at him dumbfounded before angrily snatching up more shafts. He didn't wait to find out what they had in mind for round three. He turned and started jogging for the Tree with a slightly off kilter gate thanks to the hole in his leg. He also added some zigs and zags in as he went to make the archers earn their pay.

He did his best not to swear as each foot fall raised a new stab of pain and pivoting as he turned threatened to bring him to a stop as his slightly shattered shin protested. Night was doing its part to bolster him and repair the damage, but it seemed a touch distracted.

The next volley came in high and sprouted into the ground slightly to his side and about five meters in front of him. "Going to have to do better than..." The arrows were fizzling. "Oh, crap!!!" he yelled as he dove for the ground. The arrows erupted in gouts of fury sending metal shards, dirt, and clods of blade like ice grass, tumbling up into the sky and flinging him to the side. He hit the ground with a roll that only stopped as the searing cold blades of frozen grass slashed into his back and dragged him to a stop.

A still processing corner of his brain registered the Archers cheering at this. *Rather happy bunch. I'll have to be sure to make their acquaintance and help them adjust their senses of humor after this.* The archers cheering cut off short as the gate crashed open, sending the men who had been bearing it flying as a rush of others came driving through the gate with Ai, Sen, and Reigi in the lead. He tried to make out the quick battle that followed but his eyes weren't quite up to it in the low light and he didn't really have the strength or the presence of mind to be adjusting his vision at the moment. Darkness? There was something important about that. All he really wanted to do was close his eyes and take a little nap. It wasn't like the world couldn't wait.

Mick's eyes snapped back open as Night triggered an adrenalin release and flooded his system. "The world can't wait! So stop lazing around here. You don't even like the cold!" he chided himself as he staggered back up onto his feet. Blood and iron flowed freely from his various wounds. His back was practically a waterfall with all of the lacerations and punctures that it had suffered from the grass. What with the slash from the arrow and taking the brunt of the blasts from the arrow bombs, his right side wasn't much better. There was one good piece of news. Between his mad dive and the blasts, he had been propelled well into the frozen zone. The good news was that he had made it past the fifty-meter mark and was still alive. The bad news was it looked like he still had another forty meters to go and time was funny here.

He started to take a deep breath and thought better of it. *Shallow is good.* His body felt sluggish, and it was, but it was still answering to the helm and he still had a job to complete. *No time for dying now. Death will have to take a raincheck. If he wants to collect now, he will only be putting himself out of business.*

His stumbling steps were short and slow as the night continued to grow darker. His right arm hung useless at his side as his right leg drug along behind him. As he drew closer to the tree, he could feel the earth trembling beneath him with barely contained energy looking to be released. Then again, it might have been him trembling. It was hard to be sure given the ragged state of his body and mind. He still needed to do what he had come here to do. His legs abruptly stopped and would lift no further. The ground shook with another tremor and his knees buckled, bringing him crashing down to the ground. Time was up.

"You don't get to stop," he ordered, glaring down at his crumpled legs. They seemed less than convinced of his authority over them. It was cold. So cold. A cold that crawled right into his core. And there, in his core, just before it took all of his warmth and life, it met a hunger that burned hotter than the sun and refused to be quenched. The hunger spread. Sending heat like lighting through his body. All other concerns were lost. Only the need to quench that hunger remained. And the hunger's desire was close at hand.

Mick's head snapped up. The tree loomed before him, pulsing with energy as it shook the planet and spread its roots. It was within reach, if only he could command his arm to raise one last time. It fought against him at first but then the hunger sensed his desire and seized it too. Forcing it forwards; paying no heed to his snapping tendons, tearing ligaments and muscles, bursting blood vessels, shattering bones, and his rupturing skin as the hunger sought to fulfill its need. His arm fell upon the crystal and the hunger and pain abruptly cut off. It was soon replaced by light. Searing and bright. It flashed through him, finding itself already there and then meeting with a part of it long lost and forgotten. A part which made it whole. Night flowed out of Mick.

"Would you believe that? Looks like we all finally get to rest," MacAllen said.

Mick felt his own existence flicker as Mac's remaining being flowed out of him and drifted away. Mac's memories remained, but he was gone. He turned to look to Ai'yana who was now standing before him.

"It's been short but fun. Thank you for ending this for all of us. It's not just me and Mac. All of the carriers of Night can finally rest. They are coming here now. They will leave their legacies in your hands. From the first to the last, the legacy shall live on in you. Goodbye, Mick," Ai'yana said, and then she too was gone.

He was just coming to grips with their presence being gone when the others and their memories beyond eons slammed into and through him. Each one unique and in perfect detail. He felt his own existence and being caught adrift in the flood of beings and memories, threatening to become dislodged and swept away with them. It would be so easy to just let go and go with them. To be free of his pain, guilt, and responsibility.

"Love, boy. You still have love," Mac whispered, pulling a memory of Ai out of the flood and staking it before him. *"She's waiting for you."*

Mick tensed, pulling himself back to the edges of the flood. He couldn't escape it, but the thought of Ai was enough to anchor him and keep him afloat. Slowly, the flood began to slow and then recede until not even a trickle remained. He felt washed out and exhausted. His head pounded with memories beyond years or count. But he was alive and still himself and that was all that really mattered.

As the fog cleared, he could sense himself and his surroundings again. Night wasn't gone from him, but it had changed. Into what, he couldn't fully comprehend. The crystal too remained there in front of him. It too had changed; reduced from its towering heights and size into that of a large tree. It was perhaps forty meters tall with a wide spreading canopy. The ground beneath and around it was littered with smaller crystals of every size and shape. The citadel was also still standing, illuminated in the light of the morning sun, but it was now slightly taller than the crystal tree which had once towered over it. So too stood the town and the valley beyond. And beyond that... A new world thrust upon the old reared its head. It was too much. He crumpled and fell as his eyes closed. Peace returned, but it was seasoned with trepidation about what the new dawn would bring. *Tomorrow is another day.*

Ravens! Worse than Chihuahuas
Sunday, July 11

Silence. Mick couldn't remember the last time he had heard it. Complete and utter silence. It was deep and warm and soft and firm at the same time. It was something he had lost without even realizing it. In its place had been a roar that drowned out everything else. Now... silence. He didn't want to stir and disturb that silence. Afraid that if it broke he would never be able to find it again and this time he would remember what he had lost. Click... The silence remained. Tap... The silence took note. Click, clop... The silence breathed.

"So, this is where you have been hiding." Another said in his own voice and yet not his own. The silence didn't care. *"Not the most interesting place. All black and quiet and empty. Not even a fireplace for warmth or a chair for your butt. Sure, cleaning is a breeze and there ain't no one t' bug you... but is this really what you want? There are others waiting for you."* Pictures lit up the silence. *"It ain't like this is going nowhere. You can always come back. And we both know there is too much left undone that still needs doing. There are still debts to be paid,"* he/it/they said. The silence sighed, the breeze kissed it with a gentle rustle and the silence drifted away like a morning fog on the bay.

Mick sighed and watched as color, light, sound, and knowing flooded back in on him. "You know, you are a real jerk," he said to himself. *"Yeah, but there's hardly any changing that at this point."*

Pop... Crackle... Hiss... Mick's eyes fluttered, refusing to stay open long enough for him to see anything. They felt heavy and tired beyond all reason. He had never been one to wake up slowly or feeling tired, even if he had only had a moments sleep, but apparently that didn't apply today. That his body still didn't seem to be listening should have made him uncomfortable and feel helpless, he'd definitely been in enough situations where that would have spelled his doom, but today he didn't care and felt relaxed instead. He was curious about his current predicament though and that meant that he needed to regain at least a modicum of control. He slipped from his relaxed state into a focused one and got to work. *Best to start small in these situations.*

Instead of fighting to open his eyes, he forced them shut as tight as he could. When the muscles started feeling tired, he tried opening his eyes again. This time they obeyed long enough for his to see that he was back in the room in which he had first awoken. Pop... Sigh... Pop...Mmm...

Mick's eyes opened wider this time and didn't fight to close. *Fires don't say Mmm!* It took a little effort, but he managed to get his head to roll to the side and lean forwards enough to look down the bed. They stopped in their scan as they took note of the silver furred wolf laying alongside him. The Order and wolves had an even longer and bloodier history than they did with dragons, and their history with dragons had bled rivers. Memories of lifetimes of strife with wolves flooded his vision and thoughts causing him to stiffen without meaning it to. The wolf stirred, blinking as it reared its head and yawned wide, showing its pearly white and impressively long and sharp teeth. It blinked a few more times, staring at him as he stared back. Suddenly, it jerked back in surprise and tumbled off of the foot of the bed and out of sight. Mick, still limited to moving his eyes and head, watched all of this play out. He wasn't sure if he should feel worried or amused by what had just happened. He settled for smirking. *Hey, I could move my mouth. Fezzik would be proud.*

"Oww," a lady whimpered. Not just a lady. He knew that voice.

"A...." he tried, his throat cracking and letting loose but a whisper. He tried swallowing but there was but a drip to swallow. "A... Umph," he coughed. "Ai?" he croaked out after several-more scratchy rasps. The sound from the foot of the bed promptly stopped. A hand peaked over the foot board. Then another. Finally, the top of Ai's head peeked up over it. She looked sorry, right up until her eyes met his and then tears welled up in them. A heart beat passed and then she was embracing him in a tight hug. It took him a moment, but his arms decided to start working and he promptly wrapped them around her, holding her close. He felt tears running down his cheeks and thought they were hers until he felt hers soaking into his shoulder. His hand came up and tried to brush them away, but the flood gates were broken now and there was no holding it back. He hadn't cried in over a decade and in that time he had built up a huge debt in tears that had apparently come due. He didn't know how long they stayed there, holding each other and crying, but it was a long time.

At some point, Ai regained most of her composure and opened just enough space between them so that she could see his face. A trickle of tears continued falling down her cheeks and off of her chin to land on him. They were cold but oh so warm at the same time. As she looked into his tear-filled eyes, she realized that his tears were for more than just her. She continued to hold him and sat by him through them all, wiping them away as they fell while he did the same for her. They both had a lot of tears due.

***

Ai reached down gently and brushed the last tear aside and rested her hand on his cheek. Her hand was soft and strong; filled with love, strength, and understanding. Mick reached up with his; letting one rest over hers while the other cupped around her cheek. "I'm glad that you are back," she said simply.

Mick stared up into her understanding eyes. There was love there, but also pain, loss, and concern for him and for other things. *I really am back.* He thought, probing at himself. He felt whole... complete and there was an inner peace there that he had always felt was missing but had never been able to fully understand or fulfill before. Duty, training, battle, war, and conflict had covered it, but never been able to fill it. It was now filled and he wondered how he had ever lived without it.

He was his own for the first time that he could remember. There wasn't anything taking its pound of flesh and no bonds holding him back or tying him down anymore. And yet, he also wasn't his own anymore, and it felt right. Night was there, Light was there, the memories of every bearer of Night were there also but were now simply a part of him; background information that he could access but that didn't define or influence him beyond the knowledge that it gave him access to. It was all just there for him to use like a precious tool, but it was only a tool now. Night was still Night but even it felt sated and no longer as agitated. Then there was that part of him that now felt whole that he also knew no longer belonged to him but to another and yet it fit perfectly. He blinked as that understanding dawned on him and looked back up into Ai's eyes and reached over to hold her other hand.

"Marry me!?" he said without even thinking or hesitating. "I know that we don't really know a lot about each other yet but I'm sure of this. We should probably take some time to learn about each other before we go through with it but... Please, allow me the honor of taking your hand."

Ai blinked a few times as those two simple words struck her like a pillow; firm yet fluffy, warm, and comfortable. Tears welled up in her eyes again as she felt her heart slip free of her chest and fall down to rest next to Mick's. "If you will take me, I am yours for eternity," she answered, letting the words fall free without reserve or doubt.

Mick blinked as everything that had just transpired and the implications came home. It all fit right and he had no doubts. He would face down those implications and the armies that would rise up behind them. He feared for any that should try to stand between them, for they would be crushed and even death wouldn't stop him from seeing to that. He sat up and wrapped her in his arms again and felt fresh tears of joy begin trickling their way down his face while others soaked into his shoulder.

Something says that Fate is going to conspire against us, I just hope Fate washed their neck well because if they make her hurt, my axes will be coming for them.

***

Mick wasn't sure when he had drifted back to sleep, but when he woke again, it was clearly nighttime outside his window and the moon was hanging high in the sky. There were more and brighter stars hanging in the heavens than he could ever remember having seen before. Whole constellations were revealed that hadn't been visible for a long time. In fact, according to all of his memories, he couldn't recall a night like that since the Mid-Fifteen-Hundreds. That thought sent a little bit of a chill down his spine. They hadn't been this bright for so long because of all of the light pollution that had sprung up after that as humans harnessed light and bent it to their will. Bright stars meant a dim world. He gave himself a shake to keep from chasing that rabbit. Those worries would keep or there already wasn't anything that he could do to change them.

He may not have been able to do much for the state of the world, but now that his body seemed to be back under his command, he had things that needed getting done. He slowly levered his creaking and sore body over the bed and put his feet down. He was pleasantly surprised when they landed on a pair of fuzzy home slippers instead of a cold floor. The relief triggered a memory of the fire that had been burning the last time he had woken up. A puff of his breath only added to the thought. It was cold in the room. Colder than a high summer night was supposed to be. Cold enough to warrant a fire and fuzzy slippers. Added to the brightness of the sky outside...

it raised many questions about just what had happened and where things stood. Not to mention, just how long he had been out. The moon loomed large outside his window so a decent amount of time must have passed, but was that a day or had he slept through and this was a new day? *What does it matter? A day or two won't change the state of the world and beyond what I have already done for it, there is nothing else that I can do. It's time to see to me and mine. On that note, I have some important things to see to!*

He quickly dawned the warm room-wear they had left for him to wear with his fuzzy slippers and marched out of his room; a pajama clad giant and no one had better get in his way.

The lights were on in the next room, but it was empty except for a map of the area sitting on the coffee table. It showed him the true size of the area for the first time. It was even bigger than he had estimated. There were color coated pins sticking out of it in several places along what was apparently the border to this area. The military part of his brain recognized the pins as marking picket positions and rally points without even thinking. A few of them were rather oddly placed though and he was slightly curious as to their significance. He had more pressing needs at the moment and the sounds of movement from the dining and kitchen area drew him past it with nothing more than that brief glance. He pushed open the door to find what looked to be a disinterested, yet distinctly ticked-off, raven stuck in a cage.

"What you looking at Ground Poundaa!" It squawked. "What says you just be lettin' me's out ob dis ear cage an' be abouts me's ways? Mai ju be som' in' in its foz ya."

"Deal with a raven? I'd rather trust a rat to guard my cheese," Mick said, moving his hands to quickly place a silence ruin on the cage that blocked sound from entering or exiting it. The animated gesturing of the raven made its displeasure at being shut up and cut off known. He paid it no heed and continued on into the next room.

Ai was there and so was Sen and Reigi. He only caught the tail end of the conversation as he walked in but that was more than enough. "...your hand is already..." Reigi was saying while Sen looked on with a smug smile. Whatever else he was about to say came to a halt as Mick came in, clad in plaid glory, surprising them all.

"Anyone that tries to take her hand against her will had better be ready to get it lopped off by my axes! Mountains will be laid low and armies reduced to dust, if they think they can prevent us from deciding our future for ourselves. Don't push it. I'm very accomplished at smiting things that look to harm those I hold dear!" Mick said, cutting off any comments that may have arisen and any attempts to change the subject. "We agreed to this and will see it through to whatever end it leads us to. If anyone wants to try to lay claim, refute us, or challenge is welcome to stand. I'm willing to offer recompense and apologies, but that is all. If they aren't happy with that, we can settle it in duel. I don't boast, they will lose!" There was ice and steel in his words and promise in his eyes.

Ai had come around to stand next to him and he put his arm around her shoulder, not protecting her, or claiming her, but in partnership. Sen let out a bark of laughter that cut through the tension which had descended upon the kitchen.

Reigi did his best to turn an appropriate glower on them but it shattered before the image of them standing side by side and the honesty of their emotions. "You are sure of this? There will be no going back," he asked instead of the reasoned argument that he had formulated about how it would only serve to bring them unending grief if they were together. She was royalty, and she was throwing all of that away to be with Mick. He hoped that Mick's axes were as sharp as his words.

Mick looked down into Ai's eyes as she looked up and gave him a little nod. "We're sure!" he resolutely answered for them.

Reigi buried his head in his hands for a moment before looking back up. "Never try to reason with love. I shouldn't be that surprised. Your parents were just as headstrong. I just wanted to do right by them. They trusted me to look after you and I guess I'm having a hard time coming to grips with passing the baton to someone else," he grumbled while he locked eyes with Mick. The warning was clear. If he hurt her, he would be hounded until one or both of them were dead.

"Now that is the first smart thing you've said all morning," Sen chipped in from his perch on the counter. "Reason never has had and never will have any bearing on matters of the heart," he said, giving Reigi a pat on the back while turning a smile on Mick and Ai. "I'm glad we have gotten that cleared up. And since we have that out of the way, we can return to the far less important matters at hand. Welcome back Mick. It is a rare pleasure to know the most wanted man in the world." *Oh, I just love getting to drop bombshells on unsuspecting people.*

Mick blinked. "What!"

"Oh... You didn't know. You are now the most hated, reviled, and sought-after man on the face of planet Earth. Or at least once they get a modicum of the information system back up and running, you will be. You're famous. All of this is your fault and those seeking their pound of flesh are already on the move right alongside those that want to capture the key to the most powerful source of power known to man or other beings. They are coming for you!" Sen assured, poking Mick in the sternum.

"What!" Mick repeated, the cogs in his brain, having jumped the rails, were having a hard time getting back onto the tracks.

"Oh, it's not that complicated. Shortly after you reached the crystal, we routed those that sought to keep you from it. Many were killed on both sides and few of those arrayed against you survived to be captured. But more than a few chose escape. They now see you as a hindrance to their ambitions to use the power of the Crystal to their own ends and are raising new forces with those outside of the valley to come and take what they view as theirs. Although it is now greatly reduced in size, it is still the largest accessible concentration on the planet. On the other side, shortly after you started, the barrier around the valley collapsed. We are now without its protection and when you are one of the few spots of light in an otherwise dark world, things both seeking shelter and seeking to 'take' shelter tend to flock towards you. Then there are the ravens. I believe you must have noticed our feathered friend in the other room. His ilk have long known and awaited this day or one like it. They managed to enter as soon as the barrier collapsed and quickly took note of you and the crystal's changing condition. They correctly posited that you are the key, the regulator, to the crystals enormous power and there are those that seek to control or subvert the key's power. Lastly, the world, despite the major damage and destruction spreading throughout it, took note of the place that hadn't been, until the change started, that now suddenly was. They also noted the man at the center of it. Blasted eyes in the sky! If only they had lost power a little sooner, it wouldn't have been a problem. Too late to change that now though, they got pictures of you when you collapsed. Those in power undoubtedly seek to capture, control, or eliminate the man that they also believe to be the key to the Crystal or the events that have taken place. Others simply wish to control the area because even they can tell that there is something different and powerful about it. The rest, being the remaining media who somehow got ahold of some of this information, namely your photo, and the remainder of humanity who will surely fall for their unsubstantiated claims against you, blame you as the cause of all of this. In a way, they are correct. You were late and the damage was greater than it could have been. Not that I blame you. Arrows through the leg, being blown up, and doing a spin cycle over razors tends to slow one down. That, in reality, you were trying to stop it means little to them. They know you were there, and it looked like people were trying desperately, against heavy resistance to stop you and then the end came. The satellite feed is quite good right up until that point and missed all of the important parts after that. On the plus side, the energy field swell that the Crystal released as Night fixed its levels drained all of the satellites deader than an asteroid and it is unlikely that any more of them will be being launched to replace them anytime here soon. Not going to be too fun over the next few weeks as they start coming back down though. Good thing there is a lot of water and even more area where people aren't now. Although, some of the ones in orbit further out will probably be able to be brought back on-line before their orbit degrades too far. I expect that the dark nuclear-powered ones that don't exist and are controlled by agencies which also don't exist will recover soonest. Unfortunately, it's not too surprising that the majority of humanity will react in these ways either. People always assume that the underdogs in a fight are the good guys. I blame Hollywood. But that is beside the point. The point is that you are now the face of all of this, and they aren't about to slow down and see reason. Worse, those that know better are going to encourage it. They will fan the flame and use this firestorm of anger and pain for their own ends. You and Japan are to blame, and the forces of the world are already on their way to seek their recompense and whatever power advantage that they can carve out. They see it as their just due. Apparently, Japan's own, even more severe losses aren't enough of an ante to buy in at this table. All they see is revenge to sate the masses and advantage for those in power."

"Great. I wish them luck with that. The world is a big place and they have fewer eyes than they used to. They want revenge but from what you have explained, just providing food to feed those seething masses should tie them up once the true magnitude of this smacks them in the face. They will send their tokens, but I doubt that they will have that much time or forces to spare," Mick said, shrugging. The world was a big place again and he was just one tree in the forest. *And if they come, they will learn their folly on the bit of my axes.*

"I would agree with you under most cases and if you were dealing with humans and only the outside elements of our kind. Unfortunately, or fortunately, depending on your point of view, there has been a major shift in the balance of power and many who have remained in the shadows see this as a chance to come back out into the light. From what I have been able to gather from my sources, they are already coming, and they are dragging the rest of us right along with them, whether we want to or not," Sen explained, scowling in annoyance. "I don't know how it will all shake out in the end, but I think that we can be sure that there is going to be an adjustment period followed by some new balance and mix of powers unlike anything that has ever been seen before. Enemies becoming allies, allies becoming enemies, and none of us being able to return to not knowing again."

Mick had a mental flash of battles beyond numbers from his acquired memories. The oldest ones from when the humans and Fair were both together were the bloodiest and most disturbing of all. Worse than anything in the standard recorded histories. He shivered at the thought of their like ever occurring again. Unfortunately, it appeared that the die had already been cast and there was no taking it back at this point. "Great. Just one question. How do you know all of this?"

Sen smiled at this question. "I see you aren't as up to speed on the differences between Asian and European dragons. While the Euros are all about the fire, mayhem, and Heavy Metal and Club music, we Asian Dragons are far more dignified. We work primarily with electricity and frequency. Delicate work. As such, we are tapped into most of the major information feeds around the world. We literally have two horns in the internet and broadcast sectors, a pretty big presence in the computer hardware and programming areas, and a tidy bit in the power distribution fields. We know."

Mick pondered this for a moment, wondering just how high up in the hierarchy Sen was, and nodded in agreement. He was going to have to take Sen's word for it and that fact rather punctuated a point. *I really need to hit the books on Asian Fair and get caught up. I wonder if the Onmyouji would be so kind as to let me use their books. I hope I'm not on their lists also. The Order is sure to be after me now and I don't need the other factions deciding to join in on that.*

"What I am hearing is that we have information, enemies, and probable threats to me and those that call this valley home. Even if they don't realize that they can't get close enough to harness the Crystal, they will still want to control..." Ai's hand on his arm made him stop. He looked down at her in concern. "What don't I know?"

She took a steadying breath. "The barrier went down for two reasons. Initially, it happened because the anchor points shifted faster than it was capable of accounting for. Things have settled down, but we haven't put it back up for another reason. We have the power we need. Thanks to what you did, the crystal is harnessable. Its massive draining effect is now held in check. Unfortunately, that means two things. First, the entropic sump that the crystal produced is greatly reduced now. We were able to erect the barrier because we could use that field as a foundation. The foundation is gone now, and it is too risky to try and do something like that without a secure foundation. That is bad. What's worse, is that anyone can now reach the crystal without the fear of death. Whatever you did, has made the Crystals more reserved in their hunger. They absorb free energy now but leave living energy alone for the most part. It is a little bit cooler close to the Crystal, but nothing even remotely dangerous to your health. Despite its reduced size, this is still the most massive and accessible crystal in the world. To make matters worse, it also has the largest crystal seed field. It always has been, but for some reason the propagation rate is even a little higher than average here now. Whatever Night did, it seems to have broken up the crystal in the core after the uplift settled down and pulled it up to the surface in smaller Tree Crystal fragments and those fragments are seeding. That in its own way is even worse than the trees. The trees may contain great amounts of power, but they are also stationary. The crystal seeds are not, and we now have the greatest farm of those portable and infinitely usable and valuable crystals. They will come and if they get the chance, they will be able to harness enough power to skew the balance of the world. The only plus side is that faster propagation is still slower than a snail and the amount on hand is limited. Unfortunately, what is readily available is still a scary amount to imagine falling into anyone's hands. That kind of power is dangerous even with the best of intentions!"

Mick rubbed his temples. "And here I got up looking forward to having a nice talk about dating, going out for pancakes, wedding ceremonies, honeymoons, and a wedding night," he grumbled, the mental cogs of war already turning over and computing their options. "Was that map in the other room accurate?"

The others looked between each other, Ai had a little bit of a blush now, but she didn't let that slow her down, and they nodded. "It's..." Mick held up his hand to forestall their continuing.

"Good. One question. What are the odd zones that aren't reserves or fallback positions?" he asked, recalling the map from memory.

"Tunnels into the underground. We use them as supply routes in and out of the valley. The barrier was able to bend the outside world but the powers that maintain the tunnels below are a fearsome thing and we weren't able to cut them off. We have had issues with infiltration through them in the past and it made sense to put a guard on them and, just in case things go bad, we also wanted to maintain control of the safest of them as a possible route of egress," Reigi explained.

"And how many fighters do you have?" Mick pressed, beginning to see the scale and scope of the plan that was needed.

Reigi scratched his chin at this last question. "Quantitatively, we have around a two thousand. But the Qualitative balance is greater than that. Unlike many of those who would be coming to attack us, our fighters are highly trained and many of them are exceptionally strong in their own right. We haven't set about trying to hoard power, but it has gathered strongly here. Rare and lost family lines still thrive here. Ai is a good example of that. The Dire Mountain Wolf Clans were wiped out everywhere else. They were destroyed because of jealousy of their power and because they refused to lower themselves and their scruples to match those of the lower wolves. Also, others sought to subvert their power into or under their own and they were wiped out. But here, there are still no less than five of these clans and they number in the hundreds. They are but one example."

Mick nodded his head in understanding, but he also recognized the blind spot in the argument. "That is all fine and dandy, but you just pointed out the problem with counting on a qualitative edge. Quantity has a quality all its own and we know that we will be faced with a quantitative disadvantage. On top of that, as good as our quality may be... we can't count on that always being the case. With this much power on the line, we can at least count on facing some qualitative equals and probably a few that are superior to many of ours," he warned, thinking for a moment and only seeing one real option. "We need to look at the map," he said, leading the way. He paused to open a window in the dining room and let some fresh air in. The raven glowered at them the whole time while it silently opened and closed its beak in silent yells of protest. As Reigi walked by Mick, who was holding the door, he couldn't help but smirk at the now inept bird. He paid it little heed as he continued on into the next room. Once the others were past, Mick followed after waving in the raven's direction and made sure to leave the door ever so slightly ajar.

Mick took up position opposite them and continued once they were all seated around the map. "This is a good disposition that you have put together. Overall it is perfect for what you have trained to face and for what you have available. Unfortunately, it is completely inadequate for what you have already told me that we are expecting to face. Two thousand just isn't enough people to cover an area this big. For example, even with twice our numbers, the south flank is completely untenable. The ground is too flat and there are too many small cuts and flanking routes to cover. There aren't any natural features that would allow you to funnel opponents and let our qualitative edge stopper up a quantitatively superior opponent. Even if you put all of your troops there, you couldn't stop even a slightly bigger force. They would pass through you like water and cut you into manageable packets after only a few passes..." A crash from the other room and the flutter of wings brought the conversation to an abrupt halt.

Reigi ran into the other room. A torrent of rather imaginative and thorough expletives and suggestions for anatomically impossible maneuvers as well as parentage soon followed. When he came back, it was with the cage that the raven had been cooped up in. "Good thing you put the mute on him. It's bad that he escaped, but if he had heard what we were just talking about, it would be crushing," he said, shaking his head in annoyance.

"Which is exactly why I opened the window, left the door ajar, and let the rune break as soon as we were in here," Mick said, grinning happily.

"You did what!" All three of them chorused.

"And what possessed you to do a thing like that. Do you want to see us all dead!?" Reigi demanded, charging towards Mick.

Mick didn't step down or make any move to stop him. "Quite the opposite really. I did it so that we could not only live, but win," he answered, being sure to let his confidence show while letting them know that he understood their fears.

"What do you mean?" Sen asked, stepping in and putting a restraining hand on Reigi's heaving chest. He could be quite strong and forceful for such a little guy. Then again, he really wasn't little.

"Exactly what I just said. Everything that I said before was true and I meant every word of it. Now our enemies will also know it," Mick explained, waving to the map.

"And our enemies or more accurately, for at least half, your enemies knowing where we are at our weakest helps us survive how...?" Sen prodded.

"Because now we know where they will attack. The enemy now 'knows what he knows,'" Mick explained, smiling happily. "And what he 'knows' matches with what he can see and discern. And he will be right in all of those beliefs and the facts that they are based on. And that is why he will lose. You said it yourself, this whole area hasn't just been a dark spot on the map; it hasn't been on the map since before there were maps. Almost everyone coming here will be working in the blind or off of really old intel. They will jump at information like this."

"And their knowing these things helps us how?" Sen asked, beginning to see where Mick was going. It was risky, but there was the possibility of a chance where before he had only seen eventual defeat. *Maybe he knows more of war than I thought. The question is, has he put the wagon before the horse?*

"Because we now know where and how he will attack. The reality is that there is no place that we could hold with the forces that we have. The perimeter is too big. The town is too big. Even the citadel is too damningly big. We would need at least twice as many as we have to hold the citadel, five times more than that for the town, and ten or fifteen times that number for the existing perimeter. In other words, defense is a lost cause. There is no survival in the defense. They can come at us from too many directions and somewhere they will be able to break through and then we will either all die or be forced to run away if we are lucky. Unless we can gather our forces to face them... we lose," Mick answered, looking at the three of them.

Reigi started nodding in agreement but it quickly became a frown. "But you said that even if we put all of our forces on that area, even with twice our numbers, a defense is still doomed," He pointed out.

"Exactly. The enemy will know exactly what our options are if he attacks there and he will know that it is a lost cause on our part. So that is exactly what he will do. And, that is why he will die and we will live," Mick answered, stabbing the flats with his finger.

"Run that by me. We will lose there and that is why we will win. That doesn't make any sense!" Reigi argued, furrowing his brow but no longer looking for blood.

"I said that we will lose if we stand and try to defend that area. But I never said that we were going to defend it. We're going to attack it. And we aren't going to be alone," Mick said, a predatory grin splitting his scowl. "Here's what we are going to have to do." He didn't even realize that without complaint, comment, or conscious thought on his part, he had assumed command and the others were listening.

Stand Together or Hang Separate
Monday, July 12

It was dark, cool, and quiet out. The clouds had moved in and drowned out the light of the moon and stars alike. There was but a whisper of fog traipsing across the lake and encroaching on the, somewhat worse for wear, town below. It was apparent that the lake had leapt free of its basin and washed out parts of the town and surrounding area. The local landscape remained the same in many ways, yet vastly changed in others. The mountains and foothills towered higher and the lake looked even deeper and wider at the other end, but the valley and town had remained mostly unchanged except for the damage which was rather light considering what had happened and he had no doubt that the locals were the reason for that. Now that he thought about it, there had been a lot of cucumbers being grown around town.

There were lights down there as well. A great many of them appeared to be made of different sorts of fire, but there was also a smattering of the electric lights and if he listened closely, he could make out the rumbles of a couple of generators. One area in particular had his attention though. The inn was fully lit and there was a steady flow of activity coming and going from it. Further out, in the shadows, there were darker areas that blended in a little too well where pickets had been placed. It was apparent that the town still lived and that the inn was still its heart.

So much had changed in only a few days and he had no idea about how the rest of Japan had fared except from the reports of some crows and Sen. It didn't sound good and he wondered when it would hit home for him. *I hope Jake is faring well. His dream has finally come true. I just hope that it doesn't devour him.*

"You really think they will help us?" Ai asked, cutting off his ponderings and looking at him from where she laid next to him on the knoll that they were using for cover.

Mick shrugged. "No way to know for sure without asking them. All I know is the little that I was able to learn about them in the day that I was there before you all came a calling. Considering that you have been neighbors for so long, I would think that your people would have a better feel for them?"

Ai was silent for a while. "As a whole, we may have been a little bit overly isolationist," she admitted, looking just a touch pensive. Because of her duties, she had ventured out beyond their valley more than most, but those had all been long trips to more distant areas or just slipping into town to touch base or pass a note to one of their local plants. She had visited the town a few times in the open as a local from one of the more reclusive areas and they knew her but she wasn't sure how they were going to react when they found out who she really was.

Mick arched an eyebrow and muffled a chuckle. "A little, perhaps," he agreed, giving her a wink. On the horizon the dark of night was finally beginning to be driven back by the first rays of sunshine. "Only one way to know for sure." He climbed back to his feet and started back down the path that he had first traveled only a week and a world before.

Ai scrambled to her feet and skipped to catch up with his long legged, ground eating lope. "I hope you're right about them and this idea. We have not harmed them, but we also haven't gone out of our way to help them either. And there have been times when they really could have used the help!" She grimaced remembering a few of those times. Her blood had run hot when the elders forbade them to interfere.

"Looking back and given the situation listening to the elders led us to, we never should have listened to them. I want you to know that, no matter what, I'm with you until the end. I just hope that they can understand why we wouldn't help them back then because when the forces arrayed against us come, and if we stand alone, we will fall and given the caliber of those that will likely come, they will not remain sated long. Nor will they see any reason to tolerate having a small but powerful conclave of such as these for neighbors. Then they too would fight bravely and fall!" she said in a hushed tone as they walked. She was just about to say more when her thoughts shattered as her feet were suddenly swept out from under her and the ground rapidly rose up to meet her. *Stupid!!! What was I thinking letting my guard down!* She rolled to the side just in time to see sparks fly in the dawn haze as metal met metal. There was a hollow thud and 'Umph' before one of the two silhouettes staggered back, doubled over, and sat down hard clutching at their sternum; trying to suck in air. She regained her feet as she spied others closing in; looking to the fight. She looked back up at the still standing silhouette with trepidation. Unsure if it was Mick or Foe. As the axes in its hands came around, she let out a sigh of relief.

"They don't seem too happy to see you," she said, drawing her short sword and katana, readying to meet those coming from her side. If it was a standup fight, the numbers wouldn't have worried her, but being as they didn't want to overly harm or worse kill any of those that they hoped to soon make allies of, the odds weren't nearly as advantageous. She was all ready to pounce, when the newcomers abruptly halted their charge and stopped about seven meters short.

"Is that you, Mick?" one of them asked, leery of some kind of trick.

Mick recognized the voice. "Sure is, Yosuke. Looks like you are going to have to pay up to Atsuko," he shouted back. There was a series of snickers and a bit of grumbling from Yosuke's direction.

With a forlorn sigh, Yosuke walked close enough to make sure it was really Mick before coming close enough to give him a pat on the back. He eyed Ai with suspicion as he talked. "So you leave, the town is attacked by a rabid pack of Okuri-inu, we butcher them but lose a few people tourists and take a few injured, then there's this ground tearing earthquake that seems bent on fracturing the world, but it stops just short, after that every crow and raven for what seems to be the length and breadth of Japan comes flying over, and to wrap things up, the strange foreigner that was last seen entering the woods that no one leaves shows back up here and he's brought a friend who now that I look I recognize as one of our local transients but given that she's accompanying you I now presume is also from said woods and was only acting so that she and whoever she represents could keep tabs on us," he said, ticking off questions and points on his fingers. "I hope that you have a rather amazing explanation about how this all is supposed to make sense. Because given the strange reports and information that we have coming in, I get the feeling that it somehow all connects back to you!"

"I do. We do. But all things considered, it is long, time is limited, we have been walking for most of a day, and I could really use a cup of coffee," Mick said, taking a step closer to Ai and putting his axes back away. "And, something says that Atsuko is going to want to hear this also." He shrugged and gave Yosuke a questioning eyebrow. "That and I'd hate for you to forget to make good on your bet," he added, smiling slyly.

***

Atsuko sat back in her seat and looked back and forth between Mick and Ai. Yosuke contented himself with pacing back and forth while shaking his head and muttering something about never accepting another ALT again.

Atsuko finally broke the silence that lingered between them, locking her gaze on Ai. "So, the Dire Mountain Wolfs aren't quite as destroyed as we were once led to believe; which would seem to lend credibility to your statements about your hidden village and what truly lurks within the woods. I can even understand why you wouldn't have ever come forwards or treated with us until now," she said, taking a stilling breath as she apparently put aside whatever past events that could have been prevented or were possibly caused because of them. Some of them being not so much in the past, like the recent Okuri-inu attack. "What I don't understand is why you think we can or should help you now? You have no doubt known and seen our plights over the millennia and yet you have stood by and done nothing all of this time. So, what's in it for us to shed our blood and burn our lives to help you now?"

Mick started to reply but Ai cut him off by placing her hand on his thigh and sparing him a halting glance. *We dug this hole and it is high time that we started filling it back in.* "We did what we did, and it is done. We listened to our elders and followed their orders. Now after so many of them have died and most of those that still live have become foe, it becomes apparent that we were wrong to follow them in all that they commanded. But that doesn't mean that it was wrong to remain hidden. Had our presence become known before now, unceasing war for control of the power that we guard, guard for the protection of all I say, would have consumed this land and all that lived upon it. There is no doubt about that. That war is what we stand upon the verge of facing at this very instant. The only small hope that any of us have for keeping these lands and all that we hold dear is for us to work together. I don't ask you to like us. I don't even expect you to trust us, yet. What I do hope is that you will stand beside us, as neighbors, and help to protect this land which we both cherish and our families and homes from the grasping hands, foreign and domestic, that even now descend upon us and would see us all made slave or laid forth as a feast for ravens," she answered, her voice gaining strength with every word. "As for me, I choose to fight and protect my home and people from these bandits, usurpers, and tyrants! May it be their corpses and the corpses of those that follow them that the ravens feast upon!"

Atsuko leaned back, casting appraising eyes about those assembled in the room. They finally came to rest on Mick. *I wish I could say it is all his fault and lay this all as an axe across his neck, but it would have come to pass with or without him. If even half of what they say is true, and I am inclined to believe them even if their story is a bit outrageous, then things could have been much, much worse. But it makes one wonder if fate truly was that strong or are we all simply stuck in a web so great that none of us can see it. If that is the case, just what lays at the center of that web?* She shivered and her skin prickled at the thought. *But that is all for tomorrow to find out. She is right and the time for us to dither and squat in our separate camps has come to an end.* "What do you need us to do?"

Surprise Guests
Thursday, July 15

"Well, they are here," Setsuna commented as he touched down in a flurry of detritus that got stirred up by the flapping of his three-meter-wide wings. He was on loan from the town as a scout and also happened to be one of Tobio's grandsons. Gramps was content to sit this rodeo out unless things turned aerial but his kin, and there were a lot of them, had flocked to the town and the cause in droves and were handling the scouting and insuring that the ravens were only seeing what they wanted them to see and when they wanted them to see it. This was shaping up to be a big rumble and they weren't about to let it pass without them.

Tengu may have looked just like humans with wings, although they definitely had noses to put even a Greek to shame, but their musculature and bone structures were quite different. It yielded both a lighter weight for their size as well as a surprising degree of strength. Mick knew better than to underestimate them and was glad that they would be fighting on his side. They were just as fierce of warriors as they were scouts, with their talons and razor sharp and titanium hard feathers, and he had some special plans for them that they were uniquely suited for.

"Are they approaching along the paths that we were hoping for or are they going to require a little cajoling to get them latched onto the bone?" Mick asked, passing a canteen over to Setsuna who promptly drained it. That was the Tengu's weakness. They required prodigious amounts of fluids and food to keep them going when they were putting out large amounts of exertion. In comparison, their caloric intake made sumo wrestlers look like ballerinas on a diet. That was actually the main reason why they drank so much booze. Pure liquid calories. Flying along at their standard fifty kilometers an hour wasn't a big deal, but today there were often times when they were having to maintain over a hundred kilometers an hour to stay clear of their approaching foe's own aerial units. It wasn't their max speed by a long shot, but it was still rather tiring.

"Nothing that hasn't already been handled," Setsuna said, a shadow passing behind his eyes as he passed the canteen back over. "There was a Murder of ravens that were trying to sneak around the flank, using a hill for cover. The Murder was murdered in short order. Their plumage now decorates the hillside." Ravens may have had a lack of morals and a highly defined appreciation for their own plumage, but with the payday that was in store for the victor, they were more willing than usual to match up with the Tengu in hopes of discovering something that would see them earning more shinies. "On the other side, we let them get a little deeper before raining down destruction on all but two of them like you asked. They got a good glance at the concealed positions and the reserves posted there but nothing else. They are advancing in a rough arrow shape along the path that we hoped for," he reported, grinning broadly. *I'm glad this big bloke is on our side. He plays dirty and looks to cheat his opponents wherever he can. It's no surprise Gramps likes him.*

"Good," Mick nodded, grinning ferally. *Good. Now they know where we are strong and weak and that our reserve is far too small to aid with more than one or two breaches at most. Now we just need them to...* The pickets ahead of their lines roared their attack. It only lasted a few moments before it was replaced with writhing shrieks of pain that were cut mercifully short. There was little doubt about what had befallen those that had been injured.

They still didn't know exactly whose force was arrayed before them but what they had been able to gather, based upon those that comprised it, was that prisoners would not be taken and that any signs of weakness would be met with death. Ai smiled as she vaulted over the light breastworks that they had erected and skidded to a stop alongside him. He wasn't exactly happy that she had been out there with the pickets but arguing against it wouldn't have changed anything and she was one of those best suited for the role.

She smiled happily as she came to stand by him. "Setsuna, I see that your tail feathers appear to all still be attached. Although, you do seem to be missing a few on top of your head," she said, acknowledging his presence and sending a little jab at Setsuna's receding hairline. He was about the same age as them, but his hair seemed bound and determined to lose the age long war of all Tengu against baldness.

"Ai, but at least I don't smell of singed fur," Setsuna jeered back.

Mick took note of the curly ends of her hair on the left side. "Run into a little trouble, bringing our new friends into the trap?"

"Nothing that we couldn't handle. Just some rogue Foxfire that needed a bit of quenching. Besides a few burns, we didn't suffer any casualties and I'm pretty sure that we got a nice culling with the traps. Maybe put a ding into their morale but I doubt it. These aren't the types for comradery. They will just be looking out for their own pelts and their payday. But, seeing as they are in it for themselves, they should slow their advance a little and proceed as if the whole approach is booby-trapped," she said, imitating them walking slowly on tippy-toes.

"Agreed, but don't underestimate them just because we were able to bloody their nose," Mick warned. "We still don't know who is leading this band. And sadly, they brought enough friends that even if all of our traps take two of them out of play, they will still have the numbers to overwhelm us," he admonished. A new chorus of screams that were cut short all too abruptly reinforced his point. He grinned at this but their complete lack of regard for their fallen only underscored the need for them to win this. They faced death today and Death would be collecting his quota and he wasn't known to be overly picky as to who he collected from.

"A brutal enemy makes you happy?" Sen asked, joining the group. They had tried to convince him to stay back with the guards for the families but he had flatly refused and told them that he would 'be where he was most needed!' Apparently, that meant wherever he felt like. Given his age and ambiguous status, no one had deigned to argue with him.

"No, I rather like civil opponents. They are easier to kill. But if I can't have civility, I'll settle for prideful. This headlong drive to our strongest positions means that whoever is over there feels confident that they can not only take our best punch but repel it and return it with a spear to the heart. If he" this aggressive push definitely felt like a man was behind it, "was a wise enemy, he would pin down the center and reserves, before sending forces around to take us on the flanks. Instead he drives forwards; confident that he can smash our center and work out from there. Only the prideful seek the costly and fast kill when there is no need," Mick explained, wishing that he knew just who they were up against or if there was a leader or some council of leaders. "And, it isn't like they don't know that they have us outnumbered and pinned," he added with a feral smile. "All they need to do is pierce our center and it's all over." The others shared his smile. "For now, take your positions and be prepared to move when we break. Be sure to make it look good. Bloody his nose, but don't step on his toes. We wouldn't want our opponent to think that he isn't doing good."

The others moved off to their squads leaving Mick and Ai alone for the moment. "You should be with your unit," Mick pointed out when she didn't make to leave.

"I should, but not before I make sure that you will still be around afterwards," Ai said, darting in and kissing him deeply as he began to reply. The kiss lasted several seconds before she finally pulled back with a wicked grin. "I'll see you later," she promised, darting off before he could reply. Everyone within eyeshot was looking ahead, no doubt searching for their approaching foe. Strangest of all, not a one of them looked grim and all of them were smiling.

"That's right. Smile in the face of the enemy, and they will know fear like no other!" Mick hollered before dropping into the trench next to a sickle laden weasel named Tenmen, who was grinning a little bigger than the others. "Awfully happy lot, aren't ya'll!?"

"Yep. Nothing like seeing the boss get henpecked, or should I say gobbled, by his gal to bring a smile to the troops. Can't say I've ever seen anyone blush quite that red before. Next to that you add finally getting to put all of our training and skills towards something that actually matters and we's all just tickled pink," Tenmen answered, finally looking at him and smiling balefully. "Yep, a good day, for the music of steel reeds in the wind," he said, giving his sickle a flourish and causing several notes to whistle out. "A good day indeed."

Mick knew Tenmen's worth. He had checked the overall capability of the village's and town's warriors before finalizing his plans. They were formidable. Few were blooded in battle, except for the elder members, but all were trained and knew their business. For some, the battle to come would prove beyond their training and force of will. They would break. But what remained would be enough for the day. *And we are supposed to break. For those that break early, the shock should have time to fade from most of them and they should be able to rejoin the line when it makes the second attack. Those will be the ones to watch later. Men who have ran from fear and then make the choice to turn back and face it can become truly formidable. There will be plenty of work for all of us before this day is done.*

"Movement in the trees," an excited whisper shouted out from down the line. All of the side conversations abruptly cut short as the few who hadn't already been looking turned and stared across the killing field and into the dark shadows of the forest beyond. Sure enough, shapes were beginning to resolve out of the shadows and were gathering into smaller groups or units. Disconcertingly, there were a lot of them. More than Mick had honestly expected or the crows and Tengu had reported. Not enough to overwhelm the plan, but enough that the butcher's bill was bound to be a lot heavier.

"Ready!" Mick called out to his companions. They were in a raised half trench guarded by a berm to the front but with the back open so that they could fall back easier and so that when the enemy was driven back, they wouldn't have a readymade defensible position. Once the enemy mounted the berm, they would fall back where they could make full use of their diverse skills and weapons. It would be a battle the likes of which hadn't been witnessed in hundreds of years.

The enemy across the way bristled at his call and seemed to contract towards the sound of his order. They apparently and correctly assumed that he was in command and they all wanted the glory and fortunes that would come of taking the commander's life. There was nothing for it and – anyway – it was better that they should concentrate on him in the middle.

The air stilled and turned brittle – the world holding its breath – as the tension built between them like a night-terror sweat-soaked blanket. Then came the roar as thousands of throats let loose their cry of battle on both sides and their advance resumed.

The air split with the shrieks of unexpected death before fire and explosions blossomed over the enemy force that had just entered the killing field and those still behind in the trees. Great trees, hundreds of meters tall, burst and toppled, showering those below in flesh rending splinters and crushing others under their massive trunks. The sound of the screaming hoard and the explosions were soon replaced with the concussive booms of over pressure which smacked them all down like a malevolent hand. Just as their initial shock began to fade, the world rocked again with explosions and the bloody screams of man and Fair alike as fresh ordinance rained down on enemy and ally alike. A new uninvited player had taken to the field and he had a big hammer.

Mick and his allies were luckier than their foe. Their trench protected many of them from the rain of death but not all of the screams belonged to the enemy being butchered in the relative open. He watched in horror as a napalm canister tumbled perfectly into the trench ahead of him; bursting and spilling its ravenous contents over the hunkered defenders before igniting into a searing curtain of fire, sucking the air from their very lungs while searing their flesh. A few who had some degree of control over fire quickly tamed the maelstrom, but they were too late for many of those that had been trapped within the fire's embrace.

Tenmen looked back at him, shock and horror shadowed his features as the fires hellish light danced ghastly shadows across it. Gone was the joy and enthusiasm which had burned in him just moments ago. Replaced with an all-consuming blaze of hate which burned deeply in his eyes. This was not the war that they had prepared for. "What are you orders!?" he demanded.

Mick spared a quick glance over the trenches to check on their old foe and was glad to see that they were dead, dying, or running away with all the speed that they could muster. All but one who leered back across the killing field at him. That one nodded like he had reached some kind of conclusion and then turned his gaze to the sky and hurled a dagger. One of the incoming jets staggered before pitching sharply over and crashing amongst the trees. The figure looked back at Mick and his blood ran cold. "Nephilim!" A bomb burst between them forcing him to turn aside against the searing heat and cutting off his sightline in a cloud of sod and smoke. By the time the dust had blown aside, the man was gone.

Fazed, he shook his head to clear the cobwebs of the miss and his shock at what he had seen. *It can't be and even if it is, that is a problem for later. For now, you need to save as many of these people as you can!*

To the rear, he could see bombs bursting amongst those that had been lying in wait. Above more and more jets howled by bearing stars on their wings and dropping fresh bombs on his people and enemies alike. Anywhere that targets gathered, they rained their death.

Taking a deep breath of cordite and death choked air, he focused on the task at hand. *Yes, these are my people now. We didn't ask for this war, but they will surely rue this day in which they have foisted it upon us. We will bleed, are bleeding, but they will all die for what they have done. No force they can rally will stop the reckoning which they have called down upon themselves.* As if to punctuate his thoughts, another of the attacking aircraft staggered and tumbled out of the sky, adding its flaming carcass to the chaos below. It was quickly followed by another and then by a flutter of black feathers. *Those are some brave Tengu to be tangling with Fighters.*

Tobio and his men had joined the fray. *I can't ever repay them for the cost that they will pay for us today.* For the moment, the rain of bombs ceased as the attackers found themselves tangled up in a bird fight. The Tengu had the jets beat in maneuverability but were slower in the dash.

"Now, while there is a lull, we must fall back. Gather all who live and whatever weapons and provisions can be had. We make for the tunnels. We'll regroup there and watch how things progress," Mick ordered, sending runners to spread the word.

Tenmen hesitated for a moment before nodding. "I will see to it, and when the time comes, I will stand with you when we exact our vengeance upon all those who have attacked us this day!" he promised. He gave another nod before dashing out of the trench, driving the others in their retreat, gathering all those who still drew breath and spreading the word to pullback, leaving Mick alone in the trench.

This can't be all there is to their plan. The Military wouldn't have been sent here and attacked like this unless they knew at least something about what we were protecting. They must have come to claim the power for their own. Catching me probably would only be icing on the

cake. Which means that someone who at least knew what Crystals were
must have told them at least some information and gave them at some
pointers on what they would face. The list of those that could have done
that is rather short. In fact...

A steel-clad pillar fell from the sky, landing in the clearing with
a dull thud and kicking up a cloud of dust and debris as it cratered
the earth around it. Then, another fell, and another. He watched as
death and betrayal fell from the sky; his heart growing cold with
foreboding. He caught sight of a shadow within the dust and smoke
and prayed that it was nothing more than one of the fallen that
had regained consciousness and was stumbling around. His hope
shattered as the shadow resolved into a blue-steel clad Knight, sword
already in hand and at the ready, flowing out of the haze with a
flowing grace that beguiled the plate armor encasing him. There was
a cleft shield of white with a gilded eye glaring out from between the
crack emblazoned on the shoulder-guard of his armor. Once again,
The Order of the Knight's Keeper had come to take that which he
held dear.

Without thinking, he rose out of the trench, clearing the berm
in a single step. He drew his axes and hold them out slightly to
his side as he advanced on the Knight before him. The Knight,
still dazed from the drop, only noticed him once Mick was already
within reach.

"Mic...?" the man shouted in surprise before being cut, gurgling
as a steel spike on the back of Mick's axe drove home through the
wards protecting the wearer and through the thin gap under the
helm and into his jaw.

With a crunching twist, Mick pulled his ax free and the
armor-clad Knight fell with a silent thud. He quickly slid the man's
helm free. Deen Lancy. They had trained together as youth. Deen
had always been a decent sort, even if his family had been one of
premier houses in the Order. All things considered; they had gotten

along rather well. He stood to face the others he knew would be coming and started to step away only to have an iron clamp fasten around his right ankle while cold steel bit deeply into his left calf. He instinctively pivoted, bringing both of his axes down and around at whatever had taken hold of his ankle. He grunted with pain and effort as his sinews screamed from the impact of his blow. The offending entanglement held for a moment before finally releasing and rebounding away.

Now facing his unexpected attacker, he looked on in horror as Deen regained his feet, his head lulling from side to side as his shattered jaw mended back together and the wound sealed. Proof that they were using the forbidden 'Xerox' ward. It had earned that moniker as of late because of the similarities in the processes.

Deen's eyes rolled back down and stared back at Mick with a corrupt grin to match Mick's horror. "Nifty trick, isn't it. I'm told it has something to do with continuous information copying and the ability to re-format those afflicted with catastrophic wounds so long as the extent of the damage and the necessary repairs doesn't outstrip the fallen's energy reserves or those of an assistant or surrogate if available. They named it 'Light sleeper.' It is but a small taste of the power that we now hold since those who wished to stand against us were washed under a week ago. Soon, thanks to the unlimited source of power that is now at our fingertips, we will not only be able to restore ourselves, but so much more."

"Fools!" Mick spat. "You know not what you deal with. 'Light sleeper!' Right. I take it that you think that you are the first ones to have created that particular ward!" he demanded, glaring out his loathing for the arrogance that had taken such deep roots in The Order. "It a ward, ancient beyond knowing. The 'Death Helm' and its price is higher than you know."

"You and your self-important family think you know everything. Well your time is over. Your family's dead Mick," Deen laughed.

"Don't look so sad, I'll be sending you to join them soon," he promised, lunging forwards rashly, arrogantly believing himself immortal.

Fool, nothing but God is immortal. Mick raised his axe to meet Deen's horizontal chop, moving with the blow and using its power to propel him around Deen's side. With a light rotation and all of the energy which Deen's attack had imparted, he brought his other axe around and down on the back of Deen's neck in a lightning fast chop. Deen stumbled past, laughing as he regained his balance and turned to face Mick.

"Face it, you can't beat me!" Deen mocked. He made to take a step forwards and stumbled, dropping his sword instead. He made to reach for his sword and his left leg flexed backwards with enough strength to snap his knee in two, but his body refused to fall as it continued to heal the damage. His eyes turned up to meet Mick's. "What's happening?" he moaned as two of the fingers on his left hand snapped at every joint. A bulge began forming at the back of his neck.

"Copy errors," Mick answered simply. "The ward was designed to repair damage and it does that wonderfully. But errors develop quickly. The bigger the amount of damaged repaired, the more errors occur. The ward copies the users form, but from one moment to the next, the user changes. The ward is designed to change with the user, but when errors accumulate quickly, it just keeps trying to fix the mistakes, creating more errors which it dutifully tries to correct, and it keeps on trying until the energy feeding it runs out. I'm told that it can take days and is unimaginably painful. It was once used as a means of execution for the worst offences amongst the Druids before even they came to see that it was too terrible a punishment," he explained, watching the horror building in Deen's eyes. "To the decent and honorable man that you once were, I'm sorry."

"Sorry!" Deen, roared. "Save me and I will give you whatever you want. You know that my family is powerful. The council will listen. I'll even ask the Order to let you back in and offer you leniency for your unfortunate circumstances and restore you as the new head of your family's house," he pleaded, trying to reach out but instead having his elbow shatter.

"There is a way," Mick said, watching as Deen realized that he could be saved, and hope returned to him. "But not for the likes of a murderer who has come to destroy my family. A murderer's death for a murderer. I hope you enjoy your just deserts," he said as he walked by leaving Deen to his fate. The other shadowed forms were closing in to investigate the commotion. Now wasn't the time to face them. Better to let them learn from Deen's example and wonder what he was planning.

The trench was clear of all but a few of the dead by the time he returned to it. The others had all fallen back. The bombers of the first wave had now been joined by fighters in their ongoing battle for the skies. From the sound of things, the Tengu were tiring and being forced back allowing the bombers to return to their duty of slaughtering his people on the ground. This battle was lost and there was no more point in continuing this fight. There would be other days. He fired off a flare to sound the full retreat to the caves and set off at a quick jog in the direction of the nearest tunnel but not before hearing angry shouts and retching from behind him. They had found Deen.

Dirt, dust, the stench of death, and fear hung heavy in the air as Mick arrived at the nearest tunnel entrance. It was well hidden as a crack under a boulder at the back of a small cleft in a rock face. It looked like nothing more than a small hole under the boulder that had been washed out by water but once you slid under it became apparent that there was far more space than it appeared as the hole continued to go down. Mick carefully covered his tracks before dropping all the way in. He was met with the bite of cold steel against his throat. Night immediately gathered in that area and would stop the knife from doing any more damage than breaking the skin. "You going to use that?" Mick asked, glancing to the side.

"Nope. Just needed to be sure of who it was," Tenmen answered, pulling his sickle away. He clasped Mick's arm as he turned around and Mick got his first look at those gathered close behind. It didn't look good.

"I hope this isn't everyone?!" Mick said, glancing around the ragtag group. There were ten others in sight who were standing guard and ready to stopper up the entrance if anyone unwanted happened to stumble upon it. Most of them must have come from the lines because they were a singed bunch and the smell of smoke hung heavy on them.

"No, there are more, further in. Mostly the injured, old, and kids. There were more but we got hit hard as we pulled back. Not many were killed, but we were forced to scatter to keep them from having an easy target and tracking us," Tenmen explained. "Some of the others that came with us made off through the tunnels to check on the other groups. Given the nature of these tunnels, they went in a fairly large group. This area near the surface is usually fairly safe, but you never know what you are liable to run into down here."

Mick nodded. He wasn't familiar with these tunnels, but he'd been in Labyrinths in Europe, Mediterranean, and the Middle East before and remembered just how unforgiving they were. By all accounts, these tunnels were older, deeper, and even more formidable. Unless you were a fool, you never traveled even the 'safe' routes alone. "Any word from them on the situations and who we lost yet?" he asked. What he really wanted to know was if Ai was okay.

Tenmen and all the others knew well enough what Mick was asking. "She made it back to the main fallback position with the reserves. She was lightly wounded by a run-in with some dude in armor, but it was only a light wound and she is okay. We also saw a couple of those people on our way here. You know anything about who we are facing?"

Mick's pulse raced and he must have let some of the emotional volcano he was experiencing show because Tenmen took a half step back and the others visibly flinched.

I always thought he was too calm. Now I'm glad that he wears the mask. "Mick?" Tenmen asked after a moment.

Mick shook himself. *There will be time for blood to be paid later. You have other priorities. There you go being all logical again when I really don't want to be logical.* Mick admonished himself. He took a breath, smothering the inferno that had erupted in his chest until it was no more than an ember; ready to reignite the blaze when the time came.

"Gather everyone together. We need to move out of this area," he said, holding up a hand to forestall any argument. "Don't worry. We will be back. As to who we face, I will explain that once we rejoin with the others so, it will be the short version for now. The jets are self-explanatory enough, we are facing the Americans or at least some element of their military. The others, the knights," he practically spat the word, "are Knight Watchers of The Order of the Knights Keepers. They are members of the group that I was once part of. I don't know how they came to be working with the military and I don't know who is in charge, but you shouldn't underestimate them. The Knights are formidable opponents, guarded by their armor and wards they are extremely difficult to wound, let alone kill. If you find yourself facing one alone, run if you can and if you can't, aim for the joints and seams. That is where the armor and wards are weakest. I would expect that any normal human troops that they are working with will have also been prepared in some manner to face us. They should be weaker, but don't let your guard down. Monster movie rules apply. Don't assume that they are dead, just because they look that way or aren't breathing. If you kill them, take off their head if you can and don't turn your back on their corpse if you can't," he warned. "That will have to do until we can find out more. Right now, we need to move."

The others nodded and followed Tenmen and him out. They had just rounded the corner when a grenade came bouncing down the entrance and exploded in the room they had just left. It was quickly chased by flames washing the room that they had just left with hungry fire that clawed its way forwards with a will all its own and pounced upon one of the guards in the rear of the group. It reared, readying to wash over another but was quickly smothered as Mick released a tithe of the rage burning at his core and Iron sand enveloped it, glowing cherry pink before the flames burned out as they quickly consumed all of the air trapped with them. It was too late for the man that it had attacked. He wheezed one shuddering breath as the others rushed to him, handing his weapon over to one of the other members with a smile before falling still.

Mick roared his rage wanting nothing more than to cut down those that had done this. The question of whether the normal soldiers were equipped to attack them was now answered. Flame throwers were old news, but that they had combined it with Puppet Fire confirmed that they were being helped. Tenmen laid a restraining hand on his arm and shook his head.

Mick drove his fist into the wall, fracturing stone and collapsing the passage into the room that they had just left. Even as the stones fell and settled, he could see more flames licking into the room beyond. "We move!" he seethed into the stunned silence. No one argued. Night's rage was not to be underestimated. He may have looked like just another overly big guy, but that façade was a lie, and the collapsed tunnel behind them expunged any doubts that any of the others may have still harbored about that.

A hundred meters further in, they found the group waiting for them in a large cathedral chamber. Combined, there were close to two hundred of them. Most were the young, not quite fully trained for battle, and some older members that had stayed behind in the tunnels, ready to supply them during the battle and tend to the wounded. The room was lit by several wondering blue Will-o-Wisps or the native version that orbited above them.

"We leave in fifteen minutes. Pack and make ready what you can. Stash what you can't and destroy anything that we can't take but can't let fall into other's hands," Mick ordered as soon as he entered the room. They stood there in silence until one of the slightly older members spoke up.

"Well what are ya'll lollygagging around for!? Ain't you ever heard an order before? Move!" he bellowed, sending the gathered scampering about the task. Content that they were now properly motivated, he ambled over to where Mick and the others had gathered. "We'll be ready to move in ten minutes, Sir," he assured, speaking loud enough for everyone to hear and daring anyone to come up short with his eyes.

"Good," Mick said, watching the hurried work and cracking his first smile in hours. It did his heart good to be back with friends and to be moving with a purpose. "I don't think we have had the pleasure of meeting before?"

"Nope." He answered.

Mick had to smirk at the old man's antics. "What should I call you then... Sargent perhaps?"

"Now that has a nice ring to it. A nice ring indeed, Sir. Sargent Adachi, at your service, Sir. Late of the External Guard. Spent thirty years in the JSDF familiarizing myself with their weapons and tactics. I also did stints cross training with several Special Forces in Asymmetric warfare and guerrilla tactics," he explained.

"Really now. I can think of quite a few ways that we could use a man of your experience. My only question is why you weren't out on the line today?" Mick asked, glancing at Tenmen who was fidgeting at the moment.

Adachi chuckled at Tenmen's expense. "The young pups didn't ask, and someone needed to stay behind to kick the rear area into action if a hand grenade happened to fall into the handbasket. Today's war wasn't designed to be my kind of war. It was a standup fight for the most part. Even after everything went sideways. Now tomorrow's? I'm rather looking forward to that," he said, showing a predatory grin. "I never was one to care much for honorable battle. I figure the point of war is to make the other guy dead or quit. Not to add notches to my blades," he added, pegging Tenmen and the others gathered around him with an admonishing stare. "Don't matter how you make it happen so long as you live, and he dies. Rape, atrocities, and murder ain't no good, they just corrupt and corrode your authority and beget similar reprisals against your own people and others that are caught in the wrong place at the wrong time, but terror that puts fear into the hearts of your enemy has its place so long as it is used properly. But you have to maintain the moral high ground or else it will backfire and bolster your enemy's resolve," he explained with a predatory grin and a hungry gleam in his eyes.

Mick could see that Tenmen and most of the others that accompanied him found the kind of fight that Adachi suggested distasteful and didn't seem to care much for Adachi either. But a few had simply listened and even nodded a little at his suggestions. They would require observation and guidance. *I was afraid that that might be the case. They have all been raised on the storybook version of battle and the idea that it is clean and the force of good always prevails; never stooping to sneaky tricks and underhanded attacks.* "We'll have to talk more about this later. For now, ten minutes is up, and it looks like your people are ready to move," he said, nodding towards the waiting group.

Adachi glanced to his watch and sighed. "Nine minutes and thirty seconds! A class of preschoolers would have been faster than you lot. But, in light of the extenuating circumstances which we find ourselves under, my sunny disposition, and caring heart, I shall not require you all to drop and give me twenty at this time. I'll leave it as something for you all to look forward to upon the conclusion of our imminent march," he assured them, smiling happily. "We are ready to move out, Sir. I suggest that my men take the lead while these men provide the rear guard. We know these tunnels well and are more apt to spot any changes or shifts which might have occurred."

Mick stifled the grin that had been trying to split his face. It wouldn't have done to encourage him too much at the expense of those that had bled on the lines today. "A fine plan Sargent. But half of the guard will maintain position in the middle of the group as a roving response force and in case any force tries to cut us. I'll be up in the vanguard. I have a feeling that we are going to be using these tunnels a great deal in the coming days and this should provide a good chance for me to gain some on the job knowledge of them and their idiosyncrasies. Please join me there once you have things properly moving here," he ordered, dropping into the command role that seemed to have been foisted upon him time and again since his arrival in Japan.

"Very will Sir. I'll see right to it," Adachi said and dashed off to see to the finishing touches as the group began to move.

Tenmen moved up alongside him. "You don't like him, do you!?" Mick said, once they were out of earshot of the others.

"He would have us fight without honor," Tenmen stated.

Mick rounded on him. "He would have us live. Honor and Glory are for the dead. War has no rules except to use whatever means are at your disposal to defeat your enemy. It isn't clean, pretty, or honorable. War is what happens when honor fails, and pride prevails on one side or both. I've seen more than a thousand lives and wars beyond number. There is no such thing as an honorable war. Honorable war is a lie that costs good men's lives so that Generals and Officers can sleep well at night knowing that they fought honorably while their troops scream through the night because of the cost of those same 'commander's' honor that they bought with their men's blood and the lives of their friends. I suggest that you settle whatever differences you have with the Sargent and see to learning anything and everything that you can from him so that you and yours don't have to pay 'honor's' price in blood, tears, and nightmares," he admonished. Tenmen staggered as if slapped before giving a quick nod.

"Good! Now see to your men's disposition and do your best to keep your eyes, ears, and mind open and see what you can learn from the good Sargent. It may just save your and a lot of others' lives."

"Yes, Sir," Tenmen said, jerking to an approximate position of attention before leaving to see to his men.

Adachi joined Mick a moment later. "He's a good kid, he's just been fed to much bad food. He saw enough today. After he has some time to think about it, he'll come around."

"I agree and hope so, because this world is for his generation," Mick said, sighing tiredly.

Adachi looked up at him curiously. "I can see why my niece chose you. You're an old soul with a young one's passion. It's no wonder she fell for you," he said after a moment.

Mick chuckled. "I should have guessed by your direct and headstrong manner that you were related."

"We're related you mean. You and Ai might as well be married now," Adachi corrected, jostling his elbow.

Mick looked at him in confusion. "But we haven't had a wedding or anything yet," he argued, fighting down his sudden fluster. "We should at least go on a date before then."

"So. You're serious and she accepted. You must not know us wolfs too well so I'll let you in on a little secret. We all know when we meet the right person. It's instinctual and it has caused some problems when we have met the right person too late, but it doesn't change that we know when it happens. Ai is sure, even if she hasn't explained all of this to you and as far as the clan and those that matter are concerned, you were as good as married as soon as that became apparent. You can have a wedding for the others later, but it won't change nothing. But that's for later. We're ready to move out, Sir," Adachi reported.

Mick shook his head. "Then by all means, lead the way Sargent."

"With pleasure, Sir. With pleasure!"

What Lays in the Dark
Thursday, July 15

"Halt! That means stop for those of you who are a little slow!" Adachi called, glaring back over his shoulder.

"Problem Sargent?" Mick asked, stepping up next to him. They had been walking for close to an hour already. They had a map, but according to Adachi it was 'temperamental' and it wasn't unheard of for it to give some bad directions from time to time.

Mick had seen more than enough in the last hour to give him a healthy respect for the tunnels. He'd seen shadows that formed solid shapes and moved, felt eyes unseen staring at them from the side passages, and more noises than he could count or catalog. *And this is just a shallow surface tunnel. I'd hate to be stuck down in the deep tunnels.*

"Maybe. Probably," Adachi admitted. "You see that opening ahead of us?" Mick nodded. "Well, the map don't want to show the section after it. From here, it doesn't look any different than the last time that we came this way. That would suggest that there is something in there that is blocking the map's ability to read the tunnels. Usually I would just have us jog back and make a dash past it on the surface but that isn't an option today and unless we go deeper, which I wouldn't suggest, we have to go that way if we want to reach the others."

"There aren't any other options?" Mick asked. He didn't much like being stopped here. Something in the air was making his skin crawl and Night was vibrating with anticipation at something. Neither of those things was a good sign and he didn't want to get bogged down dealing with that something and leave the chance for something else to take them from the rear and pin them down.

Adachi scratched his head. "Not really. As I said, the only other options are to head back up to the surface and take our chances in the open or go under. Either way, with a group this big, we will attract attention and too many of our members aren't fighters. They can fight, but even against a smaller force we wouldn't be a match. We can head back to that last junction and head down to a lower road. It would double the distance we have to cover and who knows what we might face down there. Again, if it was just our fighters, I'd risk it, but it isn't," Adachi explained. "We're less of a rock in a hard place than am ingot trapped between the tongs with the hammer dropping. If we don't move forward, we are going to get smooshed."

"Then I guess we move forward. Send word back. Call Tenmen and his third and fourth best men up forwards. Then have the mid-guard move up and take our position here. If we aren't back in twenty minutes, the rest of the group is to split into two groups with half the fighters going with each. The fastest members will take the low tunnels. The rest will have to chance the surface. Tenmen is to assign a leader to each group. If they are forced to move, they stop for nothing and no one!" Mick grimly ordered.

"Yes, Sir." Adachi said, setting about sending runners to see that the orders were carried back.

A grim face Tenmen and two others joined them a few minutes later and Adachi quickly explained the situation to them. It was nice having a confident and no-nonsense NCO running herd.

"So, we are going to waltz in there and smack down whatever is scaring Mr. Map so that the rest of us can take this safe route and not have to pay the butchers bill and lead unwanted eyes back to the rest of us," Adachi finished explaining, holding each of their eyes until he was sure that they understood.

Tenmen nodded his head. "So, who's point?" he asked, instead of offering to take the position himself. Apparently, the trek had given him some time to think.

"I am!" Mick stated flatly. "I have the best defense and stand the best chance of surviving an ambush." Adachi made a token attempt to argue but a small shake of the head stopped him. "Stay at least ten meters behind me. If something or someone does attack, don't move to my assistance unless I bring the fight to you or go down. If I go down, kill it if you can, but send one of you back to warn the others. Then hold it back for as long as you can to give the others time to escape!" There wasn't time for finesse. This would be over quickly one way or another.

They made their way slowly into the next room. One of the men that Tenmen had brought with him had created a few Will-O-Wisps and had them foraging ahead of each of them so that they might get a chance to see what they were facing before it was upon them. The further they went, the more Night swelled with excitement and a strange foreboding that Mick couldn't quite understand. Night apparently knew what they were dealing with and didn't like it one bit. Unfortunately, Night wasn't the best at communicating and hadn't been able to or couldn't share exactly what had it so riled up. There was something familiar about all of this buried in the jumble of his memories, but he couldn't pin it down. The Will-O-Wisp ahead of Mick puffed out of existence but was quickly replaced by a searing white orb that flooded the whole chamber with light that curved to scour away all of the shadows revealing a single person standing in the middle of the room.

Mick recognized him immediately. "Nephilim," he whispered, stopping in his tracks as his blood ran cold and Night's excitement stilled into deathly anticipation. Mick had certainly read about them, but he wasn't exactly sure how he knew what it was that he was facing. He just knew and in knowing, he knew that they were all as good as dead.

"Now, Now. I'm hurt. It isn't nice to call people by their race. How would you like it if I just called you 'human' as soon as I saw you? Hmm? Don't like it much I see," it retorted, still standing perfectly still in the middle of the room. "But where are my manners. We are civilized, aren't we?" it grinned, but there was nothing friendly or kind about the gesture. Mick had to wonder just how civilized it was behind the façade that it was wearing at the moment. "My name is... Well, you may call me Talbot for the time being."

"Messenger of Destruction. Not a name that curries goodwill," Mick said, easing a half step back. A dagger sprouted in the dirt between his feet. He stopped trying to make more space.

"Very quick. I see that your time with the Druids taught you the value of names. Oh, don't look so surprised. Their touch upon you is plain enough to see but surmising and reviewing the muddled paths that you have walked is not why I am here. I have come to talk today, and you are here to listen. If you need an example of just how serious I am, I could plant one of those," he pointed to the dagger between Mick's feet, "in one of your friends that are behind you? No? If you prefer, I could signal my forces in the tunnels to slaughter those that you left behind? Or, you can do as I say and listen!" Talbot ordered in a deafening whisper.

"Say your piece and be gone!" Mick said.

"Wise, but your manners are just like those of your ancestors, brash," Talbot said, smirking triumphantly. "I'm curious as to who sent you? Who betrayed my plans? Things have been progressing here so well for more than a millennium. The crystal's control was broken. It remained hidden from the world. It was almost ready to run rampant and usher in a new age where the human infestation had been culled down to manageable numbers. And then, on the cusp of this grand event, the one man, the one thing that could prevent two thousand years of planning appears and against all odds not only stops it, but permanently reverses the process and renders the crystal forever impotent as a means of immediate change. So, I ask once again. Who sent you?"

Mick's mind reeled as he tried to fathom the breadth of events that he had just heard. He had felt a hand pushing events from behind for some time now, but he still had no idea who or what it was or for just how long it had been working. For all he knew, it could go all the way back to Rollan. He could certainly remember enough events throughout the lives of all of the holders of Night that could lend credence to that. But if that was true, then both Talbot and whoever was working from the shadows against him were ancient beyond reason. The order itself was around twenty-five hundred years old. Its founders had created the Rune alphabet as a variant of Italic Runes to record their history and only shared their written system some five hundred years later. That was the definition of ancient. Not quite on the scale of the great libraries and their Sanskrit, but ancient all the same. "Fate. Destiny. Chance. Take your pick. Your guess is as good as mine," he answered. *Lying would just get us all killed. The truth loses me nothing and at least there is a chance that he'll believe me and let us pass. His kind are dangerous in the extreme, but they are also known for their honesty.*

Talbot's right eye began to tick, and he frowned. "So, you're just a cat's paw. Less than I had hoped, but still useful and I have to admire your spunk. It seems to be a common trait amongst your cursed people. At least you seem to be a paw connected somehow to the body and more directly than any that have come before," he pondered, clearly thinking of the best way to use him to reach whatever or whoever it was that was interfering with him. "Very well. You have given me much to think about, but sadly your payment is slightly short and given your heritage, there is much debt owed for your people's insolence. You carry their legacy and their memories so you shall also carry their payment. You'll also have to pay a price for the passage of the others. Including you and the others behind you, there are two hundred and forty-two people behind you and two pregnant women but I won't hold those infants against you seeing as they haven't earned any debts yet. Take up the dagger at your feet!" he ordered. There was an evil glow burning in his eyes, but there wasn't much choice but to comply. If there was one thing that all of the histories had agreed upon, it was that Nephilim were deadly beyond reason and not to be trifled with.

Mick looked down at the silver handled blade between his feet and carefully picked it up. The blade was so black as to disappear from sight completely. You could only see that it was there by the blank space which it occupied, yet the void of the blade pulsed with a swirling malevolence all its own that seemed to tug at his sanity, trying to tear it down. The handle itself was intricately carved with what could only be described as a scene of tortured souls.

"Good. Now for the price. For each person to pass, you must place one cut upon yourself and they must bear witness to it. It must pass the skin and taste the flesh beneath and no using Night to seal the wounds or prevent damage. For every being who passes without a cut, two are forfeit. No other is allowed to carry the cut for you, nor may they apply it. It must be done by your hand and none may aid you until you reach your intended destination, or all are forfeit. As a bonus, I can guarantee that the way forward will be safe, and no harm shall befall those who follow you or are awaiting your arrival. Also, as an added incentive, I'll let you know that your love awaits you, but I do suggest that you hurry. Her small wound was gifted to her by a 'Weeping Blade.' I doubt that I need to explain the dangers of that to you. Unless treated, she has less than three hours to live and the journey from here at a jog still takes at least an hour. I suggest you hurry!"

Adachi and the others had moved up against his previous orders. "We can take him!" Tenmen said, advancing. Talbot cocked his head and grinned in anticipation as Tenmen moved. His eyes bored back into Mick. *A cut for every one who passes or two shall be forfeit.*

Tenmen was too far away to stop. Mick fastened his grip on the dagger and quickly dragged it across his arm before Tenmen passed. The blade was sharp and true. It cut deeply without any resistance as it split his flesh but the echoes of pain that radiated from the wound screamed through him as the cries of a thousand deaths and grated upon his soul. Tenmen stopped in his tracks, now a step past Mick, and looked back as he noticed Mick collapsing to his knees.

"A fine blade isn't it! It remembers the pain, fears, sadness, and regrets of every life that it has taken. It gifts those memories to whoever it draws blood from. Only two hundred and forty-one to go. Have fun and do hurry. Ai does not have much longer to wait for you. I'd love to stay and watch the show, but there is so much opportunity to be had in this new world that lays before us and I sadly have little time to spare for the simple pleasures of life. Maybe another day when I am less busy. Keep the dagger as a gift!" Talbot ordered. He smiled and in a blinding flash, the orb of light above strobed out of existence, leaving only the Will-O-Wisp once again floating above.

"Where did he go!?" Tenmen demanded, quickly rushing ahead but seeing no side tunnels or routes which Talbot may have taken.

"It doesn't matter. He's gone!" Adachi said, walking up to Mick but being careful not to go past him. "Can you bear it?" he asked, but refrained from helping Mick regain his feet. He had met many deadly things and men in his life, but few of them were as daunting at the creature that they had just faced. All things could be killed, but there was no doubt that it had been true to its words that they would die should they choose not to heed them.

"I must," Mick answered.

"You can't be serious..." Tenmen faltered as Mick laid three more stripes along his arm in quick succession. One for each of the men gathered there. "This is madness!"

"This is the price," Mick shouted, rounding him. "Talbot, or whatever his real name is, is a Nephilim. He could see that the others didn't understand. "I don't have time to explain it now but know that if he'd wanted us dead or saw something to gain by it, we would be. I don't trust him, but Nephilim have an odd sense of honor. Most are evil, but they are honest. If they say something or make a deal or promise, they are telling the truth. They have no qualms about allowing you to misinterpret what they say or write, using pauses and punctuation to convolute your impression, but they are honor bound to exactly what they say or write," he quickly explained. "Now time is running out and if you want Ai or the rest of us to live, we must hurry. Quickly bring everyone forwards! Now!!!" he yelled. Temporarily breaking them free of their fear driven bravado and shock. The fleet footed lady who had come with Tenmen set off back down the tunnel without further word or question.

Mick stumbled slightly while they waited and Tenmen made to help support him. "Don't!" he snapped a bit more harshly than he had meant. "Sorry," he apologized, "None may so much as touch me, even a kind word of support could render all that I am about to do, void!" he warned, finding a boulder to rest against.

Adachi nodded in understanding. "You, go back and warn the others that they are not to make a sound or offer any aid at all. To do so could damn us all!" he ordered another of the men that had come with them.

"Understood," he agreed and left. Minutes later both of them returned at the head of the column.

Mick stood straight and put on the best poker face he could manage given what was about to happen and the fear that was eating away at his heart and resolve. *Be okay Ai. Lord, keep her!* "Quickly. Bring them forwards in groups of five!" The two leaders quickly set about dividing them into groups and ushering them forwards where, as per Talbot's orders, they could see what happened but hadn't passed him yet. With a final calming breath to still his mind, he readied the dagger over the top of his left arm. There weren't nearly as many veins there and there was a decent amount of space. He'd already decided that if he was going to bear these scars and the memory of this day, he would make sure that it meant something. Starting with the cuts that he had already made; he carved several more characters. The next group came. He carved glyphs. The next, Runes. And so on. Each was different and unique, but each held some meaning to him. Somewhere after the first forty cuts, he lost track of his pain and allowed the searing memories of the dagger to simply wash over him. Word spread fast and the others had been told what was at stake and why. None hesitated as they approached and they did so in silence, but their eyes spoke of their regret and tears glistened in many of their eyes, but a burning loyalty, thanks, and the flames of vengeance burned in them also. *Fight for them and they will thank you, but bleed for them and they will follow you into the darkest abysses.*

Mick's hand shook as he finished a diagonal down stroke over his heart. One last death washed over him, but this one was different, because he knew part of it now and it was clear and filled with just as much love as it was pain. The dagger had plunged home through a black guard, slicing a hole in a woman's heart. Her eyes locked on a man as she shouted for him to run. A man who Mick also knew from the memories of those that came before. Another who had journeyed to Japan long ago. Apparently, that was a rather common hobby of Night users, though it apparently rarely ended well for them. The lady's eyes turned back to her attacker. Talbot. *"You may have beaten me, but your day will come Talbot. The day when my descendants end your reign. Till the coming of that day, you shall stay with me!"* The lady swore. Smiling at the snarls of rage passing over Talbot as Night seeped away from holding back the dagger, allowing it to plunge home, but in that same instant encapsulating her and Talbot. Before the light died in her eyes, the seal completed, and Night consumed her to complete the sealing, he saw the bundle of cloth clutched close to the man's chest, the tears in his eyes, and felt Night's and the lady's determination to protect all that she held dear.

He staggered and almost collapsed; his task complete. Tenmen, who had looked away in horror took a hesitant step in his direction before stopping, remembering the warning that Mick had given him. Taking a raspy breath, he steadied on his feet and straightened, cracking wounds that had begun to clot closed back open to weep anemically. There wasn't much blood left to lose at this point. He paid it little heed. If he wasn't in time to save Ai, then nothing really mattered. "We run!" he ordered, draining his water bottle. It wouldn't help much, but it was something.

Adachi opened and closed his mouth like a fish out of water, as arguments formed and died before reaching his lips. With an angry snarl, he rounded on the others, orders flying, "You heard the man. We move as fast as we can!" He made slight changes, at his own discretion, that would let them move faster. *Fate chooses those that will change the fates of many, but for a few it seems to think that they are a one stop shop for all of its needs. Me and Fate are going to have a long talk one of these days and Fate sure ain't going to get the final say.*

"It's suicide you know?" Tenmen argued in a whisper. "We can't afford to lose him!"

Mick snarled as he turned on Tenmen. "Run! If this day I die for love, then so be it. Better to die for love than live without it. If you try to stand in my way, or try to slow me down, I will cut you down!" he promised, and the fire in his eyes and the rivers of blood running over him left little doubt in any of their minds as to his commitment to do what was needed. Tenmen took a step back as he saw the truth of the threat in Mick's eyes.

Without another word, Mick took a step towards the exit. He stumbled but kept his feet until he tried to take another and fell to a knee.

"It's impossible!" Tenmen argued.

Mick gritted his teeth and forced himself back to his feet. Without pause he took one step, and then another. And another. And another, gaining speed with every stride while blood fell like rain from his ruined flesh. The others moved to the side making way for him and being careful not to touch him or do anything to slow him.

Tenmen watched after Mick as he got further away and continued gaining speed. "Madness," he proclaimed.

Adachi smiled at him and shook his head. "The most amazing madness of all. Love. There is no force or power greater than Love. He'd already be dead if it wasn't for the love driving him. It isn't for us to judge. All we can do now is clear the path and guide him," he said, patting Tenmen on the back. "And, we'd best hurry. He seems to be building up quite the head of steam."

"Madness," Tenmen repeated, shaking his head and taking off after Mick.

Price of Love
Thursday, July 15

The world was growing dark and the wind was howling in his ears when he finally exited the tunnel into a crowded chamber filled with thousands from both the village and the town who had escaped the attack. A panting Adachi and Tenmen soon joined him. Upon noticing his arrival several people started forwards with demands and reports, but all of them fell silent in horror as they drew close enough to see his condition.

"Where is Ai?!" Mick demanded, searching the crowd.

Sen burst through the crowd but recoiled like the rest as soon as he saw the torn tapestry carved into Mick's flesh. His eyes shot to Adachi and Tenmen accusingly. "Why do you not aid him!?"

They started to answer, but Mick stepped forwards, grabbing Sen by the collar with his bloody hands and shook him until he was paying attention. "Take me to Ai now! There is no time to lose!" he demanded with a force of will that shook the air and made the cathedral fall silent as his presence washed over them all.

Sen's eyes tore away from the horrid tapestry and finally focused on Mick's eyes. Whatever arguments or complaints that he may have had died as their eyes met. "This way," he mumbled, recoiling in shock at what he had seen buried just beneath the surface in Mick's eyes. A beast like none that he had ever seen before. A creature of destruction unending. A wrath like no other. And it was almost free of the chains which bound it. Chains of honor, duty, faith, and above all else; Love. *If Ai dies, I must kill him. Even if it costs me my life. The world wouldn't survive or sate his wrath.*

Sen led Mick to a small alcove covered by a sheet and ushered him in. Ai was laying on a cot inside.

Reigi stood from the chair at Ai's bedside, turning to face them. He took in Mick's wounds at a glance but didn't comment on them. "I'm glad that you could make it," he said, laying his hand on Mick's shoulder but quickly jerked it back as pain tore through it. When he looked at it, he was shocked to see that all of the areas that had made contact with Mick had had layers of skin stripped away. He didn't have time to worry about what had just happened and he trusted Mick enough to know that whatever had happened wasn't intentional. "She wanted to see you before it was too late," he lamented, stepping to the side so that Mick could move next to her. He was careful not to make any further contact with him.

Mick moved forwards without a word and flung back Ai's blankets, revealing her and the wound.

"What are you doing!?" Reigi shouted, angrily moving forwards. An axe blade materialized against his throat, halting his advance.

"Everyone get out! Now!" Mick ordered, sparing them a single glance. With a slight hesitation, they all moved to leave. "Adachi," he whispered.

Adachi stopped, turning to face him. "Yah?"

"If I try to leave this room and Ai isn't with me, don't hesitate" Mick said, catching Adachi's eye before turning back to Ai. "Make sure that no one disturbs us!"

"You got it," Adachi promised, letting the sheet fall back closed.

Tenmen moved up next to Adachi and Sen who stoically took up position a few meters in front and to the side of the tent's entrance. "What did he mean?" he asked, looking between the two of them.

"Exactly what he said," Sen answered for Adachi. They had never been friends, but they had known each other for a very long time. "Go with your men and make sure that no one comes closer than twenty meters of here."

"Is there going to be trouble?" Tenmen asked softly.

"Pray that there isn't!" Sen warned and made a shooing motion.

"If the time comes, I'll need you to hold him for half a second," Adachi whispered to Sen.

"I'll hold him!" Sen promised, a grim set on his face.

"Good. In the meantime, I'll be praying that, Ai, walks out first!" Adachi said, matching Sen's scowl.

"I think I'll join you!"

With the others gone, Mick moved over to Ai, kneeling at her side and taking her hand while he checked her condition. She was still breathing, but her pulse was week and her skin was cold and clammy. The wound was small, little more than a nick on her left calf, but it was like a malignant seed taking root and devouring her life to sustain itself and spread. The malignant tool that had made it was called a Weeping Blade, not because of the wound that they created, but because so often the victim of them returned home victorious and hail only to suddenly die in the arms of those that loved them and had just been filled with relief at their safe return. They were weapons of terror and cowardice. That a member of the Order would stoop to using it boded ill for the moral foundation of the Order. Apparently, Death Helm was not the only concession that they had made. *I fear what other depredations they have embraced. These are not the tools of the Order. From where do they sprout? Few in the order knew or would have deigned to learn these methods. They were beneath their honor. So, what has changed and just what or who is the source of this corruption? Enough time to figure that out later and plant a blade in their heart. Now, I'm busy. You think about it.*

"Got it. So..."

Mick scowled. Weeping wounds were supposed to be incurable. The only treatment was to immediately cut off or out the affected area, but since you didn't usually know that you had faced a Weeping Blade until the signs set in, it was almost always too late by that point. Ai was definitely too far past that point. The tendrils were already entwining her heart. Which left only one option. With

Night, the incurable was curable. *If I have enough blood left.* He would have to control Night in a transfusion of his own blood and hunt down all traces of the blight that was devouring her. It was risky for both of them. Mick would have to maintain control and consciousness throughout the whole process or else Night could run amok and cause terrible damage to her. It really didn't like interacting with others. It was a daunting task considering that the Weeping Blight had already spread to her heart. To hunt it all down would probably take more than a day during which he couldn't sleep or stop for anything, including tending to his own wounds. Given the dangers involved, no distraction could be allowed, and if he failed, it would be because he had ran completely out of strength and life and he feared for those that would face Night's rampage as it sought to preserve itself through any means necessary. *Enough! There is no time for fear.*

He took a deep breath and quickly gathered what he would need from the scattered medical supplies around the room. He quickly stripped off his shirt and bound the worst of his cuts in gauze and started a fluid drip in his arm before sitting down in the chair besides Ai. It didn't take him long to find a good vein and he soon had a transfusion set up between them. The blight, tempted by new resources, immediately chased her blood towards him and tried to take root. Night was there to block its advance and hold it back on his left arm while from his right arm, black blood coursed out of him, making him lightheaded and almost pass out. It poured into Ai and spread, hunting and destroying the blight and all other maladies it encountered as it flushed her system. It strained at his control as he forced it forwards, sweeping outward through her body from the needle which he had inserted into her left arm. It was almost too much but he somehow managed to maintain his consciousness as the toll on his control kept increasing with every millimeter further away that it got. "Hang in there!" he whispered.

***

Time dragged on and the battle waged unending; every minute was an hour and every hour a week. Time stood still as Mick continued to work, losing himself in the nanoscopic battle for Ai's life and his own. Her condition was improving as vitality returned to her, washing away the dull white of death that had hung over her and returning her skin to its rosy tan. Her pulse and breathing were also steadily growing stronger. It was a good sign, but while it meant that she was getting better, it also increased the danger and demand on him as the Weeping Blight surged under the sudden return of pressure in her systems and the vitality upon which to gorge. It battered against his advance as he encircled it and drove it back towards the wound where it had first entered her. To make matters worse, while Ai's vitality gained, his was waning fast. His skin was desiccating as blood that should have been bringing life and moisture to it drained away to join the battle. His dehydration and anemia were starving his body and mind of everything which it needed to function and survive. And Night, fought against his control, seeking to preserve him through any means necessary. It had already stripped every ounce of fat from him and was starting to now devour other, less vital, parts of him to keep them alive. He was dying and his consciousness was going fast. If he lost control, Night would do anything to save them, including using the one that he loved as a resource to restore them. He couldn't let that happen. He would live, but it would destroy him.

"Don't stop!" A voice that Mick knew well but couldn't remember yelled. It was a voice that couldn't be.

"I won't. But I have nothing left. Even my life won't suffice at this point!" Mick lamented, feeling his heart begin to still. Bump, Bump.. Bump... Bum...... The air flowed out of his lungs, as all of the tension in his body flowed away and didn't come back again. His vision

contracting down to a pin prick, locked on Ai's face. *I'm so, so sorry!* He lamented, feeling a single tear, all the moisture that was left in him, gently roll down his cheek. Even in death, he could feel the gleeful surge as Night stilled in its advance and the Weeping Blight sensed its chance to surge. It rallied and hit his defenses and his attack. Tearing deeply into both.

"No!" A howl of defiance roared. *"You don't get to die yet. There is still much for you to do!"* Mick felt a warmth from somewhere else envelop him, almost seeming to massage life back into his heart.

Bump. The Weeping Blight faltered. Bump. The defense crushed it back. BUMP. His faltered and fractured attack re-coalesced. BUMP, BUMP. It raced forwards, scouring the Blight away in-front of it; all the way back to the initial wound and driving away all traces of not just the Weeping Blight, but all impurities and regenerating all damage, both new and old that had come to Ai.

Mick gasped as Night and all of the energy and vitality that it contained, flooded back into his body. His collapsed veins burst back open as blood, oxygen, and moisture quenched his tortured flesh. The force of the backwash was so great that both IV's popped free, still the remaining Night in her system leapt from the hole which the needles had made. It was all too much. The last thing he saw was Ai's eyes fluttering open. He smiled as his head rolled to the side. The relief was just too much. Just before the world went dark and he fell over out of the chair and onto the ground, he thought he saw a bone white crystal retracting back into the dirt at his feet.

"Mick!? Help!" Ai shouted, struggling to sit up and go to him, but lacking even the energy to lift her arms.

Mick vaguely heard feet rushing towards him as he slipped into the darkness. *I hope Adachi and Sen don't try to kill me while I'm asleep.*

Rebound
Wednesday, July 21

The creak of wood and the bouncing sound of tires rolling over earth woke Mick. It was dark when he opened his eyes. There were trees above him, and he could make out shapes moving around him. He tried to move, but his chest and arms screamed in pain at the slightest movement. He still couldn't move, but he could watch and listen.

"Quiet and keep the shielding up! We can't afford being seen and them calling in their aircraft," Sen whispered a warning from somewhere nearby.

"They can't have many of them left!" Setsuna whispered back, his tone making his disdain for their aircraft and the idea that they had any superiority in the air as clear as a cloudless winter night. "Between maintenance and losses, they just can't! They may have bloodied me and mine on that first day, but we gave just as good as we got and have recouped most of our losses with newcomers."

"Yes, but it would only take one to blow this whole operation. Even if we could drive it off without losses, they would know where to start looking for us when they finally get around to it," Sen pointed out. "With all of our dependents there, we can't afford that. "The Last Valley may be hidden from sight, but if they know where to start looking, they can find us."

"You're both right!" Adachi cut in, exasperation and exhaustion rasping his voice. "If they catch us moving, they will find us again," he nodded to Sen, "but if we are still out here by the time the sun comes up because we are spending too much time arguing and not enough walking, that will happen anyways," he added, scolding them both with a glare as they started beaming. "We need to move faster. Pull back in the pickets and guards and have them help the porters.

If there is anything to run into out there, it is already too late!" With a grumble, the others set about following his orders. He shook his head and stopped cold as he caught Mick's eyes. "I hope that is you Mick?" he questioned, leery and taking a step back. Just in case it wasn't, his hand had already found the hilt of his weapon.

"It's chained," Mick managed to whisper after several tries to get anything past his parched vocal chords.

Adachi nodded, apparently taking Mick's word for it, and walked over. "That's good to hear. You gave us all a bit of a scare. Night is just a might bit overprotective. Ai was the only one that it would allow near you, but she wasn't strong enough yet to move you when it became apparent that we had to move," he explained, taking a slightly choked breath. "Thank you for saving her. The Doctors still don't have any idea what it was or how they could have treated it. If you hadn't... Well, thank you," he feigned a cough to hide wiping his eyes. "Well anyways, getting you up in this cart was a real hassle. Lots of padded ropes and thick blankets were involved and a few sissy Tengu who were muttering about 'diet plans.'"

Mick chuckled at the thought. Even after shedding all of his fat and an unhealthy amount of muscle, he was still a big guy. "Oww," he moaned, as his sore chest ached, threatening to send him into a coughing spell that would hurt even worse. Night was great with the repairs when it had the energy to do them, but recovery and breaking in the affected areas still took its time. "I'll take that under advisement," he assured, managing to shift a little up onto his elbows so that he could look around. "What I would like to know is: What's happened? Where are we going? And, how many days was I out this time?" He tried not to roll his eyes at that last one. *Seems like that is all that I'm doing these days.* "But most important, how and where is Ai?!" he asked, his voice filled with love and iron determination to see her as soon as possible and confirm with his own eyes that she was really okay. After that, he was going to have to figure out how to make sure that she was safe and any door jam or corner that even thought of stubbing her toes had better be prepared to face his wrath.

Adachi scratched his head nervously. "It okay if I go in order? I think you'll appreciate the situation better then." Mick nodded. "So, we made it to the cave where the town and villagers were to gather in case everything went sideways. I think we can all agree that things didn't just go sideways, they were downright upside-down and doing spirals down the drain of a twenty-four carat Dimond bedazzled porcelain throne. You went in with Ai and we didn't hear a peep for thirty-six hours. We were getting ready to storm the room and find you both dead when Ai called out for help. We thought it was the worst and came in ready to do as you had asked, but instead we found Ai all hail except for being tired and you passed out and looking both invigorated and dead at the same time. Very vogue zombie. We tried to move to help you, but Night kept lashing out at anyone but Ai who got near you. We tried anyways," he winced. "Night can be rather prickly," he observed, rubbing a sore hand where Night had sent a needle clean through his palm. Thankfully it had been thin and had passed through cleanly. Except for being sore and smarting something fierce, it hadn't caused any real damage. "It rather pointedly made its pointed point."

"Ouch," Mick winced. "Sorry about that."

"Don't be. It was how we knew that things were actually okay. It was all defense and no attack. More like an overly protective guard dog," Adachi assured. He chose not to mention the way it had reacted when someone, Tenmen, figuring that if it acted that way then maybe they should treat it that way, had attempted to distract it with a steak. There was a slight thunk in the side of the wagon. He looked down to see a needle sticking through the outside of the wagon. The inky blackness quickly formed a picture of a dog and then put a slash through it before withdrawing. Mick hadn't noticed. "Guard..." another tendril extended his way. "Maybe partner would be closer," it withdrew. "Anyways. With you in your condition, us still reorganizing, and tending to the wounded; we were stuck. We fortified and guarded the entrances and set in to licking our wounds, but we couldn't keep eyes on what was going on in the valley and with the Crystal in particular. It was just too risky. Given how battered we were and the need to protect our families, we couldn't risk detection and them finding the rest of us in the cave. So, we hunkered down and waited. They left us alone until yesterday. Then one of the crows that had been sneaking reports into us stopped showing up. Then another. Then none. Even the ravens bugged out. Not long after that one of ours that we had thought dead stumbled in. He was bloody and beat up. He said that he had been knocked out and captured during the battle and he hadn't been the only one. There had been six others. They had come to them that morning with an offer. Carry a message for them in exchange for their freedom. Only catch was that they only needed one messenger. They could choose or when they came back in a half-hour, they would choose for them. They left two daggers in the mud between them," Adachi said, his eyes burning with a special kind of hate. "The message was simple, they 'generously offered' us a chance to surrender and yield to their supervision and administration or be exterminated. The messenger died shortly thereafter. Apparently, they had given them those cursed Weeping Blades for the culling," he spat. "I'm really getting tired of those things. Anyways, we knew that we had been found out, so we had to leave. No one wanted to accept their offer. So, we retreated further back into the tunnels and collapsed all of the known entrances. If we don't open them or they don't dig them out, the tunnels will reopen in time, they always do, but it bought us time. We fell back, using the lower tunnels, lost quite a few good people down there, but we managed to get outside their perimeter. Now we are moving over to another hidden village that we maintained as an outside training center. We can regroup there and plan how we are going to burn these thieves and murderers out," he finished, still seething but also not making eye contact.

"What aren't you telling me?" Mick asked, worrying that Ai was in trouble. He started struggling to get up.

Adachi shook his head and gently waved him back down. "Ai is fine, so stop worrying. The messenger had a second message. One he didn't think that they meant for him to hear. I'm pretty sure it involves you. By the way, they know you are here."

"What did he hear?" Mick asked, relieved that Ai was okay.

"They said that one of the ships reported an intruder. When they tried to confront and capture them, they counter attacked and cut a bloody swath through the ship until they managed to steal a helicopter. They shot the helicopter down or it was set down, they weren't exactly sure which, about ten kilometers off the cost on a rocky outcropping. When they sent a search crew, they didn't find any bodies. He didn't hear much after that, except a name. They were swearing about 'that Renalds she devil,'" Adachi answered, watching Mick carefully.

Aliya is alive. She's the only one it could be. Mick felt a weight lift off his chest for the first time since he had heard that his family was gone. If Aliya was still alive, then anything was possible. If she was still alive then the truth was that chance hadn't beset his family but that it had been the Order who had tried to eliminate them, which made more sense than that they were caught in the disaster. And with Aliya knowing that and on the loose, then the whole Order was already destined to die. Aliya was their greatest blade and strongest shield. Their folly would have removed any qualms she may have harbored and now she would be hunting for their heads. The only question was; why had she come here? "You thought right. It would seem that we now have at least one more ally. Any idea where the helicopter went down?" he asked, hopeful that it was close.

"Most we could gather was that it was somewhere off the Pacific coast of Hokkaido. Given all of the changes that have happened, we aren't really sure where that exactly is anymore," Adachi pointed out, reminding him that their little corner of Japan was but a small piece of the whole and they were really lacking Intel in that department. It was understandable given their situation, but their continued existence depended on them learning just what they faced and the situation in the world at large. *Our very own Renalds is scary enough and given how he seems to regard his sister; I'd hate to have ticked her off. With two of them, we might just stand a chance.*

Well, at least she is okay. If they didn't find the body, then out-there somewhere, she is still alive. I doubt that any of them will be sleeping peacefully from now on. "Good. If we don't know then they definitely don't. Keep an ear out though and send the word to those you trust that Aliya Renalds has come, that she is to be trusted, and don't mess with or tickle her unless you want to windup dead or with at least broken ribs. Oh, and no one had better comment on her height," Mick warned, his face going white at some old memory.

"I'll be sure to do that," Adachi promised, his curiosity piqued. "For now, you just relax and heal back up. This is the last group and we should reach the valley in another three hours. It will be close, but we should be under the barrier before sunup. Although you'll be needing all the rest you can get." There was a wicked twinkle in his eye that just screamed trouble, but he didn't offer any further information and Mick knew pressing would be a lost cause.

"Right. Then we should be about that. But if we aren't, then we will just have to be about taking our enemies heads a little sooner than we had planned," Mick growled, grinning to hide his grinding teeth as he forced himself up into a sitting position. His chest and arms burned as the taut new scar tissue was forced to stretch out.

"I've been asleep more than I have been awake ever since I came to Japan. I don't know about you, but that doesn't seem like a good way to enjoy one's time in a foreign country. I've had enough sleep and not enough fun. I think it is high time we had some fun! Wouldn't you agree, Sargent Major!?" he asked, giving Adachi a promotion at the same time.

Adachi's frown turned into a smile as he listened, and he noticed the little grins and whispers spreading around them. "I couldn't agree more, Sir. What did you have in mind?"

Mick smiled and nodded as the whisper spread, shoulders squared, and the people around him stepped off with a purpose. He knew that he should rest but it was time to get back in the game. Careful not to make a fool out of himself by falling flat on his face, although that probably would have been humorous in the moment but not great for long-term morale, he gingerly hopped out of the wagon and joined Adachi on foot. His body ached all over and screamed at him in lurid ways about the stupidity of false bravado, but he paid it no heed and grinned through it. Being sure to stand straight and let them all see that he was back.

Those that remained had all heard what he had done for them, and none blamed him for the misfortune of the last battle. There was only so much you could do when you all of the sudden found yourself in battle against a completely different foe than you had taken the field to face and he started raining death on you from above. No, they thanked him for what he had done after that and the sacrifice that he had made to save their friends and family. They would fight for him wherever he stood.

***

They reached the village just before the Dawn Sun kissed the horizon. They were tired from the hard march and all of their nerves were a touch frayed from constantly worrying about being detected, but they were more alive than they had been since they were routed. Mick had been mingling; helping where he could and making friendly banter wherever he went. He had started the day sore and tired and by the time they entered the village, he was exhausted and ready to drop, but he kept up the show. He doubted that he was really fooling anyone, but even if it was forced, it did them good to see him.

Ai found him while he was helping unload a cart of books and important documents that had been hidden before the battle. Knowledge was the most powerful weapon in this kind of war or for that matter in any war and they had gone to great lengths to ensure that they hadn't been forced to lose any of it that they had acquired over the eons. So, given his distracted and weary state, she had had no problem sneaking up on him and jumped onto his back before he knew what was happening. As he struggled against whoever or whatever had suddenly accosted him, to the laughter of all those around them, she swung around to his front as he reached back to dislodge her and gave him a long kiss as she hung from his neck. The laughter descended into zealous cat calls and bawdy shouts. She finally broke contact with a flourish, leaning back so she could see him properly. He was smiling ear to ear but the twinkle in his eyes was slightly dimmed by the pains of his injuries.

"It took you long enough!" Ai stated, giving him the most accusing glare that she could manage while smiling.

Mick smiled even wider. "I was inconsiderately delayed by events beyond my control," he defended with a sniffle.

"More like because you are apparently a magnet for trouble and an idle layabout. But, given the circumstances, I will forgive you," Ai said, serious, despite the melodrama.

"I am forever in your debt and shall endeavor to rise above my shortcomings," Mick apologized, equally serious. There were tears welling in her eyes, washing away her usually stoic shield and revealing her vulnerability. Mick was hard pressed not to wrap her up in his arms and brush her hair while he cradled her head against his shoulder. He was just about to do just that when she slid off of him, catching his left hand, and slid a ring onto his finger.

"Before God and all those present, I take Mick as my husband for all time. Any who would challenge; let them speak now or face my wrath later!" Ai stated into the sudden silence as everything around them and in the whole valley it seemed, came to an abrupt halt. No one so much as whispered. Even the cicadas had fallen silent. "Good!" There had been little doubt that anyone would try anything after everything that had happened, but tradition demanded that the chance be given.

Adachi walked up behind Mick and nudged his elbow until he turned and held out a ring. His eyes were sparkling with mischief that would have made Oliver look downright respectable in comparison. "She didn't want to wait, and it seemed like a good idea not to argue with her to the rest of us," he explained with a sheepish shrug that looked far too much at home on the old wolf.

"I guess I know what you'll be dressing up as for Halloween," Mick muttered, under his breath and took the ring and glared out into the blinding grins of all those around them. It was clear that they were all thick as thieves, the conniving lot of them. "That's right, smile while you can because I'll remember this you bunch of hooligans." He shook his fist at them all in mock fury to which they simply laughed. He let them go with a warning and turned his attention back to Ai and the ring that seemed to weigh as much as the world in his hand. It was a simple yet brilliant piece of work that's simple beauty and exquisite craftsmanship almost matched Ai's own. It was a triple braid of silver, gold, and black gold rope with two diamonds mounted in the gap where the tails of the braids met.

Careful not to make a fool of himself by dropping it, he kept a firm grip on it as he rolled Ai's hand over and faced her as he slid the ring onto her hand. "Before God and all those present, I take Ai as my wife for all time. None shall ever part us," he swore. Ai nodded and without warning or further word, he swept her up in his arms and thoroughly kissed her.

"Good!" Ai declared as the burning in their lungs finally forced them to come up for air and he set her back down on her slightly wobbly legs. She shot those gathered a glare as they clapped and continued with their chuckles and catcalls. "We will see you all later. In the meantime, get back to work! No rest for the weary or the wicked!" she ordered, already dragging Mick off like a prize-winning bull.

Mick started to debate arguing that they didn't have time and should stay to help finish but a glance from Adachi and the puppy like will with which his body followed Ai killed it. Choosing wisdom over valor, he gave in and fell in besides her so that it at least didn't look like she was leading him along by the hand as they walked side by side through the village. There was the occasional clap or whistle as they went, but he paid them little attention. At the moment, all of his mind was focused on his heart's desire.

He knew his cheeks were cherry pink and he smiled as he glanced to the side and saw that Ai's cheeks and ears were even redder. For that matter, she was so flustered that both sets of her ears were showing. She looked rather cute and he was hard pressed not to reach over and pet one of them. "How long do we have?" he asked, innocently.

Ai's cheeks got a little redder. "On threat of flogging by the whole village, they have arranged for no one to disturb us for two nights, including tonight," she frowned. *Would a whole week really have been too much to ask for!? And maybe a sandy beach and some of those drinks with the little umbrellas?*

That is more than I'd hoped for given the current situation. I wish I could give her the time that she really deserves. "We will have to make the most of it," Mick said, letting a mischievous smirk creep onto his face.

Ai started to fulminate until she saw his grin and she gave a little yelp as he pinched he bums. Her head snapped back around, looking directly forwards and she tried not to lick her lips. "You're going to pay for that later mister!"

"Oh, I look forward to it."

Maybe two days will be enough after all.

They continued out of the town and past the outlying houses and farms until they entered the woods. Mick had no idea where they were going but given the company and situation in which he found himself, he was more than willing to follow along and be patient. For a little longer at least. His knowledge of Wolf marriage traditions was a little lacking and even more so where Japanese Yokai, especially those considered extinct, were concerned.

I really need to hit the books. A helpful Onmyouji would be appreciated also. So far, my western knowledge has worked okay, but I get the feeling that that is only because I have been able to use it where weaker opponents are concerned. Soon, I will need all the knowledge and tools that I can get. Right, and that is what you should really be thinking about right now. He chided himself, giving the metronome swaying of Ai's hips an appreciative glance which was more than enough to lead him down several tantalizing rabbit holes. *I wonder...* His train of thoughts cutoff as they exited the dark, dense woods and entered a small glen. In his excitement, he really couldn't say how far they had walked, but by the sun, they had been at it for a couple of hours.

Surrounded on all sides by towering trees, with a small stream running through the middle of a green meadow filled with wildflowers of every color, was... home. That was the only term that fit it. Mick heart leapt and felt calm at the same time seeing the quaint and calm home sitting off to one side of the meadow on a small knoll. There was a small garden next to it, filled with every vegetable that he could ever want and a nicely kept yard area with a grand old cherry tree with a bench under it. The home was undeniably Japanese, yet he could also see the western influences in its design. There was a traditional wrap around porch with sliding doors opening onto it and what looked to be an open floor plan. On the western side, there were also two flagstone chimneys protruding from the rooftop. One almost in the middle and another off to the side. As they approached and worked their way around to the other side, he also caught sight of what looked to be an Onsen style bath attached to the left side porch that overlooked the creek and meadow. It had a roof and detachable shutters so that you could enjoy the view on nice days and close it up on bad ones. There was a small stream of steaming water leaving it that piped over to join with the creek which meant that it was probably fed by a real hot spring.

Ai stopped, pulling him to an abrupt halt. She fidgeted for a moment. *We are finally here.* "Do you like it?" she asked hopefully, looking up at Mick. "Are you okay?" she asked, startled by the tears gently rolling down his cheeks. She reached up to wipe them away, but never got the chance as Mick plucked her up and into his arms in a tight hug.

"Thank you," Mick managed after a moment. The sudden upwelling of emotions that had overcome him as everything that had happened became real in that moment abated.

"You're welcome," Ai said, smiling now that she knew that he was happy and giving him a peck on the lips. "So, are you going to put me down so we can go inside?" she asked, her eyes sparkling with wonder and mischievousness.

Mick gave her a smile to match. "Nope," he said, scooping up her dangling legs and marching towards the house, while Ai wiggled against his chest.

"What do you want to do first?" Ai asked as they walked in.

Mick just smiled and kept walking.

Ai looked around, trying to figure out where he was taking her. *He's never been here before so where does he think he's going?* She glanced at his grin and then looked ahead. The Bath. "Oh," she said, demurely with a wicked twinkle in her eyes.

Mick returned it and his own only grew wider as she became confused as he continued past the changing area and right up to the deep, full tub. It was indeed being continuously filled from a hot water spring that rose up in a stone pipe in the corner and washed down into the tub.

"You're not thinking of..." Ai started as Mick stepped down into the tub, soaking them and their clothes. Ai tried to be incredulous, but it only came out as a spurt of giggles as she clung against him. "You are a bad influence!"

Mick grinned back. "We'll see just how bad," he warned, pulling her into a kiss.

Awoooo
Thursday, July 22

Mick woke feeling rested and whole for the first time in longer than he could remember. He'd never realized that something was missing until the hole in his heart had been plugged. All thanks to the warm person now sleeping peacefully snuggled up against his side and using his shoulder as a pillow. She had her left arm and leg draped over him possessively and he was in no hurry to move and disturb her and just laid there contentedly, watching her peaceful sleeping face and the gentle rise and fall of her slender back with each breath. *Marriage really is a gift from God! And wow, did he ever pick a lady that matched up with me.*

He smirked at the memory of the last night and day, while doing his best to control himself. It wasn't easy. Thanks to the mountains and the small creek, the house stayed cool, even now at the height of summer, and the nights even tended to get chilly but still only required a light blanket, that had thankfully shifted off of them sometime that morning, and someone warm to snuggle with. Not that they had needed any extra incentive to snuggle close, but it hadn't hurt.

A strand of her hair tumbled down, tickling her ear and he reached over to brush it aside. Ai opened her eyes in a flutter and rose up provocatively smiling. "Don't even..."

Ai pounced before he could guard.

Mick looked around the kitchen. Ai was over by the table in nothing but a shirt nibbling on a piece of toast slathered in Nutella and sipping some tea while he worked on making a proper breakfast. Waffles with a side of country fried chicken and gravy were the order of the day and he was content to let her relax while he cooked. She'd offered to help but, on this morning, it just felt right for him to prepare the meal. He was rather impressed by the amount and varieties of ingredients that were available. Unfortunately, with the current state of the world, it was likely that many of those ingredients were probably not going to be readily available anymore.

Ai looked up as Mick swept over and quickly laid down an array of containers with different condiments and four plates, he'd been considerate enough to put the chicken and gravy on a different plate than the waffles. He sat down next to her, sliding his chair close enough that their elbows were almost bumping and looked rather proud of the fruits of his labor.

"Don't think that you can butter me up that easily, Buster," Ai warned. Mick smiled, putting on the most innocent look that he could manage, but didn't deny that that had been his intention. Still leery of what he might be up to, she dug in with a gusto as her world exploded in a mix of flavors and textures unlike any she had ever eaten before. She was no slouch in the kitchen, but this was in a league of its own. "That was really good," she admitted, patting her belly contentedly after wiping up the last traces of flavor with a bite of toast.

"I aim to please," he said, mischievously and offered her the last bite of his waffle. She eyed it and him suspiciously, but they were really good waffles. She gave up and gingerly took the bite, keeping her eyes locked on his the whole time. He shifted a little as she sat back. "Feeling a little buttered up?" he asked, setting his fork aside.

"You really think I am that easy?" Ai theatrically huffed, sitting back and crossing her arms in front of her which did anything but diminish her attractiveness.

"It certainly seemed that way yesterday," Mick countered, arching an eyebrow at her.

Ai scoffed at him. "You sir are incorrigible!"

Mick just smiled, leaning forward and trapping her against her chair as he set his hand on the back rest. "So," he whispered into her ear.

***

Mick sat with his feet in the cool stream that ran by the house, relaxing and taking a break after the activities of the last night and morning. It had come as a pleasant surprise that one of the rooms in their humble abode was a library. It was fully stocked with a rather eclectic assortment of books in several languages and according to Ai, it was alive and infinite. If something had ever been written or printed on parchment, paper, tablet, or stone; if you simply knew what to ask for, the library could call it forth. Unfortunately, it didn't do digital and conversations, unless they had been annotated. Personal memos and orders were also unfortunately hard to access unless you knew exactly what to ask for and if you already knew that, you really didn't need it. If you were just in a browsing mood, it also accepted genres. For the moment, it had provided him with a new release by David Weber.

Ai had been playfully miffed when she had found him in the library instead of chasing after her. Her exact remark was "You recently married a rather striking, nubile, and willing lady and yet here you are in the infinite library pursuing dusty old books. A less understanding lady might take offence." She'd relented when he'd turned his puppy dog eyes and quivering lip on her. She'd given up with a theatrical huff and proceeded to pull three books with rather interesting title pages from the shelf and wandered off somewhere. Mick had then discovered that the library didn't accept requests like "I want the same book as her." Apparently, it had a single copy at a time check-out policy also. He was still a little curious as to what she had checked out. Really, he should have been using the library and time to research and learn, but at the moment, he just needed some time to decompress and clear his head space.

Mick's eyes flickered away from the worlds of words as he caught movement in the tree line. There was more than one thing out there and he calmly shifted his axes, loosening them in their sheaths at the same time. He may have been on his honeymoon but that didn't mean that he was about to let his guard down for anyone but Ai. Whoever these jokers were, they had better have a good reason for bothering them and ruining the mood.

He was careful not to stare or make any real sign that he had noticed the others presence yet. People and things tended to be less cautious when they thought that they had surprised you. This was supposed to be a safe place and if their enemies had found them here, then they were probably already in big trouble. *If they are friendly, they had best have a good reason to be here and if they aren't, they are going to regret the day that they interrupted Ai's honeymoon.* He watched out of the corner of his eye as the movement consolidated, hiding in the shadows and brush at the tree line. *I guess Ai is going to be able to get some of her mad out.*

After several minutes, three Knights and a fourth man, not a Knight of the Order but a soldier by the looks of him and his uniform. The only peculiarity was that the soldier was armed with an advanced looking blocky rifle, which Mick wasn't familiar with. Clashing with the modern, he was also packing a standard looking 1911 and a well-used Cutlass which looked to be U.S Patent hanging at his side. It was a rather odd combination but was rather sensible when you were considering facing things of the Fair. *The military really doesn't ever throw anything away.*

He stayed seated as they made their way forwards but kept an eye on the other shapes fanning out in the trees behind them. They stopped on the other side of the small bridge that crossed the creek. It wasn't a big creek, but it was deep and rocky and would be treacherous in armor. On the other hand, the Para-Marine wearing a scowl of annoyance that was with them probably could have waded across it with little difficulty. He also didn't seem to be in a good mood. *I wonder if it is the orders, the leadership, the tactics that have him so annoyed, or because he has a grudge against me. Something to look into if I ever get a chance to talk to one of them alone and they aren't actively trying to kill me or mine.*

The Knights stood there for a few minutes as Mick continued reading his book and ignoring them. Finally, one of the Knights got tired of waiting for him to acknowledge them and took a step to cross the bridge. Before his foot could land, a pebble shattered against the man's helmet, staggering him backwards and eliciting a snarl of pain as a few chards found their way through kinks in his face guard. The marine's face slipped into a grin while one of the others helped steady their comrade and the other one reached for his sword and covered the other two. There was a slight stirring in the tree line but that was it.

"Apparently, you soiled honorless hedge bandits masquerading as Knights have forgotten all common courtesy. I am sorry that you have been encumbered with the likes of them and made to wear their stains Gunny," Mick said, ignoring the Knights. *Never hurts to earn points with your enemy. They may someday become your ally. Especially if they have honor and the ones who command them don't.*

The corner of the Gunny's eyebrow twitched, betraying the faintest of smiles. "Orders," he commented. *As bad as these pampered princesses are, the piper still requires his due and the ticket for the west coast is steep! Most of the boys still blame him and command and their propaganda machine just keep feeding that fire. I can see why the Knights hate him though. He has style and honor on his side. I do wonder where those scars came from though? They weren't in the file on him or in any of his pictures and they still have a bit of pink newness to them. They look rather intentional, but I don't see him being the crazy cutter type nor letting the crazy cutter type carve him up like that. Wonder what the story is behind them? If I don't have to kill him, I may have to have a little chat with him before turning him over to the propaganda machine so they can grind him up for the public's consumption.*

Mick nodded in acknowledgement. *Too bad. Disgruntled, but honor bound, and he apparently has some bone to pick or at least doesn't want to get in the way of it.*

"And what would a traitor and an outcast know of honor!" the tallest Knight who was covering the other two demanded.

"Depends on who he betrayed and what he left, Kipper," Mick retorted, recognizing the voice, family crest, and the ward pattern of the Knight. "So, why don't you all state your names and your business here or shall we just skip the pleasantries and get down to the blood and guts?"

"You and your family always were an over inflated insolent bunch!" the Knight who had first advanced prattled. "Good riddance to the lot of you."

"Coming from a pampered princess like you Axel, I'll take that as a compliment, and I'll be sure to pass your views onto Aliya. I'm sure she will appreciate them and be eager to discuss them with you," Mick said, fishing a little. He knew he was right when they all stiffened, the Gunny included.

"Empty threats from an empty and family-less man," the remaining Knight boasted.

Mick simply shrugged. "Show me the bodies and maybe I will believe you. Until then, I am content knowing that they haunt your nightmares and lurk in every dark corner for you and the Fallen Order which you serve, Page," he said, smiling icily. "We all know that death doesn't take on the Thrice Dead Paladin. But I digress and I'm sure that there is plenty that goes bump in the night to occupy your fears already. Like clowns and pink poodles or better yet having to form an original thought. So, now that all three of you have failed to name yourselves and show any signs of common courtesy, what says we get down to the blood and guts," he challenged, climbing onto the bank and drawing his axes. He was a little surprised when that didn't draw any response from the men in the tree line.

"A barbarian's weapon for a barbarian I see. Fitting. But we came to talk," Page intervened, waving back the others.

"So, talk," Mick prodded, making no move to invite them over. *Were they always this arrogant? Yes.* He relaxed but didn't lower his guard.

"Surrender," Page ordered. "There is no hope for your defeating us and the end of your little band will be at hand shortly. They can hide all they want, but it is only a matter of time until we find them and destroy them. If you surrender, we will be content to execute only the leaders of your rabble. You we will hand over to the authorities to account for the destruction which you caused. As for the others which foolishly follow you, they may take the 'Mark of Servitude' and will be allowed to live.

Mick shook his head and the Gunny shifted his leg back and rotated his right shoulder forwards. *Just more proof of how far they have fallen.* The 'Mark of Servitude' was a brand of bondage. It gave those listed under the compact control over those who carried it. To disobey would mean debilitating pain or death if one of those who were made masters by it ordered. The cruelest part was that it allowed the master to subvert control of those who carried the brand. It had been outlawed as too corrupting over six-hundred years ago. *No person should ever have that kind of control.* "How very cliché. I see that the rot has truly reached the heart of the Order. See who you stand with and those that you serve Gunny. They condemn a man for being who he is and for stopping the destruction from truly consuming the world. All to sate their desire for power and control. For their greed and nothing more. Worse, they use the false guise of justice. The stains of blood which they spill will besmirch all of your honor into mud which you shall drown in," Mick warned. "Leave now. You have said your peace and neither I nor mine accept. When next we meet, blood will spill and it will be yours," Mick warned. "You all seem to fear Aliya for the force of nature which she is, yet you also seem to forget that in sparring, I never beat her once because she always fought to win by any means necessary, including injuring her opponent while I was content to learn. We're not sparing anymore!" Mick boasted, watching as they processed that. The Gunny was the only one who didn't seem to care.

"Very well. We came seeking a peaceful accord and instead were met with threats and boasts of an honorless and condemned man who would sacrifice the innocent so as to not face justice. On your head be the blood of those you doom!" Page said, pointing his sword at Mick.

Mick's eyes narrowed as he saw the runes carved on the blade. "When next we meet," he promised. They turned and started back for the trees, but the Gunny hesitated for a moment, glancing back and giving a nod before he followed after them.

As soon as they reached the trees, Mick fell back through the house gathering supplies as he went. He wasn't surprised when Ai met him at the back door with her own supplies and a pack for him.

"We have to warn the village!" Ai said, handing him the pack and helping get it adjusted. "Then we can make them pay for interrupting my honeymoon!" One look at the loathing and frustration in her eyes was enough to dissuade any argument over proper priorities.

"Yes, but we can't go back to the village. Somebody there is a traitor. That is the only way that they could have known our whereabouts," Mick explained.

"All the more reason why we must go!" Ai said, confused by his reluctance. "What?"

Mick sighed. "Whoever it is, they only told them where we are, and they don't want to be found. They were hoping that we would be captured or killed and then they could take over. Having the village found is the last thing that they want. They figured that once the Order had me, they wouldn't worry about cleaning up the loose ends. The fact that the Order is letting us go only confirms that they don't know the village's actual location. They might have a good guess, but they are worried about walking in blind. So, they want us to lead them back to it so that they can destroy us all together. It proves that they only have a limited amount of offensive forces available and that they are probably on the far end of their supply chain. This was a rush job and they can't afford a heavy loss of men or materials. So, going back is something that we must not do! At least not yet."

Ai nodded as she followed his logic. "So, what should we do?"

"Simple. We let them follow us for a ways. Then we start picking them off. Eventually they will be forced to fall back, or they will attack. If they attack, we kill them all," Mick answered coldly. "Be careful though. The Knights have trained since birth for this. They are pompous, prideful, and arrogant, but never forget that they earned that by being deadly and powerful. They are dangerous but it is the Marines which truly concern me. They may be normal men, but they know war and have been fighting them for a long time. They are still learning how to fight this kind of war, but I fear that in the long run they and those like them will prove to be our most dangerous enemies. Don't underestimate them. Especially the Gunnery Sargent. He's dangerous," he warned. *There is something about that man. He is someone to remember to be wary of.*

Ai scrunched her brow but nodded. *Normal humans called Samurai and peasant drove us into the dark. Not the kings, powerful, or Onmyouji. They, their technology, and numbers are the great threat. Most dangerous is when one of them rises above the bounds of human yet still bears hate for our kind. They are truly to be feared.* "I won't underestimate any of them and I won't hesitate when the time comes. They killed my people, invaded my land, took my home, almost killed me, and hurt the one I love," she said softly, looking up at Mick. "We will take it back and they will regret ever coming here as invaders. They have come in greed and left their honor and justice behind them and that is why they will lose!"

"Yes, but be careful," Mick agreed, softly cupping Ai's cheek in his hand. After a long second, he reluctantly pulled his hand away to adjust his pack. "We will head towards them so as to drive them away from our home and then lead them on the merry chase," he said, leading the way.

They quickly made their way through the house, being sure to shut all of the doors and placing fire seals that could only be removed by Ai or him at every entry point. He hated doing it, but he hated the idea of any of them trespassing on his home even more. Their task complete, he was confident that none would try. They knew he was a Master of Seals and that attempting to bypass his seals would take too long and they would lose the chance to pursue him. Even if they tried to do it in spite as they passed, they would most likely pay for it with their lives. With a final glance over his shoulder at the home full of breathtaking memories, they set off across the very bridge where he had barred the intruders from crossing.

***

Mick was smiling as they exited the stream. They had doubled back and walked in it for a ways to make it look like they were trying to shake a tail and to delay them a little bit. He'd been a little startled when the Gunny had bellowed some order. He wasn't quite sure what had prompted it, but it only went to show that all was not at peace in the enemy's camp. Gunny's weren't known to do stupid things like shouting 'Sir's' out in combat situations. The only reason that Mick could think of that might prompt such an outburst was if one of the Knights had thrown a hissy fit about something silly like respect for superiors when they didn't understand why the Gunny and the rest of his men might not have been wanting to throw salutes and Sir's around while on patrol. It wasn't that hard to tell who was in command, so there was no reason that he would have done something like that unless they had done something to really peeve him.

"Sounds like the pot is already about ready to boil-over back there," Ai said, gracefully vaulting up the bank without so much as disturbing a twig.

Mick nodded in agreement. "We will lead them for the day and see how they set up for the night. If a chance to pick some of them off or better yet sow some discord should arise, we'll take it. If not, we'll just scout them out and learn how they react. Remember to stay on your guard though. They may be annoyed with each other, but that doesn't mean that they aren't still deadly. That and I don't recognize those rifles that they were carrying and that worries me."

"I know," Ai soothed. "And you can be sure that I won't take any chances," she assured with a slight huff.

Mick quirked his brow but didn't push it. *She's telling me the truth, but there is more there than just her being cautious. Something to ask about later.*

Careful. Ai warned herself. "So, what way will we lead them now?" she asked, changing the subject.

Mick looked ahead to the crags of a new range that had reared up. They were torn and ugly with the semi-toppled remains of the forest that had been on them when they were just rolling hills. To the left of those were dark and deep woods that had only gotten bigger and darker since the Crystal Swell. Behind them laid the village and to the right was the crystal tree, town, and Lake Towada. "We'll go for the deep trees. I don't much care for the dark woods but there at least, they will probably assume that their mishaps aren't our fault," he said, glancing over to Ai. She was frowning. "What?"

"In those woods, it will probably be true," Ai warned. "Even before, that area was bad. I doubt that it has gotten any better since. The crags would be a better choice!" she urged.

"It will be slow going in those falls and the crags. There is a chance that we could get trapped and they could catch up with us," Mick said, not arguing but making sure that the danger was expressed.

"I'd rather be cornered against the likes of these, than trying to lead them, attack them, and confuse them, all while having to guard against every shadow that might be hiding something even worse," Ai explained.

Mick nodded. "When you put it like that, I get your point. But the two are neighbors and if the choice is between getting trapped and entering those woods, we will go in," he stipulated, holding her eyes until she nodded. "Then let the chase begin." Mick smiled as they set off.

What Lays in the Dark Again
Thursday, July 22

The sun was low and they had traveled a lot of territory since that afternoon and both of them were sweaty from the high pace that they had set, the heat, and humidity. *And it's not like we have had a lot of sleep either. Not that I regret it.*

My hips and back are sore. Ai grumbled to herself. *Worth it. But they are going to pay for ruining my honeymoon!!!* "We should stop and get ready for the night. They are still a ways off and we will need to do some scouting around and get some rest before the night really sets in," she said, coming to a stop.

Mick followed suit, let out a slightly ragged sigh and looked around before answering. He was still on the mend from his injuries and he really hadn't gotten as much rest as he should have. *It was worth it, but they are going to pay for messing up our honeymoon.* He rubbed his sore chest. *This should have healed faster. Whatever that dagger is, Night doesn't like it.* His wounds had closed, but they were mending slowly, and Night was barely helping at all. He spotted a dark clump of fallen trees a little further up the hill and to their left. "Let's break our trail and make for those falls. We can stash our packs there and take a short break before night comes and then sneak back out and watch what they do tonight?" Mick suggested.

Ai gave the dark grove a quick once over. There was a single massive tree still standing in the middle of it. She couldn't tell if that was a good sign or a bad one. But bad things were usually more into destruction of life than saving it. *So, it's probably a good sign. At least as long as it isn't one of those man-eating trees. Those things are nasty.* "Sounds good, and I could use some food and a nap. Maybe a massage if you think you are up for it?" she enquired, with a smile.

Mick chuckled and smiled. "I don't know. I may not have the energy for that. Food would help but..."

Ai darted in and laid a lusty kiss on him. "You sure?" she asked, looking up at him with her pouty lips slightly pursed and batting her eyes.

Mick gave himself a little shake to get his mind back on the right track. "I think I can manage."

Ai smiled and pulled a little away. "Good," she said chipperly. "I'll be sure to help you stay energized," she assured.

Mick coughed, clearing his throat. "Then we should probably be off."

"Lead the way, love," Ai said, waving him on by giving him a swat on the butt.

The fallen trees formed an almost impenetrable bulwarks around the tree. Mick wasn't so sure that this was such a good idea. What had looked like random falls, turned out to be intentional construction as they drew close enough to see it clearly.

"What do you make of this?" Mick asked, looking at the crisscrossed wall. *If we get in, we will be well defended from attack, but, if we need to get out fast, this could work against us.*

Ai considered it for a moment. "I think we should ask before we enter. I don't know who lived in this area before, but they apparently feel the need for defenses. Which says that they aren't so strong that they don't need them, that they find others to be a nuisance, or that there is a danger of being caught out here without them. Defensive minded people can be tricky."

Mick nodded in agreement. "Hello?" he hollered. He glanced back at Ai when nothing happened. He turned back to shout again but stopped as three logs that had been wedged together withdrew and revealed an entrance in front of them. A moment later, an Otter came scampering out, casting furtive glances about. He stopped in front of them, standing up on his back legs and sneezed. It shook its head and rubbed its nose before turning a sidelong look on them.

"What are you doing out here in the open so close to dusk? This isn't as nice and friendly of a neighborhood as it used to be; especially at night. You smell like you are nice folks, but you also smell like trouble. Tell me who you are and your business here and maybe I will see fit to letting you in!" the Otter chirped.

Mick glanced at Ai, arching an eyebrow in question. She gave him a slight nod. "I am Mick Renalds and this is my wife, Ai..," he almost said her maiden name but changed his mind," Renalds," he said instead. He noticed a happy little smile in Ai's eyes and the way her cheeks dimpled. "I wish that we could say that we are just on a honeymoon stroll, but I can't. We are currently being pursued by the men that have invaded and taken control of the village where the great Crystal Tree is located. They hope that we will lead them back to the rest of us so that they can wipe us out and enslave the survivors," he admitted. "We are leading them away though and had hoped to dissuade their pursuit by attacking them in the night and sowing discord between their two factions," he answered, watching as the Otter frowned.

The Otter looked past them and towards the trees which they had left earlier. Apparently, he had been observing them for a while. He turned back and squinted at Mick and Ai. "And who do these invaders represent and where do these invaders call from?" he asked.

"The Order of the Knight's Keepers and the United States Marines," Mick answered. "As to who commands them, I am still trying to figure that out."

"And you, Mr. Renalds, human who is no longer, came to be here and involved in matters of the Crystal, and carved upon by a Lamentation Dagger. How are you involved in all of this?" the Otter asked. "The High Wolf Princess I can understand, but by rights, you should be an outsider to all of this or on the other side. Yet here you are at these gates. Please explain this to me?"

Mick fidgeted for a moment. Apparently, the Otter knew a great deal, including the type of Dagger that Talbot had 'Gifted' him with. "I was a member of the Order until I accepted exile, because of my bonding with Night. I then came here and, because of the connection between Night and the Crystal, I was involved in halting its expansion," he answered. Ai was starting to fidget. Apparently, she was a little disconcerted by the Sagely Otter.

The Otter nodded his head as if that made everything make sense. "Very well then. Come in and seek shelter. I must advise against venturing out at night though. If discourse is what you wish upon those who pursue you, the denizens of the night will see to it just fine without your help. If you still wish, you can observe them from here. Should they survive the night, I doubt they will stay and continue to chase you and you should be safe to return to your 'hidden village,'" he answered, turning around and retreating back into his compound.

Mick glanced to Ai, "Do you trust him?"

"Maybe," Ai admitted. "At least I don't get the impression that it means us harm or is lying to us. It knows an awful lot about things that I wouldn't think it should though. I'd feel much better if I knew who it was."

Mick nodded. "Sorry, but we have just one question before we enter?" he called after the Otter. It stopped, looking back, and gave them a wave to proceed. Mick swallowed. "Who are you?"

The Otter cocked his head to the side and laughed. "Just an Otter who remembers when a river once flowed through here. But if you must have a name, then you may call me, Gen Ryouki," Ryouki answered, turning and walking through the gap.

"Thank you," Mick replied, his mind racing through the Kanji that could comprise that name and their meanings. He was coming up with a lot of odd possibilities, but none that said that Ryouki wasn't to be trusted. All the same, he stayed close to Ai as they made their way inside.

As soon as they passed the threshold, the logs smoothly slid back into place, seamlessly closing off the entrance, with hardly a groan or a creak. Inside, the jumble of fallen trees created a domed ceiling that was about ten meters high. There were breaks left open in it to allow in light and airflow which was being funneled by colorful sheets of cloth, silk from the looks of it, which hung from the ceiling. From the outer wall to the center of the compound was about thirty meters. There was a garden and even a spring and pond contained within the area. In the center rose the giant tree that had first drawn their attention. It was easily eight meters wide at the base and rose to towering heights. The only reason that they hadn't realized its massive size before was that they hadn't had anything close by with which to compare it. The reason for its size and stability amongst the rest of the toppled forest quickly became apparent.

Mick walked up to it and ran his hand over its bark. The tree was fused and laced with Crystal. It was a true synthesis and the lines of where each began and ended were blurred and impossible to tell. Night liked it. It seemed to feel that it was natural and the way that things should be. It made sense in a way. The synthesis was much like what Night had with the Crystal and him. He looked over his shoulder to where Ryouki was watching. "How did this happen?"

"Old story. The simple version is that Sakuya planted the last seed of a forest that had been destroyed by war and disaster in the heart of a Crystal and fed it to make it grow. It grew so fast that the crystal containing it shattered," Ai looked at Ryouki in horror. When Crystals broke, they released all of their stored energy at once. The effect was devastating. He just smiled like it wasn't that big of a deal. "But the tree bound the energy and fused with it. Absorbing the crystal as a part of itself, changing it and itself until they were one and something new. It took root and continued to grow. This is the basis for Crystal synthesis. Neither remains what they were and what is left is not two but one. One plus one equals new," he explained, holding up two fingers and then laying them over each so that only one finger could be seen.

"So why does that fail when others try?" Ai asked, furrowing her brow.

Ryouki laughed. "Because what is, cannot become," he stated simply. "Or at least that is the case for most. But you three seem to be an exception born of love. Love truly is a wild card which defies reason, logic, mystery, and magic. Making what cannot be, be," he said, shaking his head. "Or maybe it is six of you if you count each expression of Night since as I said, all things change as they combine?"

"Three?" Mick asked, confused. One plus one may indeed equal new, but not three. Then it hit him like a brick fired from a cannon. He turned to look at Ai, meeting her eyes before his fell to her belly. She smiled sheepishly and nodded. He immediately pulled her into his arms and hugged her close. Then the next part registered. "Six!? You mean Night has split between us?" he asked, his head snapping back around at Ryouki. "How do you know that? How could that happen?"

Ryouki shrugged. "Love," it answered. "And it isn't like one Night has split between you. You each now carry a Night that is unique to you and will probably have unique personalities. Night has changed. It is no longer one in the same, but each is new and unique. Love truly is the Wall Breaker," he said, with a confident nod and smirk, like that explained everything. "As to how I know, I know. And my whiskers are exceedingly sensitive," he simply answered. "If you need more proof, then seek it from Night. I would have thought that you of all people would have noticed its changed behavior. The shift from guard to protector. The Crystal may be connected to it, but it has no will of its own. You of all people, the one who carries all of the memories, should know that Night is alive and has a will. It is you and yet it is it. It is a sword to attack when alone and a shield to protect when with family. It is unique. Now if you can hold off further questions for a minute, we can move around to the other side to my home and enjoy a little supper," he invited.

Mick's head was still spinning, but he nodded and followed. Walking with his arm protectively around Ai's waist.

Ryouki's home turned out to be an Ox Cart parked on the other side of the tree. Ai immediately clapped her hands together and made a happy squeal upon seeing it; as if it was the most luxuriant thing that she had ever seen.

Mick was confused but decided to give it the benefit of the doubt. He stopped next to the cart as Ai ascended the fold-down stairs at the rear and gave the cart a quick once over. The closest comparison that he had ever run into was the Old West Chuck Wagons with their infinite numbers of storage compartments and he wondered what this things trick was. It was clearly old but clean and well-cared for. There was also the smell of some kind of fish and vegetables wafting away from it that made his stomach rumble. With a shrug he went up the ladder and stuck his head past the rear flap, expecting to see a cramped wagon. Instead he was greeted with an entry leading into what appeared to be a large living room. He could even see a stairway leading up to a second story or loft. He smiled. *It's bigger on the inside. Or maybe, smaller on the outside.* It was always hard to tell with these kinds of things. He hauled himself the rest of the way in, slipping out of his boots and using a pair of slippers as he moved further inside. Ai had already found a spot on the couch and there was humming coming from the kitchen area. Ai just smiled as he walked past.

"A nice home," Mick commented coming around the Kitchen corner. He was greeted with the sight of a young lady in short-short jeans and a tight-fitting halter top. Her black eyes sparkled with mischief, her face small and speckled in freckles. Her hair was dark brown and cut short, just covering her ears. He might have rapidly blinked in sudden comprehension as his mental image shattered and re-arranged.

"Thank you," Ryouki answered in a tenor alto voice that was singsong and deep at the same time. Her smile dimpled her cheeks adding to the sparkle in her eyes. In that moment, you could still see her Otter features showing through. "I rescued, Wa, from a collapsed shed in a lost citadel a few hundred years back. It's been with me ever since," she explained. "Dinner will be ready shortly. I hope you are okay with fish curry and sushi. I know it is an odd mix, but I wasn't expecting company."

"Just dandy," Mick managed, "Thank you. If there is anything that I can do to help, let me know."

"Will do. For now, just go ahead and sit back and relax," Ryouki instructed, shooing him out of the kitchen.

Mick flopped down on the couch next to Ai. She immediately burst into laughter. "How was I to know that Ryouki was a girl!?" he defended, giving her his best reproachful look but the full effect was broken by his smile.

"You weren't, Love," Ai said, still chuckling to herself. "If it hadn't been for her scent, I wouldn't have known. It's always tough to tell with Otters." She sat back still smiling. "She knows a lot," she stated flatly, after a moment.

Mick nodded. "That she does. And I get the feeling that she is far older than her appearance would lead one to believe. But I don't get the feeling that she is an enemy or means us any harm. That isn't to say that she is an ally either. More of a free spirit that does what she wants to do, when she wants to do it, and in the way that she wants," he agreed. "I also don't want to be her enemy. I get the feeling that they meet bad ends." Ai nodded in agreement.

Ryouki came out with a tray covered in bowls of curry and small plates of sushi before they could continue. She smiled happily as she set it down. "Dinner is served. Help yourself," she encouraged, passing around bowls half filled with rice and ladling curry into it from a central pot. "Sorry about the frosty greeting when you first got here. As I said, the locals aren't the kindest of creatures. Better than the ilk lurking in those dark woods nearby, or at least not as powerful, but still a rabid lot. I was lucky that the tree decided to create this shelter and allowed me in. Killing them off in job lots every night would have grown dull fast," she commented, taking a bite. "The tree is actually the one who let you in also. It opened the gate and I came out to greet you, but it let you in. My part was more of a show since there was little that I could have done to stop you at that point."

Mick sputtered on his soup. "The tree did all of this? How?" he asked, trying to picture it and only coming up with comical cartoons of the tree walking about and moving the falls.

Ryouki chuckled at his reaction. "It snared the falls with its roots, dragged them over, stripped them, stacked them with its limbs, and tied it all together with its roots," she answered mater-of-factly. "It didn't much like those locals either. Always rooting about and trying to eat it."

Mick blinked but couldn't find any way to argue that it was impossible. *Just what isn't a tree synthesized with a crystal capable of? Flying? I wouldn't want to place money on it, nor do I have the time to dawdle and find out. It's not like I haven't seen queerer things before. Like Portland.* He gave a little shake at that memory. That whole region defied logic and reason. It was just plain weird! "You seem to know a lot about a lot," he observed. "Any reason that you are collecting all of this knowledge? Or is it just a hobby?"

Ryouki set her bowl aside and considered Mick carefully. "I'm looking for something. I've been looking for a long time now. In the pursuit of it, I have seen and learned a lot and I've researched even more. I've seen things old and new, come and gone, and thought lost. Which is worse, the old or the new, I'm not sure. I'm still looking. I thought that maybe here, where the power has welled, I might find it. Instead I just find war and destruction and the same old issues writ large," she answered, a weary sigh escaping her that for the first time revealed just how ancient she really was.

Mick furrowed his brow, "I've been around a bit. I might know something if you tell me what it is that you are looking for?" he offered. It always paid off to make friends wherever you went and even if they couldn't help you now, you never knew how those seeds may sprout some other day.

Ryouki laughed and waved him off. "I doubt it. Ama-no-Murajumo-no-Tsurugi, the Sword of the Gathering Clouds, has been lost for a long time. I appreciate the thought though."

"The sword that is part of the Japanese Imperial Regalia?" Mick clarified, surprised by her revelation and curious as to why she was looking for it here in Tohoku.

Ryouki nodded. "The Sword that is part of the Imperial Regalia. The original. The one that is there is one of them. It is the same sword, but it is not the sword. You see, there was more than one. The Imperial sword came from the Fourth Tail. The one that I am seeking came from the creatures back, its spine to be precise. It was discovered later, after the carcass was discarded in the river nearby. My family carried it for a long time. Until our river was destroyed. Our enemies used the opportunity to drive us out and the sword was lost in the battles which ensued."

What is it with family history and losing swords? People really should hold onto them better. He nodded in understanding. "You're right, I can't help you much on that. If I hear anything, I'll be sure to get word to you," he promised. Talking about old weapons reminded him of one of her comments from earlier. On a hunch, he dug through his pack and pulled out a cloth wrapped bundle and laid it down between them. "You seem to know a lot about blades. Any chance that you know anything about this one? Or more precisely the one who wielded it?" he asked, sliding it over to her.

Ryouki folded back the cloth. She hissed as she saw the dagger. "Talbot left you with one of his prized Lamentation Daggers. He is a special kind of cruel. I take it that this is the same one that did that?" she asked, nodding to his scars which were peaking out around his wrists and collar.

Mick nodded. "Talbot gave it to me to do this," he waved to the scars carved into his skin. "It was the price that he required for letting those that were with me pass unharmed. One scar for every life. Apparently, he was a bit miffed that I ruined his plans for the Crystal, but he was also curious about me and if there was anyone hiding behind the curtain. So, he let me go with this as the price."

Ryouki narrowed her eyes in thought. "You are lucky that he didn't just kill you. I would think that after that user of Night sealed him away for a few hundred years, that he would have just killed you out of hand over the familial connection. It is easy to forget that he is just as unfathomable as he is cruel. None really know what makes him tick or what his purpose is. All that is really known is that he is powerful and loves chaos. That he left one of his daggers means that you are marked as his prey. In his timing, he will definitely return to take it back from you after he has finished his business with you. Most likely that will involve killing you."

Mick smiled. "By the time he comes back, I will be ready," he swore. His tone wasn't boastful but there was cold iron in his words.

"Strong words. But can you make them reality?" Ryouki asked. "Many have tried to kill Talbot. They are all dead or worse," she warned sadly.

"Yes!" Mick said, sure that he would be. *Even if it costs my life.* He debated saying more but he noticed the pinking sky outside the window and supper was going to get cold. "Sorry for dampening the evening's cheer with this talk of doom and gloom. I should be getting back outside so that I can observe the night's events," he said, finishing off his food and gathering the dagger as he got to his feet. Putting it back away in his pack. Ai started to stand to join him. "Oh no you don't!"

"But," Ai began to protest until she saw the love, concern, and fear in Mick's eyes.

"Not tonight," he said and smiled sadly before turning back to Ryouki. "I don't mean to impose but is there someplace that Ai could rest while I am out?"

Ryouki smiled back in understanding. "I'm sure that we can handle that. Wa has more than a few bedrooms and even a rather nice bath," she assured, her pride in her home clear in her smile.

"Thank you." Mick nodded and grabbed some supplies from his pack before heading for the flap that stood in place of a door. Ai jumped to her feet and captured his hand. Several thoughts flashed through her eyes as tears welled up in the corners of them. In the end, she simply stood up on her toes and gave him a kiss before letting his hand go. He cupped her cheek for just a moment longer, flicking away a tear with his thumb before kissing the top of her head before turning and walking out.

As the flap swung shut, Mick glimpsed Ryouki coming over and pulling Ai into her shoulder and she gave him a little nod. With a heavy heart, Mick made his way over to the palisade. Several of the logs had shifted and there were now rough steps leading up to a small observation landing. Apparently, the tree had been listening in.

The last rays of light were being devoured by the shadows as he crested the rampart. Thanks to Night and the Crystal in his system, it might as well have been day to his eyes. Although, there were areas where even his eyes couldn't penetrate the inky darkness that enveloped them. Even now as the sun's warmth still lingered, some of those areas were starting to stir and move about. Keeping an eye on them, his eyes flicked back and forth between them and the far tree line for any signs of the Knight's and Marine's arrival.

He didn't have to wait long. It started as a shift in the shadows. Then came a single flash that lit up the night before it was followed by a clap of thunder followed by silence. After a pause there came the roar and crash of trees being launched to the side from several directions, shattering the fragile silence. Spears of white light pierced the night as highly accelerated rounds created clouds of plasma around them as they lashed out at stupendous speeds. When they impacted, great exploding geysers erupted. First one of the attackers, Boars from the look of them, fell. Then another. But the others continued their advance, never flinching away, but zigzagging madly to throw off the aim of the soldiers. The last Boar fell, still a hundred meters short of the nearest muzzle flash.

For a moment, all was silent again. This time the stillness was shattered by the scream of a man. It was mercifully short but was soon replaced with another. Apparently, something smaller had used the distraction of the boars to make its way in close to the Marines and Knights. The sky bloomed red as someone launched an illumination flare high into the sky, driving back the dark.

While Mick could see just fine, the battle was still taking place too far away to make out any clear details, but he was able to make out some. From the looks of things, the Knights had ordered a dispersed formation. It was better for tracking and confronting threats on a wide front, like they just had with the Boars, but was a death trap that invited defeat in details if your opponent managed to get in close and between your spread out men, cutting you into more manageable chunks to swallow. Their rifle's advantages in power and range were now suddenly disadvantages. They couldn't use them for fear of killing their own in the crossfire, and with the destructive force that they packed, necessary for dealing with the tough hided creatures of the Fair, even if their ally was behind cover, they still couldn't use them.

It looked like they were going to be overwhelmed until an all too normal muzzle flash strobed in the night. A moment later, he heard the familiar report of a Forty-Five. The shot was followed by a savage snarl and yelp of pain. Oddly enough, the low velocity and slow yet heavy impact of .45 Caliber had been found to be rather effective against creatures of the Fair. Most of the lower and aggressive Fair's defensive abilities relied on reactive flesh. The faster and more concentrated the impact, the harder its skin became, rendering most high velocity rounds ineffective unless you could overwhelm their threshold or hit them with something that negated their ability such as silver, sandalwood, or mistletoe, to name a few, depending on the creature. On the other hand, many of the slow and heavy older sized bullets were still rather effective. 45. ACP was one of the few semi-modern rounds that was effective. 50-70 Government was actually about ideal. Knowing the marines, they still had crates full of the old things and would be shipping them over just as soon as they discovered that, or the Knights thought to inform them. For now, though, the one man with the Forty-Five had created an opening, allowing the others to pull back and form a defensive area. As soon as their firing lines were clear, the rest of the remaining members opened up with their rifles again. All armor had its limits and reactive flesh or not, the tide quickly turned as rounds traveling at fraction c. struck flesh. Tanks, diamonds, and even metallic glass would have shattered under those impacts and so did the attacker, falling back or being turned into expanding clouds of gore. For the next ten minutes, he watched as the occasional burst lit up the night as they collected their fallen and wounded and either finished off the few remaining injured attackers or just put a bolt in them for good measure. Either choice was wise.

An hour after the initial attack had been repulsed, a second attack came. This one was bigger and more organized, with feints and thrust from multiple directions. But, unlike the initial surprise attack, the remaining Marines and, sadly, probably Knights also, had quickly dug in and pulled into a tight defensive square anchored on an exposed knoll of rubble. From then on, the attack never got closer than a hundred meters. During the next three hours, the attackers tried twice more, and each time were forced to break off even further away than the previous time. Apparently, someone over there had a brain and they were learning how to fight this kind of battle at an alarming rate. Fighting against an organized force or on the move would be a different battle, but in this kind of static fight, they appeared to be the superior force.

"Crap," Mick muttered. *I see a return of Maginot and Star fortresses in the future of this war. Those are going to hurt. But that is for later. For tonight, do I risk heading out there to test their abilities or do I give them their breath?* Old words of wisdom came to his mind.

When your opponents winded, don't dance with him. Get in there and hit'em in the solar plexus before he catches his breath even if you have to take a lickin'.

"Thanks Grandpa," Mick smirked as he walked to the edge of the battlements. He wasn't too surprised to find that there was a convenient ladder of tree boughs waiting there for him. *I wonder if the tree just likes me because of Night or because I'm bound with the Crystal also? A question for another day. Probably a day far down the road considering how many of those I seem to be acquiring these days.*

Mick crouched as his boots sank into the soft loam outside of the battlement. He immediately dropped into a crouch and just spent a few minutes listening and learning the sounds of the darkness. Unlike the still calm inside of the Tree's fort, this air was alive and heavy with oppressiveness. Although, it was nothing compared to the brooding darkness boiling out of the woods that they had decided to stay clear of.

Not wanting to dither, he loosened his axes and set out into the night. He had about six kilometers to cover before he would reach the edge of the dead man's land around the hunkered invaders. It was bound to be a wearing experience.

He had made it roughly halfway when the sound of the darkness around him took on a different tone. He didn't slow his pace, but he let his awareness pull back to the area around him so that he could react faster when the moment came. He didn't have long to wait.

The night split with a slash of inky darkness that lunged out at him, silvery claws extended to capture and eviscerate him. Mick rolled out of the way, tucking and rolling back to his feet, facing his attacker with his axes at the ready. He ducked just in time as another set of claws raked the air above him. He pivoted to the side and brought up his axes in an overhead cross guard just in time to catch another descending slash. The weight of the impact drove him to his knees, bearing down on him like an elephant balancing on one foot as his joints ground and his bones creaked like pine trees in a windstorm on the brink of snapping. He quickly shifted the blow down and to the side, letting the claws dig deep furrows in the ground beside him. He used the opportunity to free one of his axes and brought it down on top of the claws, snapping them off. The attacker reeled back in pain and he got his first good look it.

"I broke a nail!" it roared in anger. "Do you have any idea how long it takes to grow these?" it asked indignantly. "I just got these manicured, too! Before we were just going to kill you and eat you. Now we are going to make it hurt," it squeaked, circling around to the other side where its broken claws wouldn't be such a handicap.

Giant Groundhogs were the closest thing that came to mind as he watched these foreign creatures circle him. Groundhogs bigger than a grizzly, with half-meter claws, and a mouth full of sharp, pointy teeth. They had dark downy fur covering the majority of their body that shifted with the shadows and made them hard to focus on. His eyes kept trying to shift off of them and find something solid to focus on. Keeping a low and high guard while shifting to keep them from putting him right between them, he readied to meet their charge.

The first attacker charged in, tiring of the game and swung laterally with both sets of its claws, trying to scissor him between them while the other one lunged in from the side, ready to skewer him with its good claws. Instead of trying to block or evade the attack, he stepped into it, moving inside of the claws reach and between the Grizzly Groundhog's – GHogs as he was coming to think of them– grasp as its hands clapped together behind him. In the same moment, he moved to the side and capture its right arm with both of his axes, pulling forwards and down as he stood, pivoting back around and standing up at the same time, hip throwing it at the other GGHog and its extended claws. It squealed in pain as its companion's claws burrowed deeply into its flank before it had a chance to stop. The impaled one tried to untangle itself from the one trapped below it, but its claws kept getting in the way.

Mick wasn't one to lose the opportunity or take pity on a creature that was set on eating him. The one with the broken claws saw him coming but the other one couldn't. In an act of pure self-interest and savagery, it tore its claws free from the other one, opening deep furrows in its flank and severing muscles, tendons, bones, and arteries alike. The fallen one, panicked at the unexpected and savage injuries, tried to lash out at its partner. It was too late as its partner's now freed claws drove home into its ribs and heart as it heaved it off and to the side. It rolled desperately, trying to evade Mick's descending ax. It succeeded only in rolling into his other axe as it swept in from the side cleaving deeply into its neck below its jaw. It let out a gurgled snarl as the light died in its eyes. For good measure, he brought his other axe around and put a second chop into the back of its neck, being sure to sever its spine. After a sigh to catch his breath, he repeated the process on the eviscerated GGHog. Sometimes things got back up and he wasn't about to risk it.

Mick straitened, jerking both axes free and wiped the blood off on the coat of the GGHog before he slid them back into their sheaths. *This is going to be a long night. Too bad I don't have time to pelt these things. Mink has nothing on this fir.*

Dancing in the Moonlight
Friday, July 23

It was close to two in the morning when Mick finally sighted the edge of the killing field. He had expected to run into more things as he had gotten closer, but they had apparently pulled back for the night to lick their wounds or search out easier prey. He had been watching for close to a half hour and was just about to try and move in for a closer look when a chill went down his spine freezing him where he stood as every ounce of his concentration searched for whatever had warned him that something was off.

"You have good instincts," a shadow said, rising out of the darkness of some fallen trees just ahead and to the side of him.

Mick tensed as Gunny stepped out into the moon's light. *What is he doing here? I have no doubt that the Knights think little of the man, but that doesn't mean that they would have trusted letting him out of their sight. Especially after that outburst yesterday. Plus, if he was really the one who turned the tide in that earlier fight, which I rather suspect he was, then they have to at least know that he is far more capable and experienced with the things of this world than normal. So just what game is being played here. They have to know that the jig is up and that we know that they are following us by this point, only a blind and deaf person could have missed the show they put on, and that we will never lead them back to the others.* He didn't like it one bit.

"I like to think so, but apparently they aren't that good. You might have taken me, and you didn't. So, you don't seem to want me dead as much as the others, or at least not yet, but that doesn't explain why you are here?" Mick probed, keeping his distance and moving a little to put some small fallen logs and branches between them. It wasn't much, but little things could make the difference between life and death.

Gunny grinned. "Maybe I just wanted to say hi?" he supposed. There was nothing warm about his grin but the twinkle in his eyes spoke to his amusement over something.

Despite the tenseness of the situation, a chuckle managed to escape from Mick. "I think we both know that you have a better reason than that!" he challenged, continuing to move slowly, never stopping and doing everything that he could to keep the Gunny between him and the rest of his men on the hill while he minded his opening and got ready for whatever was coming. "Especially after saving your men earlier this night, you must have a good reason for being out here and not back there making sure that they are okay and that the 'Knights' don't waste any more of their lives," he practically spat the last part. He was sorely tempted to spit but he didn't want to create an opening.

"Aye, they did waste several good men's lives, but that shouldn't be a problem anymore and their reckoning for that will come in due time. We have come to an understanding since then. And while I might stiffen some spines should another attack or an assassin in the night happen upon us," Gunny nodded to Mick, "they are good men with brains who can handle themselves now that they aren't under stupid orders anymore. So, that left me with the freedom to come out here and meet any throat slitter that might have been lurking about," he answered, looking Mick up and down. "You wouldn't happen to be acquainted with any or able to point me in their direction by any chance?" His voice was full of mirth, but it never reached his eyes.

Mick was more than a little disturbed by what the Gunny had implied and intrigued by just what kind of understanding had been reached but it was clear that their little chat was coming to a close. "I'm not much of a throat slitter," he admitted, turning his back slightly to showcase the axes. "But I do make expectations when being pursued by those who would see all that I care about destroyed," he retorted, relaxing into a fighting stance.

Gunny's shoulders lowered a degree as he too relaxed, letting his hand fall not towards his pistol, but the hilt of his cutlass. "Aye, that's understandable. But it would seem that we are at an impasse. I have my orders and they are good boys. Which leaves me in a bind since I can't let you do that," he said, sadly. "You're just a mite bit too dangerous to be left to your own devices and I still haven't really figured out just who you are yet, and the reports seem to have been badly biased and they can only tell you so much."

"So, we speak," Mick agreed, sliding his axes free as the Gunny unsheathed his cutlass.

Mick's eyes narrowed as he saw the naked blade. It wasn't stamped or cast steel like he had expected but an intricate design of swirling Damascus steel that seemed to swim in the star light. "An interesting blade," he said, circling to the right and a little closer.

Gunny turned it ever so slightly to capture more light. "Yep, it belonged to my great-great-grandfather. He did a stint in the navy and made port in some rather unusual places. His standard issue Cutlass wasn't up to all of the things that he got into and he had this one special made by a one-armed smith who had supposedly travelled the world acquiring the secret of steel," he explained, never taking his eyes off of Mick as they jockeyed for positions." My family has a long tradition of serving our Nation against all manner of foes."

Mick found that last part exceptionally intriguing, given his own previous line of work and the limited information that he had ever been able to gather on the government's people, but before he had a chance to ask more, Gunny lunged. Steel met steel as he parried the thrust to the side, bringing his other axe around to take the Gunny across his wrists. Gunny spun his cutlass around so that the pommel and guard deflected the blow. He immediately followed it up with a pommel strike at Mick's throat, forcing him back to evade it and then brought his sword tip back around in a twirl aimed to take him between his collarbone and neck.

Mick brought his free axe back around and knocked the attack back to the side. Gunny took the opportunity to grab Mick's wrist with his own free hand and drove his shoulder into Mick's sternum, knocking the air out of him and trapping his other arm and axe down and between them at the same time. Mick went with the blow and attempted to do a reverse hip throw, but the Gunny simply rolled with it, spinning over Mick's chest and landed on his feet, still holding onto Mick's wrist and readying to bring down his now freed cutlass across Mick's arm.

Knowing that trying to fight Gunny's grip would only lose him a hand, he twirled his axe around in his captured hand and locked the base of its head over the Gunny's wrist and pulled down while moving forwards, slipping inside of the Gunny's swing while breaking his grip on Mick's arm and adding a head-butt for good measure.

Gunny staggered back but kept his sword up and forwards to keep Mick at bay while his head cleared. He had evaded most of the damage by swaying with the blow, but he couldn't stop it all and there were a few stars in the corners of his eyes and his knees had a slight wobble to them. Instead of rejoining the fight, he smiled. "I got what I needed," he said, sheathing his blade. "We can continue this if you so desire, but we both know that it would most likely end in a pyrrhic victory."

Mick cocked his head in consideration for a moment. *This is a dangerous man. I thought he was just here on orders, but I was wrong. His drive is not that shallow. He is here to bring war. Real war. He has his honor despite working with those who do not. But he is right. I can't win this fight. Not right now and at the cost that it would carry.* "On one condition," he said. Gunny simply nodded for him to continue. "What is your name?"

Gunny cocked his head to the side in consideration. Like normal, he wasn't wearing his name badge. Almost all of the missions that he had ever been on had been without names or even call signs. For that matter being in a uniform at all was almost something of a novelty; not that he didn't have the right to be in one, but he just didn't spend much time in them. This mission was a little different in that it was officially sanctioned but he still hadn't worn his badges. There were some perfectly good reasons for that, and he was under orders to keep a low profile, but he was old school and there was something for your enemy knowing who you were. It gave them something to fear. "Wilks Ashcroft," he answered, saluting with his sword. "I'd say that I look forward to the next time that we meet, but I really don't. I hate seeing good men die!" He turned to leave but paused and looked back over his shoulder. "I wouldn't suggest pressing any further tonight. Even with your reflexes, I doubt that you could dodge fast enough," he warned, giving a meaningful glance to the area where his men were camped out. "Go home in the morning with your wife. Leave this place and find somewhere nice to settle down and live a relaxed and secluded life. We will be returning in the morning. I can't vouch for the Knights, but if you leave us be, we will leave you be! But, if you choose to bring war to us, we will return it," he assured, and there was no fear or doubt as to the outcome in his eyes.

"It's in my blood," Mick said sadly. Under different circumstances, he had a feeling that they could have been friends or at least colleagues, but that sadly didn't look like it was going to ever happen.

Gunny chuckled. "From you and your family, I believe it. But remember what you have to live for and think on the offer. The Knights lied to you by the way. Your family was alive as of the last reports that we received. They were on the run and it was a while ago that I last received word on that front, so I can't guarantee that that is still the case, but they were around. Just something to consider."

With that, he turned and faded back into the night without making so much as a sound.

Mick stood there considering everything that he had learned for a few minutes before turning back the way that he had come. He'd decided not to test Gunny Wilks warning. He paused as he took a step, glancing back the way that Wilks had gone, frowning. *I know that name.* His frown deepened as he tried to place it. For a man with a photographic memory, not being able to remember something was a reason to worry. "Who are you?" he whispered onto the winds. It didn't answer, but it did shiver. "Till we meet again."

***

Ryouki met him as he returned to the Ox cart. "Was it worth it?" she simply asked as he approached.

Mick stood there for a moment pondering how he felt amount it. "Yes, but I'm not sure who got the better end of the deal." *I now know who we really need to be leery of. The Knights are a threat, but we have to get the Marines out of here before they can catch their breath. In the long run, as always, humans are still the deadliest creature on this planet. They are strong because they are weak.*

"That tends to be the way of these things." Ryouki nodded but didn't give any hint as to her own opinion or whether she even had one. "Now go get cleaned up and go to bed. Your room is upstairs, third door on the left. The bath is the first door on the right at the base of the stairs," she instructed, shooing him towards her home. Mick nodded his thanks and walked past her and started up the ladder. "Try not to drip any blood on the rugs as you head in. It stains worse than spaghetti."

Mick stopped in his tracks and looked back in confusion. Ryouki tapped the right side of her neck, just below and behind her ear. Mick copied the motion and winced as he felt a shallow fissure in his skin where he had been cut. The cut had been so clean and fast that neither he nor Night had noticed it until now. Now that he knew it was there, Night moved into it and got to work. Thankfully, unlike the Lamentation dagger, Night didn't have any problems mending this wound. It quickly sealed it back up, promoting growth and healing the wound in a matter of seconds; leaving little but a small pink scar where it had been. There was only one place that it could have come from and that scared him. "All good. No more bleeding," he assured and headed in. But he wasn't all good. For the first time in a long time, he was scared.

Ai found him soaking in the tub and slipped out of her chemise and slid in next to him. Mick wasn't quite sure what the water source was, but at the moment he wasn't about to be picky and was glad for the company. He'd been going over his encounter with Wilks again and again in his head. He had finally figured out when the wily Gunny had managed to make the cut, but that just caused more questions and doubts to popup. If he could have managed something like that on purpose, then he was capable of a lot more than he had shown him in their little bout. He was right that it would have been a pyrrhic victory, but just whose victory it would have been was the real question. He hadn't used all of his skills or even a tithe of Night's but at the moment, he wasn't feeling too confident about the answer. He let the worries fade and turned his attention back to Ai, sliding against her and holding her against him with an arm protectively around her shoulder. "Would you leave with me if I asked you to?" he asked after a moment.

Ai didn't immediately answer, but she did snuggle up closer with him. "Yes," she answered quietly, but her voice also held conviction and a hint of the pain that it would cause her if he ever did.

Mick let out a long sigh. "Thank you," he said sadly, feeling a lump in his throat but grateful that if the worst should happen that she and their child would at least be safe.

"We're going back to the village tomorrow?" Ai asked, looking up into his eyes.

Mick smiled back, and the love she saw reflected in his eyes was almost enough to crush her. "Yes. There is much to be done and some hard choices to be made," he explained but not without some sadness and a new concern in his eyes that she hadn't seen before. "Sorry about our honeymoon getting all messed up." He pulled her a little closer and kissed the back of her neck.

Ai simply nodded before sliding around so that she was sitting on his lap and facing him. "The war can have you back tomorrow," she said, leaning in and kissing him.

Heart's Conviction
Friday, July 23

Gunny Wilks, good to his word, the Marines and Knights had been gone before first light. Mick still wasn't sure what to make of Wilks and the name still itched every time he thought about him, but he was content to let that Bulldog lay for as long as he could.

Ryouki had seen them off. Ai had asked her to come with them, apparently they had become fast friends while Mick had been out, but Ryouki had politely declined. She had her own mission and battles to be about. They hadn't pressed any further and left after sharing a filling breakfast of fish hash and eggs. Mick had had a few misgivings about contaminating a hash with fish, but he'd tried it and learned the error of his ways.

They made good time on the return trip. They'd still had to be careful to keep an eye out for anyone trying to shadow them or pesky cutthroat ravens, but they hadn't seen or found any signs of either one.

Adachi greeted them with a smile torn with a frown. "I'm glad to see you. We were just about to go rescue you, but apparently that won't be needed," he said, furrowing his brow. They were a little ragged looking, but they certainly didn't look like they had been captured and somehow made an escape.

"No, it won't. Would you happen to know who became aware of our need for rescue first?" Ai asked, ice frosting her words and fire in her eyes. *Whoever they are, they interrupted my honeymoon and they are going to pay for that.*

Adachi's eyes narrowed as he understood the question. He nodded sadly. "I do." *Why? You old fool. Why!*

"Then bring us to him!" Ai ordered, barely containing her cold anger.

260

"This way," Adachi said, leading them forwards. "He'll be at the gathering on the other side of town," he explained, frowning and shaking his head in regret as they made their way.

People stopped what they were doing as they passed and started following them without question as they made their way through town. Apparently, word had spread quite far already about their 'capture' and they were curious to see what was what.

As they walked and the crowd gathered, Mick quickly saw how this was going to play out. He gently reached forwards and pulled Adachi a little back so that he could whisper to him without being overheard. Ai cast them a questioning glance, but Mick gave his head a little shake to forestall any questions. Ai seemed to accept it and continued with the building procession for which he was thankful because he knew she wouldn't have liked what he was about to do. She might have agreed but she wouldn't have felt that it made up for what happened.

Adachi arched an eyebrow as a bubble of relative privacy formed around them. "What do you need me to do?" he asked, guessing that Mick had some kind of plan.

As sharp as ever. Never underestimate the observation skills of a Sargent. Or worse a Sargent Major. Mick frowned as he thought of Gunny Wilks. "I need you to be the one to dispatch whoever this is," he answered, giving Ai a meaningful glance.

"Any particular reason it needs to be me?" Adachi asked, growing curious and a little annoyed. *I don't relish blood on my hands and especially not that of those that I have long called friend.*

"Because I can trust you to do what needs to be done and the others will believe it if it's you. That is important if this is going to work. I figured that we were dealing with a greedy snake, but I can see from your reaction that that probably isn't the case. So, I need you to do it and I need you to make it look good and real," Mick explained, putting a little emphasis on his last word and squeezing Adachi's shoulder for good measure.

Adachi caught the hint. "Real?" he questioned. Mick simply nodded. *Tough but doable. And if I'm being honest with myself, even after he endangered my niece, I still don't hate him, and I'd like to at least know why before we go doing anything permanent.* He nodded his head. "I can do that." He squared his shoulders and steeled himself for what was about to come. They were almost there. "Excuse me," he said, moving forwards and drifting back to the head of the group.

Ai fell back next to Mick and gave him a questioning look.

Mick simply shrugged. "I did what needed to be done." There was no need to drag her into these machinations.

Ai could tell that that was all that she was going to get. She didn't like it when people decided that they needed to protect her from herself, but she had been around long enough to know that sometimes that really was for the best. But that didn't mean that she was going to let it go without a warning. "Don't go getting too smart for your own good," she warned, but let the subject drop as the group slowed. They were there.

Before them, at the far end of town, close to where Ai had claimed him, a large group of fighters was busy preparing for battle. First one and then another of them noticed the arrival of most of the village and their curiosity turned to surprise as they noticed Ai and Mick at the head of the procession. Silence quickly fell over them as all their conversations and preparations ground to a screeching halt. A lithely built man with shocks of white running through his black hair like a skunk or lightning bolts, it was hard to tell which, quickly pushed his way through them to see what was up.

"Reinforcements. Good. I like your enthusiasm, but I'm sorry to say that we simply can't risk anymore men on this rescue mission when we can't be sure that it isn't a trap," he lamented, his voice dripping sincere regret as his eyes swept over the crowd. They stopped cold as they fell on Mick's towering form. He didn't even try to defend himself or make something up. He simply bolted.

He was fast. Mick's knife was faster, driving deep into the back of the man's leg right at the knee joint and locking the joint. The man toppled over with a shout of pain, rolling to clutch his leg and jerking the blade free. He tried to scramble back to his feet as he looked up and saw Ai and the advancing crowd, but his leg betrayed him and he gave up, gingerly moving into a seated position as the procession closed in on him. Mick for his part was done with this. Justice was best served by those closest to it.

"I only wanted to protect you all," he stated. Not pleading, but simply wanting them to know his reason in the end. Some of them looked saddened but none of those quickly encircling him were about to be swayed.

"Daiki," Adachi said, solemnly shaking his head as he stepped forwards. Daiki for his part straightened his spine and met their eyes. He didn't even flinch when Adachi leaned forwards and hugged him. He twitched slightly after a moment as Adachi whispered something into his ear.

"Sorry," he whispered as Adachi drew back, his dagger now red where he had slipped it between Daiki's ribs. He coughed once, a slight trickle of blood at the corner of his mouth as his head lulled over.

Adachi stood, holding out the red stained dagger for them all to see. "It's done," he confirmed. "He was wrong, but he did what he did with conviction and paid for it like a man. Learn from his lesson. Learn it well. The price of betrayal is death," he admonished. He glanced down at his old friend one last time. "Take him away. Give him to the woods. The rest of you get ready. It looks like we are about to get back into this fight." Everyone continued to stand around, still processing all that had just happened. "Move!" he barked, jogging them out of their funk. Slowly, but with gathering speed, the crowd dispersed and got back to work.

Adachi and Ai stayed and made their way over to Mick once the group had dispersed.

"What now?" Ai asked. She was still a bit wound-up from everything and needed to vent her pent-up energy somewhere. *To think it was Daiki. I wish that I could hate him for it, but he had to go and be noble at the end.*

"Now?!" Mick pondered the question for a moment. "Now we get ready. We are secure here for the moment, but that will never last. One way or another, they will find us. We can't wait for that. It is time that we toppled the invader's claim and made ours, ours again," he answered. *After meeting Gunny Wilks again, I can't leave that bulldog lay. He's too dangerous to allow any more time to get ready.*

Ai gave the area a quick once over. "You know I want to but is this really the time?" she asked. She wanted it as much as he did but she also knew that someone had to ask the question and this time it fell on her. "Wouldn't it be better to wait for more of our forces to have a chance to recover and for our reserves to gather?"

"Yes, it would. Unfortunately, I don't think we have enough time. We need to bring this to a conclusion now, or I fear that we won't be able to. It may already be too late," Mick warned, looking back at them.

Ai scrunched her brow. "Do the Knights really worry you that much? I mean they are tough, but besides playing dirty, they're nothing special. Or am I missing something?" she asked, wondering just who's fear was at play here. Something had happened last night and it had obviously had a profound effect on Mick.

Mick took a deep breath, buying time to consider how best to answer that. *I fear that we are all blind and our unknowing arrogance may very well be our doom.* "Don't underestimate the Knights. They are arrogant but they earned their arrogance. And, don't forget that

Talbot is still out there somewhere. He's left us alone, but I don't doubt for a second that he will be back," he warned. "But it is the humans that really have me worried. There is more going on there than we have seen, and I worry that we have already given them too much time to prepare or do whatever it is that they came here for."

Adachi nodded his head. "I wanted to talk to you about that when you got back. We've been careful to keep hidden, but we still have some eyes out there and what they have been sending back to us has been more than a little troubling." Humans had long been a threat to them but these were proving to be even worse than usual.

Mick stopped and turned around to face him. "What have they been seeing?" he asked.

"It's more what they haven't seen," Adachi qualified.

Mick raised an eyebrow and waved his hand for him to continue.

"I wish I could tell you, but that is just it; they haven't been able to see anything. Except for the group that came after you two, nothing has come, gone, or passed over the base that they have erected around the village," Adachi explained. "That is another thing that we don't get. We have a decent idea of how many of them there are, somewhere between twenty-five hundred and three-thousand, of which between one-hundred and three-hundred are Knights, but that isn't nearly enough men to man a base the size of the one that they have carved out around and through the village. They'd be even more stretched than we would have been and there is no way that they could shift fast enough to cover each other or stand off a full-court press. They might be able to hurt whoever attacked them, but even a smaller force should be able to overwhelm a section and make a breach. From there they would stand to be defeated in detail. It just doesn't make sense!"

Mick thought about that in terms of what he'd seen and faced the previous night. In light of that, while their disposition did seem overconfident, it wasn't necessarily as outrageous as it first looked.

"Don't underestimate them and what they can do," he warned. "The marines have a fearfully powerful standoff ability. They aren't so well prepared if we can get in amongst them but as long as we are in-front of them, we are in trouble. You mentioned that nothing has passed over them either. Why?"

"We're not sure," Adachi answered. "Since an initial flurry of activity immediately after they arrived, nothing has flown over or landed at the village. Unfortunately, that also includes our people. No one has been able to get close enough without being seen and drawing fire. That goes for night, day, and all times in-between. We also tried going underneath, through the tunnels, but ran into several stone creature of some sort that attacked as soon as we got too close and drove us back. We hit them with everything that we had, but it didn't even seem to faze the things. Thankfully, they stopped chasing us after we retreated and were content to go back to guarding the tunnel," he explained, guessing that that would be Ai's next question.

Mick frowned at the news. "Golems! It depends on how they were made, but they are tough, albeit usually rather dull. Even the puppets are of limited use in the open and they require vast amounts of energy to control and animate them. I just hope that they haven't been so foolish as to create any that can think for themselves. If they were foolish enough to do that and even more foolish to power them with their own Crystal, it could be a serious problem. The last Golem rebellion was a bloody affair and ended badly for everyone. The Dwarves have never really recovered and some areas in Europe are still rather dangerous to enter. Chernobyl was probably the worst but some of the mountain passes and valleys in the Alps are just as bad but without the radiation," he explained, shivering at the memories and stories of some of those places. "Just more evidence of their folly. I can't say that I like the idea of attacking Golems without knowing exactly what we are really facing."

"Agreed, but you're right that we can't afford to give them more time. Time will only let them grow stronger and harder to root out. As much as I don't cherish attacking the unknown and the loss of life that will go to paying for our lack of knowledge, I agree that we need to move. You never know what Intel might show up," Adachi said, catching Mick's eye.

Ai caught the exchange but decided to let them have their secret. *He'd tell me if I asked, but he doesn't because he knows that it would upset me. Adachi taught me that trick a long time ago, but if he needed to use it now, then I'll play along. I want to know, but I don't need to. Someone still owes me a honeymoon though.* "Then I guess it is settled. We all have a lot to do before we move out. I'll see to checking in with everyone and chatting up the troops," she said, excusing herself.

Mick watched her go. "I don't deserve her," he muttered, watching her walk away. "She's pregnant you know," he added, looking back to Adachi.

"That was fast work but not too surprising. I'll make sure that she is kept clear of the worst danger. Unfortunately, short of knocking her out and sealing her away somewhere, there won't be any keeping her completely away from the battle. She's wise enough not to take any extra risks. She's reasonable enough to do that, but she won't sit this one out. There is too much at stake and it is her home that we are fighting for. She won't stand by and let others fight for it while she stands aside and watches," Adachi replied, patting Mick's shoulder.

"I know," Mick lamented. "Thank you and please keep her safe," he implored.

"We'll do everything that we can, but the same goes for you; don't go getting dead. I don't know what would happen and I don't want to find out."

"Will do," Mick yielded. He let out a sigh and glanced to the woods where some of the other villagers had already taken Daiki. Let's go get this over with!"

Adachi simply nodded.

***

They found Daiki laying where the others had left him in the woods. Mick was glad to see that they hadn't been overly rough with him and had even shown his body a modicum of respect; placing it in a clear area and erecting a small stack of rocks at his head to act as a marker.

Adachi leaned over and flicked him hard between the eyes. Nothing happened so he gave his ear a twist.

"Owe," Daiki hissed moving with it and trying to bat Adachi's hand away.

"He's lives. Should I kill him again," Adachi asked dramatically, releasing his ear and stepping back.

"No, I think he has seen the error of his ways and is ready to work the problem. Aren't you?" Mick asked, holding Daiki's eyes.

"How do I know that you won't kill me once you are done?" Daiki asked. *I can't believe that I just used that line. What has the world come to?*

And now I sound like the leg breaker in some old mobster flic. Hay Guido. Get his other kneecap. Oh well. I might as well run with it. "You don't," Mick answered. "It all depends on how helpful you are and what you have to offer. Ai is still ticked-off about the interruption to our honeymoon and I'm not so happy about it myself. And I'm sure that Adachi is a touch peeved over you hanging his niece out to dry." Adachi let out a timely growl. They may have been friends for longer than Ai had even been alive but that wasn't about to get him off of the hook. "So, I hope that this was worth it?" he asked, giving Daiki a chance to offer what he considered important information. He seemed to consider it.

"Maybe I can tell you something, but first I have a question that I need answered!" Daiki countered. He knew he was courting death at this point but that was still preferable to allowing this outsider to get any more of the people that he cared about killed.

It was Mick's turn to consider. He frowned but waved for him to continue.

"I understand that you want more information, but you also seem willing to move forwards without it if you have to?" Daiki asked. Mick simply nodded in agreement. "Then I have to know why you chose to let me live?"

"Because you have a good friend and I trust his character. He wouldn't be friends with someone without principles. Which means that you probably had principles compelling you to do what you did and tried to have done. So, I'm giving you a chance," Mick answered. Daiki seemed to accept that.

"My principles said that you would get us all killed. You seem set on doing just that. So, it wouldn't be very principled of me to help you in furthering what I see as a suicide mission fueled by a personal grudge," Daiki countered. "I understand that you have principles also. I even appreciate the sacrifices that you have made for them, but this path that you envision... only blood and death live down it."

Mick sighed. "You're almost right, only blood and death live along it, but it leads to freedom. Once you run, you might as well accept that you are a slave. A slave to the fear of death and the evil that would visit it upon you. A slave whose only choice is to keep running until one day you find that there isn't anywhere left to run and are killed or conquered as physically as you have already been mentally. That is a future without hope that I wouldn't wish upon anyone and will die to keep my child from facing!"

Daiki perked up at that final statement. "Ai is with child?" he asked looking between them. Adachi simply nodded. Daiki sat up straighter at the news. "Had I known; I never would have told them. Children are not responsible for the folly of their parents. And there is truth in what you say. But you still intend to walk a bloody path with the people I love and have guarded for longer than you have been alive," he pleaded, hoping that he could still somehow convince them to turn aside from this path.

"They chose to walk this path and you know that there was no stopping them from walking it. Even if you had succeeded, eventually they still would have tried to take back what they had lost. At most you would only have delayed it and insured that they faced it separately instead of together. But that is in the past. I need to know what you know so that I can keep as many of them alive as I can. Because this is far from the last battle that we shall face and if we can't prevail now then we have no hope against the storm that is sure to come," Mick warned, making it clear that the debate was finished. "

"What do you want to know?" Daiki asked, relenting. *For all that he sounds like bad propaganda, he just may be able to back up what he says and make it happen. He certainly seems to keep exceeding reason and expectations for everything else that has happened and the fact that he managed to return goes to show that he is willing to talk and use guile to escape when needed or is far more deadly than I had thought. Either one bodes well for the outcome of a battle.*

Adachi let out a breath that he hadn't realized that he was holding. His friend would be exiled, but that was better than dead. *And the world is a funny place and all things fade in time as long as you are both still living.*

Mick noticed but didn't allow it to show. *I'm glad that we don't have to kill his friend. Again. Making him dead to all those he is leaving behind and exiling him is a heavy enough burden.* He pushed that train of thought back down. "I need to know everything that you know about the Knights and especially what you know about the Marines. In particular what you can tell me about their character, commanders and defenses. And most of all, whatever you can tell me about a Gunny Sargent Ashcroft Wilks!?"

Daiki frowned at the last request. "I'll tell you everything that I can, I fear that it won't be much though. I only met with them once and we met outside their defenses, so I didn't see much," he admitted, trying to recall anything that might be able to save some of his people.

"Whatever you can tell us will help," Adachi encouraged.

Daiki nodded. "Beware of the Marines. There is something different about that bunch. The Knights are powerful, but despite their apparent physical weakness, the Marines scared me more. Whatever it is that motivates them to be here and fight, it is a cold burning determination and the thought of what would happen if that cold turned hot is half the reason why I did what I did. Only death will stop them. I can't stop you, but for my people and friends," he glanced meaningfully at Adachi, "who will follow you into battle, please remember to be leery of them and if you get the chance, make sure you get them all," he implored.

Mick nodded. *I already planned to. I wish I knew who commanded them. If I knew that, I may better be able to understand what drives them beyond orders.* "Do you know who commands them?" he asked, hopefully.

Daiki shook his head. "I once heard a Knight refer to him as the 'Old Man.' He said it with disdain, but there was something like fear in his voice also and he clammed right up when the Marines who were present immediately stopped what they were doing and stared at him. Whoever he is, the Marines are behind him and apparently even if the common Knights dislike him, something about him has at least earned their fear if not their respect. The odd part was that for all of their fear, they almost seemed as if they were talking about someone that they had never met," he added, trying to let them understand that they were dealing with a ghost. He was sure that there was a man behind it but who and what he was, was still a mystery.

"The Old Man," Adachi mumbled, his eyes narrowing as he tried to remember something. Whatever it was, it eluded him, and he gave up with a shake of his head.

Mick felt like he should know recognized the moniker also. It was clear that they weren't talking about just any commander, but he couldn't quite grasp the memory he was looking for. There was something there, but it was foggy and stayed just beyond his grasp while putting a cold chill in his gut in much the same way as the Gunny had. Unable to recall, he filed it away for later and moved on. They needed to wrap this up before anyone got curious as to what they were doing out here and came to investigate. "What do you know of their defenses?"

"Very little," Daiki admitted. "They only met with me outside and even then, we were still over a kilometer away. It was clear that they had at least some heavy machinery though. There were track marks in the dirt of the killing field surrounding their fort and the berms themselves were too large to have been made by hand in the short amount of time that they had. Even with machinery, I have to wonder how they moved so much earth so fast."

"They didn't. They filled their defenses with the mix of everything that they cleared and layered packed dirt over the top of it. The mix of densities is better for absorbing explosions. Solid packed earth is good for stopping solid ordinance, but it isn't so good with explosive ordinance. The energy transfers too cleanly and it blows out. Mixed-density-fill allows it to absorb the energy and the blowout is smaller. There is the risk of having weak spots in the defenses, but the overall effect is more resilient and easier to construct. I wonder who they figure will be attacking them with penetrating explosive ordinance." Mick pondered the issue, but the list was long in the long-term but limited for now. "A problem for later. What it means for us is that we will have a hard time breaching the ramparts. Anything else?"

Daiki was silent, trying to remember all that he had gleaned. If he couldn't stop them then he wanted to make sure that they were as ready as possible. "You can't see them now, but while I was meeting them, there was a slight slide on one of ramparts. The cover sluffed off and I noticed that there was what looked like a shield with a void behind it. The Knights didn't seem to care much, but the young lieutenant that was with them didn't seem to like it when he caught me casting a glance that ways and stepped over so as to block my view. Whatever it was, the Marines seem to think it is important that they keep it hidden."

Mick frowned at that news. *A firing port. But what kind of weapon does it fire? It would have to be a fairly flat trajectory. Some kind of direct fire artillery or machine-gun? Or does it have a completely different purpose? Whatever it conceals, I don't look forwards to finding out.* "Thank you for the warning. Is there anything else that you can tell us?"

"That's all that I know and saw," Daiki admitted after a moment. He looked between the two of them expectantly.

Mick cast a look over to Adachi. He just shrugged. *I wish we knew more but it's more than we knew earlier, and Adachi doesn't seem to think that he was lying about anything.* With a shrug, he pulled his pack around and dug into it, pulling out several items and arranging them on a small cloth and tying the bundle together before dropping it next to Daiki. "Adachi, see to his injuries and see him on his way. I expect you back before nightfall. As for you, Daiki, I can't guarantee your life if you ever come back, so if you ever try, I suggest you come bearing something of value equal to your life in exchange," he warned, locking eyes with Daiki. "Safe travels," he added. He gave Adachi a knowing nod before heading back to town.

***

Mick found Ai busy helping the others prepare to move out. Apparently, she figured that the sooner they got this over with, the sooner they could get back to their honeymoon. The walk back had given him time to contemplate all that he knew, thought he knew, wanted to know, and couldn't know. Sadly, what he knew was far less than he would have liked, and he wasn't looking forwards to the coming battle. *And let's not forget that Talbot is still out there somewhere and will most likely return at a most inopportune time.* Ai caught his eye and brooding mood and separated herself from the throng.

"What did you learn?" Ai asked in a hushed tone as she slid up next to him, waving off the occasional catcall. "I'm telling Fluffy, about the next person skimping on work to make a catcall," she threatened. The others fell back on their work with hushed snickers and abject terror.

"Fluffy?" Mick asked temporarily side-tracked.

"Aouba Furuya, he's a Neko and the local finder. He was a bit of a pudgy kid and still has a rather full-bodied coat of fur. He is also working as our supply section and isn't one to put up with slackers. So...?" Ai asked, still waiting for his answer.

"Right. I should probably make time to meet him," Mick said.

"Probably, but you can do that later. What did you learn?" Ai repeated. She specifically didn't ask about from who or how he learned it.

"We are facing a hard nut," Mick answered. "On the one side, we are facing an ancient and deadly military organization. Once, they fought as line soldiers, together in battle, but after all this time and with the suddenness with which events have played out, I doubt that they have regained or trained much in that form of fighting. At least I hope that in their arrogance and belief in their individual strength, they haven't regained that fighting style because if they have, they will be deadly. As it is, they will probably choose to face us as singles or small groups on the battlefield. They will be dangerous and despite their arrogance, will demand a toll in blood on our part to take them down. But we can take them if they come out to meet us. The Marines are another issue altogether. The more I learn about them, the more I get the feeling that the Knights aren't really in charge and are here more as a cover or distraction even if they aren't aware of it. I saw the Marines fight off an attack last night. They were caught by surprise but once they didn't have to follow stupid orders and could fight their way, it was a slaughter. Their weapons are powerful and deadly, but judging by their defense, their utility is limited because of that power. The furthest kill that I observed was around three hundred meters away, but visibility was low, and these are Marines. I would assume that they can make shots beyond that, but they will still need to be able to see what they are shooting at so the overall range is still probably limited to what you might expect of a decent rifleman. On the other hand, cover may not be as much proof against their fire as one might hope. Whatever their rifles are, they pack a punch that even a Dragon would find daunting to shake off. In general, they don't really seem to want to fight us, but many of them, despite knowing better, still blame Japan and me for what happened, and they want their pound of flesh. When it comes time to fight them, they won't pull their punches. Also, I get the feeling that they are operating under shoot first Rules of Engagement. Add to all of that that they are trained in line, unit, squad and close quarter combat, although those tactics would have to have been modified on the fly, and I believe that they are the true threat in the short-term and will definitely be one in the long-term. They may be spread thin on the defenses, but I don't think they are truly as thin as their numbers make them appear," he concluded with a tired sigh.

Ai digested the news with a frown. "So how do we improve our odds of winning this without taking extreme losses," she asked. Defeat wasn't an option.

Mick was silent for a moment trying to puzzle that out. *This is going to be costly.* "We have to draw out one of the forces and destroy it. I still feel that the Marines are the greater danger, but we can't let them and the Knights stay together. The Knights as individuals would be able to react independently and stiffen breaches in their defenses while the Marines chewed us up at range. We have to draw the Knights out beyond the supporting range of the defenses and annihilate them. If they surrender, we'll take prisoners, but we won't take any risks by allowing them to retreat after we have engaged them. They are arrogant and prideful, so we can count on them to take the bait. What worries me is if the Marines will be content to let us fight them without interference or if they will sally to their aid. If that happens, we will have to be ready to break contact and retreat. Maybe send a smaller attacking force against the base to force them to pull back and return to the defenses," he answered. "Either of those outcomes would be costly and victory will probably be almost as or even more costly."

"I like the part where we annihilate the Knights," Ai agreed. *Especially after they messed up my honeymoon!!!* She was ticked-off, but she hadn't lost her head though she definitely had a bone to pick with them. "It's risky. I agree that the Knights are dangerous, but aren't we risking depleting ourselves before what, even you, considered the main battle?"

"Yes," Mick agreed. "But we have to risk it if we want to win. We don't have the numbers or the time for a long siege. Whatever happens, we need to remember, this is only the beginning. Who knows how long this war for control will last or how the lines will develop. We don't even know how many different factions, foreign and domestic are liable to crop up. The U.S may have gotten here first, but others will come, have already come. And then there are the local threats like Talbot and who knows who or what else that are already on the move and carving out their own domains. Japan will likely wind up more fractured than it has been since the Warring States Period. Which is why we have to make our stand, for our area here and now. We have to show them that we won't let them keep what they have stolen. This is our home and they aren't invited!" he said. His voice must have grown louder as he talked, because a roar went up from those around him and spread until it reverberated through the whole village. He looked around in awe at those assembled. They had been beaten and bloodied, their homes and lands destroyed or stolen by invaders; but they weren't broken, and they weren't done. They had come from many different places and walks of life, but the heat of battle had forged them into one people. There was no division and no going back.

"We owe it to them," Mick whispered to Ai. "We owe it to our future," he said, resting his hand on Ai's abdomen and meeting her eyes.

"Then let's make this happen," Adachi agreed gruffly. He'd snuck up at some point, his work done, and took his place on Ai's other side. "You heard the Commander. What do you think this is, a Pep-Rally!?" he bellowed at them.

"Stay," Mick asked, as they regained a modicum of privacy.

"I'll hold back to the rear, but the fate of our family will be decided together!" Ai answered, locking eyes with Mick. There was concern there, but determination also.

"Then stay safe and join me when it is done," Mick relented.

"I'll hold you to that," Ai agreed.

Killing Field
Sunday, July 25

Mick crouched at the edge of the killing field surrounding the Base. Two days had passed since they had returned from their honeymoon. He wasn't a big fan of making war on Sundays, but it had taken two days to get everything ready and in place and they didn't dare wait any longer. "It's time to go," he said, putting down the binoculars he had borrowed. He hadn't liked what he had seen. Whoever the 'Old Man' was, he knew his defenses. The Star fort had been reborn, and it was a beast. The walls were sloped but reached fifteen meters above the surrounding landscape. Before those walls was a depression that was another ten meters deep and who knew what lurked in the murky water that filled it. He wasn't looking forward to this, but there was no more time. Whispers from the south had reached them. There wasn't much news yet, but what they had heard was disturbing.

"Let's get this over with," Adachi grumped, pushing his way back into the shadows with Mick.

They quickly jogged back to the gathering area for his force. There were about one-hundred and fifty in the group. They were mostly the same men and women who had been with him the first time on the line or who had followed him through the tunnels. They would be the pointy end of today's attack and they wouldn't break until he did, and he wouldn't break until his heart stopped beating. Even then, there were things Night could do.

Mick took a moment to hop up onto a log so that they could all see him. "Let's go get our homes back," he shouted. They thundered their resolve back, their battle cry so loud that those in the Base were sure to hear them. After ten seconds of roaring their fury, they fell quiet like a water tap turned by a guillotine. The silence was deafening. He gave them a nod and hopped down. Without another word or command, they fell in behind him as they marched back to the clearing. Their steps falling in rhythm like crashing thunder.

"Halt!" Adachi bellowed as they formed a loose line just beyond the trees.

There was a light mist rising from the killing field around the Base as the sun rose above the treetops and heated the damp soil. It had rained the previous night. Not a sound was to be heard beyond the creaking of the swaying trees in the light morning breeze.

"You think they see us?" Adachi whispered with a smile as the Base broke into a buzz of activity.

"Perhaps," Mick said, looking both ways along his line. There was anticipation in the air, but no fear. *They trust me to win and sell their lives dearly. Time to prove them right.* "My flag," he called. A runner quickly approached with a standard that they had created only a day earlier. It was a simple design with the red sun of japan sitting in the left corner, the stars and moon sitting in the right, and three intertwined trees growing between them. One tree was the brown and green of the earth for humans, another was black for Night, and the last was made of mist for those of the Fair. He'd tried to argue that there was no reason for them to add a tree for Night, but the flag had already been completed and they weren't about to be convinced to change it. Embroidered beneath the trees, for this was not just a flag but their battle flag, was the date and place of the first battle that they had fought. Beneath that was today's date: July 25 home, and Victory. *Now to see if they understand the message.* The runner had also delivered a second, smaller, white flag and handed it to Tenmen.

"Shall we?" Mick asked.

"You sure that they won't just try to kill you when they have the chance?" Adachi asked, loosening his sword in its sheath.

"If it was just the Knights, I would assume that that is exactly what they would do. But, with the Marines being there also, I highly doubt that they will do something so rash," Mick replied as they started walking out into the no man's land; the mud making sucking noises with every step. Like every battle in history, he had to wonder how many souls the mud alone would reap this day. Thankfully, mud always favored peasants over Knights. "But you never know, which is why you two are coming with me."

"So that we can die together taking as many of them as we can with us?" Tenmen inquired.

"Pfft. No. So that you two can run back and bring the cavalry while I slaughter the lot of them," Mick corrected.

"Why does he get to have all the fun while we have to run back for the others? Shouldn't it be the other way around?" Tenmen asked Adachi. "Where's the propriety in that!?"

"He's the commander. Were just foot soldier aids. Our job is to take notes, bring tea, and run like scared chickens when the commander is in danger," Adachi said, educating him of the proper role of an aid.

"I want to go back to being a common foot soldier. At least then all I had to worry about was stupid orders and killing enemies," Tenmen complained with a harrumph. "Think the commander would agree to a transfer?"

"Nope," Mick said, chuckling at their byplay. He stopped abruptly, motioning for the others to do the same and handed his flag off to Adachi.

"What's up?" Adachi asked, turning serious.

Mick didn't answer directly. "Busy little builders aren't ya? Catch!" he said, pitching a rock hard enough to dent a half-inch steel plate. Adachi and Tenmen shared a glance and shrugged. "Down!" he ordered, dropping to the dirt. Adachi and Tenmen were only a half second slower than he was. He was glad to see that both had kept their flags from touching the dirt. A soft crump sounded ahead of them. They looked up to see a shot gun blast of baseball sized, dark egg-shaped items burst into the air. As they reached the apex of their flight, about a meter up and five meters away, the eggs exploded in blinding flashes sending metal balls, small lengths of wire and molten copper spraying over a roughly fifty-by-fifty-meter area. The first was quickly followed by more as eggs burst out of hundreds of the mines, sweeping the area between them and the Base a half-kilometer away and a kilometer-wide front in a rain of death.

Mick let the shroud of dirt and smoke abate a little before getting back to his feet. "I hope those weren't important," he yelled at the others, as if his hearing had been slightly affected. It hadn't.

"Just a welcoming mat," Adachi grumbled climbing back to his feet and knocking some debris away.

"You don't suppose that they may take a little offence to us clearing their minefield?" Tenmen asked, eyeing the wall. They were probably in range of those manning it at this point and while he was confident that he could evade an errant round, a fusillade might be a bit much when they were the only targets.

"Nonsense. They failed to place a warning that they had placed a minefield here to catch attackers unaware or inform us to stop as we approached under a white flag. How can they hold us accountable for the sudden and timely misfire of their improperly marked mines?" Mick asked, with a grin that would have done the Cheshire cat proud. "Oh look, they are opening the door and coming out to greet us," he said smiling as a breach in the wall appeared and five men, two marines and three Knights came out and started advancing across the field towards them. "Look sharp," he ordered. Tenmen and Adachi straitened their muddied attire and brushed off a few pieces of detritus that had landed on them while they waited, holding their flags at the ready. It was as good as they could do, considering the circumstances and their lack of uniforms.

"You think the dragons picked up the frequency to turn off the mines?" Adachi asked as the procession paused, checking that the remaining mines were properly deactivated, before continuing their careful approach.

"Probably, Mick agreed. I just hope that the frequency was the same for all of them and that each section isn't unique," Mick answered, wincing at the thought of running a gauntlet of mines like these. Given the swath the single one in the middle of the field in-front of them that he had forced to detonate had set off, any advance into that would be costly. Given the makeup of his force, it wouldn't be as devastating as it would have been against regular humans, but the injuries still would have depleted and slowed his ranks more than he would like. There wasn't any more time for chit-chat as the opposite procession drew near.

Kipper, Axel, and Page were present, as was Gunny Wilks and a Lieutenant Brently according to his patch. They came to a stop with about three meters separating their groups.

Mick shook his head and tsked. "I had hoped that the man behind the curtain would have deigned to come and greet us himself. I'd very much like to meet this 'Old Man' and share some words with him," he lamented, frowning as he shook his head slowly in disappointment. "I guess I will just have to settle for the Assassin, the three junkyard dogs, and someone who I guess is his Aid?" he prodded and probed, appraising the young Lieutenant. The Lieutenant's eyes had a slow smolder in them as they met his and worked hard not to slide in the Gunny's direction. *Now that's interesting. Apparently, the Gunny's the one in charge today. The Lieutenant's waiting for his lead.* He regarded the Lieutenant closer. He appeared to be in his mid-twenties, in good physical shape, fairly intelligent looking, and had a serious case of a simmering mad-on. *Someone to watch during the coming day and if he survives.*

"We're in charge here!" Kipper yipped.

"My bad, I didn't mean to imply that you were insignificant myrmidon," Mick jabbed back. He rather liked the way Kipper's face turned red. He hoped it induced an aneurism. He caught the corner of the Lieutenants mouth twitch ever so slightly in a smile before falling back into a flat mask. The Gunny didn't even so much as bat an eye, though it was clear that he was enjoying the show. He at least had style.

"And here we thought you had seen reason and come to talk terms. Apparently the only cure for a rabid dog is to put him down," Axel smiled in anticipation.

"But I have come to talk terms," Mick corrected, surprising them all. "It's why I'd hoped to talk with the Old Man. The only person of real significance. I guess I will have to settle for his Assassin and his aid," he answered, smiling as he saw Axel and Kipper's hackles go up again as he excluded them.

Page spared them a warning glance. "Unconditional Surrender and submission to the brand are the only terms that are acceptable," he cut in, smiling triumphantly.

Mick frowned. "That seems a mite bit severe. But if they are all that is acceptable, then I guess there is no help," he agreed, frowning sadly. "You can leave your weapons in the base and come out in single file with five meters between each of you. There will be a guide to lead you to a temporary holding area which we have..."

"What are you babbling about!?" Axel demanded, cutting Mick off.

Mick gave them a confused look. "Why, I think that is obvious. You Knights offered terms of your surrender and I accepted them. I had hoped that the Marines contingent's commander would be present so that he could speak for his force, but such is life. We are in a bit of a hurry though, so it would be appreciated if you could run back and inform the rest of the Knights of your terms of surrender and be prepared to submit to them and the brand within the next hour. There is much to be done today and little time in which to do it all. Moving back home and cleaning up after invaders is always so tedious," he lamented. Gunny finally lost the battle with his grin and the corner of his mouth quirked up a whole millimeter.

Kipper made to draw his sword and close on Mick. He stopped short as the cold bite of Tenmen's sickle tickled his neck.

"I thought you said these Knight's had honor?" Tenmen asked. "So far all I've seen them do is cowardly attack those who had no reason to make war on them, steal what wasn't theirs, threaten slavery, and now renege on an honorable agreement of surrender and attempt to attack the one who they surrendered to. Very un-gentlemanly," he said, shaking his head sadly.

"They have been going through a tough spell recently. Faulty leadership practices. Nepotism, Nihilism, and several other isms have plagued them for a while now and no one has been willing to clean house. I tried to warn them that those leadership conventions in Vegas were a bad idea," Mick lamented.

"Enough of this farce!" Page lashed out, emotion and heat finally entering his voice. "Release our man and you may yet live. Although, you may soon wish that you had died. As for your men, they can surrender now, or we will kill the lot of them later. You with that horrid flag may go back and inform them!" he ordered. No one moved. "Now!"

Mick cocked his head to the side and frowned. "I guess the game is up. So be it," he said. Page started to relax until he noticed where Mick was looking. He made to move but it was already too late.

Tenmen's blade bit deep, cutting all the way to the spine in a quick and smooth motion. At the same time, he hurled a smoke bomb at their feet, triggering a stringer of them that they had laid out as they walked out for the meeting. The air quickly filled with a concealing billow of noxious smoke and obscured them from both sides' view.

Mick heard a clash of steel and a pained yell from where Axel had been standing. Apparently, his reflexes had been quick enough to keep Adachi mostly at bay. He wasn't really worried about that at the moment. He still had one last message to deliver. The one that this whole meeting had really been about, and which would decide their fates. He didn't have to search long for the recipient.

He brought his axes around just in time to parry a slashing cutlass that had been seeking to tear open his side. "That wasn't very nice after I went through all of this to come and say hi," he said, pushing forwards so that he barreled into Gunny before he could disappear back into the smoke.

"You should have taken my advice!" Gunny grunted, taking the shoulder blow with his knees and killing all of Mick's motion. He was a lot stronger than his size implied.

"But I didn't and here we are, but I have some advice for you now," Mick countered, breaking contact as the Gunny almost won free and re-locking up with the Gunny's blade before he could slip free. They collided with another umph.

"I'm listening," Gunny said, holding his ground, still working to free his blade.

"And trying to kill me at the same time. I would applaud your multitasking ability, but my hands are a little busy at the moment. I want you to deliver a message to your commander. He has to know how this will end. Badly and with much blood. I give him this chance to pull out and leave without our interference," Mick offered.

"A good deal, but the Knights will never go for it," Gunny grunted, shifting his footing, trying to gain the advantage. *He's a quick learner. I wonder if I showed him too much last time.*

"Then leave them. We have a score to settle with them anyways. But be warned, if you aid them or make any signs of not complying, we will attack and overrun your defenses. We'll die in droves doing it, but we both know that you can't stop us if we're willing to die to the last man. I'm warning you that we're willing to take the Pyrrhic victory and it will be our victory."

"I'll let him know," Gunny agreed.

Mick felt the hackles go up on the back of his neck. He broke with Gunny, lunging a meter to the side and spun to face behind him. He was just in time to meet a flurry of rapier jabs that landed like sledgehammer blows against his axes, each blow driving him back a step and closer to the boundary of the smoke. He didn't much care to find out what would happen if he crossed that threshold. When the next flurry arrived, he met it head on, turning the thrusts to the side and bearing down on the attacker. He had several shallow cuts on his arms and legs by the time he pushed through the attack and found the young Lieutenant. He made ready to attack but stopped short as he felt a shiver go down his spine. At the last second, he jerked to the side and back towards Adachi, Tenmen, and the path leading back to their forces.

Gunny stepped out of the shadows and laid a restraining hand on the Lieutenant's shoulder. The Lieutenant hesitated for just a moment before his eyes flared as Gunny whispered something to him and he finally lowered his blade. The Gunny simply met Mick's eyes and nodded before the two of them melted back into the smoke.

Mick didn't loiter. "Fallback," he yelled and began running back towards their lines. He grabbed their flag as he passed and didn't wait or stop to look for the others. They were either okay or they weren't. He'd know soon enough and there was little that he could do for them on his own.

The others soon caught up with him and fell in alongside. Mick gave them each a quick once over. Adachi had a few nicks but nothing too severe and none of them were from a Weeping Blade. Tenmen on the other hand had a deep gash along his right cheek and was missing his right earlobe. He also had a small expanding circle of red spreading across his right pant leg. Rapier wounds.

"Have a little too much fun?" Mick asked as they neared their lines.

"The little guy is rather sneaky and quiet. He also has a rather fast, sharp, and pointy sword," Tenmen answered. "I can see that you also made his acquaintance," he said, giving Mick's nicks a raised eyebrow. "He's one to be careful of."

"Agreed." Mick's hands were still buzzing from taking the hammer blows from the Lieutenant's flurry and he had to wonder what kind of sword it was not to have snapped under the power of those blows. "I find it best never to underestimate one's opponents. Especially Marines. They are full of surprises, tenacious, and seem to attract some rather deadly individuals with exotic skill sets."

"You think the Commander over there will listen?" Adachi asked as they finally re-entered the trees and dropped into a position that they had constructed the previous night.

'Listen? Yes, I think he will," Mick answered. "But will he do what we asked? That is the real question, and I don't know. If nothing else, knowing that we are willing to lose to win, might convince him to pull out sooner if we go for the full court press."

Tenmen pondered that for a moment. "I hope he listens. I don't really fancy fighting men like that one," he said, shaking his head.

"I hope so too, but if we do, I expect that there are only a few like those two," Mick speculated. He paused and looked between both of them. What happened to my white bandana?" he asked, referring to the truce flag.

Tenmen simply smiled and pointed.

Mick looked back the way that they had come. The smoke and morning mist had mostly lifted, and he was able to see clear across the whole killing field. There in the middle of the field was a shiny spot where the sun reflected against Kippers shiny silver armor. It took a moment for him to see it through the glare, but there sticking up next to him, as if his dead hands were holding it aloft, was their small truce flag waving in the light breeze. There were red specks going diagonally across it where his blood had dyed the flag.

"I thought it was poetic," Tenmen defended.

Mick just shook his head.

"Seems to have had the desired effect," Adachi groused, pointing back towards the base.

The gate that the others had first come through was open again and shiny figures were pouring out of it and quickly forming into a blobular front.

Mick smiled as he saw that they didn't attempt to form ranks and instead simply moved forwards in a spreading amebic fashion with a few different tendrils fighting over being the point and other areas seeming to hold back. It made it harder to get a hard count on their numbers but tactically it was exactly what they'd hoped for.

"Well the turtles are out of their shell. Looks to be at least two-hundred and fifty of them," Adaich guesstimated, there was a little trepidation in his voice. The Knights were puffed up peacocks but that didn't mean that they weren't deadly. And they were about to meet that peacock with only about half as many of their own numbers. "Do you think the bulldogs will stay home or come out to play?" he asked, not cherishing the idea of facing even worse odds.

Before Mick could answer, the gate swung back shut behind the hoard of Knights and the few heads visible atop the battlements slowly disappeared. "I wish I knew. But without having met the 'Old Man' I can't really guess. One way or the other, we will know here soon," he answered.

"Stand!" he ordered. The assembled humans and Fair behind him rose and quickly formed ranks without as much as a whisper. Even the trees seemed to be keeping their peace. "Advance!" he bellowed into the silence. As one, every left foot stomped down sending a drum roll ahead of them. With a metered beat, they advanced clear of the tree line and onto the Killing Field. Today it would earn its moniker. "Halt! Dress ranks!" he ordered as they cleared the trees.

They crisply completed the evolution. The Knights had almost advanced to Kipper's corpse and the flag at the halfway point.

Mick looked both ways, giving an appreciative nod. They weren't professionals at this type of fighting, but for disparate group of skilled warriors coming together in what amounted to a militia, they were doing remarkably well. *Now to just hold them together until we meet our quarry and chaos plays its dirty hand.* "Advance!" He stepped off with the others as he continued leading them from the front. In this kind of battle, there would be little to no coordinating once the battle was met and bedlam ensued. So, for today and on this battlefield, his place was leading from the front and inspiring those that followed him.

The Knights sent up a ruckus of shouts and battle-cries. Mick's fighters met it in silence and continued to advance with grim determination. Their only reply was the stomp of their feet and their determined advance. The Knights soon fell silent as the seeds of doubt and incomprehension took root in their hearts.

At two-hundred meters, Mick shouted one last time, breaking the heavy silence. "Halt!" was the only command he gave. He looked straight ahead, making eye contact with as many of the Knights as he could. He had a good command voice and it carried across the fifty-meter void between to them. "You invaders come as thieves and honor-less backstabbers. Whatever past honor and glory you once had is over, made corrupt by your greed and pride. You brought this doom upon yourselves by allowing the contemptible to lead you and choosing to follow them. You stole what is not yours and offered only slavery in return. We offered you peace and a chance to leave, you have thrown it in our face and attacked us under a flag of truce. Your honor is dead and soon so shall you be!"

Several of the Knights stuttered as his words washed over their jostling ranks. A few seemed to hold back, but the rest pushed forwards gaining speed as their pride boiled. Their flanks began curving in as their rage focused all their attention on him. His barbs had stung their pride and now they meant to take his head and the glory. Their pride blinded them. It would be their downfall.

The Knights quickly closed to thirty meters. Mick and his men had remained silent the whole time. That all change now. "Down!" he ordered. The Knights were a bare twenty meters away now. As the first two ranks took a knee, they revealed the third rank. The rank of archers and ranged fighters. As one, fifty of them loosed their fire. Arrows fired from bows strung at over three-hundred pounds hammered against the first rank of the Knights. Many of the arrows were stopped or turned aside by the strength of the armor and the runes carved upon them but others drove home. Some shattered the armor throwing the knights from their feet, others detonated in explosions that laid low all those around them, while still others pierced through it and its wearer like hot butter and kept going through two or three more behind them. They fired a second volley sending orbs or energy of every type towards the Knights. Fire and electricity predominated; taking their toll but less so than the arrows. There was no more time for a third volley.

"Up and at them! Finish them" Mick bellowed and charged. The others quickly regained their feet and joined behind him as they hurtled into the charging crush of Knights. Lightly armored and armed fast killers with an array of abilities met heavily armored and armed slightly slower killers with a slightly smaller mix of abilities.

The world erupted in violence and death as the two forces broke against each other. The Knights' mass carried them deep into the enmeshing line of Mick's force and quickly began to flow around its flanks curving them back in on themselves and driving them towards the middle.

Only part of Mick's mind focused on those details. The plan had been made and the die was cast. There was little to nothing that he could do to change things now other than fight with all of his strength and take down as many of the Knights as he could.

Mick grunted as he guarded against a savage overhand swing from a lumbering Great-Sword, catching it in the guard of his axe and turning it to the side. The Knight tucked his shoulder and drove forwards ramming it into Mick's shoulder and driving him back. He meant to topple Mick and finish him while he tried to regain his footing. As long as their weapons were entangled, there was no escape.

Mick broke the second rule of battle; never lose your weapon and dropped his locked up axes. Freed from the anchoring force, he followed the first rule of battle; do whatever it takes to win. He pivoted to the side while reaching up and behind the Knight's head and adding forwards and downward momentum. Without Mick's resistance to slow him and prop him up, he stumbled and fell as Mick drove his helmeted head into the mud, filling his visor. He quickly recovered, pushing back to his feet while swinging behind him, where Mick had been, to keep him at bay while he attempted to clear the mud from his visor. Making little headway, he used his free hand to yank his helmet free and wipe the muck from his eyes.

In the interval, Mick had already moved to the side and recovered his axes. The Knight opened his eyes and smiled as he saw Mick crouching before him, still unarmed. Then an axe seemed to sprout from his forehead with a dull thunk. He was still smiling as he fell over.

Mick wasted no time, yanking the axe free and rejoining the battle. He was just about to reach his next quarry when Adachi caught his arm. He barely stopped Night from attacking his friend.

"It's time," Adachi yelled over the cacophony of dying men and crashing steel. "We can't hold out much longer. They have us fully enveloped!"

Mick took a calming breath and surveyed the battlefield. It felt like days had passed since the battle had begun but by the sun, he knew that only a little over a half-hour had passed. They were surrounded and being driven back into an ever-tighter circle. The Knights were falling, but not fast enough. Their mass and armor were letting them press forwards, driving Mick's force back into a shrinking circle. His fighters needed space to fight their way and that space was being denied to them as they became constricted. At the same time, the Knights were finally getting into the close quarters battle that played to their current mass and brute force approach to battle. He winced as he saw more and more of his men falling or being pulled back and replaced at the front as they were killed or injured. Soon even the replacements and rotation that was keeping them alive wouldn't even be possible as they ran out of room. He happened to catch sight of Page, about twenty meters away, through the throng. His pride wasn't all a lie, the man truly was a deadly warrior in his own right, and he was pushing hard against the remains of Mick's unit. Inflicting wound after wound with his cursed Weeping Blade. Their eyes met. Mick couldn't see his mouth through his armor, but he knew that Page was smiling in anticipation of a crushing victory and capturing or slaying him. It wouldn't be long until he got his wish and they were overwhelmed.

It was time. "ON ME!" Mick commanded. His deafeningly loud voice cut through the sounds of battle and death. The Knights flinched back in surprise, creating a split-second lull in the battle. Mick's unit who had been waiting for the order acted quickly and took full advantage of it. Instead of attacking, they shifted and formed tight ranks around him. Doing exactly as the Knights had been attempting to force them to do. Packed tightly together with nowhere left to go. "Set!" Mick commanded. "Go!"

Page's eyes frowned as he heard the commands and saw the movements, at first they had swelled with sense of imminent victory, but turned thoughtful and then worried as he saw the choreography of the movement. He quickly recognized that this wasn't some last-ditch maneuver to stave off the inevitable but part of a plan. He turned just in time to hear all of the men and women in the tight huddle stomp as one. The impact was hard and loud enough to shake the earth beneath the Knight's feet as the drum of thunder reverberated through the earth. Three times they stomped, and the thunder roared. Then silence held as the Knights paused for another brief moment. He didn't know what plan was about to unfold, but he knew that they had walked into some kind of trap and that it would be bad. He opened his mouth to order a decisive attack, meaning to kill Mick no matter what and hopefully demoralize or thwart whatever was about to come. "Kill them now," he shouted, but even he couldn't hear the command as the ground shook one more time, staggering them all.

As one, the Knights turned as the ground in a rough square around them bulged upwards before bursting into a shower of mud, rocks, roots, and a few Knights who had happened to be standing in the wrong place at the right time. The Knights stood there stunned by the surprise attack, peering into the dust. They recoiled as a fusillade of arrows and other ranged attacks and weapons pummeled them from all sides. Those left alive flinched as they heard a single high pitch howl of a battle cry rise from these new shrouded attackers. In response, a high-pitched yell answered from all sides. It was followed by the thunder of running feet. It was too much, too suddenly. First one Knight and then another stepped back in fear and horror as a new and unknown force of dark red armored shapes broke through the fog and charged them from all sides. The village's main force had come through the tunnels the night before excavating new tunnels and readying charges to clear the overburden. The Knights knew that there was no way for them to get past the

Golems and attack the base so they had grown lax and forgotten to consider other ways in which that approach might be used to attack.

A single Knight lost his nerve and tried to run as what looked to be the red devils of the underworld, in their crimson armor and horned helmets burst forth and charged them. He was soon followed by others as he fell back on the false safety of the rest of the Knight's force as it recoiled in on itself. It contracted and readied to meet this new attack; forgetting the rot left un-pruned at its core.

Page hadn't forgotten, as the Knights contracted and readied to meet the attack, he looked back at the small group of around a hundred battered and bloodied warriors that remained surrounding Mick. Their eyes met across the bare fifteen meters that now separated them. Mick was smiling as they all crouched low, caged predators readying to attack.

Mick saw Page grasp the situation, but it was already too late for him to do anything about it. *He may be prideful, but he isn't an idiot. But his fall has come today.* "Attack!" He ordered, beating Page to the punch. The tight circle burst outwards like the pedals of a deadly blossom as those remaining warriors took the distracted Knights from rear.

Mick had known that there was no way to win this fight without losses. In a stand-up battle with their full force against the Knights, he had known that they would win. But the cost would have been too high. The Knights would have faced them with too much organization or holed-up in the base and refused to meet them. Only by baiting them with his smaller unit and allowing them to sink their teeth deeply into the bait, was there a way to defeat them without breaking his whole force in the effort. They had bled and died to make this possible, now it was time to put the Knights down quickly and end this with as few additional losses as possible.

Mick's unit crashed into the Knights rear at the same time as the ambush force engaged their new front. They were still outnumbered in the center, but they also faced a much smaller front and a confused enemy that suddenly found itself between the hammer of the ambush and the anvil at their own center. Chaos reigned amongst their ranks as they fought madly to get free.

Mick swung his axe, cleaving backs, arms, and legs as he advanced through the chaos of the inner battle. He had his sights set on Page and there weren't too many more between him and his quarry. Tenmen popped up alongside him, diving the point of his sickle into the neck joint of a Knight that had been charging from Mick's blind spot.

"You take the head, I'll take the Chihuahua at his heel," Tenmen said, breaking away and closing on Axel who was likewise guarding Page's flank. The two of them were a deadly pair and far too many of Mick's unit already lay dead at their feet.

Mick was glad for the help but worried at the same time. Tenmen was deadly but so was Axel. He didn't have time to dwell on it as he entered the small ring of death that surrounded the two Knights. He raised his guard to block a rain of powerful blows as he entered Page's range. Out of the corner of his eye, he managed to catch a glimpse of Tenmen as he darted in and began his attack on Axel, drawing them apart. He was thankful for that, but still worried. With an effort, he managed to capture the next blow, turning it to the side as he swung his free axe, ringing Page's helmet. He followed it with a solid kick that drove Page back and opened some space between them. Both blows had been to Page's armor and he quickly recovered, pulling himself back up and regarding Mick. His pristine griffin winged helmet was now marred by a furrow along the left side and there was a trickle of blood running down his neck and chin, staining his white under padding.

"You should have surrendered," Page seethed, reaching up and prying his helmet free. A bloody gash now ran up the left side of his head, marring his once handsome features.

"You should have stayed home," Mick countered, lunging forwards and pressing an attack of his own. His blows rained in from every angle, driving Page onto the defensive and backwards. It only lasted for a moment, before they reached a new equilibrium; their motions blurring as they traded back and forth with attacks, blocks, and parries. Several times, Mick managed to slip a blow through only to have it turned aside by Page's armor. After a minute of neither of them gaining any ground, they broke again, regarding each other as Page slowly circled, trying to gain some advantage. Mick simply stood there grinning like a madman.

"Finally lost your mind?" Page asked, raising his guard a hair higher as he readied to attack.

"Almost there," Mick answered, sinking lower into his stance. He lunged forwards, covering the distance between them in a flash. He blocked Page's first strike with a blade on blade block at the hilt of Page's sword. A second later, his other axe smashed against Page's torso armor, only he hadn't used the axe head. The hammer struck and reverberated the armor like a gong.

Page's eyes went wide as he realized Mick's intent. Knight's armor was tough, but it came at a cost. The wards that were used to create it had one drawback. They made the armor brittle. That usually wasn't an issue because the wards protected it and made it stronger than any armor that man could fashion from metal alone. It was almost impossible to defeat it with bladed weapons in close combat. Arrows and pointy weapons could penetrate it, but only by defeating the ward in a small area. You could also kill the occupant with enough inertial trauma but even then, the armor usually remained mostly intact. Mick wasn't using a blade though, he was using the two weapons that men in armor truly feared in close combat. The hammer smashed into the armor again before Page had a chance to disengage. With the blow came the pained shattering sound of glass as a spider web of cracks raced around the shell of metal. Page was smart and didn't keep his distance for long. Despite his pride, he knew that Mick was the better fighter and that it was only his armor that had made up the difference. He had to end this now before he lost that advantage. He smiled and lunged forwards bringing down a devastating overhead chop as he saw Mick's guard lower ever so slightly from fatigue. *Even the famed Renalds have limits.*

Mick looked up as Page's bulk cast its shadow over him and smiled, he saw the fear seep into Page's heart as Page saw his smile and knew that he had been lured. Page strained to swing faster in the hope that he could foil whatever attack Mick had planned. It was too late. Mick's guard was ready, and he intercepted the swing on the side of Page's blade at the hilt, driving the blade to the side and down at the same time until it crashed against a large rock that Mick had been aiming for this whole time. "Your armor isn't the only thing with cracks in it," he said, savoring the look in Page's eyes as he realized his error as his sword struck the stone and snapped at the hilt.

Mick took the opportunity while Page was off balance to swing around behind him and land another hammer blow to the back of his armor. The hammer drove home, smashing through the armor as it fell away in pieces and landed a devastating blow to the nerve cluster at the base of Page's back.

Page immediately dropped to his knees. He still had fight in his eyes though as he scrambled for his dagger so Mick quickly followed through with his other axe and clapped him alongside the head with the flat side. Page bowled over and quit moving. He was still breathing though. Mick didn't much care except that he, they, needed information and Page would be the best one to give it to them.

With Page taken care of for the moment, he was finally able to turn his attention back to the battle at large. The Knights were still fighting hard in places, but they were quickly being cut into smaller and smaller groups, fighting ferociously and injuring far too many as they fell, but they were beaten. Assured of the outcome, he turned to make sure that Tenmen was okay.

Mick finally spotted Tenmen, still locked in battle with Axel about twenty meters away. They were all alone in that part of the battlefield. Mick had to wonder just what sort of fight they had had to have covered so much ground. "Axel!" he yelled, looking to distract him.

Axle glanced up in surprise, knowing what Mick's voice signified. He also realized that he had just made a grave mistake.

That split second was all that Tenmen had needed. With an artist's precision, he moved further into Axel's guard, ducking Axel's wild swing as he attempted to drive him back and drove the points of his sickles into both of Axel's armpits where there wasn't any armor.

Axel jerked as he suddenly found that he couldn't breathe. He tried again and was rewarded with a blood-filled cough as Tenmen twisted and wrenched his sickles free. Arterial bleeding quickly coated Axel's sides and arms in a river of red. He coughed once more before he fell to his knees, coughing up even more blood as his lungs collapsed. He managed one last soundless snarl before falling forwards into the mud. He was still clutching his sword and glaring hate at both of them as his body gave one last shudder and laid still.

Tenmen turned to face Mick across the field and waved. He was covered in small cuts, but none of them looked life threatening.

Mick started to wave back until he noticed motion where there shouldn't have been any. *"Death helm!"* he swore.

Tenmen noticed the look and made to turn. It was too late. He jerked unexpectedly and found that he no longer had any strength to turn. In fact, he couldn't seem to feel his legs at all. He looked down in time to see a shiny blade sticking out of his abdomen. Then his legs lost whatever strength must have remained in them as his own weight carried him over and off of the blade as it ground against his spine. There was enough of a slope that he rolled as he landed, strangely it didn't hurt like he had expected it too. Axle towered over him with his sword pointed down, ready to finish it. *How?* He tried to think. He vaguely remembered a warning that Mick had given them, but his mind was growing fuzzy and he couldn't seem to pull it out.

Axle looked up at Mick and smiled. He had used Death Helm just like Deen, but he knew the risks and had saved it for a moment like this. Only the Captains and Squad Leaders had been allowed to use it after what had happened to Deen and beside him only two others had decided to risk it. "Say goodbye to your frien..." he started to shout. The statement cut short, his sword still poised above Tenmen, as a spear point sprouted from his throat.

"Spinal injuries were the major weakness of Death Helm," Tenmen remembered as he saw the spear head yanked back out. *Something to do with issues reconstructing nerves due to their continually shifting electrical patterns.*

The spear dragged Axel over and to the side as it was pulled free. Axel's nerveless hands finally released his sword as he fell over. It buried in the dirt only a few centimeters away from Tenmen's shoulder.

Mick breathed a small sigh of relief as Adachi was revealed as Axel toppled over. The relief was short lived, remembering Tenmen's wound. He rushed over and dropped to a knee next to Tenmen. Axel was still twitching on the ground near them but there was no doubt that this time he was truly finished. He fully approved when Adachi put another jab through the eye hole in Axel's visor and finished him. Tenmen was in bad shape. There wasn't much that he could do with Night, but he could get a pretty clear idea of the extent of the wound. It was bad. Despite the spinal and nerve damage, the wound had been amazingly clean, missing most of the major organs, but it had nicked his liver and severed several important muscles and arteries. Tenmen wasn't human, so he had a stronger ability to heal than others but there were still limits. If they acted now, there was a small chance that he could be saved. "Adachi!" he shouted to get the man's attention. "You have to take Tenmen to the healers. Now!"

Adachi opened his mouth to argue, no doubt feeling that he couldn't leave Mick's side, but he closed it as he met Mick's eyes and saw the determination and fear for their friend there. "Don't die!" he said instead as he bent down and scooped Tenmen up in his arms. "Ai would never forgive you if you died on her and I fear the rage would vent upon the world. So, whatever you do, don't die!" he repeated, turning and setting off for the support area to the rear.

"I'll do my best not to." Mick murmured, climbing back to his feet. There was still a lot left to finish before he could rest. *Time for some answers.*

Mick made his way back over to where Page was still laying. Oddly enough, it was one of the few rises still present on the field and bordered the once quaint creek that had flowed through the town. He wanted to check on the rest of his force, but he needed to make sure that Page didn't get away or suffer any accidents before he got a chance to get all of the information that he could out of him. *Stop lying to yourself. What you really want is to make sure that Ai is okay. Sure, Atsuko and Yosuke are watching her, but by now you know her well enough to be sure that even they couldn't keep her away from the pointy end of things for very long. I Hope Page wakes up soon. The sooner that we get this over with, the better.*

A few minutes passed as Mick waited. It gave him time to survey the aftermath of the battle. They had made off a little better than he had expected. Their losses looked to be relatively light, most of them coming from the forces that he had led into the battle. The Knights hadn't faired so well. Out of the force that had attacked them, he could only see ten, counting Page, prisoners that had been taken. They were being kept apart and guarded by two men each. Whether that was to keep them from doing anything foolish or to protect them from harm; he couldn't really tell. It was probably a bit of both. After scanning for several more minutes, he finally caught sight of what he really sought.

Ai stepped out of the group of leaders that had gathered around her. They had their orders now and she had more pressing concerns. Mick hadn't shown up yet, and she had been beginning to worry. Atsuko had noticed and stepped in so that she could do what she needed to. The battle had been bloody, and her anxiety had only grown as she had scanned the aftermath. It hadn't been as bad as that first battle, but it had been even more personal. She stopped her scanning as she noticed a single mud and blood caked man standing still on one of the few rises. She couldn't make out more than his outline since the sun was behind him, but that was all that she needed. Without a second thought, she took off at a fast walk, the field was too littered with bodies and dangerous things to go any faster and made a beeline for him.

Mick smiled as Ai reached the top of his little hill, he wanted to hug her, but he was covered in the muck of the battle and didn't want to get her messy. He was glad to see that she was unharmed, and it appeared as if she had seen very little of the combat. *I'll have to thank Atsuko and Yosuke for that later.* Undoubtedly it was they who had kept her mostly out of the fray.

Thinks he's too dirty to hug his wife, does he! Ai quickly covered the distance between them and threw her arms around Mick, hugging him tightly.

Mick hesitated for just a moment before lowering his arms and returning Ai's embrace. They just stood there for a few minutes like that.

Ai finally released him and stepped back, looking around. "Where is Adachi and Tenmen? I didn't think those two would leave your side for anything," she asked, concerned by their absence.

Mick flinched. "Tenmen was badly injured and Adachi took him back to the support units."

Ai took a quick breath in surprise. It must have been a devastating injury to have made Adachi willing to leave Mick's side. She started to ask more but stopped as a groan arose from what she had thought was just another corpse next to Mick.

"Ah, he's finally coming to," Mick said, regarding the man lying near his feet. After a few more minutes of waiting, he sighed in exasperation. "Drop the dagger and sit up on your own or else I'll let my men at you!" he warned, knowing better than getting close to Page.

Page groaned once more, but slowly rose up, tossing aside the dagger that he had been shielding with his body. He held his hand to the side of his head instead, wincing as he gingerly felt at the slash on the left side and the welt on the right. He worked his jaw a little also. There were definitely cracks, but nothing felt like it was broken break. He would live. *For the moment at least. But as long as I'm alive, there will be chances to escape. I just need to buy time. If I surrender, Mick and his honor will ensure that he won't allow any harm to come to me and whoever else they managed to capture. Who knows? Maybe if I tell him enough, he'll get lax and I can kill him before I make my escape.*

Mick smiled as he watched the cogs turn behind Page's concussed eyes. He didn't need to be able to read minds to know what Page was thinking. *He really thinks I'm that stupid. Surrender doesn't protect you from war crimes you fool.* "Surrender!" he ordered.

Page's eyes lit with one last flicker of fire before he suppressed it. "Very well," he relented, reaching down and grabbing the remains of his shattered sword.

Ai moved up, standing at Mick's side and glaring down at Page as Mick stood waiting.

Page kneeled, as best as his spinning head allowed, in the mud, his armor destroyed and sword broken at the guard, leaving him only the pommel to present in surrender.

Mick started to reach forwards to accept the hilt when he caught the slightest flutter of movement from the ramparts.

Page frowned and opened his mouth in confusion as he saw the snarl spread across Mick's face. He never got the chance as a lance of light evaporated his chest and struck the ground between him and Mick, exploding in a torrent of expanding earth.

The blast launched Mick against Ai and sent them both tumbling through the air as the air around them exploded with a thunderclap. Thankfully Mick's body had shielded her and their child from the majority of the blast. As they tumbled, he vaguely noticed that all across the field, the remaining Knights were being cut down in a similar fashion. They hit the ground hard and rolled to a stop against a stump. They were still struggling to regain their senses as Mick sensed, more than felt, another rifle being aimed at them. Summoning all the strength that his shell-shocked body could muster, he pushed back up to his feet hefting Ai along with him and tried to lunge out of the line of fire and into the nearby creek bed. He almost made it.

Night rallied with all of its strength to turn the round aside, but there was just too much force. The most that it could manage was to slow the fifty-caliber sized bolt down to about five-hundred feet-per-second.

The mushroomed bullet slammed into Mick's left shoulder blade, shattering the bone and driving through into his lung and chest. Only one thought consumed him in that moment. *Ai and our child are next.*

Time seemed to slow as he pried Ai to the side with his right arm. Muscles, tendons, and bone shattered as he forced his torn body to move faster than reason would allow; casting Ai away from him, over the embankment, and into the creek below. Their eyes met as she fell backwards over the edge and he landed in the water at the bottom of the embankment. Somehow, he was still on his feet. Both of his arms hung limp at his sides as blood coursed out of his savaged back and chest. He smiled. The next round ruptured out of his chest, just below his heart so fast that you could see light through the hole, before it even had time to close. Mick teetered smiling down at Ai with all of his love and obstinately refusing to fall for a full two seconds before his body gave out and toppled over.

Ai rushed to catch him as he rolled down into her arms, looking up into the sky and her face. "No Mick!" She screamed. "You don't get to die!"

"Beautiful," Mick whispered, looking up into her eyes a single tear trickled down his cheek. He was still smiling, knowing that he had protected that which he held most dear.

Ai roared a howl of fury and grief that shook the valley from glen to glen. She glared out at the fort where the Marines still held. On the battlement stood one in particular. She couldn't see him clearly, but she had no doubt as to who it was.

***

A grizzled Gunnery Sergeant put a staying hand on the soldier besides him who had been lining up another shot. "Cease fire," he bellowed twice in each direction, so loud that even Ai could hear it, although he didn't know that. As suddenly as it had started, the sudden firestorm halted. He turned back to Ai and Mick and saluted. After a moment passed, he dropped it and turned his attention back to his men. As he walked, he pulled off his Gunny chevrons and replaced them with two stars. Major General Wilks Ashcroft was in command.

"Set the charges and prepare to pull out. We won't be able to hold the base against the coming attacks. They will die in droves if we stay and fight, but they would eventually breach our defenses and, up close, we would lose or be diminished as to no longer be able to carry out our primary mission of establishing a resource and control base for the State of Japan. We'll fallback to the taskforce and reestablish at our beachhead in Hokkaido. The Russians and Chinese are sure to throw a hissy fit, but with the loss of their primary navies in these waters, they won't be in any position to do anything about it until we are nice and dug in. The loss of the main Crystal Tree will be a slight setback and the eggheads are sure to complain, but we have already collected and readied for transport the seeded Crystals. The Tree itself is of little importance now. Call in the Air-support and move out while they are re-grouping!" Ashcroft ordered, smiling as his aids and runners scattered to be about their tasks. Those around him quickly passed the word and began pulling back to the concealed airstrip and their designated aircraft. The first heavy-lift transport carrying the Crystals, with a fighter escort, lumbered into the air before he reached the base of the fortifications. The sound of the rearguard and battle sounded behind him. *It's going to be a long day.* "Send word to command. 'Rufus' is a go," he commanded. *A long day indeed. I should have let them take that final shot. I would have before. I must be getting soft in my old age.*

Don't miss out!

Visit the website below and you can sign up to receive emails whenever J.G. Johnson publishes a new book. There's no charge and no obligation.

https://books2read.com/r/B-A-HRJI-JLPAB

BOOKS 2 READ

Connecting independent readers to independent writers.

About the Author

J.G. Johnson lives and works in Japan with his beautiful wife and rambunctious son who would even give a Tanuki a run for its money. He enjoys all things outdoors and absolutely despises being stuck in the office. People are great as long as they are real, but offices are where joy goes to die or where you write books born of pure boredom and a dire need to escape from the tedium of all things sitting with nothing to do.

Read more at nascentbooks.com.